Kevin Stevens is the author of several books, including *The Cops Are Robbers*, an account of New England's largest-ever bank robbery. A native of the US, he lives in Dublin with his family. *The Rizzoli Contract* is his first novel.

THE
RIZZOLI
CONTRACT

KEVIN STEVENS

POCKET BOOKS

TownHouse

First published in Great Britain and Ireland
by Pocket Books/TownHouse, 2003
An imprint of Simon & Schuster UK Ltd and TownHouse Ltd, Dublin

Simon & Schuster UK is a Viacom company

Extract from 'Hometown Blues' written by Steve Earle,
published by Artemis Records, New York.

1 3 5 7 9 10 8 6 4 2

Simon & Schuster UK Ltd
Africa House
64–78 Kingsway
London WC2B 6AH

Simon & Schuster Australia
Sydney

TownHouse Ltd
Trinity House
Charleston Road
Ranelagh
Dublin 6
Ireland

A CIP catalogue record for this book is available from the British Library

ISBN 1-903650-33-X

Typeset by M Rules
Printed and bound in Great Britain by
Cox and Wyman Ltd, Reading, Berks.

In memory of my father

1

I first met Bobby Rizzoli in the visiting room of MCI Concord, an ugly medium-security prison set in the idyllic hills of eastern Massachusetts. I'd heard his voice on the phone, sure, seen his face on the news, but I wasn't ready for the sheer physicality of the guy. He swaggered through the inmates' entrance with self-conscious muscularity, addressing the guards by name and razzing the duty officer with calculated charm. He was not so much led in as accompanied. The pallid guards hung on his movements, their faces gaudy with deference. Other prisoners drifted in furtively, tense but ignored, clutching packs of cigarettes and blinking like cave-dwellers in the harshly lighted room. But Bobby moved like the high-school jock who knows the coach will get him off detention. He was loose and poised. As he signed the visiting-room log he was careful not to search me out. From the get-go I could see this was a guy who played all the angles.

The duty officer nodded in my direction and we shook hands. 'Harry Donohue,' he said.

'That's me.'

'Your brother work for the state? Good-looking guy?'

'Owns a clothing factory. Even uglier than me.'

We dragged two ailing plastic chairs to an alcove, away from the smokers, fondling couples, and grubby kids in Kmart jackets. A streaked window looked on to the prison yard. Two black guys in institutional overalls were sweeping leaves from the basketball court, and a distant guard tower sat squat against the October sky. Bobby busied himself with the lame chair, but I could tell he was sizing me up. He was, after all, a crooked cop, a notorious burglar, a conman – someone well used to sidelong appraisal.

Television had misled me about his appearance. He was broader than I expected, with biceps that suggested he was making good use of the prison gym. In court he had worn a suit and tie and bifocals so incongruous they seemed to proclaim his guilt. Now he sat across from me in Patriots sweatshirt, chinos, and deck shoes without socks. He would have looked right at home mixing drinks on his boat in Revere or flipping steaks at a police barbecue. He had a classic, straight-edged Roman nose and bristling black hair carefully combed up and away from his brow. His mouth was soft, almost delicate, and seemed always on the verge of speech. His color was good, although the ridges of his cheeks were lined with broken capillaries. He had to be at least fifty, but didn't look it. Elbows on his knees, he gazed at me carefully with heavy-lidded eyes.

'Jimmy O'Leary sends his regards,' I said.

'That prick.'

'Likes you too.'

'Right.'

'One thing: he knows you can make some money with me.'

'And you with me.'

'There's the beauty of it.'

He ran a hand slowly across his hair and glanced at the bored guards. 'O'Leary knows anything about money, how come he's still grubbin' for the state when he could be sockin' away big bucks at Edwards & Angell?'

'Jimmy's doin' all right.'

'Jimmy fuckin' Doin'-all-right did his part to send me down here for ten. Let's not lose sight of that.'

In spite of the gruffness and vulgarity there was a charm that had not reached me over the telephone. His eyes were very expressive – they seemed to fix on my own yet take in the rest of me at the same time. They hinted that his words were for show, that the real message was subtle, open and even warm. There was grace in his bearing. He reminded me of the Sicilians who ran the fruit and vegetable stores in my old neighborhood and spent languid Saturdays at the Brighton Barbershop, kibitzing and studying themselves in the bright mirrors. I knew his story was marketable; now I could see he was as well.

'I want De Niro to play me.' He lobbed this comment at me, eyes flinty.

'Let's get the book written first,' I said. 'Film rights'll take care of themselves.'

'Got the feel – know what I'm saying? The real guinea touch.'

He made a *che sera* gesture with his hands and mugged gently, mouth downturned and eyes creased, a passable impression of De Niro in *Raging Bull*.

I could see he was hooked. 'We do this right, there'll be interest out of Hollywood. No question.'

'Think they'll let me outta here to do the *Tonight Show*?'

'Not for me to say. I'm sure Jimmy could help.'

He looked beyond me at the milling visitors' room, at the drab décor and peeling walls, at the slovenly guards with their cop-wannabe expressions and ill-fitting uniforms, at the drug dealers and car thieves, who were receiving contraband via girlfriends' kisses and giving earnest instructions for the outside while their children lurched among the donated toys, squabbling and bawling. He looked, and I saw in those hooded eyes a deep impatience layered with ambition, guile, and the hard knowledge that the big time had been in his grasp and now had to be earned all over again. Oh, I had him, all right.

And what Bobby had for me was a publisher's dream. Six years previously, over the hot Labor Day weekend of 1982, Hillbrook police captain Robert Rizzoli and four cohorts, including fellow Hillbrook cop Donny Donlon and an alarm man out of the Winter Hill gang, picked the lock of an optician's shop on Main Street and dynamited their way into the bank vault of the neighboring Hillbrook Savings Trust. For three sweaty nights they torched the vault safes and pried open 434 of the 500 safety deposit boxes, spilling cash, securities, gold, and jewelry into duffel bags. Daytimes they monitored the optician's shop and police scanners and established their alibis. It helped that either Bobby or Donny was on duty every minute of the long weekend, and when bank officials discovered the carnage on Tuesday morning, it was Captain Rizzoli who was first to respond, gazing at the hole in the vault roof with melodramatic amazement and demanding to know if his own box had been rifled. It had.

They cleared over twenty-five million dollars, including, it was said, substantial sums belonging to local *mafiosi*. It was the biggest bank heist in New England history and made the Brinks job look like a misdemeanor. Town and state buzzed with rumor, the Feds flew in at once, the story went national for over a week. The whole of Massachusetts knew it was a cop job, but no one in the state could prove it. The five were a tight little band, and the best efforts of the FBI, the state police, my pal Jimmy O'Leary, and the Mob couldn't break them. It was the perfect crime. They all had watertight alibis, and they handled the proceeds with the care of a bomb disposal squad. Bobby took the heat and then, after a faked accident, retired from the force on disability in 1983. He divided his time between his condo in Florida and Fowler's Marina in Revere, where he docked his twenty-foot Mako, the *Fifth Amendment*, beside the luxury yachts of Gennaro Anguilo and other made men.

The years passed and the story evolved into legend. The gang fenced the jewels and kept in loose touch. There was talk of another job but, for the most part, they kept a low profile and an eye on the calendar. The magic date was Labor Day 1988, when the six-year Massachusetts statute of limitations would run out. All was going well until Donny and another gang member, Joey Latrelli, got into the cocaine business deeper than was good for them. Using their take to set themselves up as middlemen between high-level Florida importers and New England dealers, they were quickly clearing fifteen grand profit a week. Donny, a quiet Irish kid from West Roxbury, was out of his depth. He started matching Latrelli snort for snort and got caught up in the wiseguy lifestyle. When he wasn't in the Bahamas or Atlantic City, he was throwing wild rogue-cop parties in his ranch house in South Hillbrook, complete with crystal bowls of coke and hookers from the Combat Zone.

Bobby, who wouldn't even take aspirin, tried to keep him straight, but Donny was on a spiral. He started freebasing, and his judgment drifted away in a haze of smoke. He holed up in the house, smoking all day, sending out for Chinese, and oiling his guns. He grew paranoid and convinced himself Joey was ripping him off. They argued bitterly and the partnership broke up, each claiming the other owed him money.

Everything came to a head in the winter of 1987, less than a year before my visit to Concord. The five-year federal statute of limitations had run out the previous September, and Bobby's will was focused on keeping Joey and Donny apart until Labor Day. The DA had long since closed the books on the case, so all the gang had to do was keep their mouths shut for eight more months and they were home free.

It was not to be. Coked out of his head, Donny called Joey on New Year's Eve, offering a peace pipe and inviting him over to the house for auld lang syne. When Joey arrived, Donny shot him twice at close range with an automatic shotgun. Joey stumbled onto the street with nine pellets of double-0 buck in a chest wound the size of a basketball. An off-duty cop found him in the reddened snow and brought him to St Dominick's Hospital.

Somehow he survived. Donny shitcanned the gun, but the state police found two keys of coke in his garage and took him into custody. Bobby frantically shuttled from hospital to holding cell, trying to prevent the worst happening. But Joey was not inclined to wait for Donny to screw him again. It was now every man for himself, and by the end of the week Joey had payback. In exchange for immunity from the burglary and drug-trafficking charges, he spilled the whole story. In February he went into protective custody and appeared before the grand jury. Bobby called his lawyers and waited for the indictment to come down.

As a former police captain, Rizzoli was the big fish, and either Latrelli or his handlers cast him as the ringleader. Bobby's trial had as much drama as the previous five years. Standing on the snow-covered steps of the courthouse, Latrelli peeled off his shirt and thrust his scarred chest at the television cameras, proclaiming with billowing breath that Bobby was the mastermind behind the whole affair, from the break-in to the attempted murder. Bobby's aggrieved mistress, his alibi, turned their story on its head and called him a lying-assed son-of-a-bitch from the stand. The alarm man, Benny Vogel, jumped bail; two days later his eyeless body washed up on Revere Beach. The *Herald* had a field day, assigning three reporters to the trial and featuring a series of interviews with Hillbrook residents who had lost precious heirlooms and exaggerated riches when the safety deposit boxes were ransacked. It was tabloid heaven. For the three weeks of the trial, everyone in greater Boston started the day with a cup of coffee and the latest testimony.

The jury took four days to convict, but the judge, my old law-school classmate Alex Lathrop, went light, giving Rizzoli ten years. Everyone – the media, the police unions, the bank – had been baying for blood and saw the sentence as a weak liberal response to the deep-rooted problem of police corruption.

But Lathrop, a Dukakis appointee, was not one to bow to pressure from the street. With good behavior Bobby would be out in three years, free to thumb his nose at the whole whining establishment from the deck of the *Fifth Amendment*. And if I had my way, he'd be doing it with more than a police pension in his pocket. For a struggling publisher, whose featured title that year was *Red Sox Trivia*, such a tale would do wonders for the list, and was well worth whatever royalties Bobby Rizzoli received to pay for flights to the Cayman Islands.

I had been following the whole affair from my offices on Atlantic Avenue, listening to the gulls screeching outside my window and wondering how I might turn this classic Boston opera into real money. The story was a surefire bestseller, the stuff of *Oprah* and *60 Minutes*, mass market and film rights guaranteed. The kind of book that would bring in serious dough and plenty of other opportunities in its wake. Normally it would have had all the big New York houses elbowing each other in a bid for the rights, but I saw early that, small as I was, circumstance and local connections were on my side.

Whatever money Bobby had left from the heist was in offshore accounts or his lawyers' pockets, and from the beginning the bank and its insurance company had their own law firms scrabbling for ways to recoup the losses. Any book deal would be dogged by litigation, and this was the era of the conglomerate merger, when food companies and steel mills were buying up publishing houses and editorial policy was dictated by MBAs in Gordon Gekko suits and red suspenders who never read anything more ambitious than the *Daily News*. Lawsuits, I could hear them argue, are bad for the bottom line. The New York houses were also wary of the state's untested

Son of Sam laws, which directed that profits from books by criminals be put into escrow pending civil suits by victims of the crime. So the big boys stayed away and I had a sliver of light.

As it happened, the Suffolk County District Attorney and head of the prosecution team was my pal Jimmy O'Leary. He and Rizzoli's attorney, Mickey Taylor, were close, and Jimmy worked hard to give Bobby a white hat while the grand jury was in progress. Even after the indictment he managed to put together an attractive plea bargain that would have had Bobby in a Westwood country club with white-collar criminals for less than a year. But Jimmy wasn't going the extra yard because he liked Mickey: he knew his case was built on the worst kind of witnesses – a small-time hood with connections to the Mob and a scorned mistress. There was very little hard evidence, and reasonable doubts kept popping up like politicians on St Patrick's Day. Jimmy never liked to lose, and for a DA with political ambitions, a high-profile failure in an election year would be a disaster.

The problem was that Mickey knew this too, and the prosecution cat-and-mouse just confirmed his belief he could win. He did right by his client and played the odds, although most of us on the inside guessed he'd had to work hard to convince Bobby. Mickey must have argued that even a plea bargain would open the gates to a flood of civil suits, and I'm sure he played on Bobby's perfect record at outwitting the law. So the trial went ahead and, when it was all over, Jimmy was wearing the white hat and Mickey looked like he had underestimated a public fed up with graft. Bobby, as he would, blamed his lawyer. Tough talk aside, he went to prison seeing Jimmy as a stand-up guy, and the light sentence, which Jimmy had nothing to do with, only reinforced his opinion. So I had an in.

Bobby went to Concord in June. The following month I had breakfast with Jimmy in the Parker House and pitched him for an introduction. Though he owed me a favor, he hummed and hawed for several days. There was no danger of any real conflict of interest, but voters would not see such a connection in a good light, were it ever to emerge. He told me I was wasting my time, that a book by Bobby would be a de facto admission of guilt and ruin his appeal. Besides, he argued, the bank would get all the money. But I'm nothing if not dogged, and I finally got him to agree to a single phone call – from there I was on my own.

So here I was. Three months on, I had a streetwise whizz-kid writer from the Somerville projects who'd gone to Boston University on a scholarship, edited their literary magazine, and was still young and hungry enough to write the book on a for-hire basis and sign away his copyright. I had an ex-Random House publicist with national contacts, including an old friendship with *60 Minutes* producer Jack Wambaugh. I had a network of wary sales reps wondering what the hell I was up to. I had the gossip columnist in the *Herald* speculating about a big Hollywood deal. After a dozen phone calls, I had Bobby dreaming of a seven-figure movie deal and an exclusive chat with Morley Safer. And, most important, I had a perfect way around the legal pitfalls suggested by, of all people, my sister Judy, an ex-nun and now a partner in one of the city's stuffiest Yankee law firms. The only thing I didn't have was Bobby's signature.

'Did you bring the paper?'

I reached for my briefcase. Bobby lifted a finger. 'Ah!'

'The case was searched. If they wanted to read it, they could have.'

'That's OK. Just tell it to me.'

Of course he wanted to hear me propose it. His deals had always been verbal, negotiated over cups of coffee at Dunkin' Donuts or in an idling police cruiser in the Wellington Circle parking lot. Details revealed in oblique shafts of ambiguous conversation, names rarely mentioned, plans unfolded need-to-know only. Not bad training for contract law. He sat forward, head cocked to catch soft words and extend his peripheral vision. His face had darkened slightly, and the lines of tiny broken veins intensified, like muddy water.

'It's simple,' I said. 'Your wife sets up an S corporation in Delaware. You have nothing to do with it apart from selling all rights to your story for a dollar. The new company signs a book contract with Donohue Press. Standard royalty structure—'

'Which is?'

'Ten per cent net, moving to fifteen after twenty thousand unit sales, then to twenty after thirty thousand. The Delaware company agrees to provide the materials needed to write the book and permission to use your name. I pay a writer to interview you, he writes the book, your name goes on the cover.'

'Paperback and film rights?'

'Your wife's company retains them. One hundred per cent.'

He rubbed his chin and leaned back. Everything about him was carefully casual but the look in his eyes. I had managed to move his attention from myself to the deal.

'All royalties go into a trust administered by the company, with your son as beneficiary. As sole director, your wife will have total discretion over withdrawals from the fund to cover administration costs. There'll be a tidy cash flow.'

'And the bank? They won't come after it?'

'Let 'em sue. They'll never win – not unless they rewrite the statute books between now and Christmas.'

He was doing his best to look skeptical, but his eyes couldn't hide the pleasure he took at the prospect of screwing the bank a second time. This was not just about money.

'There is one concern,' I said.

'Yeah?'

'Your wife has total control. Setting up in Delaware means that individually you're out of the corporate loop, now and for ever . . . which, in terms of the contract, is what you want. I mean, it's immunity for you.'

'So?'

'So you trust Lucinda?'

The soft mouth went tight. 'Have you met her?'

'No.'

'Then stick with what you know and tell me the deal. I'll worry about my wife.'

I'd lost ground. A blankness came over his face that I remembered. It was the look he'd had waiting for the verdict. 'You've got it. It's that simple.'

His eyes lost their focus as he considered the setup. 'What does Jimmy think?'

'Doesn't know,' I said. 'Doesn't want to know.'

His eyes returned to mine, searching for the angle. With his back to the window he had me at a disadvantage; his face lost definition against the autumn light. 'How long you known Jimmy?' he asked.

I had nothing to hide – I had come here with a straightforward proposition, determined to be upfront. Jimmy had vouched for me and the agreement truly was sweet. But as we faced each other chair to chair, I had a street sense that Bobby would not be comfortable until he discovered what I was holding back. Because everyone, everywhere, held back. The basis of his world was that no one could be trusted. He was looking for a bone here, and if it helped for him to think Jimmy was getting a piece then let him think it.

'We grew up in the same three-family on Harvard Avenue. His mother's my godmother. We went to high school together, college, law school.'

'Where?'

'Boston College.'

'Triple Eagles.'

'Triple Eagles. First two years out of law school, we shared a practice. He was my best man. You could say I know him well.'

He examined perfectly manicured nails. He looked up at me and smiled, a straight-mouthed, ironic, De Niro smile. I had passed. For the moment, he could trust his judgment of me.

'Give the contract to Lucinda.'

'You don't want to see it?'

'I'll see it when I need to. Send it to Lucy. She'll know what to do.'

Send it to Lucy. So she had stuck with him.

He was winding up. The placid, calculated stance was gone and he was suddenly restless. He glanced at his watch and at the clock. I could see he was caught between his need to move on to the next step and a desire to postpone routine. Any visitor was better than the cell. But we had reached a point where he had to be alone.

'OK, Harry, let's call it a day.'

'Keep one thing in mind. We want this story out while it's fresh in people's minds. Before summer. This'll be the blockbuster everybody brings to the beach. And the sooner we start writing, the sooner we both start making money.'

'Hey, it's not like I got other shit to do.'

He was scanning the room like a hot-rodder at a red light. It was time to go.

We stood and pushed the chairs against the wall. I put on my jacket and Bobby was gesturing and mouthing a question to the duty officer. The guards laughed. Outside, the afternoon sun had angled down above the ragged basketball court, lighting up the filthy window.

'Nice evening for a ball game,' I said.

'You goin'?'

Jimmy had a box at Fenway. Tonight, the crucial fifth game of the American League championship series between the Red Sox and the A's, the lieutenant governor and the senate president would be there. Yaz might drop by. There would be lobster sandwiches, attractive women on the make, as much Ballantine's as I could drink, and a limo to ferry me home to Charlestown. How could I say this to Bobby?

'I'll watch it on TV,' I said.

'Hey, even *I* can watch it on TV.'

He looked at me with disgust and his eyes drifted away again, back to what should have been and what still might be.

'Season ticket holder since '72,' he said. 'I was there when Pudge waved the ball around the pole. When Bucky fuckin' Dent shot us down. I even made the trip to Anaheim when Dave Henderson hit the homer that made Gene Mauch shit his pants. And tonight . . .'

'Hurst'll do it.'

'No, he won't. Doesn't have the killer instinct. Doesn't *hate* enough. A choker.' He grasped his throat, looking at the sun-spangled guard tower.

The setting sun behind me, I drove back to Boston through the prosperous suburbs along Route 2 – Concord, Lincoln, Lexington. It was hard to believe the state had set a prison in this patch of historical wilderness and late twentieth-century prosperity. I had stepped from the claustrophobic squalor of the visiting room into forests where the trees remembered Emerson and Thoreau. After the hot summer, the foliage was spectacular, and the colors layered up into the surrounding hills. Fruit stands lined the highway, with pumpkins heaped in the slanting sun and bushels of apples bunched under hand-painted signs. Grizzled doctors and executives jogged along the roadside; the passing cars sported Dukakis or Kennedy bumper stickers. The homes of Harvard profs and corporate lawyers rose out of the pines, solar panels and glass façades glinting in the sun, color schemes and architectural styles carefully integrated into the countryside. In these neighborhoods, garishness was as great a sin as fiscal recklessness. Even the gas stations and fast-food joints were up-market and tastefully zoned.

In the days when I had money (and short days they were),

I had never been tempted to move out here. There was something manufactured about the country chic, something desiccated and wan in the L. L. Bean primness of these transplanted New Yorkers and Midwestern liberals who drove expensive but sensible cars, kept their towns dry, and decorated the mini-malls with abstract art and quotes from *Walden*. They were proud of their politics and their compassion and their taste, but secretly they looked down on the children of Southie and Revere and blamed us for everything from the decline of schools to the length of lines at the Department of Motor Vehicles. They wrote letters in tortured prose to the *Globe* but kept their distance from the problems they thought they solved. Their worship of consumerism was all the more obvious for being refined. They reminded me of the prayerful dilettante in the *New Yorker* cartoon – 'I don't ask for much, Lord, but what I do ask for must be of the highest quality.' No doubt Bobby would have had a good sneer at them, roaring down Route 2 in his cream-colored Cadillac.

There weren't many like Bobby Rizzoli or me out this direction. Our parents, as they wrested power and business away from the Brahmins, had stayed close to Boston and close to the shore, as if reluctant to stray too far from the sea, as if the folk memories of Galway and Naples and Lisbon kept them close to the salt spray and the tang of low tide. From my office I could see the stretch of cold gray water between Atlantic Avenue and East Boston on one side, and the splendors of the new Lafayette Place on the other. Success for me was always measured by the graph of skyline that rose from the harbor and charted the oily interplay of politics and business, graft and gerrymander that was the stuff of

Boston public life. I drove along the smooth expressway through the heart of bluenose America confident that Bobby and I were going to do business and rescue each other from our very different slides from fortune, confident because, as a kid, I had worked summers in the canning factories and lobster hatcheries with guys like him, calling each other 'guinea' and 'harp', boozing and brawling in the burlesque houses of Scollay Square on payday, and puking our guts out side by side onto the rotting pilings near North Station while the rats scurried into the brine. No, Bobby and I were not country folk. We were port kids who'd sooner recognize a quahog than a crocus.

I drove past Belmont. The radio buzzed with talk of the Red Sox and news of Dukakis's slide in the polls. Whatever about the chances of a timid southpaw against the power of the A's line-up that night, the Duke was a goner. I would vote for him only because the habits of a Boston ward heeler's grandson die hard, but I knew it was a vote in a lost cause. He was too ethnic, too liberal, and too straight. As my dad would've said, 'Put down the mud and your opponent only will add it to his pile.' And mud was coming from Bush and his handlers like a shot off a shovel. I would vote, all right, but in my heart I knew that Bobby, incarcerated and disenfranchised, had the more logical attitude: watch the ball game, ignore the elections, and figure out how to get your own piece of the action.

For twenty-two years, since the day I took down my shingle and told Jimmy that the law was not for me, I had been looking for my slice of the roast. I'd dabbled in import-export, freight insurance, garden furniture, public relations. I ran a trucking company that was strong-armed out of business by the Teamsters. Once or twice I had come close to the big time, and a couple years ago I held the note on two parcels of downtown real estate worth over three million bucks. I was a hair's breadth from the deal that would have set me up for life when the bottom fell out of the market and city assessors came banging on my door looking for huge levies on property I didn't even own. I was still dodging flak on that one. Like Bobby, I had been close enough to smell the honey. Now I was holed-up in an old shoe factory on the waterfront, living on my wits and a salary from my dad's old print shop, publishing a line of trivia titles that were hustled over the telephone to independent bookstores by my sales manager, an Italian kid from Hillbrook, who strutted around the office in a Filene's Basement suit like a two-bit wiseguy. I was due a break.

I coasted down through Arlington Heights, and the Boston skyline loomed ahead. I loved it from this angle. Manhattan it wasn't, but for a Mick from the wrong side of Brighton, it was majestic and inspiring and at this hour especially reminded me of the first glimpse of the Emerald City in *The Wizard of Oz* – soaring, shimmering, phantasmagoric. There was a purity to it at this distance. You couldn't see the for-sale signs or littered streets or grimy panhandlers. You couldn't see the bleak edges of Government Plaza or the rusting central artery. There was just this bright curtain of polished stone and glass, trimmed of all ornament to the pure expression of wealth and influence. My heart lifted just to look at it, and I accelerated my Chrysler and swooshed along the singing tarmac into Cambridge, vowing by the reflected solidity of those buildings that this time I would make it, this time my luck would hold, this time Bobby and his story and the plan I had knit in classic Boston style would earn me my fortune and lift me at last to that shining city on a hill. So Bobby was hooked? Hey, I was too. I really was.

2

Next morning I went to Brighton for a shave and a cut. Sal Longobardi had been cutting my hair since the days when my dad would prop me on a board, light a cigar, and schmooze with zoot-suited Italians and returning GIs about FDR and Rita Hayworth. Sal was a short, dapper man, now in his seventies, with a basset-hound face and a drooping mustache. He always wore a silk bow tie and a brocaded, pearl-buttoned waistcoat. His breath was minty, and even amid the bouquet of barbershop smells – brilliantine, talcum, hot towels, witch hazel – his own cologne was distinct. His cutting style was precise and ritualistic. He spoke little, but quietly hummed arias from Puccini and Verdi as he worked. These snatches of melody, along with the snip of scissors, the slap of steel on strop, and the rough, spirited chatter in several languages, were the soundtrack of my own monthly ritual here. I came to unwind, to get the neighborhood slant on sports and politics, to take refuge in a familiar haunt unchanged through four decades.

Today Sal's brother Joe had crossed the street from his body shop and installed himself in the third, unattended porcelain chair. He was Sal's opposite: heavy and morose, with breathing that labored even when he was sitting. A tic twisted his lips at irregular intervals. He stared blankly between pronouncements, as if concentrating on the beating of a large man's suffering heart. Sal's young partner, Paulie, was shaving a shovel-headed Ukrainian I had always known as Keef, and Mick Malone, a retired cop and old friend of my dad, was sitting at the window, smoking Pall Malls and watching the sidewalk action. The talk, of course, was of last night's game.

'They pay, what, three million plus for the best reliever in the league?' Joe said to the toweled Keef. 'Then leave him on the bench while Hurst gets shelled? On the final day of the season? A chimpanzee coulda made those decisions.'

'Quick,' Mick said, 'someone get me a chimpanzee.'

'Smith ain't the best,' Keef mumbled from the towel, finger in the air. 'The Eck is. And he *was* on the mound.'

'The Eck.' Joe coughed the name, lips twitching. 'Don't do shit when he's here, then throws like Koufax after he's traded. Typical.'

Paulie turned, blade in midair. 'Smith, Eckersley – don't make no difference. A's got too much power.'

'No way the Sox shoulda been there in the first place,' Mick said from his window seat. 'Morgan Magic was Morgan Luck. They used up all their fortune in July.'

Joe sniffled and scratched himself. 'Shoulda went with Smith in the seventh, I'm tellin' you. You know, if Hurst wasn't a Mormon I'd swear he threw the game.'

'What's religion got to do with it?'

Mick stood up, stretching his legs as he lit a cigarette. He had a classic South Boston face – ruddy, leathered, squinting, with a shock of white hair, a lantern jaw, and crinkled ears.

'Listen to you guys. Who'd pay the Sox to lose? They're the masters. Seventy years of experience. Be like paying Sal there to wear his duds. Part of who they are.' He shook out the match and blew smoke into the middle of the room.

'What about you, Harry?' he continued. 'You were there. What's your take?'

I roused myself. I'd been thinking of the ingenuous eyes of a young State House intern who had accepted my offer of a lift home after the ball game. Speaking breathlessly of the senate president, she'd laid her hand gently on my forearm as she stepped with stockinged confidence from my hijacked limousine into the gas-lit antiquity of Charles Street. Young, assured, beautiful. But with the senate president on her mind, not me.

While I caught up with the moment, Joe said, 'What the hell would Harry know? He was up in his celebrity box getting shitface and trying to impress the bigshots.'

They all laughed except Sal, who pivoted gracefully from my head and pointed at his brother with his free hand. 'You keep quiet, Joe. Harry here got class, which is something you wouldn't know nothing about.'

'Hurst was fine,' I said. 'He just got a little tired. You're not razor-sharp against hitters of that caliber they'll jump on you. Simple as that.'

There was a pause in the discussion. I had moved out of the neighborhood twenty-five years ago, gone to college and law school, made friends in high places, done a few favors for the likes of Mick and Sal, kept in touch enough to earn the right to listen in – so my words carried more weight than they should have. I was seen as intellectual but streetwise, a listener and observer and a man to settle disputes. It was not a reputation

I thought accurate but, as I usually kept my own counsel, it was one that had deepened over the years.

And here I really was a listener. I liked to watch Sal work, to breathe the perfumed air, to let the jokes and braggadocio swirl about me like the sounds of a high-school band. I liked gazing at the photographs of Ted Williams, Esposito, and Yazstremski while Sal massaged my scalp. I liked to watch Paulie sweeping the cuttings from the slatted floor, elbows flapping like Art Carney's in *The Honeymooners*. I liked that Sal didn't allow girlie calendars or blasphemy. I liked the memories of my youth that hovered in the old room like cigar smoke and settled in my heart as I closed my eyes and let the conversations and expert clicks of Sal's scissors weave hypnotically around my head.

I didn't have a regular appointment. I came once a month when the spirit moved me, always on a day when I knew I needed the connection. That morning, cotton-mouthed and hung over, I had woken to a blast from my bedside phone. 'Yeah.'

'Up bright and early, huh?'

'What do you want, Eddie?'

'I guess we're lucky Johnny Rotella gets to the shop at six.'

My brother had little humor and even less tact. I didn't appreciate the early call, and his subtle claim on the family business rankled. 'Hey, you can always start the day in there yourself,' I said. 'See how a real business is run.'

'I know all about real business.'

'Good. Then stick to your own.'

During the tense silence that followed, I swiveled my legs from the bed. When hung over I could be brittle, easily offended, quick to criticize. And Eddie liked the push more than the pushback.

'I was going to suggest lunch, but maybe it isn't such a good idea,' he said.

'Hey, take it easy.' Beside my bed was a sibling photo – of Eddie, Judy, and me on the deck of our friend Leo Rooney's yacht. 'You know me, Ed. Not a morning person. So, where we gonna eat?'

Trying hard to shake his truculence, he said: 'Harvard Club.'

'*Haute cuisine.*'

'I like it there, Harry. On me.'

'I'm not arguing. What's up, anyway?'

'See you at noon.'

He hung up. Ah, Eddie. Forever brusque. There would be – there always was – a practical reason for the invitation. He wouldn't just want to have lunch with his brother. Productive, Eddie was always productive. A pain in the ass, but I had to admit it – I looked forward to seeing him. No reason needed at my end. As we grew older, each meeting was for me more moving. Slope-shouldered, gap-toothed, balding, with quick judgments and delicate hands and an unwillingness to confront anything abstract, he was, year by year, more like our father. And, as with my dad, his presence calmed me when the world got to be too much.

Sal helped me into my topcoat. Keef, clean-shaven and pink, played backgammon with Joe while Paulie swept between the chairs and Mick peered out the door.

'I'm having lunch with Eddie, Sal.'

'How is Edward?'

'He's doing well. Making children's clothing now, good stuff, like Osh-Kosh.'

'Quality, you gotta stick with quality.'

Joe looked up from the board. 'Eddie sell that Chrysler?'

'Yeah. To a teacher in Hingham.'

'Bastard. Never trust a Donohue.'

Mick followed me outside. We watched the traffic on Brighton Avenue, and he waved at a passing cruiser. 'I'll walk down with you,' he said.

He was headed for Kiley's. Mick had a city cop's gait, flat-footed and loose, and kept his right hand in his pocket. He smoked earnestly. It wasn't even noon, but I could tell he had done well to hold out this long. 'I never take a drink before twelve,' he liked to say, 'when a drink before eleven will do.'

'Hear about this case down in Shropwood?' he asked.

'The exam?'

'Yeah.'

'What else is new?'

'This is different. You know Quinn. He won't go down without taking someone with him.'

When I was a kid, Bucky Quinn was a townie with a reputation for protecting an easily bruised sense of honor with a baseball bat. He had dropped out of high school and barely scraped the equivalency. For two months one summer, he had cleaned the presses at our print shop until my dad caught him stealing paper. The night he was fired, someone smashed the windows of the family Buick. Bucky joined the service and was away for a couple years, and by the time I was practicing law he had moved to the South Shore and somehow got a place on the Shropwood force. Twenty-five years on, his powers of concentration had improved to the point where he had aced consecutive civil-service exams and become chief of police.

Shropwood was a quiet, middle-class community, dry and strictly zoned. It was close enough to the shore to smell the tide but protected from sea breezes by a fellsway ridged with pine. The population was older – retirees, state employees, folks who owned small businesses in Quincy. It was a town with little change and even less crime, but, in the previous year, it had been the scene of a succession of drug collars that didn't make sense. In the most recent case, a Haitian mule who couldn't even speak English was stopped in a stolen local car with enough cocaine in the trunk to keep the whole of Boston buzzing for days. There was sand in the tire treads and an unloaded standard-issue .357 in the glove compartment, but the mule clammed up and was eventually deported. Bucky hadn't made an arrest or followed lead one and, with each bust, the state troopers involved couldn't hide their growing disdain for his camera-hogging when the dope was displayed. I just laughed and waited. Whatever he was up to, it was bound to unravel. The guy didn't know limits.

Then the case took an unexpected turn. In June a local cheerleader accused a Shropwood cop of raping her in the back seat of the town's only cruiser. Bucky tried to smooth it over, but her parents went to the state police, who were only too happy to investigate. While searching the cop's apartment they found a half-kilo of coke and a photocopy of a police exam scheduled for the following month. Instructions scrawled across the bottom in red ink were soon identified by experts as the handwriting of Chief Quinn. The Feds were called in and a grand jury was convened.

'So what'll he do?'

'We know one thing,' Mick said. '*He* didn't steal it. Not from out in the sticks he didn't. Had to be someone in the McCormack Building, where they keep the exams.'

'Like who?'

We were standing in front of Kiley's. Mick lowered his voice. 'Anybody. Capitol cop, state employee, secretary. You can imagine how much those are worth.'

'Had to be someone on the inside. With clearance.'

'So it's a cop. That surprise you? Thing is, how many layers between the thief and Bucky? And how many other chiefs are chiefs because they had all the answers on their sleeve? Not that it hasn't happened before. But this is different. In this situation, we've got someone who doesn't buy into the code. Never did. He's a loose domino, and if there's others like him in the line we could be watching them tumble for a while. A long while. Especially when the Feds start handing out white hats.'

'Just as well you're retired, Mick.'

He stared at me. In the morning sun he looked worn and sad. 'Harry, I'm not saying I never took a free lunch. But we're into a different area here. The drugs, the exams . . . it's no good.'

He squinted at the sun, the familiar, jutting jaw locked in a certainty backed by fifty years on the street. He looked fragile. I thought he was going to ask me to join him for a late-morning boilermaker.

'Hey, Mick, guess who I met yesterday? Bobby Rizzoli.'

'Rizzoli? Where? In the can?'

'Yeah. Don't tell anyone, but I'm doing a book with him. Inside story on the Hillbrook Trust.'

He shook his head and smiled his big Irish smile. 'Harry, you son-of-a-bitch. You're just like your old man.'

I drove into the city along Commonwealth Avenue, keeping my tires out of the trolley grooves and listening to the midday news. I had that fresh-haircut feel: tingling, bristled, cool at the back of the neck. It was high autumn, time of fresh starts in Boston. There was an air of wellbeing, of football and campaigning, of moving vans and rowing on the Charles. Sharpened by my visit to Sal's, I had that openness to sensation that comes with a hangover. Slanted and precise, the October light climbed the staggered roofs of Beacon Hill until it crested in a burst of radiance on the State House dome, giving me a little trill of excitement in my stomach, reminding me I was at my own new beginning in the heart of a city in its prime.

I parked illegally on State Street and walked to the Harvard Club. Into the business district, and the city had a different feel. Here it was purposeful and parochial. Beneath the European avenues, colonial churches and glassy skyscrapers, I always felt that the center of Boston was a neighborhood – an old-boy network of bankers, lawyers, politicians, and high-level realtors, with a healthy sprinkling, these days, of pure money men who spoke the language of leveraged buyout and junk bond and made fortunes without anything real ever passing through their hands. These neighbors patronized the same restaurants, bought the same clothes, summered in the same fashionable destinations. They bought presents for each other at Tiffany's and attended the same fundraisers. They'd be deathly ordinary if not for their sparkle of wealth, which gave their every move a new-minted jangle, and raised them from the street as decidedly as the stately, gilded buildings in which they took refuge.

At the club Eddie hadn't arrived. As I was hanging up my coat I saw Jimmy O'Leary and Alex Lathrop in the smoking room. I joined them.

'Harry, what are you having?' Alex asked, flagging a white-coated waiter. He was wrinkled but robust, deeply tanned, with large ears and a heavy head. His longish gray hair and wide forehead added to the judicial mien. Even here, relaxed in a leather wing chair with a cigar and a glass of Perrier, he looked as if he had just stepped from the bench.

'Rob Roy, your honor.'

'Rob Roy for the rogue,' Alex ordered, rolling his *r*s.

'Hair of the dog,' Jimmy added.

'Not at-all. Harry here is having a publisher's lunch. Isn't that right, Harry? Isn't this where you guys do business?'

'We do business wherever there's a good story.'

'Oh, there's stories aplenty here, Jimmy could tell you that.'

Jimmy always sat at the edge of his seat, as if about to leave. He was thin and whippet-like, with nervous hands and a face scarred by acne. He was a nail-biter. In high school he had been a good athlete, but of the wiry, workhorse variety. He wrestled at 128 pounds and was state champ junior and senior years. He also ran cross-country. He was very competitive and always looking for an edge. Girls didn't pursue him. These days he was not bad on the golf course, and for several years he and I had played squash weekly until I tore a ligament.

'Harry's looking for the big story,' Jimmy said. 'The block-buster.'

He smiled at me. Though they were close, Jimmy would not have told Alex that he had put me in touch with Bobby, and Alex would not want to know, at least directly. By now he might have heard the rumors and put two and two together, but Alex's reputation for integrity rested on his mastery of the subtle lines of communication that connected the worlds of law, politics, and business. He was never seen to give or receive knowledge he shouldn't, and he was confident enough to associate publicly with whomever he wished, as if proving immunity to influence.

'If the Sox pull it out against Oakland,' I said, 'and I sell a few more *Red Sox Trivia*, I'll be happy.'

'Don't hold your breath.' Alex had been in Jimmy's box the night before but hadn't watched a single pitch. He spent the entire evening bending the senate president's ear and drinking soda. 'The Sox are on the ropes and the Duke is going down in flames. This is not Beantown's year.'

Alex had the carriage and inflection of a local boy, but he hadn't moved to Massachusetts until law school. He had come out of the University of Michigan to finish first in our class at BC, and he and Jimmy had been co-editors of the *Law Review*. He was from Grand Rapids, son of an eye surgeon and family friend of Gerald Ford. After graduation, he turned his back on his family's long-standing Republican tradition to pursue a liberal agenda, working for various city and state authorities on urban renewal, integration of public schools, and public housing. He served as general counsel to the State Ethics Commission and lectured on professional responsibility and ethics at Harvard Law School, where he had grown friendly with Mike Dukakis. The Duke appointed him Superior Court judge in 1985. He was popular, likeable, gracious with women. The kind of guy my ex-wife liked. Jimmy and I she lumped together. 'He has no commitment, no real respect for the law,' Ann continued to say to me about Jimmy, usually during awkward phone calls we felt obliged to pursue, full of disguised animosity and frustrated talk about our son. 'How someone like him becomes Attorney General . . .'

'He's the DA.'

'Oh, you can see where he's headed. His ambition is as cheap as his suits.'

Truth to tell, Ann didn't like Jimmy's style. He was a street kid prosecuting street kids, and he was going to fight like we learned in the back alleys, where anything was kosher as long as it got the job done. Of course, he also reminded her of what she didn't like about me, and for me defending him was also self-defense.

'Who you meeting?' Jimmy asked.

'Eddie.'

'Ah,' Alex said, puffing on his cigar. 'The war hero.'

'The war hero who makes kiddie clothes,' Jimmy cracked.

'Eddie's doing all right.'

Jimmy always saw Eddie, four years our junior, as the quiet kid who built model planes and collected soda-pop tops. He resented Eddie's war record. My brother was indeed a hero, with a Navy Cross and a Distinguished Service Medal earned flying navy helicopters in Vietnam. Jimmy and I missed out on war. Born in the mid-thirties, we came of age during the hysterical Eisenhower interregnum, too young for Korea and too old for Vietnam.

'Speak of the devil,' Alex said.

Eddie approached us in a dark blue Brooks Brothers suit and red tie. He had the look of a navy officer on leave: tentative, stiff, spit-and-polish. In recent years his eyesight had deteriorated, but, because he refused to wear glasses in public, he was often surprised by people he hadn't recognized. Awareness of this possibility added to his expectant look and made him appear vulnerable.

'Hey, Eddie boy,' Jimmy said, 'is it true you torched your old shop for the insurance?'

'Nice seeing you too, Jimmy.' Eddie raised a hand to Alex, almost saluting him. 'Hey, Judge.'

'Judy tells me you're going to be a grandfather,' Alex said.

Eddie beamed. 'Due March seventeenth.'

'A Patrick.'

'Or a Gene.'

'Gene?'

'Our dad was born on St Patrick's Day,' I explained.

'A true Irishman,' Alex said. 'So, Eddie, if the date holds, I guess you'll have to miss the senate president's breakfast speech.'

'There's always hope,' Eddie said.

Eddie's political conversion was the reverse of Alex's. He had been a Republican since Carter and grew more conservative by the year.

'I hear you're campaigning for Joe Malone,' Jimmy said.

'I don't campaign for anybody. I may well vote for Malone, but it's Teddy's race. Like always.'

'Don't make it sound so tragic. Course, guys like you still hold Chappaquiddick against him.'

Eddie gave me a let's-get-going look and we said our

goodbyes. He had booked a window table overlooking the harbor. He liked the sea as much as I did, sailed every summer weekend, but at the moment he wasn't looking at the view. After we ordered he was still agitated. 'What's a guy like Alex doing with him? They're always together. A distinguished judge with that little weasel.'

'Jimmy's pretty distinguished himself.'

'Like hell. Judy saw him at the Meridian with Sammy Coffola and Bill Wright. Having lunch for all the world to see.'

'Sammy's a big wheel. Jimmy wants to be Attorney General, and no way he's getting the job without the unions.'

'Coffola's a crook, Harry, and you know it. He was in the Mob's pocket forty years ago and I bet you the shop he still is.'

'Here's your soup,' I said. 'Relax.'

The waitress was plain and solid, like the Harvard Club food. She called us 'dear' and asked Eddie how his daughters were doing. He calmed down and dipped into his soup with deliberation, shoulders hunched. In his mid-forties now, he had lost most of his hair. The family joke was that Eddie was round and I was square. Though we both had Dad's bulk, Eddie had his oval head and sloping shoulders. I had my mother's boxy face and angular lines. After Dad died and she lost weight, these lines became more apparent: all elbows and knees, she sat in the kitchen in her summer frock watching the delivery trucks pull in to the Stop'n'Shop parking lot across the street, her limbs parallel planes pointing off into an infinite, suffering distance.

'I saw Judy last Friday. She's handling the action over the fire for me.'

'So I heard.'

Eddie was still trying to get his insurance company to cough up for a fire that had destroyed his previous business in Hingham, a bra factory. That was another family joke, but one he didn't much appreciate. That he had retained Judy only partly to do with family loyalty – she was a tough litigator with an excellent record in such cases. She brought a Sister Superior demeanor to the civil courts, and anyone who had attended parochial school, judges included, didn't stand a chance.

'She told me about you and Rizzoli.'

'Told you what?'

'Said he might write a book for you.'

'I'm not sure Rizzoli could write his own name. I'm trying to buy his story.'

Eddie touched the corners of his mouth with his napkin – I could see he was wondering if this was a conversation he wanted to pursue. 'I have to say I'd have a problem with that.'

I kept my eyes on my soup. 'That's why you're making clothes and I'm publishing books.'

'Hey, you think I don't come up against similar types of issues every day of the week? Health inspectors looking for kickback, zoning officials on the take?'

'So you resist the temptation to do anything illegal. Good for you, Eddie. I'm looking to publish a book, which it is my legal right to do – and, incidentally, Bobby Rizzoli's. Last I checked, the First Amendment was still in the Bill of Rights.'

A big-brother tone had crept into my response. Though it irritated him, he knew he'd gone too far.

'Judy also tell you she came up with the contract structure makes the whole thing work?' I asked.

He looked out the window. 'I don't know, Harry. I'm no fan of Dukakis, but I have to admit he cleaned things up in this state. Then you see a guy like Rizzoli, or our old friend Bucky Quinn, and you wonder if things are ever really going to change around here.'

A seagull swept against the window, startling him. The sky was so clear the horizon was sharp as a hairline.

'Dad ever catch up with Bucky?' he asked.

'Not that I know of.'

'What a piece of work. What do you make of this exam thing?'

I decided to drift with the change of subject. I didn't like arguing with Eddie. 'I gotta figure it's contained. Too many guys get their hands on something like that and you lose control.'

'Bucky wouldn't care.'

'Bucky didn't steal it. He's somewhere in the chain and wouldn't really know where it came from.'

The waitress brought our steaks. I thought about a second Rob Roy but decided I could do without another reproof. I took a bite.

Eddie was looking at me, knife and fork in the air. 'Tell me something. Straight. Was our friend over there,' he said, nodding towards Jimmy, 'in the class of '63?'

'Who – Jimmy?' I laughed. In our law-school class, the actual class of '63, there had been five guys who had bribed a secretary and got their hands on the final exam. They paid a thousand bucks apiece, though one guy, Forrest Linkliter, had welched, knowing well the others could do nothing about it. Two of them had still managed to fail, but the others, including Forrest, were practicing in the Commonwealth of Massachusetts to this day. To insiders the group was always known as the class of '63. 'Jimmy edited the *Law Review*. He clerked for the Superior Court. You may not like the guy, Eddie, but he's no cheat.'

'Judy doesn't like him.'

'I think you're wrong there. And, anyway, Judy likes passing judgment for the sake of it.' I was sorry I hadn't ordered the second drink. Something was eating Eddie. I sensed now what I should have known at once, that he had been avoiding an uncomfortable subject. 'C'mon, Eddie. You didn't ask me up here to dump on Jimmy O'Leary.'

He busied himself with his steak. Middle age had given him a cantankerous edge, but he was still the kid who made certain the tiny wing lights on the model P-51 were painted the right shade of silver. He was careful when broaching a personal subject. It drove me nuts, but I knew from experience that pushing him would only slow him further. Finally he leaned across the table. 'Judy and I spoke of other things.'

'Like what?'

'She says Mom wants to change her will.'

'How so?'

He looked at me blankly, as if at a distance. 'I guess she wants to leave the shop to me.'

'Ah.'

Eddie was the baby, and in spite of all evidence to the contrary, my mother saw him as helpless. When he was in Vietnam she used to send him the jobs section of the *Sunday Globe*. Twenty years later, she still needed to assure herself he would be looked after when she was gone. The Hingham fire had spooked her. He didn't own the building, but the machines and most of his inventory were destroyed, and he'd had to pay workmen's comp to several employees who suffered from smoke inhalation. A string of arson cases on the South Shore had made the insurance company slow to pay, and he had brought Judy to the case reluctantly. In the meantime he had borrowed heavily against the family shop to cover his losses and start the new business.

'In a way you already do own it,' I said.

'Harry, when the insurance comes through it'll all be covered. With interest.'

He was right. I didn't like the lien, but Eddie was a crack businessman, who ran his outfits like he flew his choppers – by the book. He might have lacked imagination, but he had been quietly amassing a small fortune through right instinct and sheer doggedness. The fire was a temporary derailment. And I had nothing to complain about. My mother owned the shop and, though I ran it, it was a no-brainer – my foreman, Johnny Rotella, did all the real work, and our customer base was loyal and solid. I received a respectable salary, published my books at cost, and was free to dream up the big score. But it would not do, just at the moment, to have anyone peering too closely at the accounts. Once the Rizzoli book was out, once I had a solid title, I could build the publishing side and take care of some minor bookkeeping irregularities. I just needed a little time.

'So Mom figures you can do a better job.'

'Don't be ridiculous,' he said. 'Mom has no idea what's going on. It's one of her whims.'

'So, you going to turf me out?'

'Harry, listen – I don't want it.'

'You tell her that?'

'Take it easy. You run the place – if anyone deserves it, it's you. Mom won't listen to me, but I've got Judy to explain to her that if she gives it to me I actually lose money, taxwise.'

'Would you?'

'Hard to call.'

'So you *really* don't want it.'

Eddie pretended to be hurt. 'I want to keep it like it's always been – a family business. Dad told me one time that it was part of his insurance for us. To keep us fighting so we'd keep in touch.'

This last comment, with its humorous slant and family truth, was so unlike him I was taken aback. In his mock-offended face I saw creases and puckers that mapped a whole history of sibling emotion. And a funny thing happened: the rancor disappeared, the business talk turned irrelevant, and I discovered afresh why I liked seeing Eddie, pain in the ass though he was. He put me at ease. Maybe it was the feel of a haircut, the pleasant buzz of whisky in my veins, the taste of a medium-rare steak. But I was with him and, yeah, I was feeling pretty good. Problems at the shop, sure, but a blockbuster coming down the pike that would sweep away all difficulties and bring me the success and respect that Judy and Eddie had already earned. My turn soon: I could taste it in the meat and see it in the wisps of foam on the ocean far below. My turn. I let Eddie gabble on and rode the crest of this emotional curl. I loved the guy. I did. And he loved me – how could he not? We were brothers!

So I changed the subject, asking about his daughters,

getting him to talk about his golf handicap and who was speaking that week at Rotary and how miserable the Red Sox were and always had to be or Bostonians wouldn't love them. Eddie was a drag to almost everyone, but the more meaningless his chatter, the more relaxed I felt. I let the words flow around me, like the gulls outside the window suspended on the ocean breeze, and drifted on the tone and rhythm of his voice, nearly fifty years familiar. As at Sal's, I slipped into the comfort of ritual. I said little. Here now, tangible and distinct, was a certainty I could count on. Which gave me certainty of what would be. Of my success. Yes, I was going to make it. I really was.

We finished lunch, left the club, and said goodbye on the teeming sidewalk. In the shadows of the downtown skyscrapers I watched him walk away, stiff and deliberate, his shoulders curved as if in protection against the wind.

3

I thought hard all week about Bobby's story, searching for the slant that would sell it in Peoria as well as Peabody. The right angle and this book would hit it big, no question, but success depended to a perilous degree on the co-operation of people with very different reasons for being involved: publisher, writer, lawyers, author, author's wife. I counted on money to hold us all together, but dough was first on no one's list of priorities, except perhaps my own. I didn't like depending on others for something that meant so much to me. No one knew how desperate I was to make this book happen and happen right.

Though few people knew it, the project was still in legal limbo. I had spoken twice to Lucinda Rizzoli by phone and sent her the contract. She sounded tired and distant, with wary Southern diction when I expected a local twang. During our second conversation, she had promised to drop by with the signed document the next day, but she hadn't shown up or returned my calls in the three days since. I had also left unanswered messages in Concord for Bobby. In the meantime I said nothing to my staff, who assumed that the agreement was a done deal and *The Tarnished Badge* (working title) would lead our spring list. I could do nothing but keep faith in Bobby's steely look when I queried the trustworthiness of Lucinda. They'll go for it, I kept telling myself, and then the real work will begin – keeping everyone focused on turning Bobby from a regional celebrity into a *New York Times* bestseller.

My gut told me that the hook was corruption. The details of the heist would fascinate, but what readers really wanted to know was how a decorated police captain, with three medals of valor and a pristine record of public service, had turned into one of the nation's most notorious bank robbers. Hillbrook (All-American City, 1977) was a typical Boston working-class suburb: ethnic, densely populated, organized around rituals of job, family, and class. Bobby had coached youth hockey, been an usher at St Dominick's, delivered the commencement address at Hillbrook High on the subject of integrity and the city employee. Stealing from the local bank was stealing from his own. How could he do it? I could hear that question resounding in taverns and bowling alleys, in backyards over barbecue and beer, across assembly lines and Kmart counters, in the flag-draped rooms of VFW and Elks and Local 495. If it could happen in Hillbrook, it could happen anywhere. This was a story that would stir the national obsession with blight and conspiracy. If we couldn't trust cops, who could we trust? Corruption, that was it. Americans believe so completely in the otherness of evil that stories of the worm in the apple are always irresistible.

But I had to be careful. Bobby was a smart, willful man with all day to dwell on his own agenda. One eye on his appeal, he was sure to diminish his own role in the heist and soften the hard details. I didn't want the story to suffer. If he was looking for payback, fine – Latrelli was bound to be the bad guy in Rizzoli's version, and as local color went he was a character we could feature. Readers love a wiseguy. But he couldn't become the protagonist. This was Bobby's tale, and he had to remain at the center. Behind his fall from grace was a pattern of political favor and tribal closeness gone foul. It was a pattern I knew well from my own upbringing, and it was my job to guide my writer and draw Bobby out. My plan was to play dumb and work on his ego. I wanted to give him the impression he was thrilling us with stories from the inside; I wanted him to open up and deliver the raw material for a real exposé.

However, first I had to convince my own team that we could do this book. Donohue Press was not a typical publishing house. Wedged into a corner of the family print shop on the fifth floor of an old shoe factory, we occupied a couple of old proofing rooms a shaking partition away from two pounding Heidelbergs. Our window ledges were spattered with gull droppings, and our office view was a stretch of unrenewed waterfront – hardly inspiring. We were a long way from the purpled glass and iron footscrapes of Beacon Hill, where bow-tied Brahmins rubbed elbow patches at the Athenaeum. We were ink-stained and blue-collar, trivia titles and fire-fighting picture books our stock in trade. With no rent and print at cost we were a profitable concern, but no one except me thought we would publish anything but the second-rate and parochial.

We were a staff of four: when I wasn't keeping an eye on the pressmen I did all acquisition and what passed for development; Jeff Higgins, the kid from the projects who I hoped would get inside the head of Bobby Rizzoli, copy-edited and farmed out design; Ann's college friend Shirley Van Zandt handled marketing and publicity; and good old Frankie Deluca sold my books over the phone, bargaining with bookstores and negotiating with a skeptical and canny network of sales reps. Frankie had been my first hire. Still in his twenties, he wore polyester ties and double-breasted suits and first thing each morning wiped the receiver of his telephone with a stained handkerchief. Master of the malaprop, he once told me, 'It is crucial that I preen.' He was easily excited, going pale around the nose with emotion and stammering slightly after closing a sale. A Hillbrook kid, he was proud to the point of irritation about the Rizzoli connection and couldn't keep his mouth shut. His office was bare except for desk photographs of his fiancée, Rose, and Frank Sinatra. Poor Frankie was a walking cliché, and the guys on the shop floor rode him hard. Jeff, too, they ragged for having the gall to get an education, but Shirley, who was assured and elegant and without pretension, they treated with nervous respect. They knew when they were outmatched.

This morning I had summoned Shirley and Jeff to my office. I wanted an update, but I also wanted to settle Jeff down. Since I'd asked him to write the book his attitude had stiffened, and his running battle with the shop foreman, Johnny Rotella, which he would never win, had intensified. He was becoming a nuisance when I most needed him to be a help.

Shirley arrived first. I asked her what was new.

'Sonny Volski called,' she said, looking at her notepad. Sonny was my publicist friend who used to work for Random House. 'He's having lunch with Jack Wambaugh on Friday, and he wants a proposal from us. Something short and sweet.'

Shirley was a tall, striking woman with a peach-shaped face, a high forehead, and a neck rich in substance and tone. Though, like me, over fifty, she still looked terrific. She spent good ex-husband money on French jackets, Italian boots, and silk blouses from Hong Kong. Ann once told me she had sent a nude photograph of herself to her tailor, a detail I found hard not to remember during meetings. She commanded the attention of any room she entered. She knew well the powers conferred upon her by her physical gifts, and men held their breath when she took off her coat and adjusted her dress and hair with movement as fluent as a dancer's. Up close you could see her crow's feet and spreading rear, but for me these concessions to time only increased her attractiveness.

'I'll write something and you can spruce it up,' I said.

'He says pitch it so Wambaugh can fit it into one of their categories. *60 Minutes* pieces are driven by the presenter. Is it an Ed Bradley slot, a Mike Wallace slot, whatever.'

'It's a Bradley slot.'

'How so?'

'Bradley's an actor. He loves to pretend he's amazed by stuff anybody who's been around knows all about. He'll act like the police-corruption stuff bowls him over, and Rizzoli'll lay it on thick.'

She smiled and drew back her head. She held herself so well that the slightest eye movement was a grand gesture, and what her eyes were saying now was that she couldn't quite believe we were going to do this book. Her take on me was influenced by our low-rent surroundings and whatever Ann chose to pass on during saunas at the Downtown Club.

(Ann and Shirley naked together, gossiping – I had pictured this many times.) Ann didn't like the Rizzoli project, and as my ex-wife she didn't have much faith in me. When Shirley doubted, I could only counter with charm.

'So write the proposal, Harry. I'll send it tomorrow.'

'OK. And what about tonight?'

'What about it?'

'Let me count the ways: drinks, dinner, a show. A moonlight walk.'

A tolerant smile, wary eyes, her hand at her wonderful throat.

'Isn't it time we stopped kidding ourselves,' I said, 'and yielded to the obvious?'

'Oh, it's time all right.'

The edge was there, but flirtation faded quickly. It always did. Why couldn't I get past this point with her? The work environment? Ex-wife aura? Ann's cautions? I so wanted to sleep with her. 'Where's Jeff?' I finally asked. Maybe next time.

She looked to the door. 'I think he's with Johnny. He's been complaining all morning about the heavy-metal music from the press room. Says he can't concentrate.'

'Oh, please. You know, I never figured him for a prima donna. We haven't even started and already this thing has gone to his head.'

'Harry, he wants to do well. To impress you. He doesn't have a father, you know.'

What she meant was, she didn't have a son. She was very maternal around him and, though Jeff didn't like it, it probably saved him being torn apart by Johnny.

'If you ask me, he sniffs the big-time and is afraid of failing.

So he's creating distractions. He pushes Johnny's buttons much more he'll get tossed from one of these windows.'

Shirley looked without emotion at my sad ocean view. She deserved a better context for her Florentine beauty. Body by Lippi; eyes by Botticelli. It was killing me.

There was a ruckus from the shop floor. I stuck my head out the door and asked Maureen McCarthy, one of the salespeople, what was going on.

'Johnny going bananas, like usual.'

I sent Maureen to get Jeff and went to the window. Five floors below, the old trestle bridge out to the dry docks rattled like a cage. A rusty lobster boat bobbed against the rotting wharf. 'I could still get someone else to write it,' I said, without turning around.

'Harry, stop worrying. He'll do fine.'

I sat. 'I'm glad you think so. Any other calls?'

'Gary.'

'How is my son today?'

'He has a problem.'

'He told you that?'

'He called here, looking for you. He was upset. You weren't around, so he confided. Told me he's having some difficulty down at the site. He wants you to drop over before lunch.'

'That it?'

'He needs you, Harry.'

'He needs something, all right.' Since August, Gary had been under contract with a downtown bank to build several shelters for its ATM machines on State and Washington Streets. He owned and operated his own construction business, specializing in modular kiosks and small retail units.

This was his first city contract. Up to now he had only done two-bit jobs around Dedham, where he still lived with Ann. He was coming up against the realities of the street and not handling them well.

'How old is Gary now?' Shirley asked.

'Twenty-four.'

'You know, Ann worries about him.'

'Don't BS me, Shirley. Ann's worried he's never going to make a buck and never move out of the house. And you know what? She *should* be worried.'

'So what's wrong?'

I shrugged. 'Today, who knows? Last week it was some cop hassling him about permits.'

'Isn't that something you could fix for him?'

'I try to fix this I look like I don't know shit from shinola. Keeping the cop on the beat happy is rule one on the street. Fail to do that and the whole order of things breaks down. Gary thinks the world operates like a shopping mall. He's only known the suburbs. What I gotta fix is the kid's attitude before he screws up his first good job.'

I was irritated with Gary for getting into trouble and mad at having found out about it second-hand. But I didn't have time to brood. Like a breaking window, the row between Jeff and Johnny burst into my office. Jeff arrived first, back-pedaling, his thin face blotchy with anger. Johnny was advancing, waving a copy of *Boston College Trivia* like a cop with a warrant. I stepped between them.

'Tell Joe College here,' Johnny shouted, shaking the book over my shoulder, 'that finding mistakes he shoulda caught two weeks ago is his problem, not mine.'

'I can't work like this. I can't work with this maniac.'

'*I'm* a maniac?'

'He threatened me.'

'Jeff,' I said, 'calm down.'

'*Me* calm down?'

'Harry,' Johnny shouted, 'you should know he coulda cost us the Quinlan job. I never missed a deadline in thirty years, but Mario Puzo here wants I retire without a perfect record. He took Lapich offa the job . . . he took Lapich off to proof something that's *already printed*!'

Johnny's rage was so intense it was almost comical. His face was twisted and scarlet, and his bad eye rolled wildly. With Shirley in the room he was laying off the profanity, and the effort was raising his blood pressure even further. Shirley had stepped back, notepad clasped at her bosom. I eyed Jeff to a chair and gently edged Johnny out of the office.

'I swear to God, that kid is outta control. He took George off the Quinlan job and told him to check this again.' Johnny flourished the trivia book, a book I had co-written, and threw it onto a chair like an old dishrag. '*He* told George! That little son-of-a-bitch. And you know what he did this morning? Unplugged Mac's radio. You're lucky Mac didn't break his legs.'

Johnny had been our foreman for over thirty years. My dad had stolen him from a Chelsea linotype house by offering him fifty bucks a week, and he and Mac MacCarthy started the very day in 1950 we moved the business from our garage in Brighton to this building. He could run a web offset with his eyes closed and strip negative faster than anyone I'd ever seen. The little I knew of the trade I'd learned from him. He held the place together. He kept us solvent. All he required was loyalty and the minimum of common sense. Jeff, to my dismay, lacked both. More than anything else, Johnny's work allowed me the time to devote to Donohue Press; I couldn't afford this kind of conflict. 'Johnny, I'll take care of it.'

I walked him back to his office and he calmed down, but there was a hard look in his eye. He lowered his voice. 'Harry, it's none of my business, but this cop book has this kid twisted inside-out. Walking around the place giving orders. Telling *my* people what to work on. I think maybe you want to rethink this decision.'

Johnny was funny-looking, with a conical head, a roving right eye, and a lolling tongue, but a lot of people had gone down for thinking he was less than he was – a shrewd, head-strong, experienced guy, who knew people and how to get what he wanted. His suggestion was not casual. He respected me and cut me slack, but he had been suspicious of Donohue Press since day one. He worried I wouldn't ride the salespeo-ple. He worried we would be a drain on resources. He held a slice of both companies, but he didn't trust what he didn't know. So far I had managed to sell enough books to cover print costs, but Johnny knew we would never pay commercial and told me straight whenever he got the chance that a Donohue Press success did Donohue Print no good. One of my many goals was to find a way of expanding his incentive, but first I needed my bestseller.

'Johnny, I don't know if he's going to end up being the writer on this or not. I really don't. But it doesn't matter. I'll set him right on the George thing, and if he gives you any more crap just let me know.'

I got the look I got from so many men his age who knew me through my father, the same look Mick Malone had flashed outside Kiley's. It was a look of reflected trust. *I'll go with you on this one, kid, because of your old man.*

'Don't you lose your head, Harry. Don't let this Rizzoli thing turn it all upside-down.' He walked back to the press room.

In my office Shirley was telling Jeff the *60 Minutes* news. I spoke without looking at her.

'Shirley, I'll have that proposal for you by the end of the day.'

She left, glancing back at Jeff. He had calmed down. His face had lost the blotches, and a nervous smile raised the tips of his downy mustache. He saw I meant business and thought he'd take the light approach. 'Between Johnny and Deluca and Charlie Palumbo, you and me we're surrounded by crazy guineas.'

Looking at him now, I saw the street punk he would have been if he hadn't been blessed with an ambitious mother and a way with words. He was lank-haired and skinny-assed, with hollow cheeks and darting eyes. He looked more like a pool hustler than a scholar. He should have been sucking on a joint in Union Square and giving the finger to passing cops. Instead he was scribbling beneath a poster of John Updike, the *Chicago Manual of Style* at his elbow. Which was fine, which was the American Way, but then he went and did something bone-headed like this, landing me in the soup and forcing me to wonder yet again if I had made a mistake asking him to put Bobby Rizzoli's story into words. I had reckoned his inexperi-ence was no great disadvantage – Bobby would be comfortable with someone he could lead, and I could keep an eye on the marketplace. But this war with Johnny was driving *me* bananas.

'George is a proofreader, Jeff. He is a print employee and he reports to Johnny.'

'You told me you wanted *BC Trivia* double-checked.'

'By you, not by George.'

'Harry, I'm editor-in-chief, copy-editor, production manager, and lead writer. Now you want me to be a proofreader as well. At eighteen-five a year.'

'You're starting to sound like Frankie.'

'Frankie's got it easy. He sells books that are still in your head; I'm the one has to put them together.'

He saw at once that he had strayed too far.

'Got too much on your plate?' I asked.

'Possibly.'

'Whaddaya say we find someone else to do the Rizzoli book? After all, he's just another crazy guinea you have to deal with.'

'I can handle it.'

'I don't think you can.'

'I can handle it.'

'Can you handle Johnny?'

'If I have to.'

I leaned forward. 'You have to. I can't do without Johnny, but I can do without you. There's a thousand talented writers out there who want to be the next Robert Parker. They'd jump at a shot to write this book.'

He stared at me, weighing the situation. I stared him out. I didn't like coming down so heavy, but the kid was way out of line. He needed a firm hand. Like Shirley said, he didn't have a father. The problem was, I already had a wayward son. Last thing I needed was another kid telling me how the world was getting in the way of his destiny. But my one advantage here was that I could fire Jeff, and if he had enough sense to see this I might have a chance to turn this thing around. Gary, well, Gary was another ball game. He'd call me to the rescue and then tell me how I was screwing him up. Which wasn't inappropriate, given our history.

The room cooled. Jeff stroked his mustache. 'When am I going to meet Rizzoli?'

'Don't worry about Rizzoli,' I said. 'How's the research going?'

'Fine.' He was a bad liar.

'Didn't you get the transcripts? Didn't you mention my name?'

'The clerk of court down there is a moron.'

How was he going to handle Rizzoli if he couldn't get past a civil servant who owed me a favor? I was getting a headache. I had Jeff in front of me, Gary's problem – whatever the hell it was – looming before lunch, and no contract for my make-or-break book deal. Chugging morning beers in a dark Brighton bar with Mick Malone seemed like an attractive alternative.

'We'll talk about this later, Jeff. I gotta go downtown.'

He took my weariness for forgiveness and turned enthusiastic. 'Did you hear about Bucky Quinn? The exam? I know his cousin, and we could get a meeting.'

'Jeff, Bucky once sat right where you are and called my dad an asshole. Twenty-five years ago. Then smashed all the windows in our Buick.'

'You know Bucky?'

'Knew him. Unfortunately.'

'You should call him. We could do a book on the exam scam.'

'One book at a time.' I motioned him out. It would be so easy to fire him. As he walked away, something about the shape of his neck and his sagging pants reminded me of Gary as a kid. I felt vaguely guilty for bullying him, but I was damned if I was going to let his ego come between me and the big time.

On my way out our receptionist stopped me. Carla was Johnny Rotella's niece, a large-eyed woman with stiff hair, rings on every finger, and a wide smile set in a small face. A face like a marmoset's. 'While all the yelling was going on, your mother's care counsellor called,' she said.

'From the nursing home?'

'Yeah.'

'Call her back and have her tell my mom I'll be by this evening. After seven. What's the other number?'

'A Steven . . .'

I looked at the name. 'Gurlick. What did he want?'

'He didn't say. Just left the number.'

It was an internal exchange number I recognized as the Statler Building. That meant he was either a Fed or a state agency official dealing with Health and Safety. During the summer, I had run into trouble when one of Gary's pals working for me threw a bucket of paint in our dumpster and it leaked all over the alley. This call was probably a follow-up. I stuffed the number into my pocket.

I glided down in the empty elevator, alone, breathing

deeply and doing neck stretches to relieve the stress. Head tilted back, my eyes fixed on a riveted panel above the door that I had never noticed before. Scraped crudely across the panel was the legend 'Harrys a dumb prick'. I ran my finger over the letters. I'm six-two, but I could barely reach them. They looked and felt like they'd been there a long time. I was proud of my relations with my staff. I was a decent boss. Who would have gone to the trouble to scratch, at that height, such a slur? Someone tall, like Louie, the quiet guy from Roxbury who ran the web? Louie, whose kids I took to Fenway Park twice a year? Someone on a stepladder? Jeff (deliberately omitting the apostrophe to throw me off the trail)? Was I the last to see it? The elevator door opened. I exited, one eye on those shocking words, and walked straight into a waiting woman.

She was reading the building directory and didn't see me coming. We bumped heads. She lurched back, then forward, and I grabbed her by the elbows.

'What the hell—'

'I'm sorry,' I said, 'I wasn't . . .'

She rubbed her head. Several bracelets slid down her fore-arm. She was nearly as tall as I was, a bleached blonde with lipstick the colour of a New Mexico sunset.

'You weren't is right. Hope you don't plan on driving any-where, you expect to live.'

Only now did her perfume come to my attention, musky, direct, liberally applied. It roped me back to the moment of collision with a pleasant suggestion of intimacy. She had broad shoulders to go with her height, and a large square face beneath the titanium bouffant. But she carried her size well and looked me over with the confidence of a woman who took on the world as its equal. She wore a ribbed turtleneck that matched her lipstick and a cream suit. There was something fifties about her, something Kim Novak.

'Really,' I said, 'I'm sorry. I didn't know where I was.'

'You know now?'

She smiled, hand on her hip. In spite of the make-up and clothes she had the air of a farm girl, a gal who once knew the 4-H club code and the color of wheat. I let my gaze linger a little too long and she looked back at the directory.

'Who you looking for?'

'Donohue Press.' She pronounced it Dawn-a-who, and only then did I realize I was talking to Lucinda Rizzoli.

'I'm Harry Donohue.'

'Well, what do you know? Don't even know each other, already we're knocking heads.'

'I guess you're Lucinda.'

'Lucy.'

'Do we have an appointment?'

'I was in the neighborhood.'

'Right. Why don't we go down here and get a cup of coffee?'

I led her to the lobby coffee shop, her heels clacking on the linoleum. She wasn't elegant but she wasn't ungainly. She took long steps and swung her arms slightly. Her head had the gentle bob of the large high-school girl who doesn't want to draw attention to herself, but she was a splash of brightness in the dim diner. Though it was hardly the place to bring her, I didn't want to return to the tension upstairs. I was thinking, too, of the scratched insult above the elevator door.

Tommy served up the coffee, barely suppressing a wink. We sat on electric-blue padded chairs at a narrow Formica table. She eyed the surroundings. 'I take it you get to the fifth floor, standard moves up a notch.'

'Not really,' I said.

'And you're gonna make my husband a fortune?'

I blew on the coffee. 'I'm going to make you a fortune.'

'Well, ain't that white of you?'

She took a pack of Salems from her handbag and lit up. She had large eyes, smoker's skin, and a thin mouth tightened, I sensed, by experience. Being married to Bobby couldn't have been easy. Elbows propped, she took deep drags from her cigarette, hollowing her cheeks and exhaling from the side of her mouth. Her eyes were full of disguised intelligence and a strong dose of suspicion.

'You're not from around here.'

'Perceptive.'

'I'da thought Bobby was a local-girl kind of guy.'

She arched her brows. Her eyes rivaled Shirley's for expressiveness, but they were eyes used to other levels of reality. 'Who says he isn't?'

I let that one slide. We were so close across the narrow table I could see the powdered density of her make-up. I was beginning to like her. Her banter was more playful than defensive, and she was doing a better job than Bobby had at probing me for motive.

'I'm a Texan,' she said, relaxing a little. 'San Antone. Schertz, actually. Rinky-dink town on the outskirts full of squarehead farmers. Next to Randolph Air Force Base. "Keep your pants on in Schertz," my daddy used to say to the hotshots come knocking on our door.' She smiled a Texan smile and stubbed out her cigarette.

'That's where you met Bobby.'

'Yessir. He was maintaining C-5s and playing right field for the base team.'

'And you?'

'Me? I was a seventeen-year-old looking for betterment. Like the song says, "Won't nothin' bring you down like your hometown".'

When I was at Fort Riley in 1959, women like Lucy hung around the better-class bars in Junction City, drinking vodka martinis and playing hard to get with trainee officers. They were big-boned and blonde, with wide-open Kansan accents and skin like honey. They, too, were looking for something bigger but would never know as good a time, when youth and energy and the attention of squadrons of men in their prime put them center stage for a brief, shining period. Many of them married my buddies (Jimmy was one), trading one provincialism for another and ending up homesick or bitter or perhaps content, but always a long way from prairie grass and Black Angus beef.

Lucy looked like someone who could flirt and sashay, and I could see her and Bobby leaving a little rubber behind as they roared up from Randolph in a '57 Chevy. She must have cut quite a figure in Hillbrook when she first arrived. Cut quite a figure now. But there were shadows in her face I'd not seen in those Kansas sweethearts, dark spaces that hinted at depths and experience she could probably have done without. Life with a man of several double lives would have been tough even without seeing his greed, deceit, and infidelity aired in the Boston papers, like flags on the Fourth of July, and I found myself wondering why she was still here. Was it loyalty or lack of options or the money his celebrity might bring? Money, I hoped. She could love him, hate him, wish him damned, but if money had this savvy Lone Star lady sitting in this greasy spoon then emotion was a lesser issue and I was on safer ground. Not that her eyes were giving anything away.

'Go on,' she said. 'Ask me.'

'Ask you what?'

'What you're thinking. Do I have the contract.'

She was smoking again.

'Actually, I was thinking of my army days.'

'In what capacity?'

'Oh, you know. The tenor of the times. Situations I fell into.'

She nodded in a manner that made me think she knew exactly. The way she moved her head and arms in conversation was oddly calibrated, not quite natural, as if rehearsed to cover up an innate flirtatiousness. If Bobby was the jealous type (and all the evidence suggested he was), she would have had good reason to develop such protective choreography. But I was good at making women feel comfortable and, though nothing changed on the surface, she did allow her eyes to say a little more. She reached into her handbag, drew out an envelope, and placed it so close to her overhanging breasts it would have been provocative to reach for it.

'I had several lawyers look at this,' she said, 'but you know lawyers. Tell you everything and tell you shit. So, you tell me. What's in it for Bobby?'

'For Bobby? Nothing at all. Or whatever your goodwill decides.'

She laughed. 'So you think it works like that?'

'Lucy, I don't care how it works. That's between you and your husband.'

She tapped the envelope with a brightly varnished nail. 'What if I was to say this whole thing's turning a mite complicated?'

'I wouldn't be surprised.'

I would not have liked to play poker with this woman. To mask my anxiety, I focused on the sweet curve of the turtleneck, the expanse of her shoulders, her painted fingernails drumming the coveted envelope. But whatever she was waiting for must have arrived, because, in a single motion, she pushed the contract across the table and stood, slinging her handbag over her shoulder. 'I have some tapes at the house you probably want to listen to,' she said, from a height. I scrambled up, sliding the envelope into my jacket pocket. 'Also some court reports, letters, transcripts from discovery. Bobby thinks he's gonna talk this book out of thin air, but his memory is somewhat selective. Hope you got a good writer.'

'He'll do OK.'

'Wanna do a whole lot better than OK or Bobby'll have him for lunch.'

'Don't worry, I'll keep an eye on him.'

She looked me up and down. We were partners now, and the tone of her body language had shifted. It was sharper, less ambiguous. 'I bet you will,' she said.

I walked her out to her car. In the open air she was less imposing but even more out of place against the dirty brick and rusting girders surrounding our waterfront parking lot. The trestle bridge rattled, and from somewhere high above came the sound of a wolf whistle. She unlocked the same '84 Cadillac listed on the prosecution's summary of Bobby's assets at his trial. She rattled her keys and looked up at the building. 'We do this right you just might get out of this shithole,' she said.

'That's the idea.'

'Then let's do it right.'

She drove off. I watched the big car bounce out of the lot and onto Atlantic Avenue then went inside to tell the janitor to remove the graffiti from the elevator.

4

Gary was working out of a Portakabin office in an alley off Washington Street. To meet the bank's deadline, he was building three shelters simultaneously with a crew of seven, mostly guys from Dedham he bussed in himself. The cabin was locked when I arrived, so I walked down to the corner of Washington and Franklin, where I found him examining a battered compressor in front of one of his half-finished shelters. He saw me coming and started talking before I reached him. 'Look at this – it isn't tough enough down here without this kind of bullshit?'

It was a standard, mid-sized Ingersoll compressor with the name A & H TOOL RENTAL stencilled on the side. He used it to run drills and a buffer. The casing had been ripped back so hard it was rent down the middle, and the engine had been battered with a heavy-duty hammer. Shreds of hose littered the sidewalk.

'What happened?'

Gary snorted with anger. 'That cop I told you about last week? He's responsible for this. *He* did this!' Hands on his hips, he pivoted on his left foot and looked back and forth from the wrecked machine to my face as if I were to blame, just as he'd done over broken toys twenty years ago.

'Take it easy, Gar. You said this guy was asking about permits.'

'I have all the permits. I'm by the book, one hundred per cent. So he comes back yesterday and tells me to pay him off or . . . *this*—' He gestured lamely at the compressor.

He was solid and well built, with a thick neck and my own square jaw. He'd been All-State middle linebacker for Dedham High and played on special teams at Boston College. He was smart on the field, with good instincts and plenty of drive, but top-heavy and way too slow to star on a college team as good as BC during the Flutie years. His claim to fame was being on the field for 'the pass' in the renowned game against Miami in 1984. He was put in as a tight end for the final play to help protect Flutie in the pocket, and when Phelan caught the Hail Mary it was Gary who lifted a joyous, finger-waving Flutie high in the air, an image carried on the cover of *Sports Illustrated* and in every American newspaper that Thanksgiving. In the celebrations following the game, Gary trashed the lobby of the Miami Beach Marriott, was arrested, and ended up in hospital with alcohol poisoning after collapsing at the police station. I flew down on Sunday to straighten out the mess, something for which he still hadn't forgiven me. To his way of thinking, I only appeared in his life when something went wrong. Like today.

'Gary, what exactly did he say?'

'What difference does it make?'

'It makes all the difference.'

'Dad, you always miss the point. A cop shakes me down and threatens my livelihood, and you want chapter and verse on what he said. Don't you *believe* me?'

Recently he'd changed his hairstyle, buzz-cut at the sides with a shaggy top, but it didn't suit his broad face. He had a small, crowded mouth, which twisted unpleasantly when he was annoyed, and narrow eyes. When he was three or four I used to rub his stomach like a cat and he'd close those eyes tight with pleasure. Now I avoided their challenge. 'I believe you, I believe you. You insured?'

'Of course. I have to be. But there's a twenty-five hundred deductible. Plus the premiums will rocket. I mean, Dad, I'm taking a loss on this job to begin with just to open doors. I can't *afford* this.'

He was whining now, wholly into the neglected-kid persona he assumed when I was around. Over a decade since the divorce and still he blamed me. I fidgeted, tasting the bilious mix of affection and annoyance that rose in me on these occasions. What I easily tolerated in others grated when it came from him. I suspected that, in business, he lacked all the instincts and discipline he had on the field, where firm coaching and clear rules allowed him to focus on performance only. Not the type who could make it on his own. He was petulant and indecisive, a dangerous combination. I blamed myself. If I'd been around during the slippery years of his adolescence with a little male rigor, with some fatherly iron (as my dad had been for me), it might be different now. He might have had enough sense to pay this cop off, or at least not to cry when he realized his mistake. I looked away from his crumpled face and pointed at the chrome cantilever his crew had set above the empty rectangle where the ATM would go. 'Looks good.'

'It could be the Brooklyn Bridge, Dad, but what the hell *use* is it if it doesn't make me any money?'

Why had I bothered coming down? I didn't need this knee-jerk abuse. I turned away. 'I need a cup of coffee,' I said.

The walk to the coffee shop seemed to calm him down. But my own temper was threatening, and I tried to think of reasons why I should control it. Why not cut straight to the yelling and recriminations? Why bother, as we always did, with the pretense of dialog? He lifted one shoulder as he ate his donut and wiped his fingers carefully after each bite. It reminded me of Sunday afternoons at Friendly's or Brigham's ten years ago, when we would finish off an awkward weekend with a greasy meal and a milkshake while I tried to get more than grunted responses before returning him to Ann. For his first ten years he wanted me and I was never there; for his second decade it was the other way around.

'How much this cop looking for?' I asked.

'He wouldn't say!'

'What *did* he say?'

'That a hundred-dollar permit was a bargain.'

I stared at him. For once I was really puzzled: he couldn't be this thick. 'Gary, he was looking for a C a week.'

'But I *have* the permits!'

'It was his way of letting you know how much he wanted.'

He sipped his coffee and looked out into the street. A grizzled panhandler peered at us through a window cluttered with Hallowe'en decorations.

'Dad, this is 1988 and I'm supposed to understand some stupid code like out of the movies. I took his badge number. O'Brien. Timothy J. O'Brien. I'm going to turn the asshole in.'

'Gary, listen to me. You know that wouldn't do any good.

You know that. You're angry, and that's understandable. But cut your losses and pay the guy.'

'I can't afford it!'

'You're out twenty-five hundred plus higher premiums and you can't *afford* it? A second-grader could do this math!'

'Thanks a lot, Dad.'

'You can't afford *not* to pay the guy!'

'So you pay him!' he shouted.

I took five twenties from my wallet and slapped them on the table between us. 'Sure! Here's a down payment!' Breathing hard, I stared at the crumpled bills. I became aware of piped music. The waitress avoided looking at me. I thought I could buy him off? I would have been better off giving the dough to the panhandler.

Back in the Portakabin, Gary was examining plans and talking to Eric, his carpenter. They were both smoking.

'Hey there, Mr Donohue.'

'Hi, Eric. Can you give us a minute?'

Eric left, sneaking a glance at his boss. I closed the door. 'You smoking?'

'No. The cigarette is.'

'No kidding?'

He flicked ash on the floor and let his head bob comically like those spring-headed baseball dolls. In him it was a sign of frankness. No more games, it said.

'It's stress, I guess. I keep trying to quit.'

'How's your mom?'

'You know Mom. Always on top of things. First in sales in Suffolk County and first on the golf course since she took it up last year. Can't figure why I have trouble meeting payroll or collecting receipts out over ninety days.'

'Sounds familiar. She still seeing Howard?'

'Please. That asshole.'

I could always console myself with the cruel knowledge that Gary hated Ann's current partner more than he could ever hate me. But Howard was easy to hate. All the Wasp faults and none of the virtues. 'You got that badge number?' I asked.

Gary raised his brows with suspicion. 'Why?'

'I'll see what I can do.'

'Like in what sense?'

'Gary. Can I have the number?'

He rooted through a sheaf of papers and handed me his business card with the number scrawled on the back. I slipped it into my pocket. I buttoned up my topcoat while he stabbed out the smoke. At this stage of a meeting I usually asked him if he was still considering my long-standing offer to work for Donohue Print, but I'd put my foot in it enough for one day. 'You need any Celtics tickets? You know, Jimmy's got season tix.'

'I'm busy, Dad.'

'All we got to look forward to, now the Sox have bombed.'

'They were never gonna make it against the A's. Too much power.'

'I guess so.'

Through the oval window in the door we both watched Eric watch a woman sway past. I cleared my throat. I stepped towards the door and, hands in my coat pockets, nudged him with my shoulder. It was as close as we got to a hug these days. 'The Lakers game,' I said. 'Whaddaya say?' For me a second request was unusual. A peace pipe.

'They in town?'

'Next month. Thanksgiving week.'

He looked at me warily, but smiled. 'Sure. Why not?'

'Good. I'll call you.'

So we parted, for once, on half-decent terms. Another buy-off, I guess, but at least we were moving in the right direction. And the next time we met I could tell him about the book.

I walked down Federal Street to Post Office Square, frayed in mood and stiff around the shoulders. I had an hour before lunch, so I thought I'd drop in on Steven Gurlick, the Health and Safety man at the Statler Building. I knew from dealing with bureaucrats all my life that a face-to-face meeting, with a broad smile and ready deference, always beat a phone call. Chances were, we had some mutual acquaintance; if not, a little talk of sports or politics usually created the rapport that made it easier for him to overlook unfiled paperwork or an overdue fine.

Gary worried me because he was so like me. Entrepreneurial without the eye for detail. Overly optimistic. There he was, just ticking over, doing business at a loss to keep momentum, waiting like we all were for the big break. Thank God for the Rizzoli book. I wasn't one to count my chickens, but without this contract (delivered just an hour ago by Lucinda Rizzoli, secure in my breast pocket) I would've walked away from my meeting with my son with no hope whatsoever. So the kid was screwing up. If things went right I'd move to new premises and pay him megabucks to refit the whole damn place. With no cops to pay off.

I stepped out of the fall sunshine and into the shadow of the gloomy public buildings on the west side of the square. They stood dark and solid, stone temples to the ancient Yankee gods of civic duty and sober judgment. Gods long dead like all others. Officer O'Brien was stroking Gary's crew because, in my father's time, the Irish sent these gods packing with grand gestures and tribal drama, turning these buildings into sancta of patronage and personal gain. A Boston tradition; a Boston fact. Gary was taking way too long to grasp this fundamental truth. He could've learned a thing or two from his grandfather.

Physically, Gary reminded me of my dad, a big man whose own authority went unchallenged. He'd been a drayman, a prizefighter, a navy engineer, and a longshoreman. He'd run a wholesale ice business out of Cambridge, slicing huge chunks out of Fresh Pond and transporting them across town by sledge for sale to the Italian icemen who delivered to Beacon Hill and the South End. He built a decent business, lost it all with the mass growth of refrigerators in the twenties, and went to work at the *Herald* as a linotypist. A school pal of Maurice Tobin, he secured several city printing contracts after Tobin's mayoral victory in 1941 and started his own business with a single flatbed in our Brighton garage. For as long as I could remember, he smelt of hot metal and drying flame, and the resiny trace of printer's ink. But he was well groomed and always wore a jacket and bow tie, even when he was fixing the flatbed and was black to the elbows.

Dad was big all around, but his hands were huge. Knobby from boxing, leathery and lined, with long fingers and square nails, they could pack a punch and squeeze you dry but were also delicate enough to fix the complex workings of an ailing

Heidelberg. As a kid, I saw him throw a union thug over a picnic table but, when Judy had scarlet fever, he had held her burning head all night and gently swabbed her brow with a damp cloth. She was sick during the long hot summer of 1946, and the doctors told my parents she was unlikely to survive. Dad never left her side and prayed as he had never prayed before or since. When she recovered, he always called her his angel and exalted her to such a level of saintliness it was no surprise she first joined the Sisters of Charity and later the most self-righteous law firm in the city.

Of course for me, and to a lesser extent for Eddie, those hands kept a ham-fisted vigilance over boyhood pranks and neighborhood shenanigans, and we took our share of beatings. He licked me at least once a week. But there was never any indecision or regret in the meting of his justice. He had all the certainty I lacked with Gary. His anger was precise and functional, just as his love was clear and without limits. Wartime Boston was rough-and-tumble, with plenty of trouble on offer for a curious kid like me. His authority kept me in line. But his hold was anchored in the day-to-day routine of family, the steadiness of a shared life. An hour after punishment, I was helping him in the garage or playing stickball with him in the street. What had I shared with Gary but absence? What had anger to yield to but a whispering, distant regret?

I entered the Statler lobby, with its dark marble floors and art-nouveau stylings. At reception I asked for Steven Gurlick. A young black woman with cornrows and bright eyes fingered the directory. 'What department?'

'Health and Safety, I guess.'

'No, sir. No Gurlick in H an' S.'

I fished his telephone number from my pocket and showed it to her. She asked my name and dialed. 'Fifth floor, Mr Donohue. Federal.'

Only when the elevator doors opened on the fifth did I realize my unscheduled appointment was with the FBI.

Agent Gurlick was a government-issue Fed, in blue suit and Oxfords, with the serene manner and unfocused gaze of a man not in the business of giving anything away. He could have been anywhere between twenty-five and forty. He had a bulging forehead, like the actor John Cazale, and a barely visible scar running from hairline to temple. He wore heavy-framed glasses and smelt of wintergreen. He did not offer his hand. 'No need to've come down, Mr Donohue. Could have handled this with a call.'

His voice was polite, soft, Midwest flat. Unreadable. I didn't tell him that I'd nearly turned and left when I saw where I was. 'I was in the neighborhood.'

I followed him into his office. He moved like a basketball player, his right shoulder dipped and his step springy. He shut the door behind us, sat, and peered at me over steepled hands. 'I believe you're a friend of Bobby Rizzoli,' he said.

'You get right to the point, don't you?'

'What point is that?'

'You tell me.'

He took a handkerchief from his pocket and blew his nose. He looked at me blankly.

'Bobby and I, we're big pals,' I said.

'I understand you're working together.'

'Like making license plates?'

'Writing books.'

'What does all this have to do with you, Steven?'

The room was windowless, with fluorescent lighting and wood-paneled walls. Framed diplomas and letters filled the wall behind him, and an old air conditioner hung crookedly in the upper corner of the room. His desktop was empty, except for a single photograph of an aging couple in farm clothes.

'I'm one of a task force here . . .' he waved vaguely at the office door, 'a RICO-empowered force, which is looking into police corruption. You've read about us in the papers, and what you haven't read Bobby could fill you in on. He's a regular visitor here.'

'So *you*'re working together.'

'I wouldn't say working. Exploring options.'

'Fifth Amendment must be getting in the way of your explorations.'

His skin was tinged orange by the bleached light. His teeth were perfect. He would play racquetball after work, eat light and healthy in his Beacon Hill studio, study for his degree in forensics or criminal psychology before watching a little college hoop, turning in, and dreaming bland Nebraska dreams.

'We're realists, Mr Donohue. We're out to cast the widest net we can. You have to let a few go to get the big ones.'

'Seems to me Bobby doesn't have too many places he *can* go.'

He barely shrugged, but it was enough to tell me there was something I didn't know. Or something he didn't but thought I did. Then I wondered why I was sitting there at all with this cold fish, being interrogated without the slightest sense of humor or gamesmanship. I'd known a few agents. Some of my school pals joined in the Fifties, when Hoover was waving his anti-Communist flag and looking for good Catholic boys to fight the good fight. It was like joining the priesthood, and those guys had a self-righteousness and intensity that might have rubbed me the wrong way but made a certain sense. Eddie had it. People who knew me were surprised when they met Eddie, but I knew a dozen Irish families where one brother became a rogue and another an enforcer. The Church could have such contradictory effect, though underneath the career choice there wasn't much difference between the types. But this guy Gurlick was of a new breed – clinical, cold, small-minded. The impulses, I sensed, were more self-serving. I didn't like his pale attention and I didn't like the cloudless forehead and vague stare. My nerves were frayed by the turmoil at work and my heart was heavy with Gary's wrangles with the world and himself. It wasn't even lunchtime and I felt like slamming back a couple Rob Roys and telling this suit to jump in the Charles.

I stood. 'You're right,' I said. 'We could have handled this over the phone.'

He was around the desk quickly, opening the door and handing me his card. 'Whatever business you guys do, you do. Only a matter of time before it's public record anyway, right? But if he should mention anything outside of that context . . . if anything should come up that you're not comfortable keeping to yourself . . .'

He hated asking me for anything, I could see that. It was almost like being with Gary. I twirled the card in my fingers. 'Speaking of contexts,' I said, 'don't you think us taxpayers'd

be better served if you boys spent less time running down
civil servants and more going after organized crime? Like you
say, the big fish. Bobby's doing his time.'

He stared at me. I moved away.

'Mr Donohue.'

I looked back.

'There's no difference between Bobby and Sammy McCann.
Don't kid yourself. Write your book and make a killing, good
luck to you. But don't kid yourself.'

I left without another word. As I waited for the elevator I
dropped his card into the ashtray.

5

The Friday after Election Day, Jimmy O'Leary and I continued an election-year tradition with a round of golf. I hadn't played all summer and tried to beg off, but Jimmy was insistent. 'It's a presidential year,' he said on Wednesday. 'We have to. Remember when Nixon won in '68 and I *shot* a sixty-eight?'

'Yeah, so this time you'll shoot an *eighty*-eight.'

'We'll see about that. We tee off at seven.'

We met at Brookline Country Club on a perfect November morning: mid-fifties, a little thin cloud, a northwest breeze. The air was clear, and the bare maples along the first fairway seemed etched on the sky. Starlings pecked the greens. A lone jet moved silently across the stratosphere. The course was near empty, and standing at the first tee looking down the long fairway (432-yard par four), I took a deep breath and enjoyed that rare feeling of starting from scratch, level par, even with life and the competition in a pruned stretch of bounded pasture far from the tumult of city, business, and family.

The good feeling lasted about five minutes. I sliced my tee shot into the maples, and the ball skidded along the dead leaves and dribbled out of bounds. Hands on his hips, Jimmy watched its progress a little longer than was natural. 'Take a mulligan,' he said, his voice already edged with pleasure at the prospect of a trouncing. Jimmy liked to win and win big. Though he shot off a six and I was an eighteen at the best of times, he gave me only nine strokes. We were playing for a flat hundred bucks – enough to give a loss some sting. On my second attempt, I grounded the driver, but the ball flew straight, scooting 150 yards up the fairway. Jimmy smacked his drive a ton, the persimmon clubhead clicking like a finger snap as the ball tunneled into the blue, shrinking in a second to pinprick and then to nothingness as I strained my eyes to search it out.

Jimmy was the same age as myself, though you wouldn't know it to look at him. He carried no extra weight. His face was pocked but unwrinkled, and he scowled with the hungry aggression of a junior bond salesman. He had pointed shoulders and walked with a wrestler's wariness. His terrier face was always tilted ahead, plunging into the possible. When I suggested a cart, he had scoffed. He carried his bag and played fast, assessing each coming shot as he strode the fairway, peering into the green distance with the same jaw-clenched determination he wore in the courtroom.

Fairway woods have always been my nemesis, so I whacked a couple of medium irons then chipped onto the green. Jimmy hit a four-iron just short of the pin and two-putted. I escaped with a six and the shame of the mulligan.

'Not as bad as it mighta been,' Jimmy needled. 'Coulda been three from the tee.'

'Hey. Give me twelve strokes like you should and I'll take an eight on the hole.'

His eyes sparked and his lip curled. It was the look Ann hated. 'Take the twelve and *keep* the double bogey.'

Jimmy was tough. Even in high school, when I had six inches and thirty pounds on him, he intimidated me. Under threat, his head would dip, his eyes grow narrow as a lizard's. He never lost a fight. He brought this ferocity to the mat and took the state championship twice, with ease. With his head-guard on, his teeth grinding, and his acned shoulders bared, he seemed in his element, happy in a way he would never be again until he discovered the law. Everybody, male and female, gave him a wide berth. I was his only close friend.

As was our custom, we played the front nine quickly, with little conversation. By the ninth I was already down the twelve-stroke handicap. We bought soft drinks and sat on the tee bench, waiting for an old couple who were starting the tenth. The guy wore plus fours and a tam. He hit his tee shot weak but straight, then smiled at us as he picked up his tee. 'Smack down the middle.' He and his partner tottered to the women's tees.

'Shoulda asked to play through,' Jimmy said.

'Relax.' I was glad of the break. My play was atrocious and I wanted to regroup.

Jimmy sighed. 'So,' he said. 'The Duke did all right after all.'

'I wouldn't say that.'

'Well, he took Massachusetts big. And forty-six per cent national.'

'Look at the electoral college, Jim.'

He stared off into the trees.

'Bush is a putz. He'll pretend he's moderate and end up

more conservative than Reagan. Alex and I met him at Harvard last year, at a Kennedy School lunch, and the corporate types were milling around him like shithouse rats. They could smell the power. But he's an idiot.'

'At least the House is safe. And Teddy came through.'

But Jimmy wasn't listening. In the forty-eight hours since the returns were announced he had done nothing but analyze the result as if it were one of his cases. He was known in the system for his thoroughness and grit. He left nothing to chance and would rather make an enemy than depend on someone he didn't trust. It was no different with politics. I knew he was thinking ahead to the state elections in 1990, when the governorship and other state positions were up for grabs. His ambitions had never been secret, and he had worked long and hard behind the scenes to position himself for the post of Attorney General. The current AG, Sean Devlin, was the frontrunner for the Democratic gubernatorial nomination, and Jimmy was his logical successor. But in the aftermath of Bush's landslide, the Democratic monolith in Massachusetts looked vulnerable for the first time since we were in law school. Our governor and leader had gone national and been humiliated. On Tuesday night, the state's leading Republicans had held a noisy, flag-waving celebration at the Westin Hotel, where party leaders had praised Bush and thundered out their endorsement of party ambitions. What a chance to jump on the bandwagon! To kick the Duke when he was down! I'd watched highlights on the news. It was mostly beer-fuelled good spirits and happy-days bravado, nothing you wouldn't have seen had the Democrats won. Yet it annoyed me, particularly when Nick Carducci, trying to appear grave over the panting glee of victory, led the flushed masses in the Pledge of Allegiance. It was worrying. With the Duke on the ropes and the economy tilting downward, a swing to the right would not be a surprise. I could feel Jimmy's concern through the slats in the bench.

The funny thing was, he was not particularly partisan. He was not, like Alex, committed to liberal causes out of a sense of passion. He was liberal because the state establishment was liberal. The prospect of a swing in ideology quashing his highest hopes must have been very painful for him. Like me, he had waited a long time for his shot at the big time. Opportunity comes slow in a party structure used to power, and over the years there had been plenty of bright Harvard grads and native sons trying to muscle him away from his goals. He'd fought tough and well, but it galled him still to be a DA twenty years after jumping into public life. Alex was a Superior Court judge. Pascal Rooney was a big cheese in the Justice Department. In two years Jimmy would be fifty-four, about as old as you could be in this type of race without the pundits pointing fingers and whispering. It was a crucial time for him. Sitting beside me, staring into space, he was doing no less than planning the opening stage of his '90 campaign.

'How's Judy?' he asked. He and I had been thinking in parallel: elections, Republicans, Yankee law firms, Judy.

'Good,' I said. 'She spent election night at the Welds'.'

'She knows Weld?'

'Oh, yeah. When he quit the Justice Department he took advice from Hale and Eliot.'

'Smart guy. Should be a Democrat.'

'He sees the lay of the land. My guess is he's thinking of running for governor.'

Jimmy looked at me. Every once in a while I surprised him with an insight or connection he didn't expect. Dollars to donuts he'd be on the phone to Judy on Monday, asking her how she was doing, angling for information about William Weld and his gubernatorial ambitions.

I'd seen my sister on election day. She summoned me from my office, sending out the Sister Superior call that could not be ignored. I was happy to oblige. I enjoyed her company; I liked being the only person in the world who could make fun of her to her face. We had a gently abrasive relationship grounded in imitation, as eldest son and daughter, of our parents. She was two years younger than me, unmarried, relentlessly active, on track for a prominent judicial position should the Republican shift so feared by Jimmy come to pass. She was a senior partner at Hale and Eliot, their first and only female, but bristled at any suggestion of tokenism and influenced firm policy more than anyone. She was formidable.

We met in the main conference room, the Eliot Room, beneath a portrait in oils of the dour founder. Used to the clatter of the print shop, I found the silence unnerving. We sat in soft leather at a huge oak table. A Waterford crystal bowl the size of a baptismal font glistened in the recessed lighting. From the fourteenth-floor window, I could see the Southeast Expressway, the Dorchester gas tanks, and Thompson Island, pale and hazy in the bay. Judy sat with her legs crossed and a foolscap pad balanced on her knee. Her reading glasses dangled from her neck-chain, and her unrepentantly gray hair swept up from her flat forehead. Like Bobby Rizzoli, she sat with her back to the light. 'Did you vote yet?' she asked.

'First thing, at Charlestown High. As if it makes a difference.'

'It always makes a difference.'

'Am I going to get a civics lesson?'

'Do you need one?'

She was big, as we all were, but graceful and well dressed. Her face was a city face: aware, ironic, knowing. Her smile was gap-toothed and careful. She'd been red-haired in her youth and carried into her fiftieth year the peculiar pigment and surprised look around the eyes that had made her look such a likely candidate for the convent at seventeen.

'I got all the instruction I needed from Dad,' I said. 'Every election day he'd tell me how Granddad had him painting over Storrow's campaign posters in the 1910 election. Eleven years old, running up and down Tremont Street with a brush and a bucket of whitewash until some Yankee banker with a Taft mustache grabbed him by the ear and Dad kicked him in the shin.'

She laughed – a deep, controlled laugh that rose from her throat as if spelled out: *ha, ha, ha*. 'That the time Honey Fitz gave him a ride in his motorcade through Ward 6?'

'Yeah.'

'I always wondered what Granddad was like,' she said.

'Smooth talker, I'd say. Cocky. Liked a tipple and smoked five-cent cigars.'

She shook her head. 'Where do you get these images?'

'Look at his photo. You can see it in his eyes. The one I have up in the shop. '

'The shop.'

She looked up at the portrait of Eliot. Judy ending up here, of all places, in such a male, Protestant bastion. Sign of the times. I was reminded of another photograph, a formal portrait of Judy in her habit that my mother insisted on keeping on the dresser. Sister Assumpta was the name she took. Eddie and I called her Sister Presumpta. 'Dad loved his stories, all right.'

'His favorite?' I prompted.

'Go ahead.'

'Your last night before the convent. Took you to Pier 4 for two lobsters.'

'*He* had two lobsters. I had surf and turf.'

'Surf and turf one night, obedience and chastity the next.'

'There was plenty of obedience and chastity before I got near the convent, believe me. And plenty since.'

'Was he on or off the wagon then?'

'Off. Scotch and water, Scotch and water.'

'Little twirl of his fingers to the bartender.'

'Yeah. And he had me scooping daiquiris that night – me off to Mount Carmel the next morning. *And* I was smoking like a demon, knowing it was my last chance. "I didn't know you smoked," he said, and handed me two packs of Lucky Strikes. There was a retirement party that night for some big-shot fire chief. The owner pulled out all the stops. A band, free champagne. I think if I wasn't there they would've brought on a stripper. Dad knew the chief. Knew them all. Jokes, stories, and by the end of the night he was parading me in front of all these white-haired Irish guys who kissed my hand and asked for my prayers. Then he started singing: "Mountains of Mourne", "Come Back, Paddy Reilly".'

'He loved that stuff, didn't he?'

'Oh he did. He did.'

We both went quiet in a haze of reminiscence. She blinked.

Her tone shifted. 'I got a call from Dr Larson yesterday,' she said.

'Yeah?'

'They're thinking maybe Alzheimer's.'

'Ah.'

We slid back to the present. I thought of my mother's eyes, the eyes that had said and seen so much. Eyes that stared out at me every time I looked at Eddie or Judy. Misted over now with apprehension and confusion, clouded by disease, tangled and dying like the neurons in her brain that could no longer sort the memories of a family and a life. 'I thought the treatment . . .'

Judy shook her head. 'Nothing they can do. And the problem now is that Sacred Heart can't provide the proper care. She's wandering off. They found her in the kitchen last week. Two o'clock in the morning and she's looking for a colander.' She stood and walked across to the window, shoulders high, an air of legal scrutiny about her profile. 'There's a place in Newton – Mount Judge – that offers a full-care program. It's not that far, it's the best there is. Fifty-six grand a year.'

I whistled.

'Her annuities won't cover that,' Judy said.

'Well, whatever it takes.'

Judy turned from the window. It was a courtroom turn, a rhetorical pivot as if to emphasize a legal nicety or raise an objection. 'I was talking to Eddie about the shop.'

Eddie rarely indulged in family sentiment. Judy often did, but could turn it off on a dime and launch into business talk without missing a beat. Nothing too apparent – a slight inflection, a twitch of the mouth. A stranger wouldn't have noticed, but to me, who found the mix of family and money an embarrassment, it was obvious.

'What – that Mom wants to leave it him? We talked about that.'

'Eddie doesn't want that, and neither does Mom, really. But it did occur to me that maybe now's the time to . . . to maybe look at some kind of reorganization.'

'Stop the double talk, Counselor.'

She put on her glasses and looked at the pad. She always came prepared. 'If I'm not mistaken, our newest press is twenty years old.'

'I bought the second Heidelberg in '82.'

'Bought it used,' she said. I nodded. 'And what about computers?'

'We have PCs.'

'But our typesetting, design, pre-press – none of it is computerized, right?'

'Doesn't need to be. Look, Judy, Johnny, Mac, Charlie, they're old school. They do things the way they've always done them, and they're not about to change now.'

'Have you tried?'

'I've made suggestions.'

I got the infamous courtroom glare. Fifty years of history between us was not about to exempt me.

'What's this about, Judy?'

'It's about protecting the future. It's about underwriting Mom's welfare, not to mention the staff who were loyal to Dad for thirty years.'

'You don't think I'm aware of all that?'

'I know you are, Harry. I'm just wondering about your

strategy. Eddie, me, we're on the board, and I can't remember the last time you met with us. This is still the family company. If we don't modernize, the market's going to pass us by.'

She spoke slowly, leaving the statement hanging in the austere plushness of the conference room with all the skill of an experienced litigator. With anyone else I would have retreated to salesmanship, to that oblique, offhand way I had of instilling confidence in almost anyone (especially myself) that what I was working on was big, really big, an opportunity of a lifetime that just needed that city permit or little bit of seed capital to get going. Vision! I had done; I would do. But for Judy, ex-nun to her toenails, her father's daughter, vision was for the next world. She knew me too well. Eddie I could baffle, or at least bore to the point where he would give up, but Judy was enough like me to sense the danger in my schemes and see through my pitch to the self-denial that lay beneath.

'I've been talking to Milt,' she said, when I stayed silent. Milt Solomon was our accountant. 'He says he hasn't seen the books in six months. Says you keep putting him off.'

'Milt's schedule is ridiculous. He can only come in when I'm not there, and I've been busy with the Rizzoli project.'

'Harry, we're losing clients and we're losing profits because we're not investing in the business. To be blunt, we're subsidizing the so-called Rizzoli project and Donohue Press books when we should be channeling the money back into the shop.'

'Hey, Donohue Press is in profit.'

'You're in profit because you're getting production at cost. You're riding the shop, Harry, and no one is benefiting, especially not you.'

'Thanks for the concern.'

'I *am* concerned. You should be too.'

'I'm going to make this book happen, Judy. You should know that.'

'I don't doubt it. Did the wife sign?'

'Yeah. And she's no patsy. She has tapes, transcripts, discovery documents. She'll be watching closely.'

'Not necessarily a good thing.'

'Better than dealing with a bimbo.'

She put the pad on the table and rolled the pen between her fingers. 'Well, I'm rooting for you, don't get me wrong. But this other thing needs straightening out.'

'Okay, so let's me, you and Eddie meet next week.'

'And Milt.'

'And Milt.'

'Make sure he sees the books before the meeting.'

So here was another layer of anxiety in my life, another stroke on my handicap. As Jimmy and I played the back nine, I thought more than once about confiding in him, but he and I didn't work like that. Besides, he had his own worries, from Republican resurgence to problems with his third wife. For a guy who never dated in high school, he'd had a lot of partners in his day, but he couldn't convince any of them to stick around.

I played better coming in, including a birdie on the seventeenth, but still lost by fifteen strokes. Jimmy carded a seventy-five and treated me to lunch in the clubhouse with the C note I forked over.

'You hear the senate president yesterday?' Jimmy said, sawing his swordfish. ' "Fair is foul and foul is fair"?'

'He does like his Shakespeare.'

'A joke. His own brother running the Mob in Southie and him preaching to us about police corruption.'

Joe McCann was the most powerful politician in Massachusetts, a silver-tongued, white-haired townie from South Boston whose ruthlessness and deal-making prowess were legendary in the halls of the State House. He ran the Senate with a shamrock and a shillelagh, and no one got any-where without his say-so. His brother Sammy, kingpin of the Boston Irish Mafia, had fought his way to the top of his chosen profession with the same skill set. Sammy was something of a Robin Hood figure in Southie, a neighborhood guy who had forsworn the drug trade, helped old ladies across the street, and handed out turkeys at Christmas just like Honey Fitz in the days of the ward bosses. But rumor had him taking a piece of every ounce of coke that floated in through Boston Harbor, then informing on local dealers to the FBI. Needless to say, Joe and Sammy did not celebrate Thanksgiving together.

'The Bucky Quinn case has him spooked,' I said. 'He doesn't make a stand, the Republicans will make hay.'

'Yeah,' Jimmy said hotly, 'so he makes us DAs – most of whom are Democrats, remember – look like we're letting the state go to rack and ruin. He's thinking about his own skin, not the party's.'

'Since when did you give a shit about the party?'

He snarled at me.

'Look at your record, Jimmy. You go after the crooked cops.' This was too close a reference to the favor he'd done me, but I was hoping he would open up. I needed some advice. 'This Quinn thing could be to your benefit. You'll probably end up trying it.'

'He'll be tried in Norfolk County, not Suffolk.'

'You never know. He's from Charlestown.'

Jimmy waved away the argument and ate his fish. He was edgy today. Post-election depression. We finished our lunch in silence and he called for the check. While we waited, I mentioned the first of two things I wanted to ask him. 'You know a Steven Gurlick?'

'Who?'

'Gurlick. FBI guy.'

'JFK Building?'

'Statler.'

Jimmy shook his head. He leaned on his elbows and let his eyes wander. When bored he made no attempt to disguise it.

'Anyway, this Gurlick called me. I go in there not knowing who he is, and next thing I'm getting a grilling about Rizzoli.'

'Whaddaya mean, grilling?'

'You know – what am I doing, why am I doing it.'

'You tell him anything?'

'Course not.'

Jimmy licked his teeth and propped his chin on his thumbs. He narrowed his eyes, as he used to when he wrestled. He was curt and competitive today. He was thinking about his destiny and had little time for my small worries. 'Harry, look. A: we shouldn't even be discussing this. I told you day one, this whole thing is a conflict of interest from my point of view. I can't be seen to be involved. In any way. Period. B: do yourself a favor and keep away from the Feds. Those pricks don't give a shit about you or me or anyone. They'll pump whatever information they can out of you and then indict your mother. It's the way they're built, believe me. The words loyalty and compassion are not in their vocabulary.'

'I just thought—'

'Don't think. Steer clear.'

He cut the conversation cold and paid the bill. We went out to the parking lot. A wind had picked up from the north, and the temperature had dipped. The club flag whipped in the breeze. Jimmy turned up his collar. At his car he rooted in his pockets for his keys. I had one thing left to ask and, bad timing or not, I had promised myself I would not let the opportunity pass. 'Say, Jimmy.'

'Yeah.'

'Listen, Gary . . . you know my kid Gary has a contract downtown.'

'Yeah. Bank thing, right?'

'Right. Well, he's getting squeezed. Local cop.'

'He making the payments?'

'See, this is the thing. He won't.'

'He *won't*. You've talked to him?'

'Yeah, I've talked, I've talked. Blue-in-the-face talk.'

Jimmy smiled, an easy, old-neighborhood smile. 'I don't have to tell you how much easier—'

'You don't have to tell me. It's just that the situation . . . and Gary's specific frame of mind at the moment . . .'

'You got a number?'

I gave him the card with the cop's name and badge number. He took it and opened the car door.

'Jimmy, I owe you.'

He closed the door and rolled down the window. 'Hey, least I can do after taking your hundred bucks, right?'

He looked ahead, and I saw that his attention was already somewhere else. I stepped back and he drove off, the rear of his Ford swaying as he took the corner at a decent clip. I looked at the threatening sky and headed for my office.

6

Hello?

It's me.

Hey. How you doin'?

We have a problem.

Yeah?

I think they're gonna take him for ice cream.

Who? Him?

No, the other guy. And in that situation, I'm worried what he might be capable of. The changes of behavior, the lifestyle, whatnot. What he might say.

Is the Rifleman involved?

Well, you know he's part of that . . . that group.

He's a fuckin' animal.

They're gonna take him. I know it. They want to snap a head, you know what I'm sayin'?

Why him? Why not you? Me?

We didn't drag no dealer down Revere Beach and knock his fuckin' teeth out with a tire iron.

Shirley stuck her head through my office door. I clicked off the tape recorder.

'We got it,' she said. 'They bit. Volski called and told me

Wambaugh wants to come up next week and meet with you and Rizzoli.'

Her face was bright, wide-eyed and soft. Her cheeks were flushed. Still in the world of the tape, I had to adjust to her image, as if I'd just stepped out of a movie theater. 'Congratulations.'

'Well, it's just a first step . . . but Harry – *60 Minutes*!'

She moved into the room, hoisting her shoulders and fluttering the V of her blouse; the news had raised her temperature. There was something very physical in her delight, something I was translating without thought into a sexual scenario. After listening all morning to tapes of Bobby and his fellow cops and confederates beating around the bush with wiseguy slang and cold caution, Shirley's appearance was like Rita Hayworth tossing back her hair.

'What we need to do,' she said, settling herself, 'is arrange a day when he can meet Bobby out in Concord and then have a tour of Hillbrook. He wants to see the bank, Donny's house, the hospital. He was wondering if we can take him to the police station – you think they'll be OK with that?'

'Hell, he's from *60 Minutes*. They'll throw open the jails for him!'

Two months ago I had sent Jeff Higgins out to Jake Cleary, the Hillbrook police chief, to see what he could scare up in the way of old logs and police reports. Cleary was a wily dog, and young Jeff sealed the chief's silence and his own fate two minutes into their meeting by mentioning the Freedom of Information Act. It would be a pleasure to arrive out there with CBS's finest and watch Cleary crease himself with the effort of wanting to tell and not being able to. The chief would have some stories to take to the grave, I'd always known that, but today, after living in Bobby Rizzoli's past for a full morning, I now knew what the Attorney General and the FBI and, without doubt, Jake Cleary himself had known for many years – that Hillbrook, All-American City and hometown of major-league legend Mickey Richardson, was policed by men who, if they weren't goons, weren't going to tell on those who were.

In the summer of 1987, when Joey Latrelli and Donny Donlon were smoking more money in a week than your average Massachusetts cop makes in a month, Bobby began taping all his phone calls. This Nixonian precaution was not as paranoid as it later seemed. Under the influence of cocaine, the tight little gang was beginning to unravel. By then it was clear that no one, from the Hillbrook Police Department to the FBI, would or could scrape together even the semblance of a case against any of the Savings Trust burglars.

In spite of his pleas, Bobby had not been able to keep Donlon away from the drug business, and, during the long months before the infamous New Year's Eve shootout, Bobby's task was to keep the peace as best he could while covering himself should the worst occur. The tension of the approaching date of certain freedom and the strain of negotiating daily between Joey and Donny made Bobby very nervous. So he started making the tapes, if only for the feeling of control it gave him when Latrelli started screaming threats at him in those cold waning months of the year.

After Latrelli's deal and Bobby's arrest, the Attorney General's office subpoenaed the tapes to prepare for the trial, but Bobby had been so circumspect in his conversations that they were of little use to the prosecution. His own legal team wanted to use them to discredit Latrelli as a witness, but in the end Judge Lathrop ruled them inadmissible on the grounds that the conversations were taped without the permission of Rizzoli's interlocutors. After the trial the FBI had them long enough for transcription before they were returned to Lucy Rizzoli. Now they were in my hands, where they would serve their most useful purpose. If corruption was going to be our hook, then here was our raw material. They set the tone I wanted the book to capture.

I had split the pile with Jeff and we were cataloging their contents. Many of the conversations were between Bobby and other members of the Hillbrook police force. It was not inspiring listening. There were hints of rape and graft and coercion, with names unmentioned and details left vague. I would have loved to hear Jake Cleary's gloss on those. In another category were calls to or from the gang members: Joey, Donny, and Brother O'Brien. Like Bobby, Brother didn't go near drugs, and as 1987 came to a close, a daily cycle of gang calls emerged: Bobby on the phone to an earnest, concerned Brother, to a thick-witted, coked-out Donny, and to a hyper, out-of-control Latrelli. Then variations on the same conversations an hour later. Prison had to be awfully dull by comparison.

'You want me to put an agenda together?' Shirley asked. Her voice reminded me of the third category of calls: those between Bobby and his mistress, Barbara Pavlovich. Unlike the frantic, maneuvering conversations between the men, these were low-key, whispered, certain of where they were headed.

'Call Chief Cleary at the station and set it up. I'll talk to Rizzoli.'

'Right. Good. And I'll call Wambaugh direct, get things in motion.'

Shirley had dropped the tone of skepticism that usually marked our talk about the book. Standing at my desk, mouth open, delicately flushed, she reminded me of a debutante. I wanted to ask her to dance. I was stirred. And why shouldn't she be on a high? This was a breakthrough day for her. She had scored, and with her success came the conviction that we were on to something. For once we saw this opportunity in the same light. Her eyes, so pellucid, so expressive, were free now of the screen of doubt that always fell between us. I got up and walked around my desk, gesturing at the tapes. Sordid as they might be, the conversations were like real-life words from a movie. They were hushed and colorful and muscular. They suggested a deepening vista of drama and intrigue. They cast a certain spell. 'Tell Jeff when he's done for the day to bring his tapes here. I want these locked up, in my office, every night. You wouldn't believe the stuff I'm hearing on these.'

'Sure.'

'I don't want him along on the Hillbrook tour. There's some history there. And hey – congratulations again.'

Casually, as if it were an afterthought, I touched her blouse at the elbow. Just a graze, but all the more meaningful for its lightness. She did not, as I expected, withdraw, but held her ground, tilted her peach-shaped face, and drew in her lips in a way that made me weak at the knees.

'It's going to happen,' I said. 'You can feel it.'

'What's going to?'

I paused, glanced at her breasts, lifted a hand in the direction of the tapes. 'The book.'

She took a deep breath. 'Yeah. Oh, yeah. Definitely.' With feminine intimacy she laid a hand on my forearm and raised her plucked eyebrows. As I was about to speak she said, 'I'll make those calls, Harry. We don't want to lose any time.'

I watched her walk to the door. As she was leaving she paused and leaned back. 'Talk to you later,' she said.

I stood, breathing in her lingering smell and running my own tape in my head. After a few minutes I slid back to the dark, compelling world of the tape-recorder, a sexual tingle firing my ambition, helping me dream of a Donohue Press book that captured readers as completely as Shirley's figure captured me. And *60 Minutes*! This was it! The big score! Not to mention good news to tell Rizzoli. He was getting restless, and our last phone call, the night before, had been tense.

'What's the deal?' he had said. 'When we gonna get this show on the road?'

I looked at the clock by my bedside. It was after midnight. 'They let you make calls this late?'

'My buddy in here has a cellular.'

'Not exactly secure.'

'Who needs secure? So far we got jackshit to hide.'

I turned on the bedside lamp and marshalled my thoughts. Rizzoli called at odd hours to make a point and catch me off guard. It was working. 'Bobby, we talked on Monday.'

'When am I gonna meet this Jeff . . . what's his name, Hurley?'

'Higgins.'

'I knew a Dick Higgins from Revere. Real ball-buster.'

'No relation.'

'If he's from Somerville I don't think we can trust him. Or he's got shit for brains, one of the two.'

'He's a bright kid, a good writer. Which is to say, you'll create the story and he'll get it down into words.'

'Well, so far we got a dream relationship: you tell me what a shit-hot writer he is, and then you tell him what a great story I have. Let's hope you don't get run over by a truck before the two of us actually get a chance to meet.'

I couldn't help thinking that this was how threats got communicated in Bobby's world: casual statements over a crackly cellphone in the middle of the night. Next thing I'd be climbing into the back seat of a Town Car with a couple of thick-necked goons in gold chains, talking about the Red Sox and pretending we were going to see a guy in East Boston about an idea for a book.

'I thought he sent you an outline.'

'Outline – that what you call it? What the fuck am I supposed to do with that? Let me talk to the guy.'

'Like I said, after he listens to the tapes and reads the transcripts, he'll have more reason to see you. A conversation makes sense then. By the way, I got the tapes today.'

'So I heard.'

Everything he said sounded like De Niro. Was this an act or the way he always spoke? What had Lucy told him about my visit? And why was I suddenly feeling guilty?

The previous afternoon I had driven out to Hillbrook to pick up the documents and tapes and special decks that played the one-and-a-half-inch telephone cassettes. The Rizzoli house was on Lynch Road, a long, curved street that exited directly from the fellsway and ribboned up into the hills overlooking the not-so-distant Boston skyline. They used to say that Hillbrook was where the successful guineas lived, just as the Irish moved up from Southie to Milton or West Roxbury. The houses were mostly split-level ranches, with stilted decks built out over the fellsway slopes that scissored behind the developments. In the driveways were New Yorkers and Sedan de Villes, campers and pick-ups, muscle cars for the kids. Success here was materially displayed and American crafted. Christmas featured the gaudiest lights and cheesiest decorations in the metropolitan area. Unlike the western suburbs, there was an urban density to Hillbrook, houses ample and well built but clustered together not just to squeeze a developer's dime but to preserve, I always thought, the neighborhood feel of East Boston or Chelsea.

Bobby's house was much like those beside it, though it wasn't hard to see the additional features of privilege: built-in pool, converted garage, his and hers Cadillacs, the twenty-foot Mako discreetly tarpaulined in the carport. Not bad for a city cop on twenty-five grand a year whose wife hadn't worked since Bobby Junior was born twenty-three years ago. The bank already had liens on the boat and cars, but as long as Lucy and her son lived in the house no judge would turn them out. I rang the bell, conscious of my car parked on the slope in front of the house, wondering what the neighbors thought, remembering the night Bobby was cuffed and escorted from this very door while local television stations, tipped off by state police, captured his squinting removal with bright lights and no mercy.

His son answered the door, in uniform, catching me unawares. 'How you doin'? Mr Donohue, right?'

I knew Bobby Junior was on the Hillbrook police force, but seeing him here in front of me, a younger version of his father, was almost too odd to be true. 'Yeah. Bobby. Your dad told me about you.'

'Sorry about this, but I'm late for my shift. Mom's in the kitchen.'

As he left he smiled and nodded up the half-flight of stairs that led into the open-plan upper level. He moved with a self-conscious sense of public authority, like a television cop from the Fifties who waved at old ladies from the patrol car and told tousled kids to stay out of trouble. Thick-featured and earnest. Genuine. As he left, I thought of the extra baggage he carried and wondered if his pop's claim that wife and junior had never known anything about the bank job was true.

'I'm up here.'

I followed her voice to the kitchen. She was in apron and oven mitts, negotiating a steaming tray to the top of the stove. Another Fifties image, except that on the dining table between us was a nickel-plated .38, the barrel pointed in my direction.

'That gun loaded, Lucinda?'

She removed the mitts and wiped her forehead. 'Lucy. It's Lucy. And, yessir, it's loaded.'

I moved from the line of fire. The kitchen was standard ranch, with checkerboard linoleum, table and captain's chairs, a television beside the stove, and a tiny flag of the great state of Texas pinned to a memo board. Beyond a waist-high partition, the living room was oversized and lived-in. Copies of the *Herald* and the *Hillbrook Mercury* lay scattered around a Naugahyde recliner. A half-filled ashtray and the latest *Cosmopolitan* were on a glass-topped coffee table. Boxes of legal documents sat before a sliding door looking on to the deck and leaf-strewn pool. On the sideboard were several shooting trophies and a photograph of Bobby Junior at his Police Academy graduation.

'We're kinda casual here,' she said, removing her apron and nodding at the living-room mess. 'Don't really fuss for guests.'

She had fussed over herself, it appeared – though I reminded myself that Southern women needed no excuse to pretty up. Nails and lips were mauve, jewelry silver. She wore wool slacks, a pearl-gray silk blouse, and a cashmere cardigan. Not quite a beehive, her bleached hair was swept up into a bright, imposing mass. The overall effect was metallic, smoky, *film noir*. She was of a piece with the .38, but any suggestion of hardness was countered by her body. She had the curves, no doubt about it, but she also had that slight schoolgirl ungainliness hinting at vulnerability. Women, it always seemed to me, were more encumbered than men – by clothes and accessories, by biology, by male expectation. I had always been attracted toward those whose encumbrance was significant and apparent, but who carried it well nevertheless. Lucy had an ampleness she didn't mind emphasizing. Her charm came from the tension between this Texan latitude and an innate clumsiness she just kept at bay.

'Am I a guest?' I said. 'I thought this was a business meeting.'

She sized up the comment and decided it was innocent. This was a woman who had learned to filter everything.

'Don't get any ideas. I cooked this meatloaf for Bobby Junior – one of my specialties meatloaf is – and he up and decides he's on the two o'clock shift. Where I come from you don't let good food go to waste. So if you're hungry, take your coat off.'

We ate in the slanted light of the November afternoon, the gun between us like a sundial. On her own turf, she was more relaxed but ever sharp. She talked about her son, cop son of a crooked cop, and the problems he had in town. She talked about the parade of men in suits with warrants, liens, and writs. She talked about the anonymous letters and calls in the middle of the night. She talked about everything but what I was there to talk about until the meal was long over and she was lighting her third cigarette.

'I got everything together for you,' she said, nodding at the boxes in the living room. 'Them tapes'll keep you sleepless. Few photographs in there of the principals, old pictures of Bobby, and so forth. There's transcripts from the trial – boring as hell, but I reckon you'll want a courtroom scene or two.'

The most dramatic and widely reported testimony from the trial had been that of Barbara Pavlovich, Bobby's mistress at the time of the burglary and his alibi. Barbara was a Middlesex County bail commissioner with ambitions. Bobby met her in 1980 while taking a criminal-justice class at Bunker Hill Community College. She lived with her six-year-old son on the top floor of a triple-decker around the corner from the Metro police station in Revere. Within months of meeting, they were sleeping together. Two or three nights a week Bobby left his patrol car at Metro and walked up to Barbara's. It became a Metro joke, made public during the trial. *Rizzoli's walking the beat with his nightstick.* Their affair had its own statute of limitations and ended when she forced him to choose between her and Lucy. He had never said anything to Barbara about the bank, so he assumed he was safe dumping her and refused to get a divorce.

By the time of the trial, Barbara was itching for payback. Under oath, her mouth a slit of anger, she claimed Bobby had bragged about the burglary and forced her to sign a statement saying he had been at her house when he wasn't. She said she'd been with him when he dumped blasting caps at Revere Beach. She said he had promised to take her to the Bahamas with his cut from the bank. With her high-pitched nasal voice and tilted chin, she looked like she'd walked straight out of a soap opera.

During cross-examination, Bobby's defense jumped on her. Mickey Taylor painted her as the woman scorned and full of fury; got her to admit Bobby had, in the end, chosen Lucy over her; and suggested that Barbara had changed her story and co-operated with the state in return for her current job as an officer in Suffolk Superior Court. Mickey's courtroom style was booming and theatrical, and he played without shame to the gallery. In a memorable closing sequence, he exhibited a pair of yellow plastic balls on a string that Barbara had sent Bobby after their break-up, accompanied by a hand-printed note in red ink: 'For the man who has everything but . . .'

'You *do* recognize the exhibit,' Mickey had intoned, his gray mane and wrinkled face lifted to catch the summer sun streaming through the courthouse windows. The gallery was still a-titter after his melodramatic reading of the note.

'That was supposed to be a joke,' Barbara answered.

'A joke? A month after he left you and returned to his wife, you sent this . . . this indignity as a *joke*?'

He let the balls clack together and the gallery lapped it up. Even Judge Lathrop cracked a smile. Barbara glared at him.

'You did send it, didn't you?'

'That's right,' she said.

'Because that is what you thought of Robert Rizzoli.'

'I sent it because I thought . . . I sent that note,' she squealed, 'because he is a lying-ass son of a bitch!'

Palms to the ceiling, Mickey looked slowly from jury to judge. 'No further questions, your honor.'

The media made hay with that, and who could blame them? And as defense tactics went, it was inspired. But what was Lucy Rizzoli to think when Barbara's high-pitched slur was splashed on the front page of the *Herald*? What comfort was it to Lucy that the public airing of her husband's liaison was a help to his case? What did she think of the half-dozen women who claimed on local talk shows that they, too, had slept with Bobby Rizzoli and were ready to bare all? And now I was going to push all this back in her face six years after the fact by featuring it in the book.

'I'm not so sure our readers want to be in a courtroom,' I said. 'My take on the story is corruption – that's the hook. Crooked cops in the suburbs, no one minding the minders. And the heist. They'll want to know all the details of the heist.'

Lucy took a drag of her Salem and squinted at me through the smoke. The ironic spin she gave her words was never in her eyes. They always glistened with intelligent simplicity. She had a layered, complex way of sending messages, but her eyes were always direct. She stubbed out her cigarette and looked at her nails. 'I may be just a dumb Texas farm girl, Harry, but in my experience there ain't but two things interest most people: money and sex.'

I didn't say anything to that. She stood and started clearing the dishes, so I moved the boxes of tapes and transcripts out to my car. At the bottom of the stairs was an inside entrance to the converted garage. The door was open and I could see the floor, littered with weights and bar bells. A padlocked rack holding five or six guns hung on the back wall. The room was used, no doubt, by Bobby Junior, but I could see his dad there. When I was finished I washed my hands in the kitchen sink. We had a cup of coffee and she set a document in front of me. 'This just acknowledges receipt,' she said. 'Lawyers tell me it's the best way of establishing that the sources are property of Lone Star Corp.'

I glanced over it and signed. She put it into a drawer, then folded her arms and leaned against the counter. I wanted to get up and stand beside her, but her eyes kept me where I was. 'Let's say y'all do this as planned. When does Lone Star see some money?'

'End of next year.'

'Best you can do?'

'The best – and that's assuming we get this thing written by the spring.'

'Over a year before I see any cash.'

'Soon as I have it, you have it.'

She nodded. Her smoker's skin looked tight and weary. After an hour in this house, I felt Rizzoli's presence as certainly as if he were on his son's shift. Hard to think of him doing ten years. He was a man who could extend a sense of possessiveness through the thickness of prison walls.

'I guess Bobby's dough is all tied up.'

She smirked. She knew I didn't expect an answer to that one.

'You ever think of moving out?'

'Think of it? What's to think? Bank already has everything but this place. I move and they slap a lien on here quicker than a Houston whore. Then I got nothing but what Bobby Junior takes it into his head to give me out of his two-bit patrolman's salary.'

It was the middle of a weekday afternoon with the smell of winter in the air, and she was letting her guard down. Like an unhappy princess, she was stuck in Bobby's castle in a town that peered and gossiped every time she went to Johnny's Foodmaster. And how this must have suited Bobby. What better way to keep her pinned than to have her broke and under siege? What better way to possess her? But as someone who had made a balls of marriage I knew this about possessiveness: the longer you are a woman's exclusive partner the less able you are to offer her something every other man in the world can – the sexually unfamiliar. Especially if you're locked up.

'You deserve better,' I said.

'Hey, I ain't nothin' special.' She smiled wanly and looked me in the eye. 'I'm the same as most people, Harry.'

So here I was the next day, listening to the tapes in my office, scrolling through a year of Bobby's life and getting a fast-forward version of deceit on several levels. Lucy must have listened to these. I couldn't understand why she hadn't at least held back the conversations with Barbara Pavlovich. Did she want me to hear them? When I realized the extent of Bobby's self-surveillance, I had screened the calls to his mistress and kept them from Jeff. I hoarded them. As the day passed I found myself skipping past the cop-talk and paranoia and, with a voyeur's stealth, studying these lovers' conversations, playing them over and over, thinking all the while of

Lucy locked in her Hillbrook tower as securely as Bobby was locked in Concord.

On the way home I stopped at Kiley's and watched the Bruins lose to Montréal. Mick Malone and I bought each other beers and shots of Jameson's and yelled at the television. I left the car in Brighton and took a cab home. It took me a long time to get to sleep. In the darkness, the Jameson pulsed through my blood as memories and impressions and the taped conversations swirled together. Bobby and his gang, they didn't mess around, they just went out and grabbed what they wanted. And what did I want? The big time, the respect, the show. A woman like Shirley, her open mouth hinting at sexual richness. Or Lucy, her eyes screwed as the smoke from her Salem coiled ceilingward, her elbows on the kitchen table, the gun between us. Shirley stirred me up, no question, but Lucy's pull came more subtly, more powerfully. It was deeper and darker. It suggested, as the book did, that I had arrived. That everything could happen for me as I'd always dreamed it would. And what was Lucy dreaming right now? What did darkness bring to her beyond the bitterness of what she'd been denied?

Can you talk?

Yeah. She's shopping.

Her favorite activity.

How 'bout you? What's your favorite activity?

You have a couple hours, I'll show you.

Yeah?

Yeah.

I think I can arrange that.

When?
I'm on the night shift tomorrow.
Night shift. Music to my ears.
I'll be over at ten.
You know I'm waitin' for you . . . you know it, honey.

7

The Monday before Thanksgiving I arrived at my office with a dark headache and a need for sunlight, but the view from my window was all shades of gray and rust. The day threatened snow, and something in the heavy air was conspiring against my constitution, turning the buzz of the book project into a jangling arterial tension. Today I was bringing Jeff out to Concord. I could delay his meeting Rizzoli no longer, but I worried about Bobby's response. On the surface, Jeff did not inspire confidence, and I was at a point with Bobby where I needed to give him a boost. The honeymoon was over.

As I reviewed my messages our bookkeeper, Peggy Howard, stuck her head through the door. I knew what she wanted and I knew I didn't want to talk to her. Bobby's visit was enough to worry about for one day.

'You got a minute, Harry?'

'Not really. Jeff and I are going to prison.' I smiled broadly, but she looked alarmed.

She closed the door and sat across from me, sliding a manila envelope onto my desk. 'I've completed the filings,' she said.

'Great.'

'They're two months late.'

'I know. You told me. Here – I'll sign them and you can send them in. What's the fine – ten per cent?'

'The fine's not what I'm worried about. They need two signatures.'

'Yours and mine.'

'I'm not a director, Harry.'

'Two directors? You need two?'

Her face creased with impatience. 'I told you a million times.'

'OK. Leave it with me. I'll look after it.'

'You won't let your family look at the books, how do you expect them to sign these?'

I opened the envelope and leafed slowly through the forms. She watched me as long as patience allowed before throwing up her hands with annoyance. 'Harry? What are we doing here?'

'Give me a break,' I said, looking at my watch. 'I'm supposed to be on my way to Rizzoli right now.' Then I had a brainwave. 'Besides, I've got it covered. I'll have the other signature for you in the morning.' She looked suspicious. 'I'm visiting my mother on the way home,' I improvised. 'She told me she'd sign.'

Peggy shook her head. 'This is not good, Harry.'

'What? She's a director, right?'

'How long are you going to keep up this charade? When are you going to deal with Milt Solomon?'

'Fuck Milt Solomon.'

'Easy for you to say. I'm the one he keeps calling.'

'Let's talk about this later. I really got to get going.'

'He's very insistent.' She crossed her hands on her lap. *She* was the insistent one.

'Milt,' I said. 'Right. I thought you showed him the accounts.'

Peggy and I had developed a special vocabulary around this issue. When we referred to the public records, the cooked books, we spoke of the *accounts*. What we called the *books* were the real figures, which we kept in a safe in Peggy's office. I needed to keep the private set up to date and accurate, so that when the Rizzoli book hit the street and the money started rolling in, we could quietly make the readjustments and no one would be the wiser. She'd been maintaining the double set for six months. Now I had talked her into sending the cooked figures to the IRS, turning dishonesty into a felony. Meanwhile Judy was working on Milt just like she was working on me, and he was as scared of her as anyone was. No way he was going to be happy with what I wanted to show him. He wasn't Judy's accountant for nothing. And if he got half a look at what he was supposed to see he'd blow this whole thing wide open.

'I showed him, sure,' she said. 'But he insists he has to come in and do a full review.'

'Peg, listen. Milt Solomon was a pain in the ass when Judy brought him in and he's a pain in the ass now. Don't worry about him. If he calls again, put him on to me.'

'It would take him about twenty minutes to see the accounts aren't kosher,' she said. 'And we're not just talking about your family situation. There's the legal aspect.'

Peggy was a holdover from the days when my father ran the company. She was a good bookkeeper, but she knew that what she made (after fifteen years in the company, thirty-eight and a half grand plus benefits) was way out of line. Since my arrival, she was constantly worried I was going to let her go or chop her pay, and I had been able to leverage her fear and get her to use her skills to my advantage. Besides, she had great legs.

'Forget about the legal stuff,' I said. 'I'll worry about that. You have your job – which is enough to be concerned with.'

Her face took on a pained look. 'My job? Yeah, OK. But what about your job? You're never here.'

'All the better. Milt calls, tell him to call back. Look – he has no authority. He can't tell you what to do.'

'What if he shows up here at the shop?'

'Tell him to get lost.'

'What if Judy is with him?'

Would it come to that? I didn't think so. Judy's style had always been to confront me head on. I waved my key chain in front of Peggy. 'Let's put it this way. I have the only key to the safe.'

She looked from the key to my eyes to some unfocused spot beyond me.

'Judy shows up and I'm not here,' I said, 'you can't open the safe. If she wants to wait, fine. But then it's my problem.'

'Can I give you my key? So it's the truth?'

'You're worried about the truth?'

'Somebody has to.'

'Sure. Whatever. If it makes it easier for you.'

She stood. There are some women who look pinched and tense when they sit but almost regal when they stand. Peggy wore a gold bracelet on her left ankle, suggesting a streak of daring you'd never think this timid, fastidious bookkeeper possessed. My mind never failed to race. 'Shirley here?' I asked her.

'She's on a day off,' she said brusquely. She did not appreciate my interest in Shirley. 'Her daughter's arriving from Syracuse to spend Thanksgiving with her.'

'Right.'

'Harry, I'll do what you want. For now. But if this stuff comes to light – well, you know I'd have to wash my hands.'

'I'll have the tax documents in the morning. Meantime we have the contract. In a couple months Frankie starts pre-selling the Rizzoli book, the money flows in, and then all this underhand stuff stops. Two, three months. Tops.'

'I don't doubt it, Harry. If anyone can pull it off, you can. But in the meantime don't expect me to lie. I'm just an average person and I don't want any trouble. I have to look out for myself – it's what anybody would do.'

What anybody would do. I watched her leave with a pang of lust. My business on the line and all I could think about was what it might be like to sleep with Peggy Howard. Or Shirley Van Zandt. Oh, these women and the power they have over us. Like Lucy in her ranch-house prison. The lonely eyes. The loaded gun on the table.

I picked up the documents. Now that I had to see my mother I was short on time. I called Jeff's extension and told him we were going. He appeared in Reception looking like a college kid, slump-shouldered, disheveled, dressed in black pants and a torn T-shirt.

'What's with the get-up?'

'What do you mean?'

'We're going to a business meeting, not a rock concert.'

Jeff sneered. 'A business meeting? With Rizzoli?'

'Yes a business meeting. He sees you in that gear he'll think he's dealing with a punk. Shit, Jeff. I thought you were from Somerville. You must know the kind of guy we're dealing with here. Think Frankie. Think a *smart, ruthless* Frankie.'

'Contradiction in terms.'

'I don't know, Jeff. Sometimes your head is so far up your ass I just can't comprehend.'

My patience was diminishing and my headache was getting worse. I didn't have time to drop him home for a change of clothes. I had this meeting with Rizzoli. I had to drop by my mother's new nursing home for her signature. At six I had to be in North Station to meet Gary. I was having dinner with him and taking him to the Lakers game. More family diplomacy.

Sure enough, when we got out to Concord Bobby looked Jeff and his sloppy duds up and down. 'How old are you, Jim?'

'The name's Jeff.'

'Like Mutt and Jeff. Tell me, bub,' Bobby said to him, 'what ripe old age has my co-writer reached?'

'Twenty-four.'

'No shit?' Bobby said, looking at me. '*Twenty-four*. The kid's been around.' He leaned close to Jeff. 'You been laid yet?'

'I been laid.'

'We're safe. The kid from Somerville's been laid. Knows what it's all about. Course, it'll be a while before you catch up with Harry here in that department. My guess is Harry likes his pussy.'

We were in our usual spot, beside the dirty window overlooking the prison yard. The visiting room was dry and overheated. Bobby leaned back and eyed me with pale scrutiny. He looked unwell. He was tousled and unshaven. His heavy-lidded eyes were red and watery, his lips puffy. The ridges of broken capillaries across his cheekbones were dense, as if he'd been drinking. He breathed through his mouth and tapped the side of the plastic chair with his thumb. His suspicions today were invested with all the discomforts, mental and physical, of prison life.

'I hear you visited the house,' he said to me. His look was tunneled and intense, as if he had forgotten about Jeff in an instant and was obsessed now with me and me alone.

'Got the tapes and transcripts.'

'You already told me that.'

'So I did.'

'Met the family, I hear.'

His mouth was open and I could hear him breathing. 'Bobby, our goal here is to get some work done so we can get moving on this book and on making you some money.' I gestured towards Jeff. 'I brought him out here because it's time to move to the next stage. He's finished the outline. I like it. We get into when you joined the force, the corruption, code of silence, and so forth.'

'Everybody knows that shit.'

'They don't know the details. You can give them the details.'

'I'll tell you one detail I'll give them. I did not mastermind this thing. I don't care what Latrelli says, *he* was more responsible than anybody for what went down. And he's the shitbag gets immunity.'

He had all day every day to imagine insults and nurse grudges. It was up to me to appeal to even baser instincts and ensure they were directed away from me. Money and revenge. With this book, I could give him both.

'I've been listening to Latrelli on the tapes,' Jeff said.

I waved Jeff quiet. 'Save it for the book, Bobby. This is your chance to set the record straight. *And* make a shitload of dough.'

Again the silent scrutiny. The horns of his dilemma were ambition and caution: he had let me into his life because he needed me, but he wasn't certain I could be trusted. And I had spent an afternoon with his overburdened wife, eating meat-loaf Texas-style and talking about what people deserve.

'I start selling this book in February,' I said. 'No matter where you are with it, I have to start selling. We push this as *the* summer book. The blockbuster everyone wants to read. By May it has to be written, edited, and in production. By July you'll have the networks banging down the doors here looking for interviews.'

He glanced out of the window and took a deep breath. He was beginning to loosen. I played my trump card. 'I got *60 Minutes* coming out week after next.'

'What? Here? *60 Minutes* coming out here?'

'Yeah. They wanted to do it next week, but Thanksgiving and everything.'

'*60 Minutes*. No shit. They want to talk to me?'

'Course they want to talk to you. They like what they hear this first visit, they'll bring Ed Bradley up to interview you and air the show in the new year. Perfect publicity for the book. Get it selling like hotcakes, I'm telling you.'

Bobby was shifting in his chair, tapping his chin as he imagined a coast-to-coast audience. 'Bradley. Black guy with the glasses, right? Snappy dresser.'

'Their top interviewer. Guy they roll out for the big stories.'

He set his elbows on his knees and nodded at Jeff. 'What if I call you at eight o'clock? Every night at eight. Collect. I can talk for one, two hours.'

'The way I saw it working—'

Again I cut Jeff off. 'I like that. Jeff gets the research from you each night, writes it up the next day. I like that.'

'Yeah . . . Shit, *60 Minutes*. OK.'

He was on another level. It was time to go.

Back on the highway Jeff was quiet. I knew what he was thinking. My stomach was churning with all that was happening, but I could not afford to let Jeff slip through my fingers. If I was going to sort out this mess with the shop I would need him as much as anyone. 'This is Rizzoli's book, Jeff. You're the writer, but it's his story. Let's keep focused on that.'

'I know that. I'm just worried about the time frame. I mean, he doesn't seem like a very easy guy to work with.'

'Just let him do the talking. Let him tell the story.'

He looked out at the passing trees. Snow had started to fall. 'You know, sitting out there with him? I couldn't forget the tapes. Him and his cop buddies talking about banging broads in their cruisers and kicking the shit out of niggers.'

'Hey, he's no angel. We knew that coming in.'

'Then that whole sequence about Pallotta.'

'What sequence?'

'Frankie didn't tell you? Before I went home last night,

there was this conversation, this series of conversations, on the last tape. From – I don't know – early last year, whatever. Rizzoli and some other cop called Pete talking about Paul Pallotta. Claiming he was trying to squeeze Bobby. Had been squeezing him for some time.'

'So he heard the rumours about the bank and was pushing Bobby. Had to be a lot of that going on.'

'That's what I thought too. But you listen, it doesn't feel like that. You have to hear it, but it sounds like drugs. Stuff like, "He knows I'm selling, he knows they come to me." That type of exchange. Plus, this Pete guy wouldn't have known about the bank, right? Not in the circle.'

'You told Frankie this?'

'He walked into the room. Overheard. You know how he's always talking about Pallotta being his cousin? Well, this is real-life Godfather stuff for him.'

He stuck his chin out like Frankie Deluca and gestured in a way he probably thought was Italian. Frankie inspired ethnic stereotyping, keen as he was to act like a minor character in a Scorsese film. His connection with Paul Pallotta encouraged his posturing. Pallotta owned the Pussycat Lounge, a Somerville supper club frequented by off-duty Hillbrook and Revere cops and wannabe wiseguys. He was the kind of guy who would pay protection just for the thrill of associating with the Mob but, as an underworld figure, he was strictly peripheral. He had been convicted of marijuana possession and handling stolen goods, but I don't think he'd ever done time. I knew him from my days in the trucking business. I should say I knew his voice. He heard about my union problems from a Teamster official and called me out of the blue one day to offer his services as an intermediary. He told me he would need a five-grand retainer and invited me around to the Pussycat for a free meal. I didn't take him up. Had he done the same with Bobby? A little friendly extortion? Or was there something else going on?

But it was time to address other concerns. I pulled off the turnpike at Newton Corner.

'Where we going?'

'I gotta run a quick errand,' I said.

'Harry, it's five o'clock. I'm supposed to be somewhere.'

'Hey, we're all supposed to be somewhere. Don't worry, I won't be long.'

I wheeled into Mount Judge, vaguely guilty that my first visit to my mother in her new nursing home would be rushed and mercenary. The falling snow had thickened, covering the neatly landscaped grounds. The atmosphere was comfortable and affluent. Judy had done her research well, I thought. As if it could be otherwise. It was a nice place. Of course, at fifty-six grand a year it would want to be.

My mother was watching television with a half-dozen other women and kneading the crook of her walking stick with weathered hands. Her personal attendant, Lela, a brisk young black woman in starched whites and running shoes, met me with a professional smile. We helped Mom over to a low oak table in the reading area. She fussed over her dress as Lela brought us coffee from a kitchenette behind the television. 'Why didn't you say you were coming? Look at this old thing I'm wearing.' With stiff fingers she plucked at her floral-print frock, a kind she had been wearing since I could remember.

Lela set the Styrofoam cups in front of us and winked at

me. 'You look great, Mrs Donohue,' she said. 'You keep that dress on, all the bachelor men out here be turning their heads.' She cocked her wrist, dropped her chin, and smiled, her best porchside manner. I could see this was a gal with the right touch, no matronly condescension or hospital orthodoxy, just a nicely judged professional pleasantness, though a little performed. Slow to depart, however. I acknowledged her attention with a friendly nod, resisting the impulse to look at my watch. Gingerly I held the manila envelope with the tax documents. Mom leaned back and looked at Lela, peering with the mild confusion old people never seem to shake.

'I just let you two have a nice visit, OK? Talk to y'all a little bit later.' She walked off.

I took my mother's hand.

'How's Eddie?' she asked.

'Good, I guess. You see him more often than I do, don't you?'

Through big bay windows we could see the last red and yellow leaves of maple and birch hanging on against the snow. My mom blinked slowly, her eyes moist and empty. 'I'm going to Eddie's for Thanksgiving,' she said.

'That'll be nice.'

'Judy's coming too. She's bringing her Irish yams, with green marshmallows.' She smiled. Her square face, so smooth before, was all slack and leathery. She once had the high skin tone of her daughter, a chin that was lifted with imperious certainty, a line in caustic commentary that kept the toughest of our neighborhood on their toes.

I resisted memory and forced myself to the moment. 'Mom, I can only stay a couple of minutes. I'm meeting Gary.' The way she smiled I could tell she had no idea who I was talking about. I laid the envelope in front of her. 'I have some papers I need you to sign.'

She didn't hear me. 'What time is it?'

'Five-thirty,' I said.

She looked at the television in the corner. 'There's a Kennedy special on at six. It's twenty-five years tomorrow, you know.'

'Since the assassination.'

'That poor man,' she said. 'He was here. You wouldn't remember, you were too young, but he was here.'

'Here?'

'Here at the house. In 1946, when he ran for Congress.'

She thought she was at home in Brighton. I nodded, shot through with guilt. She didn't know where she was and all I wanted was her signature. I promised myself I would return the next day for a proper visit.

'He came to the front door,' she said, looking out of the window. 'Anybody who knew Irish neighborhoods knew to use the back door and come into the kitchen, but what did he know then? No triple-deckers in his part of Brookline. So when your father heard the bell, he said, "It must be a bill collector!"'

She laughed drily. In the past, this story had sat in the context of a life, a family, a community. Not now.

I took the documents from the envelope. 'Mom, I'll come back tomorrow and we can talk about that, but right now I need you to sign these papers. They're from the shop. Routine tax papers. You need to sign them now.'

She squinted and grew restless. 'Where's Lela? I'll need my glasses.'

Attentive Lela saw my mother's fluster and came right over.

'My mother needs her glasses. And a pen.'

'I need to sign,' my mother said.

'Of course you do. You sit right there, Mrs Donohue, your boy and I get you everything you need.'

Lela led me behind the kitchenette. She nodded at the papers in my hand. 'What's this, Mr Donohue?'

'Call me Harry.'

The relaxed manner was gone. There was rigor in her stance. 'You asking her to sign anything, Harry, you should know it won't stand.'

'What do you mean?'

'She's not able.'

'Lela, she's my mother. I think I can make that judgment.'

'No, sir. Judgment already been made when you put her here. Like I told your sister.'

Mention of Judy pricked up my ears. 'Told my sister what?'

She gave me the look she no doubt gave many a man who let the women in the family take care of such arrangements. 'It's a condition of acceptance. Your mama reached that point it's best for her – best for the family – decisions be made on her behalf. So it's our policy, our condition, hand over power of attorney.'

'Power of attorney?'

'Why, yessir.'

It came to me. 'My mother gave Judy power of attorney?'

'Of course,' she said, smiling flatly. 'What you think I been saying?'

I looked across at my mom. She was nervously massaging

her walking stick and gazing at the blank television screen, waiting for the Kennedy special and the diversions of a dim past. Her distance from the present had frightened me, but at least she had refuge. Standing in the bland, insulated world of her final home, peering beyond her and out the window at the swirling snow and the onset of winter, I felt a familiar heaviness fall upon my shoulders. I had pursued the present moment and it would drag me down. Judy had raised the stakes. Pulled a fast one on me when I thought *I* was the clever one. Now what was I going to do? She was the de facto owner of the company. How could I avoid her calls in this new scenario? Mom I could manipulate, but keeping Judy's attention away from the shop until I could thicken my cash flow and cover the irregularities would be a lot tougher.

I took my leave of brisk Lela and kissed my mom goodbye. Outside I breathed deeply of the cold air and wondered where I would get the energy to up my game.

8

Back on the turnpike, I drove into a steadily worsening snow-storm, ignoring Jeff, thinking of how the rules had changed. Everything going to plan and now this. My gut had grown more knotted – less from this twist in events than from my fear of the old pattern of failure returning. Why did I always get so close, only to see success snatched from my hands? What made fate kick me between the legs at the worst possible time? Driving faster than was safe, I sluiced along Storrow Drive and dropped Jeff off at North Station. It was nearly six-thirty. I parked the car and met Gary as planned at the entrance to the Boston Garden, and we went up to the Boards and Blades Club.

'Where you been?' he said, his lip lifted above his small upper teeth. It was a look that usually raised my temperature, but I was still rubbing off the cold of the snowbound ride and news of Judy's gambit. 'You seen the weather?' I said. 'Traffic on the pike's at a crawl.'

We went straight in and took a table near the back. Gary walked ahead of me, his muscular shoulders tight, his head bobbing. Desperate for a drink, I was signaling the waitress before we had even sat down. She came right over. 'You gentlemen like menus this evening?'

She was a sports-bar waitress: freckled, tall, with a healthy face shaped by curling-tonged hair and a high-protein diet.

'Double Ballantine's,' I said. 'Gar?'

He paused, drifting between my frantic eyes and the girl's poised attention. 'Leave the menus,' he said. 'Please.' He absorbed her experienced smile. 'And I'll have a beer, I guess. You got Sam on draft?'

'Sam Adams? I can give you a bottle?'

'Sounds good.' He took the menus and watched her as she slooped away on long legs. But when his eyes returned to mine I saw that he was still assessing my latecoming and edgy entrance. He did not shake irritation easily, but my demeanor made him cautious. 'So. Dad. What you eating?'

'Not hungry.'

'Well, I am.' His small eyes idled up and down the menu. Without looking up he said, 'I finished the bank job.'

'Bank job?'

He smiled. 'The ATM shelters? On Franklin Street? Or did you think I was going into Rizzoli's line of work?'

'Good,' I said, glancing toward the bar. 'Glad it worked out for you.'

'Came in on time and on budget. More or less. Bank people seem reasonably happy. Said they might have a renovation for us in the spring, in Cambridge.'

'That's great.'

He sat tall in his chair, puffed with success. But his head tilted defensively and his eyes darted. He had rushed this good news and regretted it. Because I was still on the turnpike, measuring the snowfall, Judy's fast one, and the distance between me and my own ambition.

The waitress arrived with the drinks. 'What can I get you guys to eat?'

'I'll take the double cheeseburger,' Gary said.

'I'm fine, sweetheart, but you know what?' I waggled a finger between the Scotch and the beer. 'Why don't we do this again?'

'Sure,' she said. Oh, that every woman would respond to my needs with such professional detachment. But Gary did not disguise his alarm. His annoyance had evaporated and he held his beer with tentative concern, as if I had turned him into an accomplice in this sudden descent into hard drinking.

'You OK, Dad?'

'What, back-to-back drinks and you're worried about me? You keeping different company these days?'

He shrugged. My drinking didn't bother him – it never had. It was my distance. He couldn't figure out why, for once, I wasn't alert to his condition. He had practically invited me to badger him by mentioning his work immediately, but I hadn't bitten. And if this evening were to be an exercise in reconciliation, then the sins would have to be familiar.

But after a deep pull of the Ballantine's I felt the old stirrings: some exasperation, true, but also a desire to meet Gary halfway. After all, wasn't that why I had come?

'I've had a tough day,' I relented. 'The Rizzoli project is coming together, but it isn't easy.'

'It never is.' This commonplace he lobbed at me with false aplomb, and it was my turn to swallow irritation.

'Hey, that's great about the job,' I said. 'I mean that sincerely. How's your mother doing?'

'Oh, I nearly forgot. I got some more news. I moved out.'

'Out of Dedham? No kidding? Where to?'

'Place in the South End. Handy for downtown.'

This news really surprised me. For ten years I had seen my son as a mommy's boy who couldn't get his act together. Now it looked like he was making a go of a tough business, striking out on his own, shaping his own life – and without any help from his old man. Or only a little, anyway, and I couldn't resist reminding him. 'That cop ever get off your back?'

He blinked. 'The cop.'

'O'Brien.'

'I know who you mean,' he said, mouth tightening. 'Funny thing. Different guy started coming around. Real Officer Friendly. Couldn't do enough for us.'

'Funny how these things work out.'

The waitress appeared with our second round. I mimed another order and Gary stuck his hand out. 'Whoa. Not me. I'm good.'

She looked from Gary's alert face to the glasses lining up in front of me. Her stance stiffened slightly and I sensed an alertness of her own taking shape. 'So that's a Ballantine's?' she said to me, her tone practiced and steady as she decided to help Gary out. 'Double?'

But I knew the drill and didn't appreciate it, especially the little pause before *double*. 'Let me think,' I said, puckering my forehead. 'Was that what I've been drinking?'

'Yes sir.'

'Tell me again?'

'*Dad*.'

'Double Ballantine's, sir.'

'Then you'd better get it for me, don't you think?'

'Of course,' she said. Her expression remained the same, but the skin around her eyes had tautened. She turned to Gary. 'And your meal will be right along.'

When she had gone, Gary leaned across the table. 'What the fuck you have to go and do that for? She's just doing her job.'

I drained the first Scotch and slid the fresh one in front of me. The sweet kick of the whisky had emptied the afternoon's tension, but I could feel resentment filling the gap: at Judy, Eddie, Ann, Jeff, and most of all Gary, who happened to be on hand and whose successes had hit me at the same time as my latest taste of self-doubt. 'Her job is to take my order, not make judgments about me.'

'Nobody's making judgments.'

I sipped at the second double. 'Can you tell me honestly that you aren't?'

'Absolutely.' He spoke earnestly, almost fiercely.

His honesty pained me. Wouldn't you know it? On a day when family was letting me down, Gary had come bearing a peace pipe. I would have preferred another kick, but I shook my head and did my best to accept it. 'Well, I appreciate it. Like I said, it's been a tough day.'

The waitress arrived silently with my drink and Gary's meal. He nodded thanks and bit into the cheeseburger. Now that he was eating I did feel hungry, and I took a few fries from his plate.

He wiped his mouth with his napkin and finished his bite. 'Don't say anything yet,' he said, a finger in the air. 'I was talking to Mom. I'm going home for Thanksgiving and I told her I'd like you to be there.' His forehead was creased with purpose.

I laughed. 'I don't think so, Gar. Thanks anyway.'

'I told you not to say anything. Listen. I'm out of the house now. Finally. And I know what you've thought about my situation in the past. Anyway, this is a chance for a fresh start. You're both my parents.'

Earnestness did not suit him. It was as if he couldn't get his small mouth around the largeness of intention. 'That son-of-a-bitch Howard going to be there?' I asked.

He snorted. 'No. Tell you the truth, I think Mom's lost interest in him.'

'Well, you're just full of good news today, aren't you?'

'I don't like the guy any more than you do, Dad, but I have to admit that Mom was more relaxed when he was around.'

'You really think I give a shit she's relaxed? All I hope is you never have to put up with a marriage like we had.'

'C'mon, Dad. She's pretty mellow about you these days.'

'Maybe she's finally seeing who was the aggrieved party.'

Gary's experience didn't allow him to smile at this comment, even if my tone was ironic. Besides, he was here on a mission, and his obvious intent was making me nervous.

'So you'll come?' he said. 'On Thursday?'

I looked at my watch. 'You better finish up. It's nearly tip-off.'

I waved for the check and paid, tipping the girl a penitent 20 per cent. Half the third whisky remained. I tried, I really tried, to leave it behind, but old habits die hard on a day like that. I let Gary go ahead and finished it in a single gulp.

Right off it gave me a boost. Like a kid at his first rock concert, I walked through the low-ceilinged corridors of the Garden, floating on the first flush of a good drunk, the problems of my day suddenly very distant. I bought a program and a hot dog and shouted hellos at the journalists and cops whose faces were as familiar to me as the green seats and the championship banners hanging from the rafters. Praise the Lord for alcohol and the distractions of modern life. Gary and I melted into the flow of shouting fans, riding the excitement of the biggest show in town, the place to be. We entered the arena in a swirl of light and noise, the organ whirring, the crowd a-chatter, the buzzer banging order while giant men in garish uniforms ripped warm-ups from their legs and glared at each other with stone-faced competitive intent. The Lakers and Celtics, the best two basketball teams in the world, nationally televised. And we were in the middle of it! Even Gary was caught up in it all. 'Cool, Dad, huh?'

'Oh, yeah.'

Jimmy and Alex waved from courtside seats reserved for the influential. I headed their way.

'Not these guys, Dad. Please.'

'C'mon. Only be a minute.'

They were sitting with Pascal Rooney, Benny Rice, and two women who knew how to dress for broadcast coast-to-coast.

'Harold and *fils*,' Alex boomed. 'Here for the big game.'

'We're here, all right. But we don't have the . . . chairs you guys do.'

I blinked at them, handed my hot dog to Gary, and looked for something to grab on to. The liquor had turned me thick-tongued, and I could see Jimmy's eyebrows rise. 'Chairs?' he said.

'Seats. Whatever.'

'They *are* chairs,' Alex said, slapping the padding with a big hand. 'Veritable armchairs. Not the wooden butt-tinglers they used to have in here.'

'Hey, Harry,' Jimmy smirked, 'can I get you a beer? I'd make it a Rob Roy but I don't think they sell 'em in here.' One of the women laughed, and Gary flashed Jimmy a dirty look. Not a good idea. 'What's your boy's name, Harry?'

'Gary. My name's Gary.'

Jimmy gave him the lizard stare, slit-eyed and stock-still. I was still looking at the woman, whose dirty blonde hair and low neckline put me in mind of Lucy Rizzoli. 'Your dad tells me you're big-time now,' Jimmy said. 'Downtown construction.'

'I guess.'

'City's finest looking after you?'

Gary sneered. Jimmy stared him out then let his gaze drift to me. 'That one of your past-life gigs, Harry? Construction?'

'Not quite. Little property speculation.'

The last word didn't come out of my mouth right. Jimmy turned to the woman who had laughed. 'Harry's a jack-of-all-trades. Big-shot publisher now. Man of words.'

'Making it happen,' I said.

The blonde grinned inanely. Gary had turned his back on us and was watching the players take the floor. Alex put his hand on Jimmy's shoulder. 'Go on, Harry. Enjoy the game with your son. And listen . . .' He leaned across Jimmy, who looked squeezed and uncomfortable. 'Meet us in front of the Lakers' locker room after the game. I have a contact on the team who might be able to introduce us to a few of the stars.' He nodded toward Gary. 'Get your boy here an autograph if he's so inclined.'

If Gary heard the offer he didn't acknowledge it. We took our seats. 'Fucking asshole,' he snarled.

'Take it easy.'

'Take it *easy*? Did you have him fix that cop?'

'What are you talking about?'

'He did, didn't he? Last thing I want is that asshole doing *me* any favors.'

'He didn't do anything for you.'

'Oh. Like he did it for you.'

'Jimmy's my best friend.' These words came out slurred and maudlin. Gary folded his arms and stared at the court. 'Give me a fucking break, Dad. Case you didn't notice, he was treating *you* like shit too.'

We watched the game. Gary cooled down and I sobered up. Our seats were up high – not in the nosebleed section, but distant from the action. At half-time Gary elbowed me and pointed at a white-haired guy in a leather jacket and scally cap several rows below. 'Hey. Look who it is.'

'Who?'

'It's McCann,' Gary said, 'Sammy McCann.'

Sure enough it was the Irish Mafia boss, rings on his fingers and an unlit cigar the size of a billy club between his thick lips. He was standing in front of his seat and stretching while his henchmen looked up at him with uneasy deference. Like his brother, the senate president, he was short and compact, but coarser in looks and less flamboyant in his gestures. His face was ruddy and tight, like a boxer's waiting for a punch.

'Look at him,' Gary said. 'Just standing there.'

'What's he supposed to be doing?'

'I don't know. I mean, it's Sammy McCann!'

Gary was right: his presence was remarkable in itself. As the game resumed, I kept an eye on him. Without doing anything, he stood out. He was the only one of his group not drinking. Beside his boisterous pals, he was steady as a Buddha. He sat with his hands folded, sucking his cold cigar. He kept his cap on, removing it from time to time to smooth back his shock of white Irish hair. Whenever he spoke, his associates would lean in, tense and alert, eyeing each other with caution. It was an object lesson in the understatement of power. His very physique had an aura of controlled violence, of menace defined by quiet but ruthless achievement of what authority said was not to be achieved. Here was a man who would grasp all and grasp with impunity. And, as I looked at him, I recognized that, on a certain level, I wanted to be like him. I wanted to be someone who took what he wanted. Someone men clustered around. Someone people came to for favors. I was not a violent man, but I would have loved a slice of the power and respect you could tell Sammy the Knife owned just by the way he crossed his arms. Today of all days had taught me where my ambition was aimed. And the book could do this! Forget about Judy and Eddie and their family games. Fuck them. The book would make me part of the action! I could do it!

The game played itself out beneath my distracted gaze, and the Celtics lost in the closing seconds when Magic Johnson hit a three-pointer. Above Gary's protestations, I headed for the locker room to meet Alex. He and Jimmy were standing at the door among journalists and cameramen and assorted hangers-on attracted by the whiff of celebrity. Pascal and Benny and the women were not with them. A nervous excitement coated Alex's customary gravitas. He put his arm around my shoulders and whispered, 'Any minute now. Little closed-door meeting before they open the floodgates.'

His breath smelt of cigar smoke. 'When I was working with the housing agency in the Sixties, I used to travel to New York once a month. I'd see Kareem riding the subways, knees way up in the air. He was over seven foot even in high school.'

'Lew Alcindor back then.'

'Man of detail, Harry. Always were. Very little gets past *you*, you sly devil.'

Alex's attention felt forced. If I didn't know better, I would have thought he, too, had been drinking. But he was a player in the city and was about to get me inside the locker-room of the world champions. I felt the buzz of power. Jimmy hovered at his elbow, half deferential, half surly. Gary took refuge in my shadow.

When we got inside I was surprised at how small the room was, especially with these NBA giants walking around. The press clustered around Riley, his slick hair gleaming in the television lights. James Worthy and Mychal Thompson were already dressed, and Magic was still in the shower. Kareem sat in front of his locker, still in uniform, describing to a short white guy a termite problem he was having in his million-dollar house in LA. It was like being in a television show. I did my best not to look impressed.

Alex spoke quietly to a team official. I whispered to Jimmy, 'You see McCann in the stands?'

'Joe?'

'No. Sammy. Gary noticed him.'

Jimmy sized up Gary, licked his lips. He had his mark for the evening. 'Good eye, kid. He offer you a job?'

'Yeah. At the State House.'

'Your boy's a comedian, Harry. A laugh a fuckin' minute.'

'Take it easy, Jim.'

Alex sidled over. 'Michael Cooper's free. Come on over.'

The official introduced us. Cooper was wearing only his uniform shorts and trademark knee-high white socks. His dark skin glistened with sweat, and his lean, greyhound musculature made him look even taller than six-seven. He appeared physically aloof and larger than life, like a Sudanese prince. His hands were like a bass player's, and he smiled the easy smile of the gifted.

'Mr Cooper, I'm Alex Lathrop. We're big fans. Good game tonight.'

'Always sweet to beat the Green.' Cooper was rubbing Ben Gay into his shoulder and looking over our heads at Riley's impromptu press conference. 'It's a long season,' he said, 'but we're only here once. So it's nice to take it.'

'Only once during the regular season,' Gary said.

He looked at Gary the way Bobby had looked at Jeff out in Concord. 'I think Detroit might have something to say about that.' He pronounced it *De*-troit. Responding with a little high-handed ghetto tone to the white-bread comment. Gary didn't answer.

There was an awkward pause. Then, on this day of real ups and downs, I had my latest brainwave. 'Michael, Harry Donohue. I'm a publisher here in Boston. I specialize in sports books, and I'm very interested in doing your autobiography.'

Gary looked mortified, but Alex flashed the grin of a judge who appreciates an ingenious courtroom twist. Cooper glanced down at me with dark disdain, as if to say: *Who's this bush leaguer?* But there was a glint of interest in his eye.

'Autobiography?' He pronounced each syllable distinctly, like a preacher.

'We hire a writer, of course, to do the heavy lifting. Maybe you even have someone in mind. Someone you know. Someone you trust.'

'What you talking to me for? Magic's the man.'

'And you, Michael,' I said softly. I was on to a winner here. I could sense it. 'And Kareem. And maybe James.' I leaned in close, speaking very softly and emphasizing my flattery with slow partings of clasped hands. 'You have a story to tell. And I have a team that can make your book big. Really big.'

He slowly screwed the cap back on to the Ben Gay. 'Right now all I'm thinking about is another championship. It's like Magic says. The more we win, the hungrier we get.'

'Amen to that,' I said, a little too quickly. I could feel Gary's cringe. 'We're talking next summer, when the season's history and you got *another* ring on your finger.'

A commotion flared across the room as a towel-clad Magic emerged from the shower. The journalists clustered around him, tossing soft questions about his winning shot. But I kept my eyes on Cooper. He stared for a long few seconds, then tucked his chin to his chest and picked up his towel. 'Could be,' he said.

I laid my card beside his locker. 'We'll let you get dressed,' I said. 'Call me when the season's over.'

Back in the hallway Jimmy sneered. 'Donohue, you are so full of shit.'

But Alex was laughing. He slapped me on the back. 'I have to hand it to you, Harry. You've got chutzpah. We waddle in there like a bunch of gawking tourists, and you pull the rug out from under us by doing a deal.' He turned to Jimmy. 'You should get him back on the team, Jim. You really should.'

'Harry's a long way from a deal on this one. Besides,' he said drily, 'he already tried the law. Wasn't to his taste.'

But I was pumped up. I was too high for Jimmy's sarcasm. I turned to Gary. 'So what do you think?'

He shrugged. 'I don't see the big deal. It's not like he's Magic or Kareem.'

'The kid's impressed,' Jimmy said.

I wanted everyone to share in my excitement, so I tried to pull Gary in from the margins. But my judgment wasn't the best. 'Did you guys know that Gary here made the key block when Flutie threw the pass?'

The reference fell flat. Alex pretended to look interested. 'No kidding? Against Miami? You know, Harry, I remember you telling me something about that.' But the politeness rang hollow, and Jimmy was snickering without sound.

Gary looked at his watch. 'I gotta go.'

'Don't let us hold you back,' Jimmy said.

Gary stalked off. I jogged beside him. 'Gar, what's up? Hang on a few minutes.'

'Forget it, Dad. You've got your world, I've got mine.' He reached the exit and punched the handle so the door flew open.

I grabbed him by the jacket so that he had to stop. 'That was something, huh?' I said. 'You know, I really think Coop's interested.'

'Yeah, well, that's great, Dad.'

'Look, wait for a few minutes and we'll get a beer.'

He looked out into the parking lot behind the Garden. 'I have to work tomorrow.'

'One beer! C'mon!' My hand on his arm, I could feel him sway between duty and desire.

'Right, one beer. Let's go.'

Why did I pause? I don't know. But I looked back at the players coming out of the locker-room. The touch of fame was coursing through my veins like liquor. 'Give me five minutes,' I said.

He writhed with irritation and pushed my hand from his arm. 'I'm leaving.'

He walked out the door. I shouted after him, 'Look, I'll come Thursday. For Thanksgiving.'

He swiveled and spoke to me walking backwards, 'Don't do me any favors.'

'I mean it. I'll be there.'

'You do what you like, Dad. You always have.'

'What time . . .?'

But the door had closed between us. I should have followed him into the parking lot, but the pull of the hubbub was too much. I rejoined Alex and Jimmy. We watched as Worthy and Kareem appeared and slid into the night. Wes Mathews and Mychal Thompson. Pat Riley in an Armani suit. The group at the door shouted their names. Women followed them. Finally Cooper, svelte and imperious in a floor-length fur coat so thick it added another three inches to his shoulders. He stopped for a moment, glancing at me and nodding. Thinking he was coming our way, I felt a little trill in my stomach. But he was waiting for Magic, who emerged wearing an even thicker fur and smiling like the Cheshire Cat. He and Cooper signed autographs. Everything around them seemed to glow. Then they were off, their gait announcing power and confidence, their furs billowing behind them, their shaved heads pushed ahead as if on a fast break, beautiful women and diehard fans in their wake. Here were men so privileged, so successful, so certain of their place in the world, that they were beyond ambition, beyond yearning, beyond doubt. All their hunger aimed at more championships. And, as I watched them leave, I prayed that a little of their magic be sprinkled my way. If anybody deserved it, I did. If only because I'd made it through today.

9

I did go to Ann's on Thanksgiving. It was my first visit to the house in more than three years, and I knew as soon as I crossed the threshold that it was a bad idea.

'Harry.' Ann had a knack of kissing my cheek without getting anywhere near me. But she was close enough to smell my breath and stepped back with clasped hands and an expression on her face that hadn't changed in twenty years. 'Gary told me you were coming. I didn't believe him.'

'Yeah, well. Here I am.'

'Yes. Here you are.'

I stood in the hallway in my topcoat, a bottle of wine in one hand and my car keys in the other. Judgment filled the air like the smell of roasting meat.

'I'm basting the turkey,' she said. 'You know where to hang your coat.'

She left me standing at the hall-closet door. A football game blared from the living-room television. On an antique trestle table sat photographs of Gary as a child, Ann graduating from Babson (five years after our divorce), and a high-summer snap of Judy, Shirley, and Ann, drinks in hand, on the deck of a twenty-two-footer docked in Boston Harbor. The air was hot and dry and my face was sweating, but I waited, allowing these images to remind me of all I didn't have, before hanging up my coat and slipping inside.

Gary's buzz-cut floated above the couchback, blocking the television screen. Beside him was a shock of long red hair. Both heads turned as I approached. 'Dad. Hey.' They stood and came around opposite sides of the couch. 'This is Sarah.'

He stood on the balls of his feet, head cocked, eyes flitting between Sarah and me. I had surprised him when I called and told him I really was coming. Now he wondered if he'd done right to invite me. He was exposing more of himself than he liked. Sarah, on the other hand, was relaxed. She had a pleasant smile, alert eyes, and several inches on Gary. She stooped with a tall girl's self-consciousness, and her auburn hair framed a hollow-cheeked face that seemed to be waiting for a surprise. 'Hi, Mr Donohue. It's so nice to meet you.' Her accent was Midwestern, north of Peoria, but she had adopted a Cambridge young-liberal look: dressed-down, earnest, naïve. Maybe she was the source of Gary's own turn towards seriousness. She wore a man's shirt and baggy jeans.

I put the wine on the dining table and extended my hand. 'Harry,' I said. 'The name's Harry. I was going to say welcome, but I guess I'm not really the right person to do that, huh?'

'Why not? You're Gary's dad.' Her voice was low-toned and generous. She smiled at Gary. She liked him. And he was relaxed with her in a way that surprised, even annoyed, me. Because I liked her right away.

'How come you haven't told me about Sarah, Gary? Didn't want to give me too much good news all at once?'

He wore a pained smile and touched Sarah's arm. He was

nervous that I might embarrass him, but I was not inclined to let him off the hook. I looked around the living room, which declared the steadiness and prosperity of Ann's post-divorce life: formal furniture rarely used, coffee-table books on Ireland and Italy, Waterford crystal and Belleek china. It was hard to believe I used to watch the Red Sox in this room from a beer-stained recliner.

'How 'bout a drink?' I said.

Gary took a breath. 'What can I get you?'

'There any Scotch in the house, or did Howard drink it all?'

Ann had come in from the kitchen, carrying bowls of vegetables. 'How about some wine, Harry? I have a nice Chardonnay open.' Her voice was a strained singsong. Over a cashmere sweater and wool slacks she wore a spotless apron.

'I'll stick with Scotch,' I said, hands behind my back.

She put the bowls on the table and took the wine I'd left there. She stepped by me, avoiding my eyes. 'Honey, you want to help me inside?'

It was a moment before I realized she was speaking to Gary. Looking back at us, he followed her into the kitchen. Sarah watched carefully, green-eyed and alert. I figured her for a social worker or conflict counsellor. Someone well attuned to the high-decibel whine of family tension. 'So what brings you to Boston, Sarah?'

'I've been here for five years.'

'Doing what?' I was aware of my hands, which didn't know what to do while waiting for the drink. I walked across to the television and turned down the volume.

'I'm a clinical psychologist? With the Harris Group?' She spoke with a youthful, self-aware tilt of her head and the little interrogative rise at statement's end that my generation has never gotten used to.

'In Boston?'

'Newton? We run an outpatient program for Newton-Wellesley?' She leaned over the back of the couch, her hair falling forward, her lightly freckled face showing the glow of good circulation. Gary had done well. I should have been happy for him, but her freshness and good nature simply reminded me of how long it had been since I'd had the unambiguous attentions of an attractive woman.

'Newton-Wellesley. Sure.'

'Gary says you run the family print shop?'

Gary would say that. I smiled. 'Print shop's the bread and butter, but these days I'm spending most of my time building the publishing arm.'

'Book publishing?'

Gary came in with my drink and a Coke for Sarah.

'Yeah,' I said. 'Sports titles mostly. But right now we're working on a book about the Hillbrook Savings break-in.'

'The cop robbery?' she asked.

'It wasn't a robbery,' Gary said, handing us the drinks. 'It was a burglary.'

I took the drink from Gary and sipped it. It was heavily watered. 'Bobby Rizzoli's writing it for us. An insider's view.'

'Rizzoli? The guy in prison? He's writing it for you?'

'He isn't writing it,' Gary said. 'Some ghostwriter is. He's a real lowlife.'

I couldn't resist the opportunity to bait Gary. Watering down my drinks. Afraid I might treat Sarah as I had treated the waitress at the Boards and Blades.

'He's no angel. But spend some time with him and you can't help but be fascinated.'

'You've met him?'

'We're working together.'

'Gary, how come you didn't tell me this about your dad? It's so exciting.'

But Gary was looking at the silent television with a linebacker's intentness. 'What did you turn it down for? The Vikings are like killing the Lions.'

Ann appeared with the turkey. 'Leave the TV off, Gary. Please, everybody sit down. We're ready to go here.'

While Ann carved I wandered into the kitchen, found the bottle of Scotch, and poured myself a real drink. Another picture of Judy was pinned to the refrigerator door. I gulped the drink, topped it up, and joined the others at the table. Gary was opening another bottle of wine. Ann glanced at my glass as I sat across from her.

'Sarah doesn't like dark meat, Mom,' Gary said. 'And I'll take a drumstick.'

'Actually, I don't mind. Whatever's going.'

'You told me you didn't like dark.' Against his will, his voice was assuming an adolescent whine.

'I prefer white. But whatever.'

She preferred white. Clear-cut in her tastes, and she had chosen Gary. Well, why wouldn't she? Ann passed the plates and we helped ourselves. Sarah tucked her hair behind her ears and heaped up hearty.

'I forgot to tell you,' Ann said to me. 'Shirley called earlier. Told me that you have to give Chief Cleary a call.'

'The Hillbrook chief?'

'Cleary. That's all she said.'

'What, today? He wants me to call him today?'

Ann paused with the long knife and puffed out her cheeks. 'Call Shirley, Harry. I just gave you the entire message.'

The television flickered from across the room as men in purple cavorted – another touchdown for Minnesota.

'Must have something to do with *60 Minutes*,' I said. 'They're coming up here on Wednesday.'

'*60 Minutes* are coming here?' Gary said.

'Producer first. Jack Wambaugh. Has a look around, works out how the segment is going to go, then comes back with Ed Bradley and a crew. Bradley's their top interviewer, you know. Guy they roll out for the big stories.'

'This is for the book?' Sarah asked.

'Yeah. They're going to do a story on the heist and feature Bobby in an interview. Dream publicity. My pal Sonny Volski and this producer go way back. So I set this up. Knowing Rizzoli, he'll do a great segment.'

'That's so cool,' Sarah said. 'My friend Lena? She works at Little, Brown? All she does all day is fact-check books on art and architecture.'

'Lena is an airhead,' Gary said. His shoulders were bunched, and his face had the same frown he'd worn the day the compressor was smashed up. 'Thinks because she went to Harvard she has a right to success.'

'Little, Brown's a dinosaur,' I said. 'Gotta be small these days to move quick.'

The dinner cooked and served, the wine poured, Ann could finally pay attention to the conversation. When we were married she could never relax, but I noticed that since she shed me, earned her MBA, and made a bunch of dough, she had no problem kicking up her heels. She finished a mouthful of food and looked at me. 'Little, Brown's a dinosaur?'

I saw her near-smile. She could see through my bullshit faster than Judy could. 'Hey,' I said, 'I got Rizzoli, didn't I?'

'You really are going to do this, aren't you?'

Was it the house? The Scotch? I was hearing tones in her voice I thought she'd stopped using with me years ago. Part puzzlement, part suspicion. 'The book? Yeah, I'm going to do it. And I guess Judy and Shirley think so too.'

I saw from her eyes, screwed up with obvious irony, that I had touched the truth.

'It doesn't bother you,' Gary said, 'working with a criminal?'

'How's it different than working with anybody else? He's doing his time for what he did. This is extra-curricular.'

He pointed at me with his fork. 'He's profiting from his crime. What about Son of Sam laws?'

'Got 'em in New York. Don't got 'em here.'

'Isn't it a First Amendment issue?' Sarah said. 'Freedom of speech? I mean, how can you stop someone telling a story? As long as it's true.'

She was charged by this news, I could see it. Gary snorted.

'Sarah,' I said, 'I couldn't agree more. Gary, you could learn something from this girl. She's a smart cookie.'

Gary put a hand on her arm, as if to keep her from floating away. 'I don't see what freedom of speech has to do with it. This is just one more crook you're hanging around with.'

Sarah stopped chewing. Ann swallowed in the silence. 'No

offense, Dad,' Gary back-pedaled. 'What I mean is, it's not just the cops. Business and politics in this town are run by crooks.'

I wiped my mouth. 'So. Which of my friends are crooks?'

'I'm talking about the general situation. Your contemporaries, I guess.'

'Don't you think you're exaggerating a little?'

Gary put his elbows on the table. Sarah was tilting away from him, wine glass in her raised hand. 'Look at the news just this week. Cops stealing civil service exams. Detectives getting paid off by bookies on Blue Hill Avenue. Politicians extorting from the 75 State Street developer.'

'I can tell you for a fact,' I said, 'that McCann is clean on 75 State Street.'

'What about Finnegan?' Gary fired back.

'Finnegan I couldn't say.'

'If he's dirty, McCann has to be.'

'Don't believe everything you read in the papers.' Gary leaned over his plate, his fingers knit so tightly their tips were white. I laughed. 'Hey, loosen up. It's what makes life interesting in this town.'

'You can see that Gary's father enjoys the company of the city's finest,' Ann said to Sarah.

'Who says I'm keeping their company?'

'You're certainly thick with Rizzoli. And whatever about politicians, he's the worst of them all.' She turned again to Sarah. She had leaned way back, aware by now that there was more going on at the table than talk of Boston politics. 'This is a man who violated the public trust in the worst way. A police captain who burgled his own community's bank.

Who was mixed up in drugs and extortion and organized crime. And who got a paltry ten years from Harry's old pal Alex Lathrop.'

'Sounds like a good story,' Sarah said. Good for her. This girl was rising in my estimation by the minute.

'It's a story, all right,' Gary said. 'A dirty story.'

'The best kind,' I said.

Gary turned in his seat and watched the television. Sarah gazed at me with something like admiration, and I shook my drink so the ice tinkled. Alert to the tension, Ann asked Sarah about the clinic. Gary kept his eyes on the TV. After a while I went into the kitchen to freshen my drink. Ann walked in as I was unscrewing the cap on the bottle. She closed the door behind her. 'What are you baiting Gary for?'

'Me baiting *him*? Did you hear his crack about my friends?'

'And you're making a show of yourself in front of Sarah. He brought her here for our approval. Can't you see that? Or are you too drunk to know what you're doing?'

'Hey, I approve, I approve.' I ignored her jibe and poured myself another. 'What does the kid want from me?'

Her face was flushed with anger. 'He wants his father to behave appropriately. To say the right things. Not to embarrass him in front of his new girlfriend. God, Harry, you would think after all these years I'd have some clue about why you do the things you do, you'd really think so, you know? But I'm still mystified.'

I tried to think straight, to be fair, but my brain was muddied. The two of us stood silently, locked in postures almost as old as our relationship. What has made me think today would be any different? Gary's will? This house and its history were much more powerful than any need he had suddenly stumbled across to have his mother and father smile at him over mashed potatoes while he basked in the gaze of a girl he'd probably known for less than a month.

Ann passed a hand through the air despairingly. 'I spoke with Judy this morning.'

'I thought you guys gossiped *every* morning.'

'I told her you were coming over. She's at Eddie's today.'

'One big happy family.' She was setting me up. I knew her too well.

'She said Milt Solomon's coming in to the office on Thursday?'

'You asking me or telling me?'

'I'm telling you what she said and asking if you're aware of the arrangement.'

'I don't see how it's any of your business,' I said. There was a lull. I tried to soften my tone. 'I think my mother and her situation . . . Judy's taking stock of everything. There are some family decisions that have to be made.'

'I don't think Judy knows you want to make those decisions with her. I think she's worried about you. And with your mother—'

'Leave my mother out of it,' I snapped.

'Harry, you brought her up.' She looked at me helplessly. Her anger had cooled, and I sensed that she really wanted to help. But, as long as we were on our old turf, the emotional background would be too complex to allow me to open up. Before I could say anything else, the phone rang. Ann looked at it for several rings before answering. 'Oh, hi . . . Yeah, a real family day.' She stared at me blankly. 'He's here. Gary invited him . . . I gave him the message, but I think he wants to talk to you.' She handed me the phone. 'It's Shirley,' she said, and left the room.

'What's this about Cleary?' I asked.

'Happy Thanksgiving to you too, Harry.'

'And many happy returns, Shirley. But what about Cleary? Does this have anything to do with Wambaugh's visit?'

'He called the office yesterday. I think he just wants to confirm the meeting next week, but he wouldn't tell me. He's one of these man-to-man guys.'

'Like me?'

There was a questioning pause. 'No, Harry, not like you. Not that you don't have your faults.' She had read something in Ann's voice. How these women rallied around each other at the slightest provocation. Something men rarely did. 'Anyway, he wants you to call him at the station.'

'Today?'

'No harm trying. It's a police station, isn't it?' She gave me the number and we hung up.

I dialed. It was answered at once by a voice stiff but friendly. I asked for Cleary.

'I'm sorry, the chief is off until Saturday.'

'Would you tell him Harry Donohue returned his call?'

There was a pause. 'Mr Donohue? This is Bobby Rizzoli.'

For a confusing, Scotch-soaked moment, I thought I was talking to my author.

'Bobby Junior,' he said.

'Sure. Bobby. How you doin'?'

'It's the holiday,' he said. 'Chief's at home, killin' the bird.'

'It's the *60 Minutes* thing, Bobby. We're set up for next week, and I just found out he was trying to get hold of me yesterday. I'm worried there's a problem.'

'I wouldn't know.'

'What are you doing at the station?'

'The short straw. I got the two to ten.'

'How's your mother?'

'OK, I guess. We had an early dinner and she went out to Concord.'

'She home now?'

'Have to be. Visiting hours finished at three.'

I checked the kitchen clock. It was nearly five.

I returned to the table. The TV was off and the three of them formed a tense triangle. 'Something's come up,' I said. 'I gotta step out.' Gary said nothing. Sarah shook my hand and said goodbye. 'Take it easy, Gar.'

'Right.'

Ann followed me to the hall. I took my coat from the closet. 'Where are you going?' she said.

'Clear my head.'

'You're not driving, are you?'

I settled the coat on my shoulders and buttoned it up. 'Ann. I'm a big boy now. Not like when we were married.'

She decided to let that one go. 'Harry, I'm sorry. I didn't mean to drive you away.'

'You didn't.'

'Judy and I, we talk. She's my friend. Normally, you know, I wouldn't say anything. It's not my business – I agree. But I thought today was different. Gary setting this up, you making an effort.'

I shook my car keys and opened the door.

'Will you give Gary a call next week?' she asked. 'Maybe it would be better if you two met on more neutral territory.'

'I took him to a Celtics game last week. He mention that?'

'Yes, he did. That's great. He needs you, Harry.'

'The kid's doing great. He doesn't need me.'

'You're wrong about that.'

I drove back into the city slowly, then headed north toward Charlestown. But when I got to my exit I kept going, out toward Sullivan Square. Traffic was light and winter darkness was descending. The orange glow of Route 93 channeled up into the hilly shadows north of Boston and layered into late-November twilight. I drove deliberately and well under the limit. The engine knocked. To my left, the lights of Somerville glittered with the sort of promise that attracts the lonely to bars on Thanksgiving Day. Where Paul Pallotta grumbled when his exotic dancers demanded double time though the crowd was only half its usual size. I had become reacquainted with Paulie's rasping voice that week as I listened to the taped conversations Jeff had discovered. It was a voice with sweat on it.

I ain't gonna lie to you, Bobby. They mean business.

If I was to deal with anybody – and you know I don't, at all I don't – I wouldn't deal with them. What? I'm gonna walk into a fuckin' lion's den?

This is what I told them. But they scooped me, and when they . . . when they do that they don't let you go to tell anybody. I'll tell you the truth, I thought I'd never walk again.

Ah, Paulie. You had to love the beady histrionics.

And I pay you what you say and they . . . they walk away.

I can arrange this.

They won't want the merchandise?

You won't hear from them again.

Paulie, listen to me: I got several friends in my basement – I think you know who I'm talking about . . . friends that don't let nobody muscle me. Nobody. So tell them to go fuck themselves, Paulie. Tell them straight.

By now I knew where I was going. I took the Fellsway exit, passed a church spire dark against the sky, and looped back into Hillbrook. I was clear-eyed and clear-headed and no worse for wear after about a quart of Scotch. I stopped at the Hillbrook Store 24 and bought mints, an Entemann's cake, and a carton of Salems. The sleepy-eyed Pakistani behind the counter smiled and wished me a Happy Thanksgiving. As I left I popped a mint into my mouth. I could see the police station glowing across the square.

Lucy opened the door without surprise. Blinded by the porch light, I couldn't see the expression on her face, but she stood in a way that neither barred entry nor invited me in: right hip thrown, elbow against the door, forefinger of her free hand tapping her chin. It was a stance that said, 'Come in if you dare.' She wore what looked in the murk like a jogging suit. The light from the living room frosted her high hair.

'Well, look who it is.'

'I was in the neighborhood.'

'Hunting turkeys.'

'You could say that.'

'I could say a lot of things.'

I squinted at her, starting to feel drunk again.

'You gonna stand there like a border guard or come on in?'

She swiveled and swayed up the split-level stairs. As I followed I glimpsed Bobby's gun rack in the weight room. *I got several friends in my basement.* What sort of merchandise was Bobby peddling? Or Paulie imagined him selling? In the light of the kitchen I saw she was wearing a creased cotton one-piece suit, an exotic outfit that pinched at the wrists, waist, and ankles and puffed out everywhere else. She also wore big, looping earrings. An open bottle of Southern Comfort sat by itself on the table. There was no sign of the nickel-plated .38. I took the cake and cigarettes from the bag and set them beside the bottle. 'Didn't want to come empty-handed. It being a holiday and all.'

She looked down at the gifts, touched, it seemed to me, and vulnerable, her eyes dropping their wariness for once. Like a woman who hadn't received much of late. She turned the cigarette carton on its side and finally looked at me. 'Why, thank you,' she said. 'So kind of you.' She kissed my cheek. I encircled her waist, my hand on the small of her back. The press of her breasts and the scent of her bare neck were enough to make me hold her, gently but firmly, long after the kiss was over. I was still in my topcoat. Beneath her perfume were traces of lipstick, hairspray, and breath both sweet from the liqueur and edged with the metallic trail of tobacco. I wanted to taste that breath, but I stood still as a sentry. We were both breathing audibly.

'Bobby Junior's at work,' she ventured finally.

'I know.'

'You know?'

'I phoned the station earlier. About the *60 Minutes* visit.'

'60 Minutes.'

Everything depended on this moment. Intentions judged, motivations weighed. While in the arms of a tall man no longer young, reeking of whisky. Alone. Much like herself. Then she smiled – out of one side of her mouth, to be sure, a smile of irony and experience, but a smile all the same. I took off my coat.

We went straight to her bedroom. *Their* bedroom, though everything about it suggested a woman on her own: vanity spilling over with make-up, terrycloth bathrobe draped over the easy chair, piles of women's magazines on both sides of a bed covered sloppily with a pink bedspread. An ironing board stood folded against the closet door, and a pair of fur-trimmed slippers lay on the floor. No overflowing ashtrays or dirty glasses, I was glad to see, just a comfortable woman's retreat. I guessed she left the worst of her loneliness in the kitchen with the liquor. But what did I know?

I knew what I saw, and I saw her turn, look me in the eye, and unbutton the one-piece so it fell to the floor like soot from a chimney. I started to undress myself as she removed her underthings and stood before me naked but for her earrings. Lucy was a well-dressed, sexy woman, but I expected women my age to take off their curves with their clothes. Lucy looked even better. Freed from support, her breasts moved out but not down, lovely, full, expansive. The sweet curve from rib to waist came round again in perfect symmetry in the swell of her hip. Clothes off, she seemed loosed from gravity; in spite of that splendid ampleness she looked buoyant and light-footed, as if she might float away if not embraced. Her face was frank and clear and empty of all calculation. She was before me in spirit as she was in body, unencumbered, untethered, willing.

At my age I've learned not to expect fireworks from every brush with sex. Sometimes it's good, sometimes not. On rare occasions it's as wonderful as anything can be (and better than ever imagined), heightened by realism, experience, and respect for the mystery and elusiveness of passion. Lucy came to me without shame or weariness. Once decided that we would do what we would do, she shed all doubt and reservation and gave of herself with all the fervor of a woman who loved life and hadn't gotten the best deal from it. And me? I was overdue. I was ready to trust her. Our need arced to the same blissful apex; we were like lovers in a song. Slowly, steadily, but at the most intense pitch, we made love with all the stored energy of long loneliness, and I saw in her ecstatic face the joy of moments sheared from all others, suspended outside the normal, grinding chain of days and years.

Only afterwards, as she smoked and I stroked the curve of her hip, did I sense an alien odor, the spoor of another's masculinity clinging to her skin. It was Bobby's territorial scent, left over from his departure or carried back today from her prison visit. I did my best to ignore it, but it hung around like smoke on a battlefield.

'You're good,' I said.

'We're good.'

'Yes.'

She touched my chin. 'You ever a smokin' man?'

'No.'

'This bother you?'

'Only because it's keeping you from something else.'

'Ambitious.'

I kissed her shoulder. 'You got that.'

The phone, on her side of the bed, rang like a dropped plate. Her eyes narrowed. 'I gotta take this.'

I nodded toward the door.

'No. Stay.' Her naked back to me, she picked up the receiver.

'Hi, sugar . . . Nah, fell asleep . . . In bed . . . You know it.'

Her voice betrayed no difference I could detect, but she was clutching a fistful of bedspread with her free hand. My own heart was thumping. I wanted to touch her. I also wanted to flee.

'Well, why don't you ask them about that? Or put in an application. Medium security, all I've heard, they can make arrangements. Especially on holidays . . . I could, I guess . . . Yeah, *sure*. They're banging down the door here . . . Bobby, please . . . All right, an unfortunate choice of words . . .'

Her voice was flat and defensive. She went quiet as the conversation followed a course I imagined it always did: a little probing from Bobby, just enough for him to construct in his own mind a reason to attack, followed by monologue that she would usually construe as paranoid. Only this time he was right. I could feel it. Thick prison walls and ten miles of city and suburb were not enough to stop his seeing. He was like some comic-book villain with super vision. The master of deception, he saw it with ease in others. He *knew*.

She hummed assent to his rant for several minutes. I looked at the ceiling and didn't move. When she finally hung up she said nothing, stood, and visited the bathroom. I heard the toilet flush. She returned and lit a Salem. She was earth bound now.

'He knows, doesn't he?'

She blew smoke from the side of her mouth. The weariness had returned. 'He doesn't know jack.'

'You sure?'

She didn't answer, but looked away. 'Conjugal visits,' she murmured.

'What?'

'He wants a conjugal visit. But he's waiting for me to do all the work. Like I'm the one in jail with all day on my hands.'

I reached and stroked her. She didn't pull away, but she didn't respond. 'Hey,' I said. 'He's a long way away.'

She sighed and managed a smile. 'No, Harry, he's not. But you're closer, aren't you?'

'I am.'

'I'm glad. I'm glad.'

Bobby Junior's shift ended at ten, so I had to be out of the house early. But now what? I could hardly return to Ann's. I couldn't face my cold apartment. For a while I drove aimlessly, taken over by circumstance more powerful than my will. Something was in motion, and not even the stars could tell me where it was headed. And though Lucy's smell was still on my skin, her form still bright in my mind's eye, against the dark Hillbrook streets, Bobby's brooding face was just as evident. Why, so close to the simplicity of good fortune, had life become so complex? How, the next time I faced him, could I keep the obvious from my face? He would know! He had phoned, while I lay naked beside his wife, and asked her for a conjugal visit! I kept checking the rear-view, as if expecting him to roar up behind me in his Caddy with killing in his eyes.

I returned to the city, wheeled onto Storrow Drive, and followed the parkways west. I joined the turnpike at Cambridge, where I paid the toll to the slot-eyed attendant and eyed the fall garlands festooning the booths. I could have been heading south, down through Sturbridge, past Hartford and New Haven and on to the enveloping anonymity of New York City. But I wasn't heading to bright lights big city. I turned north on 128, then west on Route 2. The red lights of the Waltham television masts blinked in the dark. A plane droned far above.

I pulled into the prison parking lot, cut the engine, and rolled down the window. There was nothing but the sound of crickets and the ticking beneath the hood. The night was cold. My breath billowed black against the stars. Lucy was gazing at her ceiling, sliding down the same slope of thought that had me out here, staring at prison walls, reassured for the moment by their height and solidity. The guard towers were dark – it was, after all, medium security. But the walls were thick. I needed to see them. Yet I also needed, for some strange reason, to be near the man whose story would make me a fortune while I dreamed of his wife's ample, uplifting form. Did more than dream. Ah, Lucy. We had some thinking to do, didn't we? But we both knew that while we agonized we would do again what we had done tonight. Once tasted, you couldn't put that drink down. In one blissful swoop it had us in deep. Deeper than I'd ever been.

10

Jack Wambaugh was everything New York used to be: elegant and charming, muscular and streetwise, full of energy and irony. So I could pick him out at Logan Airport, he told me to look for an old, bald guy in a brown coat. When he emerged from the eight o'clock shuttle I saw that the coat was a fur-collared chesterfield and the bald head a tanned and gleaming dome. In one hand he carried a faded, soft-leather carryall monogrammed in gold; in the other, a plush brown fedora with a satin band and the front brim angled way down. No doubt he was wearing cashmere socks. He put the hat on his head to shake my hand. 'Used to spend a good deal of time up here,' he said. 'My Masters is from Harvard.'

'In what?'

'Philosophy.' He winced – at the memory of 1940s Ivy League rigor or in acknowledgment of the gulf between then and now I couldn't tell.

He had mobile, intelligent eyes underslung by wrinkled, plum-colored bags. His lips were fleshy but not carnal. His head was fringed with a nimbus of white hair, yet his eyebrows were full and black. He was thick in the middle yet graceful, a fullback's frame, with large hands that trailed fluently behind his speech. He was even taller than me. There was an old-world air about him, something Middle European, pre-war. Gracious and attentive, he listed toward me as we walked from the terminal, catching every word, replying in an urbane New York accent, and watching the passing travelers with the seasoned attention of a native Gothamite.

'Is Durgin Park still around?'

'Sure.'

'Waitresses surly as ever?'

'More so.'

'Ah, tradition. How about lunch there? On CBS?'

'You've twisted my arm.'

New York Jew and Boston Irish, by afternoon we were American pals, swapping tales over lunch of Scollay Square taverns and Kansas City jazz joints. He was like guys I had met in the army: worlds away in background and experience but so like me in ways that counted. He was an operator, a lover of the big picture, a sentimentalist. A ladies' man (I sensed) and a city boy. On the way to Concord he insisted I take Cambridge River Drive. As I drove the curving parkway he looked through the bare trees at the granite of MIT and redbrick of Harvard, wistful and content, hands folded over his generous belly, full now with Durgin Park pot roast, mashed potatoes, and Indian pudding. The day was sliding by effortlessly, like a vacation day, and you'd never guess he was building a story that would hold the attention of thirty million Americans for twenty minutes on a precious Sunday night. During the morning we had visited the Hillbrook Savings Bank, the optician's shop beside the bank, the offices of the *Mercury*, and the Hillbrook police station, where we had a memorable encounter with Chief Cleary. Jack was tactful and sharp wherever we went, tough when he had to be, expertly gathering what he needed while gazing at the world of Bobby's criminal past like a tourist on the Freedom Trail. Everybody liked him. They told him what he wanted to know. He was a pro.

He sighed as we passed the Harvard boathouse. 'I rowed intramural. Four months of torture.'

'Not easy.'

'Up at five, two hours of practice, Heidegger and Kierkegaard at eight.'

'When was this?'

"Forty-seven. Hasn't changed much, though.'

'I was in the fifth grade. We used to mitch school and come down here during the regattas to throw apples at you guys.'

His eyes twinkled. 'Always wondered who those urchins were. Now look at you, Harry. Successful publisher consorting with the underworld. Maybe I'll have Reasoner talk to *you*.'

I had managed to keep Jack away from the shop. I could do without him taking that elevator ride and contemplating the desolate view from my office. Shirley was miffed, as she had worked so hard on the day's arrangements, but I promised she would join us for dinner. I looked forward to it. If he was this gracious with me, I could only imagine the charm he'd lay on her. 'When did you leave?'

'Here? 1948. Went straight to CBS. I was a stringer in Europe for two years. The whole time I was there I heard only one name: Edward R. Murrow. He was back in New York by then. A legend, an absolute legend, among American journalists in London and Paris. When I came back I got the break of my life. Joined the staff of *See It Now* and worked with the man himself for eight years. A truly great man. I'll never forget the way he went after McCarthy. All to lose, and he went after that son-of-a-bitch and beat him at his own game. Television had real journalists back then.'

The last sentence had teeth in it, but also the same wistful echo as the sigh near the boathouse. He bounced his hat on his knee and stared at the new apartment blocks beside Mount Auburn Cemetery. 'Rizzoli,' he said. 'Bobby Rizzoli. How old you say?'

'Around fifty.'

'Wore his belt buckle on the left side. Listened to Johnny Mercer. Smoked Luckys. Lost his cherry in the back of a '46 Nash to a full-lipped broad named Luisa in a polka-dot dress and two-toned saddle shoes.'

'Baseball player. Played his way through the air force.'

'Still plays the field. If he wasn't in the can, that is. Married to a dark-haired butterball with big teeth and a high-pitched voice who gives him no joy.'

'Not quite.'

'Wants to be a star, though, right?'

I nodded. He was working now.

'And . . . and he wants everybody to think he's a nice guy.'

'It's not that he likes to be liked,' I said. 'He has real reasons for portraying himself as a patsy. Doing-time reasons.'

'How are you handling that?'

I paused. I had to be careful here. 'No one's going to make him say he was the ringleader, if he was, or that he's not repentant, which he probably isn't. We're focusing on the corruption, the environment, the code of silence among cops, and so on. Forget about what Cleary said this morning. It's stuff Bobby knows about, and I'm betting he can convince himself that *we*'re convinced he hung around with the wrong kids on the playground.'

Jack laughed. 'This is going to be fun.'

Fun was not what I expected. The more we talked about Bobby, the more nervous I became. The countryside sped by. The prison loomed into view. Without thinking, I pulled into the same parking spot where, a week ago, I sat until well after midnight staring at the prison walls. My palms were sweating; my breath was shallow. Jack was selecting papers from his leather bag and humming an old song. On my own, I would have turned around and headed back to Boston. Or Hillbrook.

It was the seventh day of my new life. Balanced between obsession and complication, I had no choice but to ignore any reality other than Lucy and her body. At least, for as long as I could get away with it. What she offered, what I pursued relentlessly without reference beyond the moment, was more intense than anything I could remember. It was certain and spontaneous. Exhausting and regenerating. We knew what we were doing and we knew nothing. My skin tingled just thinking of her. My breathing quickened just hearing her over the phone. And when I was with her it was almost too much to handle. She did whatever I asked. Over and over again. We were both retreating from something, we knew that, and the frenzy of our escape was all-encompassing. It allowed nothing to trespass the purity of the physical. Twenty years ago, I would have mistaken these feelings for love. But ours was not a love affair: it lacked the conventional sentiment – a lack that made it all the more powerful. All feeling was centered on the act of sex itself, and thus was supremely thrilling. We had none of the complications of youth or scruple. None of the usual equivocations. What we did have was the shadow of Bobby. The other reality.

Though we rarely mentioned him, he was always in the room. Jail made no difference: he was present, in the air and on our skin, especially in the coasting moments after orgasm, when our loss of breath and the dry air of her bedroom returned to our attention, and the ordinary world of knotted sheets and dripping faucets reminded us, if only for a moment, where we'd come from. Since Thanksgiving my head had been spinning and not just because of Lucy: Bobby was part of it too. He scared me. As the week went on, sexual thrill modulated into fear. I would have to face him. And prison walls, my great physical ally, were no consolation. They would sharpen his suspicions.

So preoccupied was I with these suspicions that I behaved all week in a way that could only feed them. At work I avoided his phone calls. At home I screened calls with my answering machine. Tuesday I canceled a visit after weeks of telling him we had to prepare for Wambaugh's arrival with a lengthy session. 'It's crucial,' I'd said in my old life, 'absolutely crucial.' I worked him into a state of anxiety and then failed to show. Jeff, poor unsuspecting Jeff, I sent to Concord like a virgin to a volcano. Bobby was not impressed. While I, instead of fulfilling my obligations to him and to the project, was sleeping with his wife and seeing his reflection in her eye.

Time had run out on me. We went through the prison visitors' routine, interesting to Jack as a first-timer but tedious by now to me: registration at the front desk; the long wait for our names to be called; the move through a series of barred electronic gates that clicked and slid and slammed; the search; the request to leave belt, laces, and ballpoints behind. With pencils and pads of paper and the sound of my shoes flapping (Jack wore Italian loafers, with tassels), we walked into the overheated visiting room and gave our names to the duty officer.

Bobby acted as if I wasn't there, while doing his best to embarrass me. 'Jim, a pleasure.'

'It's Jack.'

'No shit? Jack? Harry here told me Jim. Not so good with details is Harry.'

'We're very pleased you're working with us on this, Bobby. This is a hell of a story.'

'I just want people to know the facts.'

'Thirty-two million Americans watched *60 Minutes* last Sunday. The people will know.'

Bobby looked over both shoulders. This was the kind of moment he dreamed of, and just his luck the only witness was his dirtbag publisher who, for some reason (there was a reason, there was always a reason), had kept him on the outside at the most critical point in the project. He shot me a savage look, half triumph, half threat. Waiting for today had not been easy for him, but I could see that his anger had nothing to do with being cuckolded. I filed away my relief and concentrated on repairing damage done.

'So, when's Bradley coming up?' Bobby asked.

Jack didn't answer. He was looking down the line of cons, mostly young blacks and Hispanics in for drugs or burglary or assault. 'Medium security here, right?' he asked.

'Yeah.'

'I would've thought, with your status, maybe a more secure facility.'

Bobby lifted his shoulders and tapped his chest with both hands.

'What they got to worry about? I'm not going anywhere.'

'I was thinking about your own welfare.'

Bobby shrugged. 'I'm in isolation here. And these guys,' he nodded at the guards, 'with most of them I get on OK. They look out for me.' He fidgeted, clearly impatient to get to the where and when of his stardom. 'So how does this work? Bradley comes in, we talk about what I'm going to say?'

But Jack, for the first time that day, looked distracted. It was as if he was waiting for someone else to appear. 'We'll get to that, Bobby. First there's some business to attend to.' He drew some paperwork from his pad and leafed through it slowly, sliding out three releases he needed Bobby to sign.

I excused myself and called the office from the only pay-phone in the room. Carla answered, 'Harry, I've been trying to reach you. Milt Solomon and your sister were here this morning.'

'The appointment's for tomorrow.'

'I know. I told them. Said they had to talk to Peggy. Wouldn't take no for an answer.'

'Put me on to Peggy.'

'She's at her mother's. It's Wednesday.'

'Right. Shirley, then.' I spoke to Shirley, confirming the time for dinner and waiting for her to tell me something. But she wasn't giving anything away about Judy, and I wouldn't risk too deep a probe.

'How's it going out there?' she asked.

I looked across at Bobby, who was studying the releases like a bad student at exam time. Jack, the patient school-teacher, was pointing out specific clauses and whistling between his teeth. He was pressing all the wrong buttons, but he knew it. 'It's going. Jack's a player.'

When I returned to my seat, Jack was bundling the signed forms together and Bobby's jaw was clenched. Now Judy was banging on my thoughts, just when I needed all my wits about me.

'I just talked to Jeff,' I said to Bobby. 'He says chapter three's looking good.'

'Good of you to let me know. The kid didn't have much to say yesterday. Course, least he was out here.' He stared at me. He was not acting like he wanted Jack to think he was a nice guy.

Jack broke the silence. 'I've been doing some reading, Bobby. What the papers say about the trial—'

'Screw the papers.'

'You know what struck me? Maybe you can shed some light on this: not one of the articles I read said anything about motive. Now, I find that interesting, because my gut tells me this whole thing wasn't about money.'

'It wasn't for the fun of it.'

Jack leaned back in his chair, like a farmer on the porch with his day's work done. 'I don't just mean the burglary. But afterwards. You trying to keep the gang together, the Latrelli shooting, the whole thing falling apart in the final months. I mean, you guys were home free! All you had to do was keep your mouths shut! It was like you had a death wish. It was like you *wanted* to be caught.'

Bobby peered at Jack as if he'd been challenged, as if it had just dawned on him that *60 Minutes* wasn't there simply to stick a camera in his face and let him tell the world what a great guy he was. Or what a chump he'd been. Now he had to decide, immediately, which way to spin it.

'Jack, let me tell you something . . . this wasn't about wanting to get caught. I'm not excusing what we did but, once it was done, there was a bond. Right? The last guy you expect to break such a bond is someone you consider your best friend.' Jack was nodding, leaning close, giving Bobby the feeling of an audience. 'I don't use drugs. Never have. But the way I see it, the coke made Latrelli paranoid just like it made Donny homicidal. Now what was I gonna do in that situation?' He lifted his arms, like a priest beseeching the congregation. 'I did what I could. The house of cards came down. And Latrelli, that son-of-a-bitch, whatever about sending us all down the river – which is maybe, just maybe, understandable in terms of him being blown open by Donlon, painful as it is for me to say – Latrelli, that rat, tells the grand jury and the Feds and the judge and every two-bit reporter in Boston with a pencil in his hand that I – that *I* – masterminded this fuckin' thing! Anything else I could live with. Prison doesn't mean shit to me. But the guy that talked me into the job is the guy who says – who *testifies* – that it was the other way around. Now, who could live with that? Justice, sure, give me justice. But that . . . *that* is treachery.'

Bobby had talked himself into a stately rage. Jack was as casual as before, but there was a shine to his eye. He said nothing, leaving Bobby floating in the wake of his rhetoric.

'I did the crime, I'm doing the time,' Bobby said. 'But I just want the truth to be known.'

'Truth's a funny thing, Bobby. I'm sure Latrelli has his own version.'

Bobby reared back, lips drawn from his teeth. His color was high and his eyes flat as a snake's. 'You talking to him?'

Jack let the question echo. 'No, this is your story. Is there anything between you and Latrelli that isn't out there?'

'Like what? Like I was screwing his wife?'

I waited for him to look at me. One little turn of the head and I'd know that I hadn't been paranoid. Or was he more subtle than that? My heart thumped and my stomach fluttered. Then it was clear to me: he didn't *need* to know. Lucy and I knew, and that was enough to keep me shackled in fear. He was my rival, whether he knew it or not. And he could find out at any moment.

'Why don't you ask Harry? He's spent the last month listening to my old phone calls. Right, Harry? You must know my old life inside out by now.'

Truer than he knew. Now it was my turn to weigh a response. Something to settle myself down, something Jack could use, and something to mollify Bobby. His bitterness wasn't making me look good.

'The way I see it, Latrelli was the first one to talk himself into disloyalty,' I said. 'When Donlon shot him, all he had left was to convince himself that you and Donny were in cahoots. After all, you and Donlon were on the force together. And you are friends.'

'*Were* friends. That fuckin' moron set the whole thing in motion.' Bobby turned to Jack. 'Harry's right about one thing. Latrelli's a rat. No way I was gonna put even one guy away to protect my own ass.'

'No matter what was happening,' I said, 'at Hillbrook station or anywhere else, the code of silence was a given. Breaking that is the worst crime of all.'

Bobby nodded. Was he beginning to forgive me? Was the road to his ego that short?

'Chief Cleary told us Hillbrook is clean now,' Jack said.

Bobby smiled. 'So you met Jake, huh? How is the old bastard?'

We had started our day with a tour of the scene of the crime and arrived at Hillbrook police station at ten-thirty. Jake Cleary had been trying to get in touch since before Thanksgiving, when he had caught wind of a *60 Minutes* visit. He led us to his office with a heavy swagger. He was an old-fashioned, steak-and-eggs chief, with flat feet, quivering jowls, and gnarled fingers. He wore his thin hair straight back and oiled. His puffy Irish face and horn rims made him look like a labor leader or big-city politician, a George Meany or Richard Daley. The only thing missing was a big cigar. He wore a blue blazer and red polyester tie decorated with the Hillbrook crest. He sweated easily. But he was sharp and likeable, and, at first, he and Jack hit it off like the city kids they were.

'Gotta show you this,' he said, as we sat at his cluttered desk. 'My secretary gave it to me last Christmas.' He lifted a stained coffee mug and pointed at the printed legend with a smile. It said, 'YOU KNOW YOU'RE HAVING A BAD DAY WHEN *60 MINUTES* VISITS YOUR OFFICE.' Jack returned the smile and Jake's belly laugh bounced off the walls.

'Didn't mean to ruin your day, Chief.'

Jake cleared his throat. It sounded like a command. 'This is an honor. I'm just a small-town cop trying to convince people there are no more skeletons in the closet. Listen, did Harry Donohue here show you around Hillbrook?'

'We had a look at the bank, the optician's shop, the ice-cream parlor,' I said.

'Nice-looking place,' Jack offered.

'All-American City 1977.' He lifted a bent finger. 'And we're Democrats here.'

'Nice to be in one of the few states that went for Dukakis. Too bad the rest of the country couldn't see things that way.'

'Don't support a native son, you're in trouble,' Jake said. 'And I wouldn't feel sorry for the Duke. He got national exposure like you could never purchase.'

'Not always a good thing. Take it from someone who knows.'

The chief rearranged the papers on his desk. When he was sitting, his sports jacket bunched up at the shoulders and his thick neck strained over his collar. There was a little trench of bristle between chin and lower lip where the razor couldn't reach. His complexion was rough, mealy, the color of blood sausage. 'I guess this Rizzoli thing means a little national exposure for us.'

'Part of the story.'

Jake stood, took a frame from the wall, and set it before us. It was a citation from the Attorney General's office, a clean bill of health for the department dated four months earlier. 'When this whole thing broke,' Jake said, 'my first concern was for the department. And the town. Two bad apples and everyone in the state was pointing fingers at us. I personally insisted on this audit.' He tapped the citation with his fingernail. 'Don't know if you've heard, but there's been a lot of rogue-cop stuff popping up this year – drug dealing, stolen civil service exams, not to mention our little situation here. Something like the burglary comes to light and the Feds go to town, which they should do. It's their job. But one incident gets public, the do-gooders start looking closer, more stuff surfaces, and all of a sudden the whole state thinks all cops are crooks. Isolated incidents are happening all the time, but they have a tendency to be revealed in bunches. So not only do you have to *be* clean, you gotta *look* clean.'

'What about the competency issue?'

'What do you mean?'

'This all happened under your nose. In your town.'

Jake shook his head. 'I wasn't chief at the time. Appointed in '85.'

'You were a captain,' I said.

Jake looked at me like I was a kid who couldn't figure out a math problem. 'You're a lawyer, Harry, right?'

'No.'

He ignored my reply. 'Lawyers and reporters are the first ones to tell us cops we don't know the Bill of Rights. I had my suspicions about Donny and Bobby. Everybody did. But if the FBI, the state police, the Attorney General, and everybody else couldn't prove anything, then how the hell could we? And what were we to do but presume innocence? What would you have done?'

He let us chew on that one. But Jack had done his home-work. 'There have been allegations of corruption here since the Sixties,' he said, looking at a notepad. 'Drugs gone miss-ing, two of your officers in detox last year, ATF investigations. And correct me if I'm wrong, but the chief down in

Shropwood – the one who's been indicted for stealing civil service exams? – at the time of his arrest he was allegedly carrying a gun registered to an ex-Hillbrook cop.'

Jake nodded genially. Nothing new there. 'Jack, save yourself some grief. I've read those stories, and they're way off base. We're a clean department. My guys, they got their problems like everybody else. Rizzoli's son is on the force here, and I swear some days I think I'm the only one in the world who knows he's nothing like his pop. It's his nature. The kid's straight as a die. But I also know his old man, who woulda shielded the kid from all the other stuff. No doubt on that, take it from me. The world isn't black and white, you know.'

The last sentence came as he was lifting his huge frame from the chair. He stuck his head out the door and bawled, 'Angie! Angie, get us some coffee down here.' He returned to his seat, loosening his tie. 'Harry, tell me this guy isn't a Yankees fan. Anything else I can live with, but not that!'

'Methinks the chief doth protest too much,' Jack said afterwards in the car, to himself more than to me. We were driving into Boston on 93, the late November sun behind us. To my left I could see the wooded ridge that sloped fellsward and hid the upper development, where, at that moment, Lucy was having coffee with the only woman in the neighborhood who would still talk to her. That she was thinking of me was weak satisfaction, winter sunshine when I wanted the full heat of her Texas skin. There was little chance of being with her today, though we had agreed to talk by phone that night.

'Where'd you read that about Bucky Quinn?' I asked Jack.

'Who?'

'The exam cop. You said he had a Hillbrook cop's gun?'

'I must've read it in the wire story about the indictment. Are you hungry, Harry?'

'Sure.'

'Let's go to Durgin Park. I think better on a full stomach.'

So now Bobby was asking after Jake with a smirk. It was the look of a man who knows, who knows you know, and who knows you can do nothing with the knowledge. It made me nervous. You didn't mess like that with a guy who'd grown up on the streets of Brooklyn and read Plato's dialogs in the original Greek. I could see Jack turning an ironic glance into a watertight story. He was as fine-tuned as Bradley and Safer were heavy-handed. Though why I was worried it was hard to say. This whole conversation was win-win for me. The harder Bobby fell, if that's how Jack decided to play it, the more I stood to gain. Any publicity was good publicity, and the truth, to the extent Jack could find it, was best of all. But I wanted Bobby to be happy. I wanted him diverted. Brooding, he might direct his energy toward other truths, and I'd be falling with him.

But Jack seemed to have all he was looking for from Bobby. He stood, hitched at his beltless trousers, and peered at the prison yard through the dirty, rime-scaled window. The basketball rims were edged with fresh snow, and the guard towers hunched in the distant glitter of the winter sun. 'We'll need some continuity shots,' he said. 'You and Bradley, walking in the snow out there. What do you think? That be a problem?'

'Hell, no.' Bobby was on his feet, staring afresh at this scene he had come to hate, thinking about Bradley and himself in parkas shooting the breeze while America looked on with awe and respect. This was more like it. He nodded at the duty officer. 'Ask Cyril there. He'll make whatever arrangements you want. I talked to him about it this morning.'

Jack went over to the desk. Bobby and I were alone for the first time.

'Knows what's he's doing, huh?' I said.

He wasn't going to let my presence spoil the moment, but business was business. 'You're lucky, Harry. Today's another day. Did the kid give you my message?'

'No,' I said, and I was telling the truth. I had deliberately avoided Jeff.

'Bullshit. You're lucky I'm still doing this book. Yesterday I was *out*.'

He leaned close, teeth bared, and I could smell the after-shave that still lingered in the Hillbrook bedroom. 'I know you're not going to believe me,' I said, 'but I pissed you off on purpose. I knew if you were bullshit, you'd have the right impact on Wambaugh.'

'You expect me to believe that?'

'I don't care if you believe it. All I care is that you get on *60 Minutes* and I sell a shitload of books. And don't tell me it didn't go well today.'

My lie was so off the wall it might have been true, and Bobby frowned at me, head tilted. Jack came back and put his arm round him. 'You got a good guy in your corner here,' Jack said, jerking a thumb in my direction. 'All day I've been hearing what a great story you have, and now I see he isn't exaggerating.'

'You think so?'

'Hey, you guys are going to make a bundle together. I'd bet on it.'

He'd bet on it. Those words hung in my head the rest of the day. Was Jack telling it like he saw it or doing me a favor? Or was it in his interest to keep Bobby on my side? He was not an easy guy to read, but was I glad he was there. With anybody else, under any other circumstances, I don't think I could have brazened Bobby out. As it was I left the prison in a sweat, my teeth clattering and my armpits tingling. In my new life I was seeing the world as Bobby saw it. I took nothing at face value. I assumed everyone had a hidden agenda because *I* had one. When I wanted something, I was good at fooling myself that whatever I had to say to get it was true. I trusted people even as I deceived them. But this deception was on another level. I had lost the insulating layer of self-belief. I was playing Bobby at his own game, but without his experience.

I drove Jack to the Marriott Long Wharf. We had an hour to kill before dinner, so I had the drink I sorely needed while he showered and changed. I'd reserved a table at the hotel restaurant and arranged to meet Shirley in the bar. The crowd was thin, a mixture of tourists, financial district types, and visiting business people. I called Lucy from the lobby pay-phone and got her answering machine. As people drifted past, I listened to the polite Southern lilt of her message. 'Hey, it's me,' I said, hollow with need. 'I'll call you later.' I hung up, stranded by her artificial tone and the metallic inadequacy of technology.

As I returned to the bar I saw Shirley looking for me, her round forehead creased and her lovely neck straining as she scanned the room. She wore a red power suit, cut to look feminine, and a ruffled blouse. She clutched a leather-bound clipboard. I caught her eye and waved. Without acknowledging, she ducked out of the rear entrance. Just when I was wondering what else the day could throw at me she returned to the bar with Judy.

They turned a few heads, the two of them, striding through the sparkling murk of this high-ceilinged, big-city hotel lounge: Judy tall and purposeful, her gray hair frizzed out and swept back, her wide shoulders padded to an even more imposing mass, her pale-eyebrowed, startled-looking face squinting as she approached; Shirley a half-head shorter but no less formidable, stepping carefully in high heels, full hips swaying confidently, her peach-shaped face and big eyes catching the muted light to the best advantage. I didn't have a chance against these women. If blood didn't get me then sentiment would. I surprised them both by kissing each on the cheek. This was not a ploy. Even under normal conditions, this hour of the day was a vulnerable one for me. After a drink, especially, I felt like one of those plants that opens its leaves at twilight and exposes its heart. I needed Lucy. 'This a coincidence or a conspiracy?' I said.

They let the question fall between the physical rituals women indulge in when they settle in somewhere: the opening and snapping shut of purses, the smoothing of skirts, the straightening of hair, the careful arrangement of posture. Shirley was always scrupulous about such preparations, especially in public. Judy's head was raised, looking for the waiter, probably to avoid answering my question. In from the cold, her color was high.

'Where's our guest?' Shirley asked.

'Washing the smell of prison from his skin. Did you come from the office?'

'I went home. Tanya's been up from New York with her boyfriend, and tonight's their last night.'

'How's she doing?'

'*She*'s doing fine, but he's an unemployed actor who seems to like the trust fund her daddy set up for her.'

'Either that or something else,' I said. Tanya was nearly as voluptuous as her mother.

'Or both,' Judy chimed in. She might have been an ex-nun, but she had also defended the First Amendment rights of the biggest strip-club owner in the Combat Zone. She ordered a Coke for herself and a glass of Chablis for Shirley. She didn't ask what I was having, so I ordered a third Rob Roy, more out of spite than desire.

'Heard you were by the office. You forget our appointment was tomorrow?'

'I don't forget appointments, Harry. I had it written down.'

'You don't forget and you don't make mistakes?'

She gave me the hard stare, the stare my dad gave union goons who dropped into the shop from time to time with 'suggestions.'

'Oh, no. I make mistakes all right.'

'Well, we're all human,' I said.

Shirley sat with her legs crossed and her eyes moving back and forth between Judy and me. Her place in this scenario was complex. She worked for me, but it was plain Judy had confided in her. She must have known about Judy's power of attorney and the failure today to get to the books. Were the two of them up to something here? I guessed not. It was more likely that Judy found out about the dinner and suggested tagging along. Shirley would hardly say no. But she was also aware that Donohue Print and Donohue Press were separate legal entities; the Rizzoli contract and all it might bring would remain mine no matter what happened. And it's not every day that *60 Minutes* comes calling at your invitation.

'Today was a good day, Judy,' I said, as the drinks arrived. 'Let's not spoil it.'

I insisted on paying for the round. Judy sipped her Coke stiffly. She was about to respond when Jack arrived.

He had the look of a lucky man: on the road, his day's work done, ready for no more than a Manhattan, small-talk, and a plate of Boston scallops, and look what fate should throw his way. But he was the kind of guy who dressed for opportunity. He had changed into a camel's hair sports coat, linen shirt, and a silk cravat. His bald head glistened and his deep brown eyes drank in Shirley. I made introductions. Hearing Judy was my sister, and no doubt sensing the tension between us, he took a moment to reconnoiter. I could almost hear him thinking: something's going on here – but play it as it lays and see what happens. He was, plain to see, an adventurer.

He sat beside Shirley but was courtly and attentive to both women. He reviewed the day, emphasizing the careful preparation of the agenda. He was generous in his praise of me, and only because I had spent the last twelve hours with him could I sense that the high words were said principally to reflect on himself. He was intelligent, successful, good-looking, charming, and still willing to share the limelight. Though limelight was not the reward he was angling for now, and judging from the way Shirley raised her chin and touched her neck as she leaned toward him, he wasn't doing too bad.

'Who will you have do the interview?' she asked.

'I think your recommendation was inspired, Shirley. Ed is a solid reporter, but he also has the sense of drama to bring this story to life. You must meet him when I bring him up.' This suggestion was addressed to us all, as he swept a big hand through the air and let it come to rest at his highball.

'And when?'

Here was a small hesitation, as if he'd noticed a speck of dirt in his drink. 'The new year, I think. Let's get the holidays out of the way.'

The waiter approached with news that our table was ready. 'Judy, you're joining us, I trust,' Jack said, and he certainly meant it.

'Sorry, Jack. Big trial starts tomorrow and I still have to review my opening argument.'

'Such a talented family.'

Judy, for one, would have begged to differ. I told Jack and Shirley to go ahead. I thought he was going to kiss Judy's hand, but he dropped his head graciously, wished her luck in court, and accompanied Shirley to our table.

Judy watched them walk away. 'He married?'

'Why?'

'He's romancing her.'

'All men romance Shirley.'

'Not true. All men want to *sleep* with Shirley. Jack's romancing her. In the old-fashioned sense.'

'I wouldn't know. Not much romance in my life, these days.'

I could have saved myself the lie – Judy had on her court-room face and was thinking of business. She rubbed together thumb and forefinger of her right hand, a tic from her smoking days. Knowing how her mind worked, I expected that she was sitting across from me – back straight, head high, cheeks flushed – with several options. Which she'd choose depended on me. However it fell, she would walk out of the hotel knowing in her heart that I had forced her hand.

'Harry, I know you want to be as open with me as I've been with you. I know you want to make the best decision for the shop and for the family.'

'As open as you've been?'

'Yes.'

'Trying to squeeze Peggy when I'm not there, you call that open?'

'I'm in court tomorrow; I would never have agreed to an appointment. It was today.'

'That could have been calculated.'

She threw her hands in the air. 'Harry, listen to yourself! I'm not one of your back-room cronies looking to cut a deal. Now, are we going to talk about this sensibly or not? I have Mom's welfare to think of, and Eddie's just as concerned about you as I am. You're just not being open with us.'

'Send Milt in to me next week.'

'Look, you've been a little creative with the books, whatever, I really don't care. But you've got us all wondering what it is you're hiding. And why you're acting like an adversary instead of like a brother.'

'And you're acting like a sister?'

Now I got the Mother Superior stare. She gathered her bag. 'Either you have the books at my office by nine a.m. or I'll get an injunction.'

'You serious?'

'You think I won't play hard ball?'

'I know you would. But an injunction? What would Mom think of you doing that?'

She stood, and from her full height spoke loud enough for those at neighboring booths to hear. 'She'd wonder why you were doing this to the family. She'd wonder why you were turning your back on your own flesh and blood.'

These words seemed to suck from the air whatever chance there was of resolution. I stood, trying to fill the absence. Her eyes were angry. If I'd any sense I would have sat her back down and nailed a compromise. But by then I'd drifted a long way from common sense. 'So do what you got to do,' I said.

She walked off without another word. I watched her leave the room, shoulders and head lifted high, and went in to see how Jack was progressing with Shirley.

11

The next morning, the first day of December, was cold and overcast. After coffee at the hotel, I drove Jack to Logan. We didn't say much on the way. I'd sunk a shitload of Scotch during and after dinner and left Jack and Shirley in the hotel lounge long after midnight, Jack still chattering brightly about CBS News and Shirley holding on to her poise through glass after glass of Pouilly-Fumé. My blood hot with alcohol and the image of Shirley's crossed legs, I called Lucy as soon as I got home. She had the answering machine on, and in spite of my condition I knew enough not to leave another message.

I said goodbye to Jack at the Eastern Shuttle and watched him head off for his flight. As he approached the security check, he stopped and came back. So abrupt was his about-face I thought he was holding something he didn't want to bring through the metal detector. He put a hand on my fore-arm. 'There's something going on,' he said. 'Under the surface. Trust an old newshound, there's more to Bobby's story than we're assuming. Now, I'm not saying we won't do the piece as planned, but if I were you I'd give Latrelli a call.'

'He's in the witness-protection program.'

He coughed, and the bags under his eyes, a deeper shade of

purple after last night, trembled. 'All the more reason. See what you can find out between now and the holidays and give me a call.'

He walked away without looking back, a kid-gloved hand fluttering a so-long beside his gleaming head.

I drove back to the city confused. On top of all else, I now had this ambiguity. What was he talking about? What did he want me to come up with? Latrelli was the last rat I wanted to mess with. I had a solid story going with Bobby, and I didn't want to screw it up by contacting the guy my author hated most in the universe. It was true crime I was publishing, not investigative journalism. If I read Jack right, he was threatening to hold the story on a hunch. So he was *60 Minutes* – hadn't I brought the story to him? Wasn't it complete and compelling in its own right?

But the day left little time for analysis. After more than a week away from the office, I had scheduled a staff meeting for ten o'clock. By the end of the morning, my sister would have filed the preliminary paperwork for the injunction (with Judy there was no such thing as an idle threat), and I had arranged to meet my attorney, Moe Sommer, to discuss my options. Most importantly, despite not being able to reach her, I expected to see Lucy at home for the first time since Sunday, as Bobby Junior was back on the two-to-ten after three days off.

I hung up my coat and went straight to what we called the library for the meeting. This old room, a shaking chalkboard partition away from the biggest press, was full of old legal texts from the days when my dad was printer of choice among the city's Irish law firms. We still did a little bit of legal work, but the room had been divided into proofreading carrels and a meeting area. The books stayed as furnishing. But before I got there, Peggy grabbed me outside her office and drew me in. She looked haggard and pale, and her make-up was off-center.

'You heard about your sister?'

'Yes. I saw her last night.'

'I told you this was going to happen.'

'And you did exactly what I asked, Peggy. It's OK.'

She sighed. Her mother had Crohn's Disease, and Peggy was the only one in her family who would look after her. Every Wednesday afternoon, she collected her mom from Beth Israel, brought her home for dinner, and took her for a drive before dropping her back at the hospital. Thursday morning, without fail, Peggy appeared at work looking tired and washed out. She avoided eye contact and fingered her jewelry absentmindedly. She was a pessimist by nature, prone to depression, and this year had not been a good one for her. She was lonely. I knew the symptoms well. Hitting more and more of the critical moments as her forties progressed, without a partner. Since her break-up with her ex-husband ten years ago, I had never known her to have a boyfriend.

'I was embarrassed,' she said.

'How's your mother?'

'Same as ever. Harry, I appreciate all you and your father have done for my family, but I could do without this aggravation. I'm stuck in the middle when right now I need smooth sailing.'

Didn't we all? 'I have a tough day ahead, Peg, but I want to talk to you about this. You know what a family situation is.

You know my family so well. Why don't we have lunch tomorrow?'

She nodded, but appeared so resigned, her face so tubercular white, that I went into the meeting with the fear that she was losing her nerve.

Frankie and Jeff sat on opposite sides of the conference table.

'For me it just doesn't have the excitement of the college game,' Jeff said. 'And the Celts are old, Frankie. Just plain old.'

'Your problem is you got no loyalty. Loyalty is about maintaining a certain aspect of faith at all times. In a sports type of context, it's about the home team. Am I right, Harry?' Frankie looked up at me, his large head cocked at a young-Sinatra angle, his hair close-cut and tightly curled. The buttery light from the carrel lamps caught his pug-nosed face from beneath, giving him the look of a bull. I could smell his cologne from halfway across the room.

'Harry is such a loyal Celtics fan he goes to the Lakers' locker room,' Jeff said. 'We doing a book with Bird or Parish? No – with Cooper.'

'We're doing a book with Bobby Rizzoli,' I said, 'if you two guys don't screw it up in the meantime. Where's Shirley?'

'She called in sick.'

Hung over or embarrassed? Had she stayed with Jack? He had certainly given nothing away that morning. I shook the inevitable pictures from my head. In fact, her absence suited me. I had some delicate manipulating to do, and she was awful quick to smell a rat. 'We had a good day yesterday. Very good. By the way, Jeff, Bobby said to apologize for his temper.'

Jeff looked skeptical. He had recently cut his lank hair and taken to wearing striped Van Heusen dress shirts (cuffs rolled to mid-forearm), faded jeans, and penny loafers, often without socks. From weedy projects kid to hip author in one smooth change of image. If he needed glasses, he'd choose John Lennon frames.

'He's a little frustrated,' I said. 'He thinks we're going too slow.'

'That's not what he told me.'

'Forget about what he told you. He likes to play people against each other.'

'Listen to Harry,' Frankie said. 'He knows the street.'

'Sure, Frankie. Just like you.'

Jeff was smart and capable (if directed), but he had no experience to speak of. Who does at that age? His image of himself was lifted from the movies, or maybe from characters in novels he read for his watered-down degree in English from BU: Nick Carraway, Holden Caulfield, Frederick Henry. He had no right to look down on Frankie, whose own self-image was easier to mock but truer to his roots. Frankie's needs were simple and set within a world of clearly defined limits. He came to Boston to work or to catch a ball game, but he was a Hillbrook kid who would never leave the neighborhood. Jeff was not a kid from the projects, not a college boy, not an urban up-and-comer – he was all of these, with just enough self-loathing for each contradictory part of himself to make him far more difficult to handle than Frankie. He was a young man of talent and ambition, but with confusion at his core. Yet he had his level. We all did.

'Jeff, listen,' I said. 'Your structure has, what, ten chapters?'

'Twelve.'

'Two down, ten to go. You'll have to write a chapter a week.'

'*What*?'

'Frankie, I want you pre-selling from today.'

'I can't write a chapter a week!'

'Start with local bookstores,' I said, ignoring Jeff, 'especially the mall shops – Hillbrook, Assembly Square, Revere Beach. Concentrate on the North Shore. I want to see some big orders.'

Jeff was half out of his chair and leaning across the table. Frankie was taking notes with a fountain pen, his stained handkerchief clutched in his left hand. From behind the partition, rock music suddenly blared at press-room volume.

'What the hell is that?' I said.

'This is what I've been trying to tell you. How am I supposed to write with that racket?'

I sent Frankie out to get the music turned down. His gait was jerky and animated, his wide nostrils flared. I was finally letting him loose on what he'd been dreaming about since the day I first mentioned the book. Calling up his hometown bookstores with such an offer? He'd be in his own movie. Jeff, though, was not so easily thrilled. 'Harry, you know what you're asking me to do?'

Since our face-off in my office, Jeff had become more careful about the way he put things. But his thin face was flushed, his long upper lip (so much resentment could funnel to the tip of such a lip) extended.

'I know it hasn't been easy,' I said. 'I know it's a lot of work. But I'm prepared to give you a royalty of one per cent on the hardcover if you can hit this deadline.'

Money. The level we all reach at one point or another. He sat down slowly. I could hear the figures tumbling in his head, louder in their way than the whining guitars from the press room.

'Retail?'

'No, no. Net. But think of it this way: the book sells a million copies, you make a hundred grand.'

Big bucks to a kid on eighteen-five a year. But Jeff was shaking his head. 'It won't sell a million.'

'The better it is, the more it will sell. And this is pure gravy for you. I'm already paying you to write it!'

The music stopped and my voice echoed. I looked around, but George Lapich, deaf as Beethoven, was the only proofreader on duty. Jeff assumed his streetwise look – puckered lips, wrinkled chin, eyes tight with feigned caution – but I could see he was hooked.

'Ten weeks?'

'Has to be done by the middle of February. That's the only way I can justify Frankie pre-selling before Christmas.'

'I thought late spring was better timing for this title.'

'Not from what Wambaugh was telling me yesterday. They want their piece out by February, and the sooner we follow with the product, the more we benefit from the publicity.'

Frankie returned, his mouth off to the side in a way that told me he'd been thinking. 'Harry, the reps! What about the reps?'

'Tell them March. They'll have copies in their hands at the beginning of March.'

'How you going to manage that?' Jeff asked.

'We'll typeset it as we go along.' I set my hands, palm

down, on the table. 'Both of you, look: we'll be flying by the seat of our pants, but if we pull this off, we'll all do well – you know that. You're going to hear some things, especially from the print side,' I said, jerking my thumb toward the wall. 'It's complicated – it involves family and Johnny and other stuff – but let's just say there are people who don't want us to get this thing done. We just gotta keep our heads down and pull it off. Right?'

Frankie was nodding vigorously, his lips pushed out like a fish's. Jeff was pulling at his hair, but I'd won him over. I stood up. 'Don't mention anything to Shirley or Peggy or anyone else. I have appointments for the rest of the day, but we'll work out a plan.'

Who can resist an intrigue? Or, better yet, money? These kids were in the middle of something exciting, and they knew it. I hated depending on them. They made me vulnerable. But without them I was even more exposed.

Frankie followed me to my office. 'Harry?'

I was pulling on my topcoat.

'I . . . I ran into Paulie Pallotta last night.'

'You hanging out at the Pussycat, Frankie?' I said. 'Rose know you're going there?'

'I met him at a family function. He's a distant close relative on my mother's side of the family. It was a wedding reception for my mother's cousin, Jimmy Guidone.'

For a salesman it took Frankie an awfully long time to get to the point. 'So?'

'So I happened to mention we were doing the book—'

'Ah, Frankie.' I threw my keys on the desk and turned to the window. 'Did you talk about the tapes? Did you?'

'Harry, no, I swear to God. I told him nothing that isn't in the public domain.'

'You told Pallotta!' I said, still facing the dull view of the harbor, the rusted trestle bridge and rotting pilings.

'He wants to meet you.'

'What for?'

'He says he has some information you might be interested in.'

I turned around. 'Look, Frankie, I have to be somewhere. Don't call him, don't talk to him. If he calls you, play dumb. We'll talk about this tomorrow.'

He tucked his tie into his suit coat and leaned towards me. The smell of his cologne was chemical and metallic. 'Harry, there's stuff on those tapes that nobody, I mean nobody, knows about. Jeff doesn't realize what he's sitting on. He's from the projects and thinks he knows all about the street and so forth but, like they would say about him in certain circles I'm aware of, he's an Irish punk.' He blinked at me. 'No offense.'

'You sell books,' I said. 'That's what I pay you to do. Keep focused on your job, and you'll make some dough with me. Don't sidetrack, Frankie.'

'You gonna call him?'

'I told you, we'll talk about it tomorrow.'

I caught a cab outside the aquarium. The dirty clouds were low and linty. December cold had consolidated: cars trailed steaming plumes of exhaust, the subway vents blew heavenward. The ageing metal superstructure of the central artery looked tight and brittle in the frigid air. People hurried through the streets, bundled and blinkered. The overheated cab smelt like spilt liquor, and the cabbie nodded at the rants of a right-wing radio talk-show host. I, too, was coiled tight. A fortune to pursue, a tryst to observe, a family feud to avert. And so many dogs of so many colors snapping at my heels. I pinched the taut muscles beneath the topcoat collar. Early winter I always fought a stiff neck and shoulders, and this year I was shackled by all sorts of further agonies and ecstasies. Or their anticipation, at least.

Moe's office was on Court Street, but he asked me to meet him at the State House, where the senate president was holding a press conference that he said would interest me. Moe was a skilled and longtime observer of local politics, an ex-criminal defense lawyer who left his practice in the mid-Seventies to teach at Boston University. When he returned to the law from teaching, he stuck to civil. He told me that he couldn't stomach associating with the violent anymore. While he was at BU, his daughter had been raped on a New York rooftop. It was seven in the evening, midtown Manhattan, and dozens of people must have heard her screams. No one emerged to help and, after an hour of terrified sobbing, she stumbled in her torn clothes down to the super's office. Yet when Moe offered a ten-thousand-dollar reward, five witnesses came out of the woodwork. They never caught the guy, and the cops suspected he commited several more rooftop rapes and perhaps a murder.

When I first told him about the Rizzoli project, Moe warned me that I might be lifting a few rocks better left unturned. I remembered the hanging lower lip, the upturned hands, the raised shoulders. Gestures as old as Jerusalem telling me to be careful. Maybe Pallotta was such a rock. As the cab bumped along Congress Street, Frankie's message wouldn't leave me alone. Outside, the dirty puddles of city water were scaling over in the cold. (I so wanted the warmth of Lucy's bed. The directness, the simplicity of that bed.) With so much on my mind, I had not paid full attention to the tapes. I searched them for clues to Lucy's world when I should have focused on their business possibilities. Pallotta and Bobby had been up to something, and who knew where it might lead? As comical as Frankie could be, he was a salesman with the right instincts about this particular market. Maybe he was right. Maybe I should meet Pallotta, if only for the adventure. I had to admit I was curious.

I climbed the granite steps of the State House, as I always did, as if ascending the summit of my tribe's achievement. On the surface, it was all so Yankee classical: redbrick walls, Ionic columns, the golden dome beaconing the hub of civilization. Another Brahmin temple, appointed with stained glass and marble, gold leaf and Honduras mahogany, statues and paintings of Adamses and Winthrops. But beneath the elegant façade, Bulfinch's masterpiece was a warren of deal making and power broking, where the rules of the ethnic neighborhoods had been lifted to the heights of influence, and the names on the smoked-glass office windows read Galvin and DiMarco and Harakis. The Duke in the governor's office (lame now, it had to be said) and wily Joe McCann at the golden-eagled rostrum of the senate president. Inside, voices echoed, and the domed air smelt of leather and old wood, floor wax and cigar smoke. During the war years, when the shipyards were buzzing and my dad's pal Maurice Tobin was mayor of a thriving Beantown, Donohue Print (such as it was, a flatbed press in our Brighton garage) got a fair share of municipal printing contracts. City Hall bumped Dad up to Beacon Hill, as any good Irish Democrat would expect, and he often took me to the top of these steps, introducing me to ruddy-faced, cigar-smoking politicians from his neighborhood; telling me how he'd been in the public gallery of the Senate Chamber during the 1929 earthquake, when the pendulum clocks stopped at 12:17; pointing out the tiny office where his own father had arrived, after years of loyal ward heeling, as an aide to newly elected state senator Honey Fitz Fitzgerald. '"No Irish Need Apply" signs still hanging on factory gates and workshop doors,' my dad said more than once, 'but your granddad had an office in the biggest Yankee stronghold of them all. So how do you like them apples?'

Moe was waiting inside, in front of the 1798 model of the building. 'C'mon,' he said. 'You know McCann, he always starts on time.'

We walked quickly to the Doric Hall and sat at the back, near the door. Moe brushed some taxicab lint from my sleeve. He was a considerate, solicitous man, bred to be gentle though with a stevedore's toughness in the muscles of his upper body. The son of a rabbi, he was reform in persuasion and conservative in temperament. But he was tolerant, kind, and amused by the petty hatreds of the Irish and Italians who came to him looking for legal revenge. And who had made him wealthy.

'You're going to like this,' he told me. 'McCann is establishing an Ethics Commission. With the Duke on the wane, he wants to be seen to be leading the charge against civic corruption.'

'This doesn't have anything to do with 75 State Street? A smokescreen?'

Moe shook his head. 'He's clean there, believe me. This has more to do with legislators taking kickbacks, town treasurers on the take from banks, payoffs on state building projects. The very things that make this commonwealth great. There's been a run of big-publicity cases this year, and the papers now got these spotlight teams. You got a gaggle of *Globe* reporters just out of journalism school trying to be the next Carl Bernstein and, with all that digging, you know stuff will turn up. The boys are running scared, even old pros like McCann. From a legal point of view, the senate president will always be pristine, but he wants the world to know he's making sure his own house is in order.'

Moe had a strong, high forehead, black eyebrows joined at the center, and a narrow chin. It was a tapering face, a little skull-like but fierce in its light and intelligence. It would have been at home bent over the Torah. His coloring was Ashkenazi pallid, almost anemic, but his lips were a vigorous red. The gentleness came through in his eyes, which were soft and probing. His neck was muscular, like his chest, but not thick. Women liked him. The balance of intelligence, strength, and tenderness (not to mention his law-office income) gave him plenty of sex appeal. He had married four times.

'Wait'll you see who he's appointing. You'll be surprised.'

'Who?'

'You'll see.'

Microphones and a row of padded chairs were lined up in front of the two Minuteman cannons and the Bicknell portrait of Lincoln (McCann lost no symbolic opportunity). Dressed for the weather, reporters and cameramen sweated beneath the lights and clustered in the first two rows of seats. At the rear, lawyers, up-and-coming politicans, and a few members of the public sat and waited. Two guys in identical blue suits sat bolt upright way over to the left, conspicuously isolated, beside the statue of Washington. One looked familiar.

'Who are the suits?' I asked.

'That's Dick Erpelding, the US Attorney. His office has been doing the heavy lifting on corruption cases for years; you know he's going to want to hear what McCann has to say. Depending on the nature of the commission, it could seal evidence from Erpelding's office and give Devlin's team a chance to make up some ground. With this year such a disaster, everybody's got his eye on the '90 election. There are even those who say Dick has his eye on the governor's chair.'

'Republican ticket?'

'What do you think? The good guys don't much like the Feds.'

The Feds. The second suit looked across at me; I recognized the blank stare of Steven Gurlick, the FBI guy who had pumped me for information about Bobby. I looked away. There was a murmur from the crowd, the clicking of cameras, and Joe McCann made his way to the microphones, followed by Alex Lathrop, Jimmy O'Leary, and Sean Devlin, our disheveled, slack-jawed Attorney General.

'Well, what do you know?' I said.

'What did I tell you?'

'Last time I met Jimmy, he told me McCann was a joke.'

'Politics makes strange bedfellows. Look at Devlin. You think he wants to be up there? Our probable next governor playing second fiddle to McCann? This had to be orchestrated by the Democratic committee. A show of party solidarity.'

'Yeah, but why Jimmy? He's only a DA.'

'Lathrop, that's why.'

McCann cleared his throat and stared us into silence. No man could control an audience more completely. He had the presence and voice of a pre-electricity orator. Silver hair swept back in a modest pompadour. Tough smile. Built like a fire hydrant, with not a wrinkle in his face or clothes. Sharp tenor voice that had the knack of making his harsh Boston vowels sound patrician. The mikes were a prop – he needed them as much as he needed the unconsulted script he let droop in his left hand. His style was high rhetorical, his language ornate. He always came thoroughly prepared. His eyes – small, hard, ice-blue – remained fixed on his audience, and his right hand rose and fell with the Latinate cadences of his speech. He used silence to great effect. He was the latest and best in a long line of Irish blue-collar classicists, raised from the pinched alleys of South Boston's lower end by dint of street smarts and a scholarship education with the Jesuits. In the State House, he was the man.

'"Foul deeds will rise, though all the earth o'erwhelm them, to men's eyes",' McCann intoned. He paused, staring brilliantly as the Elizabethan English echoed in the pillared hall. 'The words of the poet tell us that maliciousness in public life, though cloaked in deceit and the trappings of privilege, will out. There will not be, there *cannot* be, even a whiff of corruption in this august house,' he lifted a trembling hand high against the backdrop of Lincoln's long body (cameras clicking on cue), 'or in any building, or on any street in this commonwealth, where the people's servants perform their civic duties.'

He was soaring from the get-go. And kept soaring. As the rhetoric ascended its stately spiral, Jimmy sat behind the senate president, perched at the edge of his chair, elbows on his knees, chewing his lip and staring at no place in particular. How well I knew that look. Alex sat beside him, looking pretty august himself in charcoal wool suit and green silk tie, his graying hair combed behind his ears, his handsome, leathered face tilted back with judicial reserve.

'The Lathrop Commission will have such powers as the people of this commonwealth see fit to assess the extent of corrupt practices and to recommend the legislation that will extirpate such venal conduct from the fecund soil of public service.'

Moe nudged me, smiling in profile. As McCann reminded us of Judge Lathrop's sterling record on the bench, Alex held his head stiff with false modesty. Devlin got a token reference, but Jimmy's name went unmentioned until question time, when a *Herald* reporter asked bluntly why the Suffolk County DA was sitting there. Alex stepped to the mike.

'District Attorney O'Leary is probably the most experienced prosecutor of public corruption cases in the state,' he said. 'I was proud to recommend his inclusion on this commission and I look forward to letting him loose on the evidence.' He smiled and looked back at Jimmy. 'You need a terrier in this kind of group. This is not an academic exercise.'

'What about police corruption?'

'Absolutely within our remit.' Alex said, 'Allegations of exam stealing and conspiracy are as serious as any facing the commonwealth at this grave time. And, as the senate president said, we're here to weed it out.'

'Didn't you grow up with O'Leary?' Moe whispered.

'Yeah. Same triple-decker. Harvard Ave.'

'Brookline?'

'Brighton.'

'The tough side of the tracks. You know, I do business with guys I grew up with all the time. Big wheels now, but when I meet them, all I can see are the snotty-nosed kids who tried to look up my sister's skirt.'

'If Jimmy tried to look up Judy's skirt she would've killed him.'

'Still, he's one of these guys with something to prove, right? You can see from the way he's sitting, there's still a pimply adolescent inside him worrying about the size of his schlong. Alex must've had an awful big favor to call on with McCann to get *him* included.'

Moe was another of Jimmy's critics. He had a way of getting me focused (almost against my will) on my friend's insecurities. And it was true. For me, Jimmy still was that skinny kid who always had to win. And I was the same for him. Even though we were lifelong friends, he still resented my knowledge of his dad's drinking, his bed-wetting, his relentless bullying of Eddie. He wanted me to succeed, he was loyal as a hound, but he always had to be a notch above me. Two to be on the safe side (not hard given my track record). He always had to have that edge. Was always trying to move beyond his origins. But I, too, was part of his origins. I was like the scars on his back from the acne that seared his teenage years. There was a memory. Jimmy stalking the wrestling mat in his blue singlet and headguard, slender and ferocious, but looking so *sore* where those ugly eruptions ranged across his back and shoulders. It unsettled his opponents. When they noticed those sores they'd get the strangest look on their faces, part curiosity, part pity, part squeamishness. It was a look that enraged Jimmy, and he'd learned to use that rage to his advantage. Those pimples helped him become state champ.

'Say what you like. He'll never let you down.'

'No, Harry. He'll never let *you* down. He's the loyal type, all right, but if you're not in his camp he'll make chopped liver out of you.'

As the questions ended, an army of McCann aides passed out copies of the official press release. He was the only politician I knew who didn't distribute releases in advance. He didn't want his audience reading when they should be listening to him. Moe and I stood. I tried to catch Jimmy's eye, but he filed out quickly in McCann's wake, as if eager to begin cataloging the public sins of the commonwealth.

Erpelding and Gurlick left their seats and, as we were near the door, approached us. They looked like Mormon missionaries with their short haircuts and identical suits. Erpelding had the press release rolled up like a baton and was tapping the base of it against his palm. He was tall, at least six-four, with swinging shoulders and a halfback's waist. He had a head-coach look: face thrust forward, teeth clenched, eyes always on the field. He walked a half-step in front of his subordinate and, when he noticed Moe, gave him the subtlest of acknowledgments, a mild flaring of his efficient eyes.

'Counselor Erpelding,' Moe said. 'How goes the battle?'

'Tough, as always.' He waved the press release. 'And this doesn't help.'

'Afraid of a little competition?'

'We're all on the same team, Moe. Or should be. It doesn't serve justice to fragment resources and keep secrets from each other. That's just what the other side wants.'

Moe stepped back to allow me into the circle. Gurlick was standing with his hands folded at his crotch, smelling of wintergreen and blinking ponderously behind his heavy-framed glasses.

'My friend Harry Donohue,' Moe said, 'a denizen of the world of book publishing.'

'We know Mr Donohue,' Gurlick replied. Neither of them extended a hand. 'How's your friend Bobby Rizzoli?'

'That's funny, I was just about to ask you the same thing.'

Gurlick pushed his glasses up the bridge of his nose. 'That particular avenue didn't work out for us. It appears Rizzoli's agenda is too complex to allow him to work with us.'

'What the hell does that mean?'

Gurlick just blinked. There was something in the air that I couldn't identify. It was like a chess game where no one wanted to make the first move. Or even acknowledge that there was a game going on.

Moe, always polite, tugged us back to the issue at hand. 'A guy like Alex Lathrop brings experience and credibility to such a commission. Don't you think, Dick?'

Erpelding snorted and moved his head from side to side, the coach dealing with a callow recruit. 'With all due respect, Moe, this is a publicity stunt. A typical McCann exercise. Sure Lathrop's experienced – though not as much as people give him credit for. But that's not the real issue. The senate president is looking at the elections. What the nation discovered in 1980, Massachusetts is only learning now. The Democrats are splintered. So he's thinking about votes, not about indictments.'

'And you have no such conflict of interest?'

'I – my office – has the power and objectivity to do the job. We have RICO, which is an enforcement tool the state doesn't have. We have investigators from outside who don't have to worry about putting away friends of their friends. And we have the full weight of federal law behind everything we do: we don't have to wrangle any legislation past people like DiMarco and St Angelo.'

He was doing his best to sound off the cuff, but he was even more on the stump than McCann. The last sentence was delivered with particular, some might say racist, emphasis. Dominick DiMarco and Barry St Angelo, the East Boston and North End state senators respectively, sat on the Senate Judiciary Committee. They were both criminal defense lawyers who numbered among their clients reputed Mafia lieutenants. They were a powerful alliance, and it was virtually impossible to get any law-enforcement legislation through the committee without their backing.

'Dick, I take your point,' Moe said. 'But politics is politics. O'Leary and Devlin are up there, and you – you're down here.'

Oh, Moe was masterly. Gentle, considerate, tactful, he still couldn't resist the jab, and delivered it with all the irony his Jewish sensibility could muster, hands flowering domeward in a sublime gesture of political fatalism. He might as well have said 'Governor Devlin' or 'Attorney General O'Leary'. We all knew, standing in that tense quadrilateral, what today was about: strengthening the Democratic monolith and perpetuating the ethnic coalition that, towards its own ends, had mastered the very arts McCann was promising to expose. And Erpelding? He felt his hour was nigh, and he was right about the coming changes. But he was also scared he would be no more than John the Baptist when he so much wanted to be the Messiah. And McCann would love nothing more than to serve up his grimacing head on a plate.

Erpelding leaned close to Moe but looked me straight in the eye. What did these guys know about me anyway? And what were they trying to find out that they didn't already know? 'Any time you feel like it – and it's as easy as reading a back issue of the *Globe* – just compare federal and state sentences on corruption cases. It's instructive. More – it's criminal in itself. These guys look after their own, no matter what they've done. That prick O'Leary is the worst of them. He's no good. And in this situation, he's out of his league. Way out.'

He loped off without saying goodbye. You could see the tension in his shoulder blades. Gurlick paused and lifted a finger. 'You still have my card?'

'Actually, I don't.'

'Well, you know where to find me.' He was as close as Erpelding had been. I got a strong whiff of wintergreen and hair oil and a good look at the thin, pale scar running from his high hairline to his temple. 'Just don't leave it too late,' he said, and trotted after his boss.

'Interesting,' I said.

'What's that?'

'Erpelding didn't even mention Devlin. Sean's his rival, but Dick seems hung up on Jimmy.'

'Harry, I'm surprised at you.'

'How so?'

'You don't see it?'

'What?'

'He hates Jimmy because the two of them are so alike.'

We went to Moe's office to talk about the impending injunction. I suggested a cup of coffee at the Parker House, but Moe needed familiar surroundings. His special orthopedic chair, his Italian desk topped with lacquered walnut, his baseball autographed by the 1967 Red Sox (he was a big fan), the view of City Hall Plaza: these physical details helped ease him into the inductive frame of mind that made him one of the best lawyers in Boston. I sat in the client's standard-issue leather chair (how well I knew this seat) and summarized the situation at Donohue Print and Press. I didn't hold back: he would find out everything sooner or later, so I told him all. As he listened, he tossed the ball from one hand to another, stopping only to ask a question.

I was never one to turn legal matters personal (or the other way around). At times, I'd sought redress in anger, but usually someone else was going after me with a hot head. I'd learned to stay cool, allow the lawyers to do their job, and let the wheels of the law spin. My attitude was, you win some you lose some. Whatever the outcome, life goes on. But I'd never had a legal battle with family, and it didn't seem right starting one today. Family feuds were supposed to be passionate and personal. And conducted in the kitchen. That way, they got solved – at least in my family they did. My parents battled over Eddie going into the navy, over Dad's bullheadedness about unions, over meddling priests and drunken cops dropping by the house once too often. After my father's death there had been several tense discussions about the shop around the kitchen table (and Eddie had said it, hadn't he? The shop was Dad's insurance for us – to keep us fighting so we'd keep in touch). There were yelling matches and hurt feelings and the occasional grudge. But legal action? Unthinkable, at least until last night.

So my soul was not in the narration, and Moe knew it. Today, Jimmy (esteemed prosecutor for the Lathrop Commission) was the wiry kid who could spit from our back porch to the window of Mary Kiley's bedroom across the alley, a good sixty feet. And Judy was my kid sister, stretched on her sickbed, incoherent with scarlet fever, grabbing wildly at my arm while I told her the plot of the latest Tom Mix movie. She was the tearful eighteen-year-old heading off to the convent, to the great pride and fear of her mother. She was the whizz-kid legal student at Suffolk University who corrected her professors and wrote articles for the *Globe*. She was, with Moe, one of my own legal advisers, the sharpie who had come up with the contract solution to the Rizzoli book. And she was now suing me! My own sis!

'What's your rationale for holding back on the records?' Moe asked me.

'She sees those, she'll go nuts. They're cooked, Moe. *Over*cooked.'

His head reared back in mild surprise. 'But with all you've told me, how you going to stop her?'

'Why do you think I'm here?'

He nodded, tight-lipped, and set the historic ball carefully on its Plexiglas stand. 'I have to tell you, Harry – from a strictly legal point of view? I'd advise you to cut your losses and come clean before the injunction gets issued. From what I know of Judy – and I don't have to tell you this – if she's seeking a legal solution it'll be ironclad. Everything is in her favor on this one. And, given the personal element, I'd be even more inclined to nip this in the bud.'

'What's the best I can do?'

He shrugged. It was not an encouraging gesture. 'String it out. Put her through the loops. It'll buy you time, but it'll also piss her off. And it'll cost you. I wouldn't advise it.' He touched his lips with steepled fingers.

'How much time?' I asked.

'Three, four months. But what's the point?'

'I don't want her to know how much the Press owes Donohue Print.'

'Why?'

'It's a family thing. I don't know – I'm her big brother, maybe. Let's say I don't like her calling the shots.'

Moe raised his heavy eyebrows at that comment. He stood and, rubbing the base of his spine with the flats of his palms, walked around and leaned against the front of the desk. 'Harry, I'm your legal counsel.' What he really meant was *I'm your friend*. 'Hell, *you're* a lawyer. You have to see you're not making sense here. She'll find out eventually.'

It was an appeal from the heart. Moe liked me. Hey, I was a likeable guy, good at getting friends to make excuses for me, not bad at using my charm to keep the wolves from the door.

Except with Judy. I stood and looked Moe in the eye. 'She *won't* find out. Three months will get me the Rizzoli book. It'll give me the time to create the cash flow to make things right with the books and make the Press independent.'

The soft eyes took in these words; the keen intellect weighed them against all I told him, all he knew of my history. And me? Well, this was what I wanted, what I believed. I had to believe it.

'I'm no accountant,' he said, 'but from what you've told me, that'll take a lot of dough. Not to mention my fees.'

'It's a hell of a book.' I looked at my watch. It was time to see Lucy. 'I gotta go. You'll set the wheels in motion?'

He pushed himself up from the desk. 'I'll do whatever you tell me to, Harry,' he said, with a gentle gesture of Jewish resignation, a little wave of the hand, a lifted shoulder. 'I'm your lawyer.'

12

A week into our love affair, and Lucy and I already had our rituals. Many were around secrecy. She didn't want my car near the house, so I parked at the base of Lynch Road, in the driveway of a Boston Edison sub-station just off the expressway. Her front door was also off limits. From the sub-station, I walked along a muddy trail that cut through the woods behind the development and led to the rear of her house. On Thursday afternoon, after driving straight from Moe's office, I made my way carefully along the trail, through pine trees and poison ivy, carrying a bottle of white wine and thinking of Bobby in his musty cell. To my right the fellsway ridge dropped away to clotted ravines. The slatted fence behind the Rizzoli house had a gap that let me check out the sliding door without being seen. Lucy and I had agreed that, if Bobby Junior was late leaving or if she had an unexpected visitor, she would hang a red pool thermometer from the door handle. Otherwise, I would slip through the gap, cross the yard, and tap on the glass door.

Lucy was my first married woman, though I didn't use that phrase when I thought of her. The first week of our relationship had introduced me to the shadow world of the cuckold, with Bobby Junior standing in for his old man. Sex became a daytime pursuit, everything revealed in clean afternoon light, at a time when I was used to sitting at a desk or lingering over a late lunch. The strangeness of lying naked with another man's wife, on another man's bed, bodies perspiring in the dry heat of an indoor suburban December day, was nevertheless *appropriate*. Because to be in the throes of such an obsession at fifty-two was also strange. Sex was not the occasional treat, the reward for things going well, the end of a good night out. It was the only reason for being together. It was, for those few hours, the center of life, sweeping aside all other responsibilities and concerns, taking over my life, bringing me to where, without even thinking about it, I stood at the edge of a suburban wood, staring with dry-mouthed anticipation through a broken fence at a glass door at three-fifteen on a midweek afternoon.

The door handle was free. I trotted past the pool, dodging puddles, and climbed the redwood stairs of the deck. Five feet from the door, I stopped. Through the glass I saw the figure of a man sitting in Lucy's Naugahyde recliner. I knew at once it wasn't Bobby Junior. Though he sat back in the chair, his big shoes splayed across the raised footrest, he wore a scally cap and brown raincoat, wrapped around a big stomach. He was smoking. I couldn't see his face. His head slid from side to side, as if he was trying to look round a pillar. As I watched, he wagged a finger. His head stopped moving as Lucy stepped into view. Cigarette between her lips, she counted off something on her fingers, then took a deep drag and looked straight at me. After the briefest hesitation, she exhaled the smoke and opened the door. 'How long you been out there?'

'Just got here.'

'Well, get inside. Colder than a well-digger's ass today.'

I stepped in and slid the door shut behind me. The man was out of the chair and on his way to the door. 'See ya later, babe,' he said. He let himself out the front.

Cigarette still between her fingers, Lucy embraced and kissed me. 'Who was that?'

'Friend of mine.'

She had her arms around my waist and was leaning back, head tilted, looking up into my face. Her eyes were heavily shadowed, her hair sprayed stiff, and the musky smell of her perfume rose from her cleavage like heat off a desert highway. I felt a loosening in my thighs and a tingling in my scrotum. I felt warm and wanted and excited. But uneasy. 'How come you didn't hang out the pool thing?'

She disengaged but let her fingers linger on my coat. She had that department-store smell women have, lotions and cosmetics and creams layered under the heavy perfume and cigarette smoke. 'You don't have to worry about Mike,' she said.

'So he knows about us?'

The strained, careful look of our first meetings returned, a hardening of the mouth and a tightness at the corners of her eyes. 'You telling me *you* haven't told anyone?'

'Well, no.' I hadn't. Who would I tell? And had I thought about her telling anyone, I would have expected it to be another woman. Not a fat guy in a scally cap who called her *babe*.

She stepped back. 'You turning in' one these men wants explanations for everything?'

She took a stiff, loud drag, like snatching breath before a plunge. I was never a smoker myself, but I understood how tobacco was more than habit or addiction. Like alcohol, smoke could receive need, give it shape, and provide reassurance. Lucy smoked deeply, like a man, taking plenty in and exhaling through her nostrils in thin jets. The smoke kept coming for several breaths.

'No,' I said. 'I don't think I am. Just got a bit of a surprise, that's all. Then him shooting out of here like that.' I could still see the front door closing on the wrinkled seat of his raincoat, the oiled hair edging down his neck from beneath the brim of the cap. She nodded, and stubbed out the cigarette. In the ash-tray, beside the white, lipstick-edged Salem butts, were the mottled brown remains of four or five Marlboros, smoked to the nub. Lucy brushed ash from her V-neck sweater, and the movement of her breasts brought me back to reality. I felt a little flutter of panic: I'd let my focus drift from the crucial. 'Hey, I've missed you,' I said.

She smiled. Only then did I notice the smells of cooking: roasting meat and rosemary and mint. I handed her the bottle of wine. 'Now you're talking,' she said. 'Let's eat.' She walked past me, trailing a hand along my arm. I watched the old-fashioned sway of her hips. Maybe they still walked that way in the South, but not in bluenose Boston. Or Irish Boston, for that matter. I took off my coat and laid it over the recliner. I followed her to the stove and hugged her from behind, breathing in those odors of ampleness, cupping her breasts in my hands, letting the movement of my own hips describe my need. It had been two long days; the food would have to wait.

After we made love, she lay on her back and blew smoke at the stained ceiling. Her breasts tugged gently to the sides but kept their shape and smoothness. One knee raised, she revealed a curve of thigh and hip as to the point as any laconic Texas pronouncement. I kissed her elbow in the afternoon light. Her arms were fleshy, lightly dimpled. The bedroom windows were high and uncurtained. The phone was on the answering machine. I'd asked her to take it off the hook, but she had to know if the phone rang. Had to be prepared to confront Bobby with whatever detail she could put together. What we did might have started spontaneously, but it continued with utmost calculation.

'Sally called me yesterday.'

'Who's Sally?'

She peered at me. 'My best friend, that's all.'

'You never mentioned her.'

She propped herself up on an elbow. 'Sally Robidoux?'

'Nope.'

Bemusement crossed her face, like wind through wheat. She leaned to the night table on her side and tapped ash from her cigarette. Her back, reddened in lines by the sheet's creases, somehow showed her age. There was a slight bow to it, suggesting an invisible weight.

'You tell her too?' I said, grazing her back with my knuckles. I intended my tone to be playful. I wasn't sure it came out that way.

'I surely did.'

Her irony was folksy and puckered. I could hear it emerging between creaks of a rocking chair on a deep west-facing porch in the Nacogdoches Valley. Sheet lightning jolting in the distance and the lowing of longhorns beyond the fence. Warm electric air and crickets ratcheting in the moonlight.

'She asked you have plenty life insurance.'

'Don't even joke,' I said.

She settled back, arm behind her head, the bed shifting with her weight. 'You can't joke about that, honey, you shouldn't be here.'

'You know why I'm here.'

'Oh, I know,' she whispered.

Whenever she touched me I felt a slackening inside, a loosening of organ and muscle that led to a complete, dizzying unraveling, where everything that had been worrying me trailed away like loose yarn. She made me forget the world and live within those physically heightened minutes as if there were no future and no past. Afterwards, as she smoked and resettled, and I watched her or straightened the sheets the briefest brush of skin against skin would spark us off, and we would pursue again the moments when all was excluded except the other, moments made longer and even more intense by the physical challenge of performing yet again. Though this was not performance: it was too natural for that. It was like breathing.

But the world would intrude. The phone rang, her answering machine clicked into action, and though she had the volume turned down, we both knew who it was. She went quiet. I used the bathroom. When I returned she was rooting through the night-table drawer. Bits of paper, bobby pins, and pencils fell to the floor.

'What are you looking for?'

'Aspirin.'

'Isn't it in the bathroom?'

'It's still my house, honey. I know where I keep the aspirin.' She stood and shook the little yellow box of pills a little closer to my face than I liked. She walked past, smiling tightly, and got herself a glass of water. In this mood, brought on suddenly by the ring of the telephone or an ill-considered word from me, her nakedness altered: she was freighted by her fullness, cumbersome. I waited. She usually bounced back pretty quickly.

'He won't understand why I'm not out there today. No matter I told him I was sick as a hound.' She sat at the end of the bed, one leg folded beneath her. She was nudging her hair into place with both hands, lifting her breasts, revealing recently shaved underarms. With every different pose, every new piece of clothing, each phrase or gesture I hadn't heard before, I coveted her anew.

'Forget about him.' It sounded hackneyed as soon as I said it, and she didn't react. She picked up a bobby pin from the floor, breasts pendant, and resumed attention to her hair.

'I've been listening to the tapes,' I said.

'You do anything else?'

'I can't help it. It's like a window into his life. *Your* life.'

She nodded. After sex her eyes narrowed and her jowls grew slightly puffy, giving her a remote, nocturnal look.

'I don't understand why you didn't get rid of them,' I said. 'You've listened to them, right? You know what's there?'

'Didn't bother. Why would I listen to them? I *lived* them.'

On Friday I had come across a conversation between Lucy and Joe Latrelli. It wasn't pretty.

Lucy? Yeah, this is Joe. I'm only gonna say this once, so listen to me.

His voice was high-pitched and racing. He was clearly coked up.

Bobby's not here, Joe. You're wasting your time.

Fuck him. I don't give a shit any more if he's avoiding me. That's his funeral, that scumbag ratfink.

He's real fond of you too.

Forget about him. I don't care if he's there or not, this is for you. Bobby is screwing Freddie Laconti's wife. Do you hear me, Lucy? Do you hear me? He's fucking Cynthia Laconti right underneath your nose.

I thought you were only going to say this once.

He shitcanned me and he'll shitcan you. Make no mistake—

She cut him off mid-flight. The next call was to Bobby Junior at the station. It might have been hours later, but it followed immediately on the tape. Lucy wanted to know, in a voice like Vivien Leigh's, if he was coming home for supper.

'You have any idea where Latrelli is?' I asked her.

'I do not. And I'll do my level best never *to* know.'

'He ever call?'

She had a bobby pin between her fingers and was twisting it out of shape. Naked, gently swollen with whatever was released within her by our contact, she was less intimidating. I don't think I would have mentioned Latrelli if she'd had her clothes on.

'What you getting at?'

'Professional interest.'

She lit another cigarette. 'I'm not going to tell you how to do your job, Harry, but seems to me you got as much Joey Latrelli as you want in your story already.'

'I'd like to know what motivates a guy like that.'

She snorted and touched her tongue with her little finger. 'I can tell you that. Rage. Little-dick male anger. Like a kid on the playground. Like guys I've seen all my life in the army, on the force, on the streets.'

'Bobby like that?'

She tilted her head back and looked at me, funny as it sounds, like a teacher. A bleached blonde, full-breasted, chain-smoking schoolmarm, sitting naked in the afternoon with a man not her husband and talking about men murderous and disloyal.

'This might sound like a crock of shit, but I respect Bobby. This . . .' she waggled a finger between us, shorthand for so much, '. . . this is not about lack of respect. But Latrelli? Hell, he doesn't deserve the respect you'd give a *worm*.'

The conversation stalled, and I sat there wondering how I had led her to where she was silently considering her respect for her husband. She shifted on the bed. I stroked her knee. But her mind was less than playful.

'I thought you needed to get this book finished by February, hell or high water.'

I sighed. 'I'm only thinking out loud, Lucy.'

'Well, stop thinking. Bobby thought you even mentioned Latrelli's name he'd be telling me to tear up the contract.'

Another rock in the pool, and again I looked at the ripples a little too long. But sometimes changing the subject isn't as easy as it seems, especially when you go before each other unclothed.

'I know what I have to do,' I said quietly.

'What's happening with the shop?'

'I thought you said stop thinking. One of the things I love about being with you is I don't think about all that crap.'

Johnny Rotella was my latest headache. I didn't know if Judy had got to him or if he'd been talking to Peggy, but he caught me on my way out to the press conference that morning and grilled me Rotella-style about the current crisis. Johnny was no dummy. 'Maybe it ain't my place to ask,' he had said, 'but what's this I hear about you selling the shop?'

He had heard no such thing of course. 'What, you interested, Johnny? Management buyout?'

He scratched his cone head, trying to look as bumpkinish as possible. But his good eye had me pinned. 'Maybe I am. And one guess my first act as owner.'

'What's that?'

'Fire Joe College.'

'You're buying Donohue Press as well?'

'There's a difference?'

'Last time I looked.'

Like that he had me roped. One swift twist of a verbal lariat. He pushed his mouth to the side and bobbed his head. The funnier he looked, the more careful you had to be. But I was already trussed tight as a steer.

'If there's a difference, tell Peggy to settle the *Red Sox Trivia* job.'

'That still outstanding?' Eyes to the ceiling, head rocking, he feigned a little mental calculation. 'A hundred and fifty-six days, and counting. A record.'

'I'll talk to her when I get back.'

His eyes gave me straight what his lips were holding back: get the accounts in order or no more print for Donohue Press. As part owner of both companies, Johnny could make life difficult for me if he chose. And, technically speaking, he wasn't even my employee any more. His loyalty was tribal in its intensity and descended from his time with my dad. It found its keenest expression in his harangues and comparisons: 'Your old man wouldn't have put up with this' and 'Your dad never woulda allowed that.' When he went quiet was when you had to worry, and he was saying very little to me lately. I was losing my protected status.

'Lucy,' I said, needing more than ever her touch, 'I don't even want to think about that place. Be with you and get the book done. That's all I want. Make some dough. For us *both*.'

She kissed me. 'Let's eat,' she said. She drew on her bathrobe. When your lover's been naked with you for hours, putting on clothing is as sexy as disrobing. I grabbed her. '*Harry*! I'm hungry.'

She went into the kitchen and I pulled on my pants. Among the litter on the floor she had spilled from the drawer was a wrinkled slip of paper. I picked it up. It was a long list of names with checkmarks in pencil beside most of them. The last names looked familiar: Hartigan, DeLasalle, Ribero, Jensen, Quinn, Cleary, Martorano . . . On it went. About twenty in all. 'Hey!' I shouted. But she was banging pots in the kitchen and didn't hear me. I slipped the list into my pocket and finished dressing.

Before we ate, she dressed and made herself up. I drew the curtains and uncorked the wine. But the sound was hollow. We had reached that stage in the day when the clock was against us. She served the dried-out meat and sat at the table, subdued.

'What are you doing tonight?'

'What do you think? Watch the news and *20/20* like the rest of bored America. Course, most people don't have the privilege of knowing their husband's gonna pop on to the screen one of these days and talk about how his best friend and mistress shafted him.'

'That would be on a Sunday.'

'Thanks for the clarification.' Her voice was hoarse. She finished her wine and held her glass out for more.

'That's not how it's going to go,' I said, as I poured.

'I really don't care how it goes.' She drank and then let her head fall forward. Toward the end of my visits, she often grew despondent. I hadn't yet discovered what I could do to cheer her up. Conversation, like the meat, grew dry. I remembered the list in my pocket but didn't think it was the right time to ask her about it. But those names – where had I heard them before? I found myself thinking of Frankie and our conversation that morning. Frankie, who grew up a stone's throw away from where I was sitting now. 'Guess who wants to see me?' I said.

She shrugged.

'Paulie Pallotta.'

'Well, you're going out of your way to mention all the lowlifes tonight, ain't you?'

'He says he's got something for me.'

She looked at me wearily and stood up from the table without replying. She put her plate on the counter and lit another cigarette. The puffiness in her face had somehow coarsened with the drawing of the curtains and the loss of light. She looked like one of those tough but good-hearted women who frequent taverns and tend to have a drink too many on a Tuesday night. 'Harry, you're giving me something I can hang on to. So don't get me wrong. But just today – well, you're sounding like Bobby did when I started losing him. Don't start acting like a wiseguy. You got a good thing going here, and a greaser like Pallotta's only going to sidetrack you. At *best* he's going to sidetrack you. What could he possibly give you that you don't have already?'

'A bigger story.'

'Your story's big enough. Too big, if anything. You don't stay on top and all this is gonna fall around your ears.'

Then I remembered the list – and it suddenly occurred to me what the names on it had in common. I waited for a moment before mentioning it. Then I knew I wasn't going to say a word about it. 'You know something I don't, Lucy?'

'I know plenty you don't know. And you know plenty I don't. What's dangerous is someone wanting to know it all. Like the kid in the story who tries to fly to the sun.'

'That a Texas story?'

She eyed me. Condescension was dangerous with a woman like her. 'Hell, far as I know it ain't even American,' she said. 'But it's true.'

On my way home I went through the names as if assembling a jigsaw: Jason Ribero, Pete Martorano, Tommy DeLasalle. It all made sense. Those I didn't know I could figure out. But I was also thinking how, for the first time since Thanksgiving, Lucy wasn't the only thing on my mind as I drove home. And the list burned in my pocket. My first betrayal. My head clear, I drove into the city, the lights of Somerville glowing in the gloom. I made a mental note to call Pallotta in the morning. Maybe I did want to know it all. But I knew now there was more to this story than I expected.

13

He might have wanted to see me, but it took a week to get Paulie Pallotta to commit to lunch. We met on Friday at a Portuguese restaurant in Union Square in Somerville, opposite the Vietnam memorial triangle. The venue was his suggestion. Not his first, mind you, but there was no way I was going to meet him at the Pussycat Lounge. Whatever about him wanting to meet me, he had no idea how much I wanted to see him. So I had some leverage. His taped conversations with Bobby had assumed new meaning. My discovery of the list of names opened up a new world of deceit, and a few careful questions to Paulie would confirm that I was on to something huge. I was in the fortunate position of being able to meet him without looking eager, with the appearance that I was doing *him* a favor. I had a chance to con the conman.

The waiter led us to our table but, true to stereotype, Paulie ignored him and chose a table at the rear of the restaurant. He sat with his back to the wall. 'I read about you in the *Mercury*,' he said. 'You're the guy has Hillbrook Savings pissing and moaning how criminals got more rights than victims.'

'Hey, I'm a businessman.'

'We're all businessmen. Rizzoli, I called him. Day after the robbery, I call him and I say, "You son-of-a-bitch, you want your head on a platter?" As a friend I make things very clear. "Do yourself a favor. Do the right thing and give the appropriate men their cut." Which is to say not just a cut. On account these men – and you know who I'm talking about here – on account a number of these men have safety deposit boxes in that very bank. Which is to say Rizzoli had actually stole from *them*. Do I have to spell it out? As a friend I am very concerned, so I offer my services as a go-between. Considerable personal risk, given the involvement of certain individuals, but there is a history there you should not, as a friend, deny. So I make my offer, and what does he say?'

'I can guess.'

'He denies all knowledge. Like I'm a lowlife from the papers. Denies what I know for a fact he did, what he is now writing a book about admitting to the very details I projected day one after the heist.'

The rhetoric was different (no wiretaps to worry about here), but the purpose behind the words was similar to the terse circumlocutions of the telephone tapes.

I pay you what you say and they . . . they walk away.

I can arrange this.

They won't want the merchandise?

You won't hear from them again.

The merchandise. I had thought all along that Paulie had been trying to extort jewels or other Hillbrook contraband from Bobby. Playing up his Mob connections to land a little sweetener for himself. The same game he was playing with me now. For a while, Jeff had got me thinking they were referring to drugs, but that never felt right. Donlon and Latrelli's drug dealing brought the gang down, and Bobby had done all he could to distance himself from that activity. But now I had the list. The names raised fresh suspicions, and I listened to Paulie's harangue with new ears. His chatter was a testing of the waters. He was a master at talking about one thing while referring to something else. But was the something else what I thought it was? The only way to find out for sure was to butter him up. The only thing slicker than Paulie's talk was his ego.

'Harry – I believe I'm right on the name, it is Harry? – it's me should be doing a book with you. I'm not saying I could tell everything, not if I want to stay alive, but even ten per cent of what I know would make you a fortune.'

'That might not be such a bad idea.'

In five minutes he had worked himself into a sweat. He pulled a red handkerchief from his coat pocket and patted his forehead. Paulie Pallotta in the flesh. I knew the voice so well from the tapes that I had a hard time connecting it with the puffy, nervous, roving-eyed guy sitting across from me. He wore a dark green double-breasted jacket with heavy brass buttons and wide lapels. An open-neck canary yellow shirt with the standard gold crucifix tangled in his chest hair. On one hand his Everett High School ring (class of '63); on the other a chunky signet with overlapping Ps. He moved his fingers with a heavy man's delicacy, shifting the silverware and tugging his sleeves with prissy needlessness. He worked his lips when he spoke, and there was something soiled about his speech, a dirty tone that put you on your guard. He would have been the first kid in school to bring in smutty pictures or tell stories about the single nurse who lived beside the river.

'We're always looking for good book concepts,' I said. 'We expect Bobby's to open some doors for us.'

He looked at me squarely for the first time, ruminating. His breathing was wheezing, asthmatic. 'This like a bestseller?'

'Definitely. And in this business, these days, a book's only the tip of the iceberg. There's film rights, TV, video. A lot of money to be made.'

The waiter put breadsticks and a jug of water in front of us. Paulie snapped a stick in half and ate it. 'I have to be honest with you, Harry. It's my nature: I cannot deliberately mislead. This story Rizzoli's telling is not the whole sausage.'

'You been looking over his shoulder?'

'Don't have to. It's a question of circumstances and realities. The withholding of details out of his particular situation. He *can't* tell the whole story.'

'And you can?'

He poured water into his tumbler, took a sip, and swished the water around his mouth. 'I could contribute certain insights.'

The sweating voice on the tapes was full-blown before me, skewed, outlandish, narcissistic. With a bloated, oily face to match. It was tempting to see Paulie as no more than a stereotype, a cartoon version of men far more subtle and dangerous. But the truth was, he served a useful, very real role within the underworld. You had to give him credit. It suited the big boys to have guys like Paulie operating on the margins, running strip clubs and used-car lots and local rackets, not just to generate a little tribute and launder a little dough but, more importantly, to help blur the lines between the public face of the Mob and its true power base. Guys like Paulie were a buffer. They played the part and attracted the gossip. They even got their piece of the action, limited though it was. But their real role was to protect the inner circle from too much scrutiny. To be a success in this business you had to appear unsuccessful. It was like politics. The real power lay with the guys who didn't draw attention to themselves. From listening to him, I knew Paulie wasn't a player. He was too eager to appear connected. He took risks to boost his image, and it made him easy to manipulate. And I knew he could be manipulated because I had heard Bobby doing it.

'Right now,' I said, 'there are a lot of very interesting things happening in this state. Some dynamite stories about corruption, criminal drama, and so on. It's been going on since the beginning of time, but now it's a *topic*. The public want the detail. They lap it up. Someone like you, a legitimate businessman who happens to know a lot about what goes on, someone aware and intelligent, could put together a proposal that I know my editors would take very seriously. Maybe now is not a good time, but in the future . . .'

'How come not now?'

'Well, we have Bobby's story, which we're featuring on *60 Minutes*—'

'No shit?'

'Yeah. Ed Bradley's coming up for the interview next month. That's between you and me, Paulie. I wouldn't like the *Mercury* catching wind of it until I'm in a better position to use the publicity. So right now we have our hands full, unless something really big breaks. Like the Bucky Quinn thing or, well, you know what I mean . . .'

The waiter approached and asked if we wanted to order a

drink. Paulie waved him away and took another sip of water. 'What about Bucky Quinn?'

'What about him? He's sitting on a powder keg. Everybody wants his story, but Saul Richards is representing him and Saul has him zipped up tight. *He* knows what's worth what.'

Paulie shook his head, fleshy lower lip pushed way out. 'Bucky doesn't know shit.'

'He knows who sold him the exam.'

He was shaking his head again, but this time in an attempt to control himself. There was a lot he could say, a lot it would make him look good to say. But he had to be careful. So he shook his head and thought about his next words. 'A lot of guys know who sold him the exam,' he said. 'Maybe not a lot, but key people. So what? The real questions are, where did that particular salesman acquire the merchandise? Who else did he sell to? And what other activities are this group of individuals tied into?'

The merchandise. As the word echoed my suspicions were confirmed. 'This is what I'm saying. With a story like that,' I said, 'Bucky could make himself a rich man. He can bargain for immunity and then bargain with the publishers. Who'd've thought getting caught was maybe the best thing could've happened to him? Bucky fuckin' Quinn.' I threw my hands in the air in a how-do-you-like-that gesture right out of Fifties television.

And he fell for it. He was blinking at me, licking his lips. He was getting frustrated, and he pulled out the handkerchief again and slid it across his mouth. 'Harry, listen to me. These details are not in Bucky's knowledge. He's a cell. An isolated cell.'

It was my turn to sip water. 'Well,' I said, 'we have no choice but to wait to find out.'

We were the only patrons in the restaurant, but after Paulie's brush-offs the waiter was keeping his distance. Paulie stared over my shoulder. He bunched his napkin in his pudgy hand. His eyes beaded down, and he shifted into a different mode. 'What if I told you I could give you that story?'

'With all due respect, Paulie, we're here to talk about Bobby. I'm not averse to hearing what light you might be able to throw on the story of the heist, but let's stay focused here.'

'Forget the heist. It's small change compared to what I could bring you.'

I wriggled in my chair and peered over my shoulder. 'Paulie, can we order here? I'm starving, I gotta tell you.' I flagged the waiter. When he came I dawdled over the menu. We ordered and I told the kid to bring me a double Dewar's on the rocks. Paulie was sweating. By now I knew I only had to wait.

'I could lay the whole thing out for you,' he said, after the waiter was gone. 'Names, ranks, and serial numbers. And it is big.'

I allowed myself to turn serious. '"Big" is a word I hear every day, Paulie. You're going to have to be more specific.'

He swallowed. We could hear the waiter shouting our order in the kitchen. His face assumed a kind of fearful earnestness, and I could see he had decided to tell me more than he knew he should. 'Police chiefs all over Massachusetts owe their jobs to one guy. One guy they all got exams from and they all owe big-time. Not to mention how he could hold them over a barrel he wanted to. So they do what he says.

Which is to say if there's a shipment of certain goods needs co-ordination statewide, if there's a question of certain hardware needing to fall into the right hands, if there's amounts of revenue channeling out of a situation this individual feels it is his prerogative to share . . . well, no question but these chiefs do the right thing. On account of what is being held over them.'

He was crouching in his seat, pointing from one side to another with a thick finger. I was sitting back in my chair like the guy who knows he and his date are going straight from the table to her bedroom.

'And you're prepared to name this individual,' I said.

He shrugged. 'For the right price.'

'And how can you prove you're right?'

'Harry Donohue. Be realistic. However, I will say this unconditionally: I can display details that in a totality you would be a fool to argue with me. You would be convinced, no question.'

Convinced? I already was.

All they want is a percentage?

On the terms discussed.

And they'll keep their word?

If you will, they will.

He would. They would. And so it went. I had been pursuing the wrong story.

Back in the office, I couldn't concentrate on my work. Johnny Rotella was lurking around Reception, kibitzing with Carla and letting me know, it seemed, that he was waiting for payment on the *Red Sox Trivia* job. Jeff and Frankie were at the door every few minutes, asking questions they should have answered themselves. I kept hearing Pallotta's sweaty voice in my head. I kept seeing his oily face and sidling eyes floating in front of me. Now that I knew what I knew, I was compelled to act, but I had no notion of my next move. I was swollen with my new information, desperately in need of a drink and a neutral ear. I was thinking of heading to Kiley's when Carla buzzed and said that my brother was on the phone.

'Eddie. So nice to hear from you.'

'I thought maybe we'd have lunch Monday.'

'Next week's bad. I'm busy.'

An Eddie silence. I could see him squinting in his bare office as he slumped in the big leather chair his daughters had given him for his forty-fifth birthday. Friday was Rotary day, and he would be wearing his Rotary uniform: blue blazer, gray slacks, red tie decorated with nautical crests. 'We have to talk, Harry. If you can't make lunch then let's do it some other way, but we have to talk.'

'So we'll talk. Shoot.'

I heard him take a breath. 'Look, I don't like this situation any more than you do, but it has to be addressed.'

'What situation is that?' I was staring at the photographs on my desk: Gary, a recent one of my mom, my dad in his prime. None of my brother or sister.

'Judy and I met yesterday with Milt Solomon and two guys from Hale and Eliot. I'm not even supposed to be telling you this, but the whole thing seems so ridiculous. And I told them that.'

'That was white of you.' I had picked up the phrase from Lucy, and it threw Eddie into another breathy silence. 'So,' I said, 'did the family brain trust determine my future?'

He found his bearings. 'Don't get defensive. Judy said you would, but you and I know it doesn't have to be this way.'

The directness was unusual. He'd been doing some thinking. 'The last time we met,' I said, 'you told me how you wanted to keep the shop a family concern. You said if anyone deserved it, I did.'

'That's right.'

'And now you're sitting in that fancy Hale and Eliot boardroom plotting with Judy and her pals and talking about how I'm screwing up. Are you in on this injunction?'

On Wednesday I had received a registered letter on Hale and Eliot stationery informing me of Judy's intention to file and giving me one last out. I had forwarded the letter to Moe Sommer.

'What does "in on" mean? Judy's the one with power of attorney.'

'Do you approve? I mean, Eddie, do you think it's going to *solve* anything?'

His weariness clogged the phone line. Oh, for the clarity and lines of authority of the navy, his silence said. Where enemies were enemies. But family! Shouldn't there be clarity between brother and brother? Eddie was a black-and-white guy, but he was taking a deep breath, filling his lungs with the air of compromise. It wasn't an easy role for him, and I wasn't making it any easier.

'I want us to work things out without litigation,' he said. 'I mean, what if Mom heard about this? It would kill her.'

'That's what I said to Judy.'

'Harry, do you think she likes all this? Don't you know it's killing *her*?'

'Then why did she get power of attorney without consulting you and me?'

Eddie couldn't lie. He was driven by duty, not politics. Courageous, certain, he had picked out targets in the Vietnamese night and led his chopper to where it had to go, but he couldn't pretend he didn't know what he knew. Especially not to his brother. So when he didn't answer my question I knew that he *had* been consulted. I was the odd man out. When he said he didn't want litigation, what he meant was that he wanted me to capitulate. Eddie was here to make peace, but he was a guy who drew lines in the sand, and there was no doubt on which side of the line he stood.

That conversation sealed it. I had no choice but to flee to Kiley's and its dark certainties. I needed to talk to Mick Malone.

Kiley's was an old-fashioned, no-frills neighborhood tavern, where you could count on darkness at high noon, a bartender who spoke only when spoken to, and an eight-ounce chaser for thirty-five cents. When I walked in at four o'clock the booths were mostly empty, but the bar stools were all occupied by sagging, wrinkled men in flat caps and worn coats. The bartender cocked an eye, but before I could order I heard a familiar croak from the opposite end of the bar. 'Give the kid a Rob Roy, Dinny. He looks like he could use it.'

The kid. Only here would a fifty-two-year-old be called 'the kid.' Heads lifted. I leaned on the bar, staring at my hands, until the drink arrived (heavy, I could see from its hue, on the Scotch). I hoisted my glass. 'Cheers, Mick,' I said, and drained it. Chest tingling, throat tight, I pointed at the glass. 'I'll do that again, Dinny,' I said. 'With a draft this time.' With two fingers I blessed the line of glasses between me and Mick Malone. 'But first, scoops down the line for Brighton's best.' I walked behind the drinkers as Dinny set to work. They twisted stiffly in their seats to inspect their benefactor (*he reminds me of . . . who's this he reminds me of?*). Retired firemen and cops, tradesmen and city workers, men who had refined small-talk and daytime drinking to a subtle art, they stared with eyes dulled by drink and boredom but rich nevertheless with curiosity and experience and the yearning of those who, more and more, knew only sadness and pain outside the hours on these stools. The proper audience for my state of mind.

I sat next to Mick, who set his Pall Mall in the ashtray and reached across with his left hand to grasp my own. 'Always thought you were straight no chaser,' he said, grin stretching from ear to crinkled ear.

'The times that are in it, Mick.'

'With you there, pal.'

I laid a fifty-dollar bill on the counter as Dinny lined them up. Drinks on me. One of the fundamental adult-male gestures, like lighting a cigar outside the barbershop or signaling for the check at the Parker House. My dad pulling into the Texaco station on the Old Post Road and telling the grease monkey to fill it up with regular. Or tipping the State House cleaning ladies at Christmas and asking after their renegade sons. As a kid I longed for the day when I would move through life with the assurance my father had at these moments. Thus I measured maturity. And I wasn't far wrong.

The feeling put me in mind of Gary. He was out in the

world, doing his best and taking measure of his own maturity without any help from his old man. Let him succeed on his terms, I said to myself. Let me not get in his way. I resolved to give him a call.

I sipped the fresh drink. It felt good to be here. Behind the bar I noticed the touches of local color that hadn't changed since I was a kid: a two-dollar bill taped to the wall; a street sign from County Clare; a dusty bottle of Jameson's Redbreast surrounded by a set of pewter measures. John Paul Kiley and his son Liam, the current owner, believed that a drinking establishment was a place where men counted on one kind of familiarity and escaped from another. There were no signs of Christmas in here, nothing at all to indicate the time of year except the results of the college football pool. No piped music. No seasonal brewery promotions. In the mirror behind the serried fifths, I could see the reflected faces of my dad's old drinking buddies, stoic and pallid, keeping an eye on me without appearing to, one or two still working out who I was.

'So what's the big occasion?' Mick asked. From the side he looked like Spencer Tracy. You couldn't see the tender, inflamed nose or the tired eyes set a little too close together. I nodded toward a booth and we moved across.

'Between us, Mick.'

'Oh-oh.'

'I'm in a situation.'

'This have anything to do with that book you're doing?'

'You could say that.'

Mick shook a cigarette from the pack, stuck it between his purple lips, and lit up, all with his left hand. The year before retirement he had hurt his shoulder breaking up a brawl outside the Golden Harp, and now he could barely lift his right arm. 'Only need one hand to drink,' he'd say. Through the smoke I watched his eyes, watery, bloodshot, but with a rare glint of interest. I had made his day, dropping in and singling him out for a mysterious head-to-head.

'I've come across some interesting information,' I said.

'Interesting information is usually dangerous information. What kind?'

'A list of names.'

He winced. 'Watch out. Any I'd recognize?'

'More than recognize.'

'My own on there?'

'I wouldn't be talking to you if it was.'

He took a wadded handkerchief from his pocket and blew his nose. Even in the dark of the bar, his skin looked raw and nubbled.

'This gonna be twenty questions?' he asked.

I gripped my glass. I was giddy from the liquor and my secret. I took a breath and tried to keep my tone even. 'It's a list of police chiefs,' I said. 'From all over the state. And from what I can determine, they all bought exams.'

He whistled quietly, looked across at the bar, and dropped his voice to a whisper, 'Keep your voice down. From what you can determine?'

I nodded.

'Bought from who?' he asked.

I told him what I understood from Paulie Pallotta: that Bobby had been either selling or bartering civil service exams to cops who had used them to climb the ladder to chief. Over twenty chiefs of police across Massachusetts looked like they owed their positions to him. Over twenty chiefs who would be more than inclined to do him a favor, like moving dope or acquiring guns or looking the other way while Bobby or another associate cherry-picked what he wanted from the town. From there it was easy to guess the next step: Bobby would use his underworld connections to move his spoils and protect himself. But, just when he had it in place, jail had screwed up his plans. Just when he had all the angles covered. It was the Hillbrook heist writ large, a network of crooked cops with power and access and allegiance to no one except an ex-captain currently in the clink. Hungry to get out so he could start collecting tribute from what he had worked so hard to create. The look in Bobby's eyes I'd noted that first day out in Concord was only partly about the money he'd make with me. He had another stash waiting for him, and the book was crumbs compared to the toast of that scam. This, this was the big score.

The words came in a rush, and Mick kept nudging my voice down with a spread hand. After my careful silence, being able to talk made me feel I was on the inside. Like being with Lucy. But Mick had lost the glint in his eye. His lips were tight and his eyes quick.

'Did you talk to Quinn's lawyer?' he asked.

'I haven't talked to anybody except Pallotta. But I don't have to, Mick. I've got the list! And the tapes. It's a lock.'

'A lock? What's that supposed to mean?'

'It's the story of the year. The decade!'

'A story you can't prove.'

'What, I'm a prosecutor? For myself, there isn't a shadow of a doubt.'

Mick rubbed his unshaven, lantern-jawed face and stared across the bar. 'Where did Rizzoli get them?'

'I have to figure he stole them himself. He's a qualified locksmith. He's the one in the Hillbrook gang who picked the lock on the optician's beside the bank.'

Mick took a deep drag of his cigarette and let the smoke drift from his mouth as he continued staring. He was doing what my dad said no guy did better: building a picture in his head, assembling all the pieces, examining them carefully. 'So a Capitol cop's in on the deal.'

'Maybe. Or maybe Bobby just snowed a pal into letting him wander around the McCormack Building.'

Mick took a gulp of his Scotch and some went down the wrong way. He had a coughing fit and turned crimson. He spat phlegm into his handkerchief and gave me a hard look. 'So. The million-dollar question,' he said. 'What are you going to do with this information you can't prove but you know in your heart to be true?'

'I don't know.'

'Let me put it this way. You plan on telling anybody besides me?'

Coming here, I hadn't thought this far into the conversation. I had imagined shouting out the news to Mick, a guy from the old school, and then listening to the echo. I hadn't considered the hard questions. He was giving me the look – avuncular but tough – that I guess he thought he owed me. He reminded me of my dad on those disappointing occasions when I went to him with a big balloon of an idea and had it gently but quickly punctured. 'Not for the moment.'

'Not for the moment,' he said. 'How 'bout later today?'

'This is big-time news, Mick. I want to keep my options open.'

'I thought the Rizzoli book was big-time.'

'It is. But this is a once-in-a-lifetime big.'

Mick stubbed out his cigarette and shifted in the booth. 'Harry, let me lay out a few realities here. Speaking to you as a former law-enforcement officer and as a friend. Number one: you are in possession of incriminating evidence, and know it to be incriminating. So you found it among Rizzoli's papers – it's still in your hands. Two: you had a conversation with a known felon who in effect confessed to involvement in a high crime. The law is very clear here: you report what you know to the appropriate authorities or you become an accomplice. It's like accepting stolen goods. And the fact that Pallotta knows you know takes away your deniability. So, practically speaking, it would not be a good idea to sit on this.'

'Like Pallotta's going to turn me in?'

'Someone's gonna turn someone in. Bucky Quinn. Rizzoli himself. The very fact that you know this means it's gotten out of hand. Someone's going down. If no one else knew that you know, I'd say shut up and pretend you never heard. Though I would be concerned that I was now in the loop. *Am* concerned. But you don't know what Pallotta is going to do. And forget about him. If he knows, then the big boys know.'

'What big boys?'

'Both sides of the fence. And they find out you know, you better hope it's the good guys get you first.'

'But nobody knows I got the list.'

Mick waved his hand dismissively. 'Forget about the list. That's just one more reason to kill you. You gotta get rid of it.'

It was the kind of talk that should have quickened my pulse, but I knew where it was headed. 'So what would you suggest?' I asked. I had come for his advice? Well, I was going to get it. Yet, as I asked, I felt tired, weighed down by afternoon drink, knowing that the answer coming was not the answer I wanted to hear, suspecting it was advice I would not heed, in spite of my respect for Mick.

'Let's look at your options,' he said, sticking up a twisted thumb. 'You can sit on it. But we both agree that would be foolish.' He gave me the nodding stare he'd give a drunk after throwing him in the hoosegow. 'You could go public in whatever publishing fashion you have in mind, though my guess is you're a bit fuzzy on the details. And you know what? It ain't gonna get any clearer. Or safer. Or,' he said with finality, 'you could do the right thing and go to the authorities.'

'Who?'

He lifted his empty glass in Dinny's direction and nodded his order. He had probably been drinking steadily for five hours, but he was as steady as Dinny's stare.

'You got a few options here too. Attorney General's office, one of the state DAs, the Feds. There's this new commission with Lathrop that your pal Jimmy O'Leary's on. They'd love a bone like this.'

'But what can I prove?'

'You don't have to prove anything. Just give them the list and tell them where you found it. You've done your duty as a good citizen. And look at it this way: the publicity can only help your book.' He drank. 'Problem with anybody local,' he continued, 'is they know where the bodies are buried. Plus, their loyalties are complex. Some would say contradictory.

Ask your old man in your prayers tonight, he could tell you a story or two down that line.'

Dinny slid our drinks in front of us and glided away.

'All things considered,' Mick said, 'I'd have to say the Feds. They may be bastards, but they don't owe anybody.'

I thought of Erpelding and Gurlick at the press conference, staring at me with scaly indifference. They didn't owe anybody. Wasn't that their problem? 'I met an FBI guy last month who told me they were working with Bobby. He was talking out his ass, but they must know Bobby knows something.'

Mick shook his head. 'Harry, if your old man was here he wouldn't mince his words. The more you tell me about this the worse it sounds.' He chugged down his drink in a way that said his position was not going to change. And the more we talked, the worse I felt. I couldn't think straight. The possibilities unveiled by my conversation with Paulie seemed distant now. I was drunk and confused and sorry I had come to him. I had wanted the Mick who kissed my mother on both cheeks and did an Irish jig in our kitchen while my dad clapped and sang. Not the Mick who broke up bar-room brawls. I left Kiley's caught between my respect for him and the sharp fear that I would not do as he suggested. This was the big one. How could I lose it? I had lost enough already. As my dad used to say, in for a nickel, in for a buck.

It was six o'clock when I emerged from Kiley's, negotiating my options for the evening ahead, suppressing all thought of what was going wrong. Not an easy task. It was very cold, but dark, at least. Thankful for small mercies, I moved up the road. There is nothing quite as disorienting as being drunk in daylight, and I was confused enough. I decided to put off all decisions until the morning and looked for a payphone to call Lucy. Though, best I could remember, Bobby Junior was at home that night. I was running out of sanctuaries.

14

I was like the poor kid who finds a hundred-dollar bill on the street. I had the break of my life but no idea what to do next. What would I spend it on? Where would I begin? Who would believe that it was really mine?

Mick had brought me to earth with a thud. I sat in my apartment all weekend, nursing a bad cold, drinking more than I should have, gazing out at the cold waters of Boston Harbor. On Monday, I returned to work, checked up on Jeff's progress, sat in my office and schemed. I did not tell anyone else of what I knew, as Mick had suggested I should. I clung to the conviction that I could turn this opportunity into real money. I sifted options, dreamed of confidences and dark deals, riffled through the friends I could draw into an intrigue that would break this town wide open. But Mick was right. It didn't get any clearer. And when I was done thinking, I knew there was only one guy who would understand, one guy who knew the possibilities here, one guy I could turn to.

But he wasn't anybody Mick had suggested.

So on Wednesday I found myself on the familiar route to Concord, gripping the wheel, teeth on edge, climbing the hills west of Boston with the engine of my Chrysler knocking like secret police in the night. An army helicopter hovered above Hanscombe Airfield. The day was dark and cold, with patches of dirty snow scattered on the margins of the highway like old newspapers. My body temperature was up, and I had a metallic taste in my throat reminiscent of childhood fevers.

Bobby knew I was coming. I'd called him. He would be shuffling reasons for my visit like a pack of cards, but I had deliberately left the purpose unplanned, and somehow this ignorance gave me the illusion of advantage. Whatever he guessed would be wrong. Or wrong at least for that moment. But one thing I did know: I would leave Concord later that afternoon with a certainty I'd been missing all week. The issue, whatever it was, would be forced. I would have to do something.

I also knew where we'd start. When was *60 Minutes* coming up from New York? This was Bobby's first question every time I called. Where the hell is Bradley? And I would feed him a line, knowing he knew I was, happy to have him cursing my dumb Irish ass when he could have been looking into my soul, seeing my guilt proclaim that, yes, I had kissed the wonderful breasts of his lonely wife as often as I could. But now I was wondering about *60 Minutes* myself. Shirley had caught me on my way out the office door and told me something that pricked up my ears. 'Jack Wambaugh called,' she said, pushing at her hair with splayed fingers. 'He wants to set up a conference call with you and Rizzoli.'

Her tone was flat and careful. She had changed her make-up in some way I couldn't pinpoint – lighter mascara or heavier liner, something that made her eyes look even more probing. She held a clipboard at her chest, not defensively but attentively, like a conference hostess. I stood at the shop door and looked into her eyes. Our relations had altered in recent weeks, but I wasn't sure what was going through her head. After our hotel dinner with Wambaugh, she had made herself scarce, partly, I suspected, because something had happened between them that night, partly because of my problems with Judy. Our talk was measured and arm's length. Yet here she was, in the office. She had chosen to hang with me, at least for the time being. I needed that assurance. I needed to know that someone besides me believed that this book was going to make money.

'He called you?' I said.

'Yes.'

'And he wants to conference with Bobby and me?'

'That's right.'

I let the door close. The air between us was filled with several histories and an uncertain, trembling future.

'About what?' I asked.

'I'm not sure. Dates, I would think.'

'Dates?' I smiled.

She spoke carefully. 'The next visit. The interview.'

Behind her, Carla was filing invoices and eavesdropping. I nodded toward my office and we went in. I kept my topcoat on. 'How come he didn't call *me*?'

'He did. Several times. Harry, you're never here.'

'You've been missing a little yourself.'

She smiled. I had missed that smile. It told me that she craved my sense of her beauty, no matter how crassly expressed. It reminded me of the spark of irony and attraction that survived her friendship with my sister and my ex-wife.

And it wondered why I no longer paid her the refined, detached, sensual attention that, since Lucy's arrival, had disappeared from inclination.

'It's not my fault,' I said.

'What isn't?'

I shrugged, overheated in my coat, burdened all of a sudden by the winter light and derelict view beyond my window. Waiting to go out to the prison to say something to Bobby as yet unformed. 'That they're taking so long – *60 Minutes*. Bobby blames me.'

'So maybe the call will clear that up,' she said. 'Like I said. Dates.'

'If this was about scheduling a visit, he wouldn't need Bobby in on the conversation.'

'I'm just the message-bearer.'

'But you've got his ear.'

She sighed, dropped her shoulders, and tilted her head. Now what was coming? 'What I've got, Harry, is a problem. Is it me he's interested in, or the book? Don't go paranoid on me. You're still signing my paycheck.'

I weighed that one up, feeling much, I supposed, as Lucy did when I dropped a compliment. Start deceiving and you begin to suspect everyone of deception. 'I'm actually on my way out to see Bobby right now,' I said. 'We have five chapters finished, you know.'

'Yeah. I heard about Jeff's schedule.' Another slight smile, a tuck on one side of her mouth. 'Don't you think it's a little ambitious?'

'I'm an ambitious guy.' I took a deep breath. 'I'm going to make this happen, Shirley. I'm going to make it happen and it's going to free me from all this shit with Judy and Eddie that's breaking my heart.' My tone was frantic. I couldn't hide it. Moments like this were why I hated coming to the office.

A trace of pity flickered around her eyes, made exotic and unfamiliar by the change in make-up. 'Harry, don't take this the wrong way. I'm worried about you.'

'Hey, I can take care of myself.'

'Ann told me about Thanksgiving.'

'Oh, *great*.' And I thought Shirley was wondering why I wasn't lusting after her anymore. 'I have to go out to the prison. I'm late as it is.'

'It's not as bad as you probably think. Gary told her he wants you and Ann over to his place for Christmas. He's afraid to call you after what happened.'

'He wants me over for Christmas? He said that?'

'Yes.'

'Jesus. After what I did? That wasn't my best day, you know. He brought this girl of his over – girlfriend, I guess – and I got shitfaced.'

'Ann told me.'

'Is there anything she doesn't tell you?'

She raised her eyebrows at my naïveté.

'I know, I know. I owe Gary a call. He's reaching out and I'm acting like an asshole.'

'Harry, if you know all this then why do you do it?'

'Why do we do anything? Look, this is a tense period for me right now. I need to get the book out and get past this business with Judy. I shouldn't even be talking about it with you.'

She put the clipboard on my desk. There was a crease in her

blouse where it had pressed against her breast, and this little indentation, in such a perfect curve, made me yearn to be held close. For a dangerous moment I wanted to tell her about the list, about Paulie Pallotta, about my new score. But I held back and watched her eyes, eyes that, like Lucy's, showed the layered nature of womanly response, the balance of sexual power and intuition and defensive intelligence. The complexity of a good mind in a beautiful body in a man's world. But unlike Lucy's, there was no hardness there; rather, weary gentleness and a surprising sympathy. 'So we won't talk,' she said. 'But you should call him.'

'Good. I'm out of here.' I opened the door.

'So when shall I set up the call?' she said.

'With Gary?'

'*No*. With Wambaugh.'

'Oh. Say, Monday. But let me talk to Bobby first.'

She nodded slowly and, with a long look from those deep eyes, left my office. I watched her sway past, and her movement stirred in me a huge desire, tinged with loss and guilt. Was my lack of interest pushing her to hint at what might have been? Would I ever learn? Would I ever get it right with women? As I headed to my car, my thoughts turned with swift inevitability to Lucy.

Lucy. Subtly, slowly, I was losing her. She was making excuses not to see me, claiming Bobby Junior was at home when I knew, for a fact, he was on duty. When we were together, her heart drifted at critical moments. She was not finishing her kisses. Her eyes kept me dead in their sights, denying all past and future in their intensity, but her lips were pulling away a split second sooner than in those first searing weeks. And through this tiny opening, I could see a vista of concern where I had no presence, where I could bring no real solace.

As I hammered through the western suburbs in my ageing car, running away from the dictates of my heart, I admitted what it would have been wiser, for the moment, to deny: that, since my discovery of the list, the urgency of our attraction had diminished. It was my fault. I was the first to hold back; she sensed my withholding and reacted as a woman of her experience would. Her intuition told her I could not be trusted. And too late I discovered how much I needed her – beyond the sex, beyond the companionship. I had been distracted. As I had been with Shirley. But what could I do? The world was sucking at me from every direction. Something had to suffer. I pulled into the prison parking lot and slid to a stop in front of the wall. Instead of being with Lucy, I was heading for her husband and an altogether different affair. I reached for a fresh pint of Scotch from the glove compartment, took a long pull, and went inside.

He made me wait. I took a seat in our usual spot and looked for a good ten minutes at the overheated room and peeling walls and dirty snow in the prison yard. I was light-headed and flushed from the whisky and the heat. I removed my coat and folded it over the back of the plastic chair. A thin, frizzy-haired guy in corduroys and an open-necked white shirt was stringing holiday decorations from wall to wall. Cardboard Santas and gold stars, tinsel and colored lights. A surprisingly full and well-decorated tree sat in the corner. The guards looked at him disdainfully; he was probably a social worker.

The Hispanic inmate helping him smoked menthol cigarettes and stroked a thin mustache. There were more kids visiting than usual, and the sounds of their play and the social worker's cheerless directions gave the dry air an even more oppressive weight. Christmas in prison. The compassionate time of year.

When Bobby appeared, he was surly and pale. There was dandruff on the shoulders of his sweatshirt, and the broken capillaries in his cheeks were a royal purple. The clothes that had looked crisp and summery on my first visit were losing their shape from prison launderings. I stood as he arrived but he ignored me, walking past to retrieve a chair and glance with baleful eyes at the fresh decorations. He set his chair directly across from me and leaned close, elbows on his knees. His breath was sharp. The skin between his eyebrows was raw and flaking. He said nothing, preferring to see how I would react to his stare. I was sure he could smell the Ballantine's on my breath. To keep my mind off Lucy, I thought of the list. I had no idea how I was going to play it, so I stuck with what I knew.

'Wambaugh wants to talk to us next week. A conference call.' He kept staring. 'I guess he wants to set a date to come up,' I continued.

'He needs a conference call to work *that* out?'

I shrugged. 'I guess. I don't know.'

'Sounds like you're communicating with him about as good as you are with me.'

'What do you mean?'

He let his head drop to his knees and ran both hands through his hair. I leaned back, but I could still see the stiff black bristles spring back up as they slid from underneath his palms. I could smell hair oil. He raised his head, sucked in his lips, and opened them with a pop. 'What do I mean?'

I was finding it very hard to concentrate. Liquor and anxiety were making my head spin, so I said something I would normally have avoided. 'Forget I asked. I know what you mean.' I slid my chair back and crossed my legs. 'You want to know ahead of time, *you* call him.'

He smirked and shook his head. *Drunk fuckin' harp.* He might as well have said it. He said it often enough on the tapes. *Never trust the Irish. Can't keep their mouths shut and can't stay off the juice.* He held his hand out and calibrated index finger and thumb as tight as they'd go. 'I'm that far . . . *that far,* Donohue, from saying *fuck this* to the whole deal.'

Two months ago, such talk would have panicked me. Not now. The conflict was a relief. I wasn't running. And I wasn't being silently scrutinized. 'Go ahead,' I said. 'But don't forget who controls the rights to the story.'

'I do. *I* own the fuckin' rights.'

'And you can't do shit with them without me. Not for three years.'

He bobbed his head, still rubbing thumb and finger together. He was regrouping. This was the first such outburst I had risked with him. It occurred to me that we had only ever met in this exact posture: facing each other on cheap plastic chairs in a stuffy room full of convicts and their haggard girlfriends, me having driven through some of the wealthiest suburbs on the east coast, Bobby having walked down echoing halls from his narrow, brooding cell. Was it any wonder he was like a zoo animal? And me? I had passed through reminders of all I didn't have to the only guy who could help me escape failure. A couple of caged beasts. It was no surprise our conversations were tense and predatory. Then along came Lucy, and Bobby turned into the last guy in Massachusetts I wanted to see. My choice was between pursuing passion or success, and trying to have it both ways had strung me out. So here I was, trying another angle, eyeing him up, resentful of his hold on me, but still wondering what the hell I was doing out here and what it was I wanted.

Bobby sniffed loudly and rubbed his chin. He may have looked edgy and rumpled and a little bloated, but his arms were lean and muscular, coiled tight with the ability to deal a quick blow. 'You know, Harry, I'm down this room two, three times a week. Sometimes it's my wife, sometimes an old pal, but every time I'm down here I swear to God I'm thinking of you. Back to my cell, I'm thinking of you. In the mess, some crackhead yappin' at me like a monkey, and who's in my head? You and this fuckin' book. You're like some broad I'm banging I'm thinking of you so much. Then your pissant writer, this Somerville kid not old enough to yank his chain, he calls me and asks me his screwy questions, and when I ask him to pass me on to you, you're not there. I call you at home, I get your fuckin' answering machine.' A long pause here, eyes like a cheetah's. 'I call my wife, she tells me . . . she tells me she never sees you. The woman who will control all this so-called dough you told her and me we'd be making. I ask myself these questions: why is he avoiding me? Why is he avoiding *her*? What the fuck has Lucy ever done to *him*?' Another pause. 'Finally, you decide I'm worth a visit. You come out, and you treat me like some piece of dogshit. Who the hell are you to be treatin' me like that? I thought we were partners.'

Coming from Bobby, this was high rhetoric. Both diversionary and aggressive. 'I've got a lot on my mind,' I said.

'You got a lot on *your* mind?' He glared at me with savage openness. 'I'm in prison. My whole life is *on my mind*.'

I wasn't prepared for the burrowing intensity, or for the emotion it carved in me. His look reminded me of the news clips of the final moments of his trial, when he was led from the courtroom in his blue suit and reading glasses, a grizzled Mickey Taylor whispering unheard in his ear, his eyes focused with fiery concentration on something beyond the courtroom, beyond the buzzing crowds, on the cramped gray space of his future, so swiftly defined by the simple phrases of the foreman of the jury and Judge Lathrop. Under such a glare I let my guard down. I wavered. 'We're getting it done, Bobby. We have five chapters out of twelve. *60 Minutes* is coming up. We're on our way.'

He wasn't listening to me. He had seen in my face and heard in my tone what I'd managed to disguise in the past. Maybe it was pity, or fear. Maybe guilt. Whatever it was, he recognized it at once and knew what to do with it. 'What's eating you, Harry?'

'What do you mean?'

'Something's going on. What is it?'

He was the kind of guy who used the direct approach only when he was going in for the kill. His eyes roped me to the chair. Bring on the bloodhounds. He smelt something on my fingertips and he would know if it was his wife's scent. He would know and he would act on the knowledge.

'I met with Bucky Quinn yesterday,' I lied. The words came from nowhere. I hadn't even been thinking of Bucky. He paused for an instant but came right back with a lie of his own.

'Who the hell is Bucky Quinlan?'

The name change was the stroke of a master. But my scrambling subconscious had gone him one better and saved my skin; now he was on the defensive.

'*Quinn*. The Shropwood chief going down for possessing a stolen exam. Don't know who he is? You must be the only one in the state.'

'Rings a bell.'

'He wants to do a book with me.'

Like *that* he was back on the street, sizing me up, mulling his next move. This time I had thrown him. But at what cost?

'And what the fuck does this have to do with me?' he said.

We had arrived at where my whole week had been aiming. My whole life, you could say. And I had no idea where I was going with this.

'Quinn seems to think it has a lot to do with you.'

'Oh yeah? How so?'

'I don't know.' Something told me backing off would get me more. 'He's there with his lawyer – Saul Richards, you know Richards, don't you? – he's there with Saul, who keeps shutting him up every two minutes. Keeping a very tight hold.' For all I knew, Bobby *did* know Saul, and would be on the cellphone to him as soon as I was out the prison door. But to my muddled thinking, the lie was getting more inspired as I went along. 'He's very clear about wanting to do the book, however. Only thing is, says I can't do it as long as I'm doing yours. Something about conflict of interest.'

'On the part of who?'

'You. At least, that's the impression I'm getting.'

Bobby assumed the face he thought would tell me he was confused. 'I still don't get it. He's saying what he has to say is gonna contradict my book?'

'Either that . . . or maybe that you're going to figure somehow in the story *he* has to tell.'

Bobby stood and looked out the dirty window, hands grasped behind his back. The seat of his chinos drooped. A little kid was crying in the corner and I could hear the social worker offering her a candy cane.

'What I've been hearing about this case,' Bobby said softly, without turning around, 'it's gonna take a while to come to trial. You're telling me you'd jack in my book to wait for that?'

'Bucky's been indicted, Bobby. He wants a contract *before* he talks to the grand jury. Before the cat's out of the bag.'

'What cat?'

'I thought maybe you could tell me.'

He turned around. 'You don't know what he has to give and you're talking about dumping *me*?'

I stood so as not to be at a disadvantage. We were inches from each other. 'I'm not dumping anybody, Bobby. I got too much invested in this project. I was hoping maybe you could enlighten me about this whole exam thing and we could move on. I mean, maybe there's even more dough in it for both of us.'

I had said the word. *Exam*. Eyeball to eyeball, I had said it, focused on those bloodshot, flaking eyes with all my attention. I saw nothing but a fierce, desperate calculation. Not a lot different from what I was feeling myself.

'How the hell can I enlighten you?' he said.

'Someone is going to tell this story and make a lot of money. Why not you? You must know something about it.'

He exhaled sharply and let his attention drift to the ugly, crowded room. The ambition I had seen in his eyes two months ago was clouded now by impatience. There was a tiredness in the shape of his shoulders that I knew instinctively could be turned to my advantage. I had stumbled into a plan. I had derailed his scrutiny. Now I needed to push him into one more golden concession. We sat again, and he rubbed his eyes with his palms.

'We got this conference call?' he said. I nodded. 'When?'

'Monday.'

'You coming out here?'

'I was planning on hooking up from my office.'

'Why don't you come out early? We'll have another conversation.'

'About what?' I asked.

His lips were tight. 'Monday.'

I put both hands in the air. 'Give me something,' I said. 'All these balls in the air, I gotta know something about what's coming.'

He gazed at me for a long time, then leaned close. 'Whatever it is Quinn can give you – and I seriously doubt he can give you anything at all – whatever it is, I can go better, ten times better. But . . . this thing is bigger than you can imagine. And dangerous. Money is money, but your health is your wealth, you know what I mean?'

He sat back, his hands on his thighs, looking worn and pale. He had meant to sound mysterious and inscrutable, but my improvised ruse had fooled him. I *could* imagine how big

this was. I knew exactly the danger involved. I had the list.
And, for the moment anyway, I had regained some control.
The excitement had returned.

'Monday?' I said. He nodded, stood, and, thumbs hooked
in his belt, pants drooping, looked over at the finished decorations. The social worker and the little girl were singing
'Jingle Bells.' He looked flat and bone-weary and burned out.
I picked up my coat. I would get no more from him that day.

15

On Friday morning I was at my desk, drinking coffee and reading the *Globe*, when Carla peeked in. 'Uh, Harry? There's these two guys here to see you?'

'Who?'

'I never seen them before.'

I sipped my coffee and kept reading. 'Tell them I'm in a meeting.'

She was back in seconds. 'I think you better.'

'I better?'

Her marmoset eyes were even bigger than usual. As I rose from my seat, a thin guy in a camel's hair overcoat edged past her, one hand on his stomach, the other clutching a pair of kid gloves. 'That's OK, sweetheart, we just want to have a look at the view.'

'Hey,' I said, putting my Styrofoam cup on the desk.

The guy had a narrow head, small ears, and slick black hair. He wasn't even looking at me. He lifted his hand from his gut and pointed out the window. 'Right there,' he said. 'Like jumping from twenty floors up.'

Behind him was a dog-faced goon in the same coat, but blue. An LBJ type with a deep chin, pocked cheeks, and a five o'clock shadow. He was pulling at his scarf and looking frazzled. 'Heat in here is a killer,' he said, glaring at me. Carla had retreated.

'What is this?' I said. 'What's going on?'

Tan was still pointing at the Tobin Bridge. 'See, they've built one of those cantilevered mesh fences underneath, supposed to put them off but doesn't stop them jumping. One a week. Like clockwork, one a week one a week one a week.'

'*Cantilevered*,' the dog-faced one said to me. 'Where the hell does he get them?'

The overcoats were a snug, almost feminine fit, knee-length with tight waists and shoulder pads. Fit right in with the greased hair and bad skin. I was looking for bulges near the armpit.

'So,' Tan said, still facing the window. 'Harry Donohue. DON-AH-HUE.'

'That's me.'

They looked at each other. 'He knows who he is,' Blue said.

'Smart guy. You a smart guy, Harry? Or a dumbshit, like my friend here.'

'He doesn't look too dumb to me.'

'Don't condescend, Harry. He may be stupid but he's got,' he wiggled his forefingers near the little ears, 'good antennae. Flawless. I bring him along because he's my lie detector.'

But Blue had edged around my desk and was staring sourly at my photographs. Gary as a teen, mop-haired and self-conscious, holding a football on the steps of Ann's house. My mother in a summer dress in front of St Gabriel's. My dad and me in black and white, the summer I campaigned for JFK, me skinny and slit-eyed and ambitious, my dad staring off-camera, shirtsleeves rolled, arms tense. A guy eager to get back to work. Fortunately there were no photos of Lucy. Not that there would be, but it was the way my thoughts were tending. I was trying to figure out who had sent these guys; if I knew that I'd know what they wanted. Though I was smart enough not to ask.

Tan pocketed his gloves and unbuttoned his overcoat. He swiveled from the window, loosening coat and jacket to reveal a light blue shirt, Paisley tie, and red suspenders. Straight on, his face was like a hatchet, sharp, tapering, notched. Blue's eyes had the misted distance of the self-absorbed: he would be focused on his limited role. Tan's, on the other hand, ranged where they wanted with scope and savvy. They widened now as he squeezed his nose, preventing a sneeze. He was definitely the one in charge. I closed my office door. 'How can I help you, gentlemen?'

Blue nodded at the open newspaper. 'You read this shit?' Whether he meant the *Globe*, broadsheets in general, or any paper at all, I wasn't going to ask.

'This,' the other said, sweeping a hand across my desk, 'is what our friend here means by being in a meeting.'

'Like, maybe he doesn't want to see us.'

'Hard to know with Harry. His wants, his desires. Would take something of a mind-reader.' He smiled coldly.

Annoyance was beginning to overtake caution in me. 'What do you guys want?'

Blue raised a corner of his mouth and looked at the other. Tan sat down and crossed his legs. 'We want to talk to you about your recent whereabouts. We want to make you aware of a few realities.'

If I was lucky, these guys were PIs hired by Hillbrook Savings Trust or its insurance company. They would have the power to make my life uncomfortable, but I would not be in any real danger. The other end of the spectrum I didn't even want to consider. 'And how is that your concern?'

'You'd be surprised at what is our concern. And I think you'd be surprised at how much it is in your interest to have a dialog here.'

I sat. Blue leaned against the wall, smiling, hands folded at his crotch. It was show-time.

'You seem to be spending a lot of time with Lucinda Rizzoli,' Mr Tan continued.

'We're business partners.'

'And just what business is that?'

I waved a hand at my bookshelf. 'The publishing business.'

He eyed the titles. Blue lit a cigarette, and snapped the lighter shut with an expensive click. 'Is that why you sneak into her house from the back?' Blue said. 'You a back-door man, Donohue?'

I shrugged. Blue blew smoke across the desk. 'Is that why, yesterday,' Tan said, 'you drove from the Shamrock Bar in a blue '82 New Yorker, which you parked beside the Boston Ed station on Fellsway West at, oh, say seven-thirty-two in the evening?'

Blue started to laugh, then fell into a coughing fit. I looked at him and he kicked my desk just hard enough so that I jumped in my seat. 'The phone calls,' he rasped, still catching his breath. Tan ignored him and kept staring at me.

'So you're following me,' I said, looking from one to the other.

'*Following*?' Blue sputtered. 'You think we're a couple foot soldiers sit in a fuckin' car all day?'

Tan sat up straight, waving his partner quiet. 'Harry, interrupt me at any point if you think my details are inaccurate. At eight-thirty last night – this was about ten minutes before you left the house on Lynch Road – Lucinda Rizzoli, beloved wife of Robert Senior, called a pizza joint in Hillbrook and ordered . . . well, you know what she ordered, don't you? Though you didn't stick around to share it with her.'

I was in trouble.

'She wouldn't fuck you, Harry, would she? Not like the other times. Beginning to lose interest in your dick. So you took off. And you know what happened in between the time you left and the time that pepperoni arrived? She had a conversation with the aforesaid Robert. A very interesting conversation. Kept her on the phone while that poor pizza kid was banging to beat the band on the front door.'

Real trouble. I found it hard to breathe. I was trapped. Right then, all I wanted to do was to call Lucy and tell her she was in trouble too. Though I owed it to her to remain cool and to find out everything I could. Because I *had* been with her yesterday. Cocky and salted with Scotch, I had gone there straight from the Shamrock. It was all as Mr Tan said, to the minute. I looked at his hatchet face and wondered if his devices had also captured the words between us, the stuff, as it happened, of our first disagreement.

For the first time since Thanksgiving we had not gone to bed. Though she usually had a drink waiting for me, she was not impressed when I arrived with booze on my breath. It was snowing as I drove into Hillbrook, and I tramped through the muddy woods with a pocket flashlight, tripping once over a dark log and soiling the knees of my Brooks Brothers trousers. The dark snow melted against my cheeks. She met me at the sliding door and told me to leave my boots on the deck. As usual, she had the heat cranked up high. Drunk and dizzy and cold, I reeled into the sitting room.

'Well, look what the cat dragged in.'

'I . . . I fell.'

'That a fact?' She looked from my knees to my face. She was wrapped in a terrycloth dressing gown and had her arms folded across her chest. She wasn't wearing make-up, which made her look sickly.

'You feeling all right?' I asked.

'I'm feeling fine. Looks like you're the one on a little medicine.'

I didn't answer but stepped carefully into the kitchen and draped my coat over a captain's chair. I was hungry, but the kitchen table was bare, and there was no evidence of any food going. The coat slid to the floor.

She picked it up. 'Why don't you take those off?' she said, pointing at my dirty pants.

'Hey, be taking them off soon enough, right?' Drunk though I was, I saw the flash in her eyes.

'Take it easy, Harry. My day could've been better,' she said.

'My *week*.'

She sidled over to the counter and shook a cigarette from a fresh pack. With her back to me, she lit up and said, 'Maybe tonight isn't such a good idea.'

I concentrated on appearing sober. 'I saw Bobby on Wednesday. We had a breakthrough.'

'That so?'

'We're stretching this story right out. Whole new dimension, whole new ball game. Big bucks.'

'How can you *drive* when you've had this much to drink?'

'You're not listening. Bobby and I are on to something big.'

'There's hearin' and there's listenin', and I don't *want* to listen. I don't want to listen to talk about Bobby and I don't want to hear you blabbing about might-bes all over again. You understand, Harry? Or are you too liquored up?'

Aggression lengthened her chin and creased her eyes. She did look unwell, swollen beneath the cheeks and slightly blurred. The tone of her looks was off.

'You're sounding more like my ex-wife every minute.'

'Maybe I'm beginning to see why she *is* your ex.'

'Look who's talking,' I said.

She smoked fiercely and stared. That's how it happens. A little mud on your knees and Paradise loses its leaves.

She disappeared into her room. The way her bathrobe trailed behind her brought a stir to my loins, and the whole focus of the day shifted. Always the way with me. One gesture, one breath, and I'm suddenly clear that I have it all wrong. I drew a glass of water from the faucet and sat at the table. The grand fantasies that had danced in my head all weekend faded. My head throbbed. Should I tell her about the list? Should I come clean? Would that win her back?

She returned and picked up the phone. 'I'm ordering a pizza,' she said, as she dialed. 'You want one?'

'I'm trying to keep the future in mind,' I said. 'The money, and what that means to you. And to me.'

'You want a pizza?'

'I want you.'

She ordered, hung up, and faced me, hands on hips. 'Do you have any idea what this is like for me? You seeing Bobby, then coming here and spouting off like I have no feelings? I don't want to think about him. Bad enough you're working with him. Then you turn up like this and it gets me thinking, when are you gonna get loaded and ride on out to prison to tell my husband what is really going on? Because of some shit-for-brains plan you got hatched. Harry – write the book, publish it, *get it over with*. Stop scaring me.'

'Let's go to bed.'

'You better leave, Harry.'

'Please.'

'Hey. Just go.'

So now I sat before Mr Tan's intelligent and dissecting gaze, wondering what the chances were that a new archive of Rizzoli tapes was in the making, with that night's desperate conversation the latest installment. With another of my secrets on cold display. And for whom?

'So what's your point?' I said to Mr. Tan. 'You know my private life, and now you're telling me you know. What is it you want?'

Blue shook his head like the big dog he was. He had no patience with this kind of challenge, and I sensed he was looking for permission to do whatever it was he got paid to do. But Mr Tan saw the reasonableness of my question. After all, if they were here to break my legs they would have done it by now. They wanted something.

'You and Mrs Rizzoli . . . well,' he shrugged, 'we're men of the world, my friend and I. We know how these situations arise, needs, opportunities . . .' He let a hand trail toward the window, an ironic gesture of tolerance. This part of the game, I sensed, was what he liked best, and I would do well to be patient. 'We *know*, of course. More than you would expect. Even now, with one of our cards on the table. This is one of the realities I spoke of. *One* of. When we act on this knowledge, how we act – you'd be surprised how little control we have over such details.'

'And how much control I have,' I said.

He looked at Blue with raised eyebrows. It was impossible to judge the grade of his irony. How well, after all, did he know me? 'Did I tell you this guy was smart? Did I tell you? You know, Harry,' returning his gaze to me, 'we're busy men. We do appreciate it – or I do anyway – when an effort is made to be co-operative.'

I nodded. Patience.

He stood and walked slowly to the window. 'The problem is, Harry, you talk too much. Full of theories and speculations that are all well and good in the privacy of your own home, but which, in the public domain, impact on men, powerful men, in adverse ways. And you are a man,' he waved at the bookshelf, 'who lives in the public domain.'

'Just trying to make a living.'

'As we all are, Harry. As we all are. But it is important not to make it at the expense of others.'

'You mean Bobby's book?'

He smiled. He could see I was trying to make it easy for him, to do whatever it took to get these guys out of my office so I could breathe and think and plan my next step. 'Bobby's paying his debt to society. If he wants to pass his time by writing this little fiction with you . . . well, we really don't care about that particular story. But I think you know what I'm talking about.'

He buttoned his coat and slid his hands into his kid gloves. As if on cue, Mr Blue bumped Gary's photo flat and very deliberately stubbed out his cigarette in my son's face. I made sure not to move a muscle. There was an acrid whiff of melted Plexiglas. Blue hitched at his coat, crossed the room, and opened the door. Mr Tan was staring at me, the half-smile still playing on his face. 'I know I don't have to tell you this, Harry. But men and their loved ones have suffered for indiscretions far smaller than those you have indulged to this point.' He looked out again at the bridge and shot his cuffs. 'One a week take a dive. Can you believe it?' He turned on his heel and walked out without looking at me.

Frightened to my fingertips, I stared at the phone. Beside it lay the damaged photograph, a smudge of burnt plastic where Gary's face once smiled. I had to call him. But if they had bugged Lucy's phone, they had probably bugged this one. I sat paralyzed for a long moment, then sent Carla out for more coffee. Who could I turn to? What could I do?

Frankie Deluca stuck his head in the door.

'Not now, Frankie.'

He had his handkerchief in his hand and a pen behind his ear. His tie was loosened. He was in big-deal mode. 'I got something going on, Harry.'

'Great, Frankie, but I'm busy right now. I'll talk to you later.'

'Franklin's? The big New York chain? They're willing to place a substantial order, in advance, on the basis of knowledge that the *60 Minutes* special will air before May. F-f-fifteen thousand copies.' He was pale with excitement. 'A call from you could close it.'

I got out of my chair. 'That's great, but let's talk about it later.' I all but pushed him out the door.

He looked at the open newspaper over my shoulder. 'Paulie told me you two got together.'

Now I did shove him. He tripped and nearly fell, then looked at me with total surprise. I held a finger of warning in the air but, of course, Frankie had no idea what was going on. 'Don't ever mention him again,' I hissed in his ear. '*Don't!*'

He stared in shock at my twisted face. He was about to speak, but I put the waving finger to my lips and pointed down the hall. He ran away.

I was shaking. My palms were damp. All the control I had screwed up during the meeting with the two coats suddenly uncoiled. My bowels loosened. I ran to the bathroom and sat in the cubicle, ashamed, desperately trying to recall the phrases traded with Paulie Pallotta and Mick Malone. Mick . . . Mick couldn't have. It had to be Paulie. What was I thinking? How stupid could I be! I had listened to Frankie Deluca!

I had to get out. Frankie would tell Shirley and Jeff about my outburst, and they'd be down to my office, asking questions, while the tapes rolled. I was now convinced the office was bugged. I grabbed my coat and headed for the elevator. It opened as I got there and Carla emerged with a tray of coffee. I brushed past her, telling her that something had come up and getting into the elevator. Down I plunged. On the riveted panel above the door, faint but still legible after the janitor's half-hearted attempt to scrape it away, was the story of my last three months: 'Harrys a dumb prick.'

I got into my car and headed down Atlantic Avenue with a pounding heart and a scrambled head. I could follow no train of thought, but hopped from fear to fear: Gary, my mother, Lucy, Judy, Ann, Eddie. I had infected everyone associated with me, brought danger to all who had the misfortune to be related. I had to call Gary. I had to call Moe. I shouldn't call anyone. And who had sicced these guys on me? Who had told them? Paulie's restaurant might have been wired. Bobby could have told the wrong prison guard. Someone could have been sitting in the next booth over in Kiley's. It didn't make any difference! All that mattered was the here and now. *What would I do now?*

I checked the rear-view repeatedly, and nearly back-ended a UPS van. I ramped up onto the elevated central artery and drove north. The twin flagpoles and yellow-brick façade of the Boston Garden loomed to my left, and a flock of pigeons, stirred by an arriving trolley, wheeled across the highway. The city seemed sharper than usual, almost surreal in its precision. My city. Each landmark a mine of the most personal memory. The Garden, Tobin Bridge, the Bunker Hill monument. My impulse was to run, to head to New Hampshire, Maine, Canada, but as soon as I was up, I went down again, taking the Storrow Drive exit and heading west toward Back Bay. The CITGO sign flashing in the distance. The Esplanade. Longfellow Bridge arching into Cambridge against a disturbed sky. Yes, my city. All I knew and all I had ever really known.

I turned on to Beacon Street and parked beside Boston Common. White Christmas lights, already glowing in the afternoon gloom, draped the bare trees, and skaters swayed across Frog Pond. I got out of the car and wandered with false casualness across the Common. At the Park Street T station, camouflaged by students and Christmas shoppers, I huddled at a payphone and called Gary. At the sound of his voice a lump rose in my throat.

'Listen, son,' I said, 'if anyone unknown calls you or comes to the door, don't let them in. You understand?'

'Dad? What are you talking about?'

'Gary, please. Listen. I've been acting like a prick lately, I know. It's to do with me, not you. I've been going through a rough patch.'

'Why don't you come on over to my place? Where are you?'

'That doesn't matter. Go to your mother's for a while. Lie low. I'll explain later.'

'This is too weird, Dad. Let's meet.'

'No!'

There was a pause. I imagined Mr Tan craned over a listening device, drinking in every word. 'Please, Gary, do what I say. I have to go.'

I hung up. My hands trembled. Had I added to the danger? Put my son at further risk? What kind of a father was I? I thought of my own dad. What would he have done? What would he have told me? *Always stand by your friends, Harry, and they'll never let you down.* Fathers fall away, but the tribe is always there. As long as you don't reject it. And then it was clear to me. I dropped another dime and called Jimmy O'Leary.

Even as I dialed I felt better. Jimmy would know what to do. When we were kids in Brighton and Italian gangs wandered over from East Boston to kick the shit out of us, Jimmy was never afraid. He would spit blood, even teeth, from his mouth without a complaint. He taught me when to stand and when to run. He taught me how to take a beating. And he taught me the most important rule of all – that the tribe sticks together.

He answered on the second ring. With a tremor, I asked him to pick me up at the entrance to the underground parking lot beside the Common. For a moment he sounded put out. But he must have sensed my panic because he agreed quickly and was there almost as fast as it took me to walk across the park. I climbed into his Ford and told him to drive out to Storrow or the Mass Pike, somewhere where we could keep moving and have a private conversation. He looked at me sidelong with a smile, chewing gum.

'What's with the cloak and dagger, Harry? You got someone on your tail?'

'As a matter of fact, I do.'

'Not going paranoid on me, are you pal?'

I slumped low in the seat as he went left on Beacon. As we turned onto the embankment, I heard the rumble of cars ramping into Kenmore Square and the Fenway from Storrow Drive. The urban familiar was somehow more than I could bear. I knew too well where danger might lie. I wanted escape from the city's nooks and angles. I wanted the freedom of flat, unknown vistas.

'Gary's in danger, Jim.'

'Gary? What are you talking about?'

'I'm a little lost. Every time I think I have it worked out, something happens that tips the canoe over. It's like I'm never going to be allowed to have it, you know?'

'Slow down, Harry. What are we talking about here? What's this about Gary?'

'I know you're not supposed to discuss it with me, but I'm in a real jam in this Rizzoli situation, and you're the only guy I can go to.'

He looked straight ahead, but I took his silence as instruction to continue. The pocked face and lean jawline were reassuring. Over the years, whenever I pictured him I saw him in profile: walking beside me on the streets of Brighton, looking for soda bottles; face to face with a wrestling opponent, elbows out like a big ugly bird's wings; at my side in Coolidge Corner movie house as we watched Bogart or Sinatra or, bless her soul, Rita Hayworth. A profile that inspired trust and confidence. No one was going to get one over on Jimmy. The political tide might have been against him, but for my money he was our next Attorney General, and who knew what after that? He was a guy who had the bases covered, and I had been a fool not to go to him as soon as I learned about the list.

I told him the whole story, straight, as the city skyline receded to our left. Bobby, Paulie Pallotta, the shop, Mick Malone, the two goons and their threats. He drove, eyes sweeping the crowded parkway, jaw working the spearmint. At home on this drive past railyards and elevated roads and the steaming backsides of college buildings and light industry. A city boy, like me, but one who didn't waste time pondering his place or trawling the past. Jimmy, then and now, always stayed focused on the present and what its careful manipulation could bring in the moments and months ahead. A good man in a tight spot. A good listener. Though when I told him, as I had to, about Lucy and me, he turned and stared, mouth open. 'You're sleeping with Lucinda Rizzoli?'

'And these guys, whoever they are, they know it. They know phone conversations, the whole bit.'

'Harry, Harry, Harry.'

'You're not one to talk, Jimmy.'

'No? Nothing on my record *this* stupid. Do you have any idea . . .?'

What could he say? I finished my account. Stated so baldly, sitting in a gray government car on a gray winter's day, it sounded pathetic, like the stories traded between cops and reporters in Foley's on a Friday night. The only detail I fudged was how I found the list of names. I told him I'd discovered it in the box of transcripts.

'These guys this morning, they didn't ask for the list?' he said.

'No.'

He nodded, chewing vigorously. 'So they must not know about it.'

'You think so?'

'If they knew about it, they would have asked, believe me. Where is it?'

'Jimmy, I'm scared.'

'Where's the list?'

'I have it with me. In my wallet. I'm worried about Gary and Lucy. I'm worried they'll tell Bobby.'

He shrugged. 'Do what they say and you got nothing to worry about.'

'I'm telling *you*! I've already *not* done what they said!'

His eyes slid in my direction with annoyance, lizard-like.

He never liked hysterics. I could see the tension in his neck and the pulse of blood beneath the tight skin of his temple. He wore a wrinkled Burberry over his suit, trying to look natty as his political aspirations grew, but he was still the funny-looking kid on the mat. Lean and wiry. Still wound tight. 'Take it easy, Harry. Think about this. You've done the right thing. You got that?'

'I know. I hope.'

'You have. In fact, you should've come to me a long time ago. The Lathrop Commission was set up for this kind of business, and you're not telling me anything we don't already know. We've had our suspicions about Bobby, and so have the Feds, but so far the only clear shot we've had is Bucky Quinn, and he's not giving away shit.'

'Mick told me I should go to the Feds.'

He sneered. 'With all due respect to the great Mick Malone, who seems to be dedicating his retirement years to drinking himself to death, the Feds are the *last* people you want to go to. They'd handle something like this with a sledgehammer.' He arched his pointed shoulders with clear disdain and went dark and silent. He took the Cambridge exit onto the turnpike, paid the toll, and drove west. Ahead, low clouds threatened storm. Now that my story was told, I wondered what I was looking for. Protection? Advice? A kick in the pants? Jimmy had the same studied look he had when lining up a putt.

'Your list is evidence,' he said, with a distant voice, as if trying to sound neutral. 'The kind that will help the commission. We can use it and no one will ever know where it came from.'

'What about Lucy?'

'If she knew about it, it wouldn't've been laying in a box of court documents.'

'It was in her possession.'

He waved away my concern. 'We won't involve her. I can promise you that.'

We drove silently, the highway hissing beneath our wheels, the steeples of Newton poking the gloom. The route out to Concord and Bobby. I felt a fresh tug of fear. 'This comes to light,' I said quietly, 'who's to say they won't go after Gary, or Ann? Or me?'

Snow now slanted from the squall ahead. Jimmy hit his lights and wipers with a little flare of his wrist. A guy at home with the mechanical detail of driving and the physical distraction it provided. Like his rituals on the golf course.

'Harry, they, whoever they are, won't find out. The commission is all sub rosa. If indictments come down, they will be on the basis of all the evidence amassed, not a single piece, and none of it will be public anyway. You have nothing to worry about as long as you keep your mouth shut and don't mention this to anyone else. And that includes me after you get out of this car. As far as you're concerned, that list *doesn't exist*. Do you understand?'

The wipers squeaked. He glanced across at me and continued, 'If there was danger, I would provide protection. You know that. But it would be foolish now. It would be like shouting you went running.'

'I did go running, didn't I?'

'You ran to the right place, Harry. Trust me. Too bad you didn't do it before you went to Pallotta.' He laid his right hand on my arm, eyes straight ahead.

My eyes misted with emotion and self-pity. The maudlin side of me Ann distrusted. And with good reason. It was the side that made it so tough for me when the big decisions came up. The blindness of heat and the impulse to run.

Jimmy exited at Watertown and looped back to the east-bound lane of the turnpike. The city was gray and distant, blurred by the weather. The snow whipped past, melting as soon as it hit the ground.

What was I going to do now?

'What about the book?' I said.

'What about it?'

'What's going to happen now? How am I going to continue?'

He lifted and resettled himself at the wheel. I always needed a little more leading than Jimmy thought should be given. 'You have to continue. Don't you understand? Everything has to go on like you never saw me. I mean, we're having this conversation because we have to, but once you're out of this car it's like it never happened, right? Life goes on.'

'What about Bobby?'

'Same as before. He's your author, right? I presume you have a contract.' I lifted a hand. 'Don't answer that,' he said. 'Look, we've talked too much already. You leave this to me.' He paused and cleared his throat. 'Do me a favor. We can't talk. But if you hear anything else, if Rizzoli says a word about any of this, call me. Tell me you're having trouble with Gary and we'll meet at the same spot. Otherwise, I don't want to hear. Not until the book is finished, I'm done with the commission, this is all over.'

His tone was severe, almost savage. 'OK,' I said.

We said no more until we were off the highway and back

downtown. The snow was like a shield over the city; heads were down. I felt safe again. 'Jimmy?'

'What?'

'Who do you think they are? The two goons.'

He shook his head and flicked a look out of the driver's-side window. We were nearly back at the Common. 'If I had to guess, I'd say low-level wiseguys who caught wind from Pallotta. Getting kickback maybe from corrupt chiefs, see you horning in and upsetting the apple cart. In which case, you have even less to worry about than I think. These guys are easily scared off. But I don't think it's going to come to that, not if you do what I say. And don't ask me to speculate. After today, we can't talk about this. For about twenty different reasons. You have to put your head down and ignore it ever happened.'

'What if they reappear?'

He double-parked near where he had picked me up. He glanced in the rear-view and vigorously rubbed his neck. 'If they come back,' he said, without looking at me, 'you can call. You can call.'

Now he looked worn, and I felt guilty for dragging him from court. He was one of the busiest guys in the city and I had him driving all over the suburbs solving my two-bit problems. 'Thanks, Jimmy.'

'Forget about it.'

'How's Elsa?'

Left hand draped over the wheel, he jiggled his right, a gesture I knew well. Nothing new there.

'Well, pal, thanks,' I said, and opened the door.

'Harry?'

'Yeah?'

'The list.'

'Oh, right.'

I took it from my wallet and handed it to him. As he took it, he turned his head and I caught his eyes, straight on. The eyes his adversaries looked into: close-set, tight in their sockets, hard and small and flecked. And, like the glassy surface of the city's newest skyscrapers, I saw reflected there the world at large, and the ambition Jimmy had to fill it with his presence. My ambition, I was reminded, as I had been so many times in our friendship, was no match for his intense yearning for so much. But I could accept the difference. He was looking after me. Let him ride the commission and the corruption and whatever he could squeeze out of my fear to the governorship if he wanted, I didn't care. He was looking out for me. I owed him.

16

The two goons turned my life upside-down. Everything I'd hoped for was now unimportant. Everything I'd shunned was a priority. After my ride with Jimmy, I went back to the office parking lot and fetched my car. But I didn't dare go home. I drove around the city in thickening snow, stopping at pay-phones from time to time to call Gary and Lucy. Neither was answering. I did not risk leaving messages. Had Gary taken my advice and gone to Ann's, or was he screening calls? Whatever the case, I didn't worry. Jimmy had reassured me. Jimmy I could trust. But a long night lay ahead. I spent an hour cruising the snowbound streets, listening to the wail of sirens in the distance.

I ended up in an Irish tavern on Canal Street. The place was packed with office workers and civil servants from the federal buildings. Friday night, ten days before Christmas, it was party time: the air was full of toasts and high spirits. I wedged up to the bar, hoping to remain unrecognized, and ordered consecutive doubles. A professional basketball game was on the soundless television, and I watched the lithe, silent players descend on the basket in swooping strides, jamming the ball home and prancing back up the court with faces fierce and noble. I thought back to my locker-room encounter with Michael Cooper, which I knew now would lead to nothing. I had been playing celebrity bingo while pushing aside Gary, whom I'd invited to the game, who for once had admitted he needed my attention. And I had let him down.

I'll go to the kid's place for Christmas, I promised myself. I'll get him and Sarah a nice gift, I'll stay off the sauce, I'll do right by him. With blurred but intense logic, I concluded that nothing would happen to him tonight. I had done nothing, so no harm would befall him. So Jimmy had promised.

Drinking was all that was left to me, and drink I did until closing time. The bartender took my car keys and called a cab. When I got home I fell asleep on the sofa in my clothes.

I woke to light so bright it hurt my eyes. It was nine o'clock. I lurched to the kitchen and poured a glass of water. My apartment was in a new development on the site of the old naval yard. The sun lit up the scrubbed boardwalks, and its rays glinted off snow-capped bollards, painted bright green to match the paint scheme and sculpted junipers of the development. These units had been built in a nautical style, with high ceilings, skylights, and big bay windows to catch the salty light of the harbor. Beyond lay the cold ocean and the city skyline, placid and glittering from this southern vantage.

Events of the previous day came to me as I finished a second glass of water. Again I called Gary. Not even the machine this time, just the monotonous drill of unanswered rings. Again Lucy, and again the machine. I listened closely to her singsong message. This time I ignored my certainty that the phone was bugged and spoke after the tone. 'It's Harry, Lucy. Please call me. I'm at home. Please.'

I turned and faced the light-filled apartment, soundless now except for the ticking of the kitchen clock. Outside, my beloved skyline stood in Saturday uselessness, sheared by winter winds and the lost dreams of a city long changed from what I'd hoped would endure. For me and for it. Empty offices high in a colorless sky. And me below in a still life of indecision.

I showered with the bathroom door open, in case Lucy returned my call. My mind empty and despairing, it turned against my will to images of Tan and Blue, their pocked faces and tight coats. What could they do now? Much, of course, to me and others, and as I toweled down I checked the apartment, looking self-consciously for evidence of surveillance.

The phone screamed. Still naked, I answered.

'Harry!'

It was Frankie Deluca. No mistaking that nasal bark. My spirits drifted to the floor. 'What do you want, Frankie?'

'You didn't hear?'

'Didn't hear what?'

There was a long pause. I could hear him breathing heavily and easily imagined his round-shouldered, intense form over the receiver, the handkerchief clutched in his paw.

'Bobby Rizzoli was killed.'

Hearing this news was like being in a car crash: time slowed, my body locked, part of me was outside myself, looking on. Images flooded my mind, fleeting but vivid as a dream: Mr Tan instructing his corrupt prison-guard contacts to put a hit on the only person in the world who could scrape me from the bottom; me holding Lucy, clutching her close while television cameras looked on; *60 Minutes* doing the definitive follow-up, the focus on the Donohue Press connection; me in the dock, taking the Fifth. There was no denying it – the thoughts that arose unbidden at that moment all had to do with me, full of details to do with my fears and desires. But words, plain words in response to Frankie's news, I couldn't come up with.

'Harry, this isn't even public yet. My cousin Lou, he works for Western Regional Hospital, and he was there when the body came in from the prison at, like, the early hours. Pronounced dead in the ambulance. He knows my connection in this regard and just called me. He's putting his job on the line on this, so you gotta keep in mind—'

'Frankie, slow down! Rizzoli, what . . . he was murdered?'

'I don't know. Knife wounds or shiv wounds, whatever.'

'Shiv wounds? Was he shanked?'

'Harry, we gotta be asking, how much of the book has Jeff finished?'

'*Frankie – was it a fight or a hit?*'

I had carried the phone to the window and looked down at the wooden walkways and iron railings bordering the opaque water. Water that reflected nothing. My stomach fluttered, my head was light, and I could taste my own fear, dry and mustardy at the back of my throat. An old guy in a headband and MIT sweatshirt jogged past, but otherwise no one was in sight. The development was set out so that no apartment overlooked another, but I still felt watched. I moved back from the glass.

'I don't know,' Frankie said. 'Lou just called, and what do you think? I get right on to you. What I know is what I told you. Naturally, you're the first person I think to call.'

'Listen to me, Frankie.'

'I can't believe this. This is, like, so big.'

'Frankie, *listen to me*! Don't tell anyone else. Just sit on this until it breaks in the news, and if anyone asks, you haven't talked to me.' As I said this, it occurred to me how stupid these instructions would sound over a wired phone. 'You understand?'

'Harry, take it easy. I understand.'

'I have to go,' I said. 'I'll see you in the morning.'

Lucy. Poor Lucy. Did she even know? She would have to, they would contact a wife at once. I had to go to her. She would need me. But I couldn't move. I had reached that supreme level of urgency where action seems fruitless. I looked around at the apartment, my sterile single man's apartment, and moaned. 'Now what?' I said aloud. 'Now what?'

I ran downstairs. Then it hit me. What if Frankie's cousin was wrong? Or what if good old Lou was playing a joke on his gullible cousin? What if Frankie dreamed the whole thing up? No, even he wouldn't do that. But who knew what was true? I turned on the television and flicked through the channels. No news. I called the *Globe*; if they knew anything they weren't saying. Then I called Western Regional, posing as a reporter from Channel 7. I finally got through to a tired doctor with a patrician accent.

'We did have a DOA from Concord this morning,' she said after much pestering. 'I will tell you that. But details are being withheld pending notification of next of kin.'

'Was it an accident or a killing?'

'Mr . . .?'

'Lewisham.'

'Mr Lewisham, I am a physician, not a detective.'

'Were the wounds consistent with a stabbing?'

'I don't recall saying there were wounds.'

'So there weren't?'

'Mr Lewisham, please. I am not authorized to release any information. Have your station go through the usual channels. Good day.'

Lewisham, I thought. Where did I come up with that one? So it looked like it was true. And Lucy still might not know. They were probably calling her and getting the answering machine, just like me. Did they send someone around? A priest? And I couldn't risk phoning her. What if she answered? What would I say? Though I should have waited for confirmation, I couldn't stay in the apartment any longer. I left the apartment and headed for Hillbrook.

Out on the highway, my chest thumped so hard I imagined having a heart attack and careening down the fellsway slopes to a fiery death. One way of making the six o'clock news. Would they lead with me or Bobby? Bobby, of course. '*And in a bizarre and possibly related incident, Rizzoli's publisher, Harry Donohue . . .*' My thoughts might have been flippant, but, at that moment, I felt the presence of death as never before. Stories of Joey Latrelli taking a shotgun blast at point-blank range, of Benny Vogel's eyeless body washing up on Revere Beach, of Brother O'Brien wasting a small-time coke dealer with a tire iron were just that – *stories*. Verifiable they were, on the record, the worst actions of despicable men, but they had been transformed by voyeurism and casual discourse into barroom chatter and tabloid fodder. By me as much as anyone. Until Mr Blue came along and crushed his cigarette on my son's image; until Bobby was (who knew?) cornered in his cell and executed summarily; until I found myself close to the moment when I had to confront the dead man's wife, my lover, wondering what I would say, what she would say, what we two would do in the face of a reality I'd taken so lightly and to which I was so closely connected.

Someone had killed Bobby while I lay drunk on the sofa. He was in solitary for his own protection. If he was shanked, who could've done it except a guard? Or an inmate who had stolen the keys. Or an inmate who'd been *given* the keys. But the man who shoved the knife in, I reasoned, was likely nothing but the last, lowest link in a chain. Someone had to have ordered this. A Mafia *capo* with a stake in the network of crooked chiefs Bobby had engineered? The same guy who sent Blue and Tan my direction? Had my blabbing about the list been Bobby's death sentence? And was I rushing now to the last place in Boston I should be, both for my sake and for Lucy's?

I didn't try to answer these questions. I didn't really ask them. I wheeled into Saturday-morning Hillbrook as if onto a movie set. The streets were sleepy. The bare trees clutched at the pale sky, and the winter sun cast long shadows. Sleigh-riding Santas and faded reindeer were screwed at odd angles to the housetops, and new snow softened the hard edges of muscle cars and metal awnings and chain-link fences. I pulled up in front of Lucy's house in a cold sweat. Bobby Junior's Camaro was not in sight, but Lucy's Caddy was out front, one wheel up on the curb. I turned off the engine and discovered I needed a drink. Though whisky-breathed was hardly the way to approach Lucy on this day, I finished the glove-compartment pint.

The front door was ajar. A thin wreath circled the knocker, and a string of dusty lights framed the hall window. I pressed the buzzer, heard nothing, then knocked lightly. The door nudged open another couple inches and I stepped inside. Standing on a white shag rug in the split-level hallway, I peered over the half-flight of stairs leading up to the living room and kitchen. The gun-and-weight-room door on my right was closed (*friends in my basement*). There was a dangerous peace to the place.

'Is that you, Bobby?' It was Lucy's voice, a weak, quivering, middle-of-the-night voice.

As soon as I heard it I knew the news was true, and that she knew. I mounted the stairs just as she appeared from the back hallway, haggard and disheveled in her blue bathrobe. I paused mid-flight. 'It's me,' I said.

She shook her head, as if contradicting my presence.

'I heard,' I said.

'Heard what?' She was listing, off-center, one arm hanging in an odd way, the other hand stuck in her bathrobe pocket. Her face had shadows I hadn't seen before, and her body looked bloated.

'About Bobby,' I said. 'Bobby Senior.' There could be no doubt she had heard, but the look she flashed was tired and puzzled.

I climbed the last couple steps, and she lifted a hand like a traffic cop. 'Don't even think . . .'

I stopped and put my own hands out, half suggesting contact, half showing I was keeping my distance. She swayed, as if being pulled down on one side. All the confusion of the ride over seemed to gather in me and surge in my throat as pity and affection. I wanted to hold her, but her eyes kept me away. 'Lucy. Lucy, I want to help.'

'Help? *Help?* Get away from me!'

She stumbled into the kitchen and I dared follow. There was a small artificial tree on the kitchen counter, bedecked with thick tinsel and white bulbs. It looked too green in the hot, stale air. The Lone Star flag was gone. Breakfast things littered the table, half-eaten bowls of cereal, as if the news had interrupted the meal. One chair was knocked over, asking to be picked up, and a coffee-stained Sunday *Herald* draped over another. Where was Bobby Junior? Why would he leave her like this? She leaned on the counter with one hand, her back to me. I approached slowly and ventured a touch to her arm. She spun on me and pushed me away. Her jaw was crooked with grief and her hair was brittle and tangled.

'What happened?' I whispered.

Again she shook her head, then jerked her hand from her pocket. At first I thought she held a kitchen utensil, but it was the nickel-plated .38 she raised and pointed at my chest.

'Lucy,' I said, backing up. The gun was shaking wildly; her trigger finger, I knew, was tense. My mouth went dry. As I back-pedaled, I hit the overturned chair and fell on my elbow. Pain seared through my shoulder and Lucy was shouting. There was a huge ringing in my ears and I thought she had shot me. I lay clutching my arm but keeping an eye on her. I saw she hadn't fired. Her face was puffy and red, her mouth jagged. She stood over me and aimed the gun at my heart.

'*That*'s what happened. You came along and screwed everything up. *You!* He was all I had, and *now look what you've done!*'

'Please put down the gun.'

'I'm going to kill you like you killed him. I'm going to end up where I shoulda been all along, and I'll be happy there because you'll be dead and all this shit will be over!'

I kicked her feet apart and she fell back against the chair, grabbing at the tabletop and sending milk and cereal flying. I scrambled to my feet and moved to restrain her, but she was up as quickly as me and had the gun leveled. Her bathrobe was open and I could see her breasts and stomach. They looked heavy and pale, pulling her down like everything else. 'Why?' she sobbed. 'Why did you have to show up?'

I averted my head. I was in such pain I couldn't lift my arm. Two shots rang out in quick succession accompanied by the shattering of glass. The bangs were enormous and split my ears. The smell of cordite was dense and choking, and when I looked up Lucy was lying across the table, still sobbing, the gun sitting in a shattered bowl.

I heard a shout behind me and Bobby Junior came running up the stairs. He went to his mother and lifted her off the table, adjusting her bathrobe and glancing back at me with a cop's neutral look of concern. The sliding doors to the deck were a jigsaw of broken glass, and cold air flooded the rooms. An upright shard leaned out from the frame and fell to the deck, startling me again. Bobby had his arm around his mother and was peering into her crushed face. He was dressed in a loose sweatshirt and jeans, but I could see his musculature beneath the cotton, more impressive even than his father's.

'Bobby, all I want to do is help here.'

The pain in my elbow was terrible, but it was nothing to the feeling I had in my stomach. For the first time since Frankie's phone call, I saw what had happened, how *real* it was, how isolated it would leave me.

'Mr Donohue, I think it would be a good idea if you left.' His voice was soft but firm. Lucy had laid her head on her son's shoulder and was moaning, a low, deep moan that came from somewhere long ago, long before I had anything to do with her or her husband, and filled the draughty room like a siren. It was like the ghost of bad news, and it terrified me.

'I'll call a doctor,' I said. 'Let's get her some help.'

Bobby reached out and grabbed my coat lapels with his left hand. With great strength and control he pulled me closer, keeping his body between me and his mother. I could smell his mouthwash and see the suffering in his eyes. My elbow was in such pain I wanted to cry. Lucy's moan had spiraled louder and higher.

'Mr Donohue, you gotta get out of here. *Now!*'

He thrust me back. Cradling my injured arm, I backed away and left the house. I got into my car and closed the door. I couldn't move. Slumped over the wheel I felt the bright sun and the eyes of Hillbrook on the back of my neck. Even with the car door closed, I could hear Lucy's keen filling the pale sky.

17

Bobby was buried in Redstone Cemetery four days before Christmas, the shortest day of the year. The funeral, I learned from the page-three *Herald* obituary, was at St Dominick's in Hillbrook. When Gary dropped me off, I recognized its spire as the one I'd seen poking through the pines when I parked at the Boston Edison sub-station and took my backwoods walk to Lucy's. It was windy and warm, and a four-inch snowfall from the previous day had turned to slush. I wasn't early, but there were very few cars in the church parking lot. Gary helped me out of his Malibu and headed off for breakfast. He'd return for me, he promised, but there was no way he was coming inside.

At the church door, an old priest in alb and stole sniped at two young ushers before glancing at the parking lot with a puckered face. He rubbed his hands and retreated inside.

Churches at Italian funerals, even a big stone neo-Gothic like St Dominick's, were supposed to be overflowing. Tribal celebrations. Cops and gangsters usually got the biggest turnouts, but as a denizen of both worlds, Bobby probably scared away the usual guests. I steadied myself on the sidewalk and looked up the street. My arm was in a full cast and strapped to my body. The fall at Lucy's had broken my elbow, a clean but awkward break that still hurt so much I was on painkillers. There was no sign of the cortège. I could hear the expressway traffic beyond the trees, tires whipping through the melting snow with a sound like bacon frying. I stepped gingerly up the stone steps, entered blinking into the gloom, and took a seat at the rear of the nave.

The body language of the people filing into St Dominick's betrayed their confusion. They looked around as if in a church for the first time and walked hesitantly up the aisle, wondering where to sit, fingers grazing the flower-decorated pew ends. They were older couples for the most part, friends and relatives of the Rizzoli family, no doubt, who squinted through thick-lensed glasses and dressed in dark, old-fashioned suits and dresses. They didn't like being here, that was obvious, but you could see that, for them, a funeral was an obligation. No Jake Cleary that I could see. No cops in uniform. Nobody from the mayor's office or VFW. Just these older folks, close enough to death themselves not to worry about being seen at the funeral of a murdered felon. The core of the Hillbrook tribe. But you could see their hesitation as they paused and held trembling hands to their chins. Those already seated were whispering and shaking their heads. Murder was on the minds of the congregation, and you could feel it like a chill emanating from the stone flags and granite pillars.

Murder was on everyone's mind, especially mine. Since Monday I'd been holed-up in Gary's flat. He had taken me in without hesitation, fixing me a bed in his living room, helping me dress and use the toilet, staying beside me as he ran three construction jobs from his apartment phone. Sarah had gone to Saginaw for Christmas. Gary cooked BLTs and hamburgers, which I ate one-handed and washed down with glasses of warm milk. No alcohol. No contact with the outside world. I didn't even watch the news reports, though Gary heard my name mentioned on several occasions. By Tuesday the news of my whereabouts had leaked and the phone started ringing. Friends and relations. The papers, television stations, *60 Minutes*. Jack Wambaugh left three increasingly intriguing messages, all designed to appeal to my ego. I wouldn't talk to anybody except Moe and even refused to see him until after Bobby was buried. A couple of reporters camped at the front door, and Gary and I had to sneak out the back way to go to the funeral of a man whose killing I just might have had something to do with.

The church was less than half full when Lucy arrived. The coffin nosed in first, not carried but wheeled on a stainless steel cart by the funeral director, a stooping old man with wire-rimmed glasses, cuffs to his knuckles, and a dusting of dandruff on the shoulders of his black suit. Lucy followed immediately. I wasn't prepared for what I saw. Flanked by Bobby Junior and a guy with a double chin and thick neck, she faltered up the aisle in sunglasses, hat and dotted veil, and a long black fur-trimmed coat. I sat at the aisle end of the pew, so was close enough to see the badly applied make-up and red blotches mottling her neck and face. My elbow throbbed and my throat tightened. I wanted to reach out and touch the hem of her coat. I willed her to look my way. But she didn't. She moved slowly, stiff and weak-kneed, gripped firmly at the elbows by her companions. If I could only hold her now, at this moment of greatest encumbrance. Not in ecstasy but in consolation. This was my need. If I could only make things right. But I would never, at the elbows or anywhere else, touch her again. Worse still, I would never be allowed to explain what it was I hadn't done and never intended to do.

Among the telephone messages Gary had taken while I lay on the couch was a terse sentence from a guy who didn't leave his name. *'Tell that asshole, tell him, if he goes near Lynch Road again I'll fuckin' kill him.'* It was several hours before Gary could bring himself to pass the message on, and, when he did, I saw he was shaken. After the news about Bobby and a close look down the barrel of my former lover's .38, however, it didn't make much of an impression. Hell, it made sense. Look what I had done. When I asked Gary to bring me to the funeral, he tried to talk me out of it. But how could I not go? Gary couldn't understand because he didn't know the whole story. Nobody knew, except maybe those who killed Bobby. And if they could get him in solitary they could easily get me in Gary's apartment, or St Dominick's Church, or anywhere else. 'You've got connections,' he told me that morning. 'Call Jimmy O'Leary. Get some protection. Have them trace these calls.' He was scared himself. But what was I to do? I was at the end of the line. I had finally gone too far. There was nothing left except the funeral.

During the service, two red-faced guys slipped into the pew across the aisle. Reporters, I could tell at once. One kept glancing my way, so I left early and went looking for Gary. To tell the truth I was eager to get out of there. Seeing Lucy like that was too much. Gary's car was parked in front of a coffee shop across the street, behind a black Crown Victoria. I crossed the street, and as I approached I saw a telephoto lens sticking out of the passenger-side window of the Ford. It was quickly withdrawn. Gary came out of the coffee shop, wiping his mouth with a paper napkin, and opened the door for me. I got in carefully, but something kept me staring at the other car. 'Who's that?' he asked.

'Government vehicle.'

'Where we going?'

I recognized Steven Gurlick sitting in the back seat. He wore sunglasses and was hunched over, trying to appear nondescript. But it was him all right.

'Whaddaya know?' I said. I leaned across and pressed Gary's horn for several seconds. The blast echoed down the street.

'What are you doing?'

'Feds,' I said. 'Fucking Feds.'

I hit the horn again. The photographer was peering back at me and Gurlick was leaning forward, speaking to him. I leaned out the window. 'Hey, Gurlick! Get a shot of me. Go on!'

'Dad! Dad! What's going on?'

'Take off your sunglasses, you prick. Let everybody see who you are!' I kept my hand on the horn. Mourners were spilling from the church and staring across at us.

Gary pulled my hand from the steering wheel and squealed away from the curb. 'Are you *nuts*? What did you do that for?'

'Sons-of-bitches,' I said, trying to look back, restricted by the cast. 'Taking pictures at a man's funeral. At a man's *funeral!*'

'Calm down, Dad. I'll take you downtown.'

Though I was late for an appointment with Moe, I couldn't

leave Lucy yet. 'We're not going downtown. I want to go to the cemetery.'

'No way.'

I gripped his arm fiercely. 'We're going,' I hissed.

We waited at the cemetery entrance for the cortège to arrive. Gary kept the engine running and the heater on, even though it wasn't that cold. But my teeth were chattering. I kept looking for Gurlick. I would kill him if he showed. I would batter him with a tire iron. Gary and I said nothing for several minutes.

'How's the elbow?' he finally said.

'OK.'

'What was it like in there?'

I shrugged. 'Empty. People aren't interested in a loser.'

'I heard it was a hit.'

Over and over I had imagined, against my will, those final moments of Bobby's life in a dark cell. 'What else? A squabble over laundry duty?'

'A Mob hit. On account of they had so much money in the bank.'

Gary was testing me. He thought I knew something and was curious. 'So why would they wait five years to hit him?'

'I thought you might have an inkling.'

I looked at him for a long second then returned my gaze to the slushy grounds and gray headstones. 'Gary, I remember when Jimmy and I were in law school and our criminal law professor took us to our first real trial. The McNeely brothers' murder trial at the federal courthouse on Congress Street. Two brothers from Hyde Park who'd killed a black sanitation worker because he dropped a garbage can near their Cadillac and splattered their white walls. Then he wouldn't clean it up after they called him 'boy'. The professor wanted us there because it was a landmark race-relations case. The defense team was all Irish, but so was the prosecutor. Hotshot kid down from Washington. Climate at the time being what it was, Bobby Kennedy told him personally to make this stick and stick good, even though the only witness was an old drunk and the black guy had a knife on him. What black wouldn't have in that neighborhood? I don't care if it was ten in the morning.

'Anyway, we went every day for a week and, on our way in each morning, we were supposed to hand in a two-page précis of the previous day's testimony and what it meant to the trial. The principles of sound jurisprudence. *Lex loci* versus *lex terrae*. Other stuff we were studying. I didn't turn any in. Not one all week. Couldn't write them, and nearly failed the course because of it. Every night, when I sat at my desk and tried to recall the proceedings, all I saw was the face of the murdered guy's wife. She sat right across from us, identical seat every day, a very elegant woman who wore the same dark suit to every session but was always clean and fresh-looking. Her hair straightened in the way black women wore it back then. Hands always crossed in her lap. I could see her wedding band. Sitting upright, staring at the judge, this look of total determination on her face. Looking for justice. Looking to be proved wrong for once in her life. For once! When I sat down to write, all I could see on that paper was her face, that look on her face, and I couldn't think. Jimmy, he wrote them up like they were love letters, so good the professor would read them out in class, looking up at me the whole time, the sentimental dunce. But I couldn't get past that face.'

I was crying. 'She loved him, Gary. Maybe she pretended she didn't, but she loved him and he was all she had left. And I come along and use him and I use her, all because of what I want for myself.'

'How were you using them?' He thought I was still back in 1962.

'Always my problem,' I said. 'I get this vision of what could be, what I can achieve, and everything else gets clouded over. I did it with Ann. With Judy. I did it with you.'

'Dad, it's OK. Take it easy.'

He put his hand on my arm. I wiped my eyes. 'I was part of this,' I said, gesturing vaguely at the headstones. 'Part of it all and didn't do a damn thing to stop it.'

'What could you have done? What?'

'Could have been more like Jimmy. More detached. Less railroaded by my own ambition. Ambition and sentiment. And I always thought *Jimmy* was the ambitious one. But if I could've been like him all this never would've happened. She'll hate me for ever now. Like she loved him.'

Gary stared, puzzled. When the cortège arrived we followed it in. I got out and watched the burial standing beside the car. I thought of going graveside, decided against it. I kept an eye out for Gurlick, but he didn't show. Not even he would be that brazen. But I was here, wasn't I? Was I mourning? If so, for what? I could hear the drone of the priest and see the black backs of those at the grave. Only a dozen or so. Lucy slumped between the two men.

They were out there for ages. Lucy bent to throw dirt on the coffin then collapsed into Bobby Junior's arms. An old newspaper cartwheeled in the wind and the gulls shrieked. Always gulls in Boston, wherever you went, always there to comment. The priest closed his missal and consoled Lucy. From this distance, the scene was like theater. I was crying again. As they approached the cars, Gary suggested I get in. But I stayed where I was, waiting for Lucy. I had to see her and speak to her. I couldn't let it end like that. I called her name. She looked up, but I couldn't see her face because Bobby Junior leaned between us and steered his mother away from me. I took a step in their direction. The second man left her side and confronted me. I saw now it was Mike, the guy in her house with the scally cap and rumpled raincoat. The guy who called her *babe*.

'I just wanted . . . I wanted to express . . .'

'No way, pal.' He was a big man with oily hair, deep creases at the corners of his mouth, and eyes like an eagle's. He stood like a fighter, just out of my reach, weight on the balls of his feet, hands out from his body. A mouth familiar with disdain. Not a guy to mess with.

'Maybe you think she doesn't, but I have to talk to her.' I went to step around him, but he cut me off. He was breathing heavily, steeling himself for whatever action was necessary.

'Listen, bud,' he said very quietly, 'don't make me break your other arm.'

'The name's Harry.'

'The name is shit as far as I'm concerned, and you can take it from me that Lucy feels the same.'

He had a hand on my good arm, ready to twist it and send me flying. Gary opened his door and stepped out of the car. It was a bad moment, a moment with little of the rational in it. But seeing Gary pop up and become part of the danger, I knew what to do. I could back down from a fight, especially one I was guaranteed to lose. I stepped away. 'Tell her I'm sorry,' I said, my breath catching in my throat. 'Please.'

He stared at me. I moved back to the car and got inside. Gary was still standing, sizing up Mike.

'Gary,' I shouted. 'Let's go.'

That was the last time I saw Lucy.

On our way into the city, neither of us spoke. I didn't know what was on Gary's mind, but against my better judgment I was reviewing my afternoons and nights with Lucy, thirteen altogether, each of which I could recall with at least one memorable detail. Invariably physical. Her shoulder in the afternoon light. The way she lit a cigarette in bed, propped on an elbow. The touch of her hand on the small of my back. The lightness of her step when naked. The last thing I should have been contemplating, but I couldn't help myself. I was exhausted, tense, and hollow.

Gary left me at City Hall Plaza, and I walked down Court Street to Moe's office. Groups of government and office workers were heading off to lunch, and there was a Christmas party buzz in the air. My elbow was sore and my head was aching, so I swallowed a couple of painkillers at the lobby water fountain in Moe's building. In the elevator I looked at my trussed, rumpled reflection and tried to focus on the business at hand. She was gone. As sure as Bobby was. It was time to leave self-pity aside and consider my legal situation. Three days of couch-bound introspection had not helped my position. No doubt the cops wanted to talk to me. Not to mention the Feds. Gurlick had my photo and was speculating at that very moment about the cast. I would be subpoenaed, at the minimum, and Moe needed as much help as he could get to prepare. This time I was ready to listen to him. This time I was ready to do the right thing.

When I walked into his office, Judy was sitting in one of the big leather chairs, an arm thrown over one of the wings, her frizzed hair shining in the light of the big windows. I hadn't seen or spoken to her since the night with Jack Wambaugh at the Marriott Long Wharf, and I had not expected to run into her here. I tensed as she stood and faced me.

'Harry.'

'Hey, sis.'

She embraced me carefully. I clutched her with my good arm.

'What happened here?' she said, pointing at the cast.

I shook my head. 'The least of my troubles.'

'Gary tell you I called?'

'Yeah. I wasn't talking to anybody.'

Moe was leaning against his desk. 'Not a bad strategy under the circumstances,' he said.

I looked closely into Judy's face. She looked healthy and rested. There was a softness around her eyes I hadn't seen in a long time, and an ease in her posture. Her hands, thin, liver-spotted, decorated with several rings, rested elegantly at her sides, ready to wave away a problem or caress a point of casual discussion. Her eyes were bright with sympathy; whatever reason she was here, she was offering a sign of peace. But I knew she could cut this ease dead in an instant.

'This about the injunction?'

She took my measure. 'No,' she said, 'it isn't. I came here

for other reasons. I didn't know you were going to be here until five minutes ago.'

'That's true,' Moe said. 'And we don't have to talk about anything today you're not prepared to.'

He looked at me with those tactful dark eyes, and I could see he was telling the truth. 'That right, Judy?'

'Oh, c'mon, Harry. I never wanted it to come to this anyway.'

I sat in the free chair. From the corner windows I could see the Tobin Bridge, Charlestown, the Bunker Hill Monument, and the blue expanse of the winter bay. The silent gulls and flowing air currents at thirty storeys. I was still off the sauce but, after the funeral and cemetery, I was light-headed and a little muddled, as if I'd bolted a couple small ones after a hard day.

'Moe,' I said, 'any chance of a cup of coffee?'

'Of course, Harry.' He left the room.

'Send Milt in on Friday,' I said. 'I'll tell Peggy to get everything ready.'

She waved away the request. 'All that will wait until the new year, Harry. You have other concerns right now.' She looked at me closely with her pale, intelligent face.

'I just came from Bobby Rizzoli's funeral.'

'That couldn't have been easy.'

'No.'

Below us, ugly and colorless, was Government Center, a mass of concrete where the high life of Scollay Square used to be. Memory traveled back, past Lucy's body and Bobby's face, to less ambiguous times. 'Do you remember the day they buried Uncle Julius?'

'Sure,' Judy said. 'Driving down to Woonsocket in that snowstorm. Mom crying the whole way.'

'And Dad reminiscing. Mom asking him ten times to be quiet, but Dad talking about Julius the whole way, how they fell through the ice on the Charles River and had to be rescued by the fire department, the time Julius fell asleep in a whorehouse in Providence and woke up in the middle of a raid, the two of them crap-shooting with sailors on the wharf and winning a thousand bucks.' Judy was laughing as I spoke. 'All the things Dad had told me not to do, and here he was, describing himself and Julius doing them while the windshield wipers squeaked and Mom cried into her linen handkerchief.'

Judy was smiling and shaking her head. 'Harry, these memories. *You* should write a book.'

'I think I'm through with the book business for the time being.'

Moe returned and handed me my coffee. 'What you need to do,' he said to me, 'is take a step back. Don't rush into any decisions. Deal with what needs to be dealt with, enjoy the holidays, and let your arm heal. One step at a time.'

'I gotta figure there's a few agencies out there want to talk to me.'

Judy pointed to the door and raised her eyebrows. I shook my head. I didn't mind her being here. I could use another legal mind.

'Yeah,' Moe said. 'So they'll get their depositions. I'll be with you. I'll tell you what to say. He was an associate; this has been a big shock for you, personally and professionally. You need to be afforded space and consideration.'

I sipped my coffee. I felt guilty. I felt like confessing all, related to the case or not. 'What if I'm a suspect?'

Judy stiffened, but Moe smiled. He wasn't easily shocked. 'I think it would be easy enough to establish you weren't at MCI Concord on that Friday night. But we'll cross that particular bridge when we come to it.'

'What *did* happen?' Judy asked.

Moe moved to his high-backed orthopedic chair and picked up his autographed baseball. 'I talked to Jimmy O'Leary this morning. They've got a guard who's testified that Rizzoli and another prisoner had mixed it up in the yard that day, and the guy is now in custody.'

'I thought he was killed during the night,' I said.

Moe shook his head. 'Early morning. A second guard saw Rizzoli and this same guy heading back toward Rizzoli's cell. A typical prison drama. You don't think this kind of stuff doesn't happen all the time? Buddy of mine lives in Walpole, says he hears the ambulances going in and out two three times a week. These are savage places. But we never hear about it. Bobby is news because of his history, corrupt cop and so on.'

'I hear I'm news too.'

'Nothing substantive. Channel 7 mentioned the book deal. Maybe one other item since Sunday.'

'You can't tell me this wasn't a hit, Moe.'

'I'm not telling you anything. This is straight from the horse's mouth.'

'Someone took him out.'

'Harry, it was two guys fighting over an insult in the yard, some minor point of honor. It's unfortunate for everyone concerned, but it is what it is.'

'You've been hanging around Bobby Rizzoli too long,' Judy said.

'I won't be hanging around him any more.'

'When did you see him last?' Moe asked.

I didn't have to think about that one – I had replayed the visit in my mind over and over during the last three days. 'A week ago. The fourteenth.'

'That's deposition material, all right. But leave that to me.' Judy stood. 'You guys have stuff to talk about.'

'How's Mom?' I asked her. I didn't want her to leave.

'I met with Dr Larson yesterday.'

'Abe Larson?' Moe said. 'From Newton? He's Jewish.'

'For us, Moe, only Jewish doctors,' she said, with a grin. 'Doctors and accountants. Lawyers, on the other hand, we only go Irish, so don't ask me how Harry ended up with you. Maybe that's why things haven't gone so well for him lately.'

'Yeah, yeah.'

'So what did the doc say?' I asked.

She widened her eyes and bobbed her head, mouth down-turned. 'Improvement. Definite improvement. They do these memory exercises, short-term memory exercises, and it has really helped her awareness.'

'I gotta get out to see her.'

'He's revising his opinion. Says it may not be Alzheimer's after all.'

'How old is she now?' Moe asked.

'Eighty, eighty-one,' I said. 'Nobody really knows for sure. *She* doesn't know. Fudged so often she confused herself, and there's no birth certificate.'

'I wrote to Cavan for her baptismal cert,' Judy said.

'She arrived in Boston in 1923. Roomed in Chelsea with a Jewish family. Did I ever tell you that, Moe? That says something about her. Judy thinks the son – who, Hymie? – asked her to marry him.'

'He did. She told me.'

'Stranger things have happened,' Moe said.

Another moment of quiet, and I saw then that Moe and Judy had been nursing me through the meeting. And what I must've looked like, coming into Moe's office in the bulky cast, wrinkled raincoat, with the look of despair brought on by thoughts of those thirteen trysts and Bobby's final dark moments. Judy patted my shoulder. 'Call me, Harry.'

Moe helped her into her coat.

'Judy?' I said.

She turned. 'Yeah?'

'I want to straighten things out at the shop. Come clean.'

'We'll work something out,' she said, pulling on her gloves. 'Find an investor, maybe a buyer. Who knows? But I will need your help on this. You know that.'

Oh, my sis. Tactful as she could be tough, when she wished. Tall and imposing in her gray wool coat and leather gloves, she furrowed her brow. 'What are you doing for Christmas?'

'I was thinking maybe Moe would invite me over.'

'Sure. You can light the Hanukkah candles.'

'Why don't you come to my place?' Judy said.

'Thanks, Judy, but I'm spending it with Gary.'

'His new place?'

'Yeah.'

I got up, and Moe and I walked her to the door.

'Moe,' she said, 'we'll talk. Look after my brother.' She

stopped at the door, leaned, and pecked me on the cheek. 'I'm sorry about Rizzoli, Harry. It's a tragedy for his family, and I know it's not good news for you either. It would've been a good book.'

'The book doesn't matter.' I said. 'Would have been something to pull off, though. And thanks to you, I nearly did.'

'Thanks to me?'

I turned to Moe. 'Judy figured out how the contract should work. Have Lucy Rizzoli set up an S corporation in Delaware. Now she'll probably sue me. Her and everyone else in the city of Boston.'

Judy's head was tilted. She lifted a gloved finger. 'I didn't suggest that.'

'Sure you did. That night at Eddie's.'

'No. I know I told you, but it was Jimmy's idea.'

'Jimmy? Jimmy O'Leary?'

'Yeah.'

'How come you didn't tell me?'

'He told me not to. Said it would be a conflict of interest to get involved. But he had it all worked out.' She looked at her watch. 'Oh, I'm late. See you, boys.'

Moe closed the door behind her. The room darkened as the sun retreated behind a cloud. 'C'mon, pal,' Moe said. 'We got work to do.'

18

On Christmas Day Gary cooked lasagne and garlic bread, but I wasn't complaining. I could only eat with one hand anyway. And the kid continued to surprise me – the food was good. He bustled around the kitchen in an apron, slicing tomatoes and stirring pots, while I listened to classical music and watched two guys across the street digging a car out of the snow. Ann and Judy called. I spoke to my mother. Eddie sent over a bottle of brandy, which I could tell from the wrapping was a recycled gift from one of his suppliers. I allowed myself a snifter after dinner, and Gary contributed a pair of Cuban cigars he'd got from a buddy who worked Customs at Logan. Not a bad holiday meal. Not bad at all.

We exchanged presents as we smoked. I gave him a gift voucher for Jordan Marsh and a framed photograph of the two of us taken when he was in high school. It was one of the few pictures from that time where he looked comfortable with me. He stood slouched in his football uniform, long hair tousled, face streaked with dirt, helmet held at his side by the mouthguard. I had my arm stretched around his massive, arched shoulder pads. There was more pride on my face than

I would permit myself these days, but that was OK. If I could go easy on him, I could go easy on myself.

He went into his bedroom and came clanking out with a new set of golf clubs, which really astonished me. 'I figured by the time your arm's healed, the snows'll be gone.'

'Wow, Gary, I'm impressed.'

I examined the driver while he put the photograph on the mantel. He looked at it for a good minute then sat beside me. We smoked in silence.

'So,' he said eventually. 'What about Raul Ortiz?'

I figured we'd get to the name eventually. The day after the funeral, Ortiz had been charged with Bobby's murder. He was a serial offender from New Bedford who had spent more than half of his thirty-four years in prison. This time round he was serving concurrent twenty-year sentences in Concord for armed robbery, possession of heroin with intent to deal, and aggravated assault. A lifer with nothing to lose. 'Took *me* by surprise,' I said.

'What's a guy with his rap doing in Concord? He shoulda been in Walpole.'

'Maybe there was a reason. Maybe he's a patsy.'

Gary thought for a while. After all, his dad, injured and in his care so to speak, had significant links to a murdered con. 'You worried?' he asked.

'Gary, I'm worried about making a living. I'm worried about the shop. I'm worried about you.' And, though I didn't say it, I was worried about Lucy. 'About Raul Ortiz I couldn't give a shit.'

'Don't you think they'll want to talk to you? The investigators?'

'Moe's working on it.' I sighed. 'Hey. It's Christmas.'

Gary poured me another brandy. The guys outside were spinning tires in the snow and cursing.

'So,' I said, 'how's Sarah?'

'She's in Michigan.'

'I *know* that. How are the two of you getting on?'

He stood, smiled, and drew an iron from the golf bag. He took a slow practice swing and pretended to follow his shot into the distance. 'April,' he said.

'April? What about April?'

He was grinning. 'That's when I figure I'll kick your ass on the golf course.'

'If I were you, son, I'd set your sights a little higher. Beating me is no great achievement.'

'Hey. It's a starting point.'

I was wondering whether I should bring up Sarah again when the phone rang. It was Jack Wambaugh. This time I decided to take the call. 'Jack. What's a guy of your persuasion do of a Christmas Day?'

'What I do every year, Harry. I'm reading Shakespeare. *Julius Caesar.* "Here comes his body, mourn'd by Marc Antony, who though he had no hand in his death, shall receive the benefit of his dying."'

'There a modern parallel here?'

'You tell me.'

'I'll tell you this, Jack. You and the senate president would get on like a house on fire. Both fans of the Bard.'

'He knew the hearts of men.'

'I wish I did.'

Through the open kitchen door I could see Gary cleaning

up, moving from table to dishwasher with the hunched, intent posture he brought to everything he did. Pleasantly light-headed from the brandy, and less alert than I should have been to Jack's words, I watched my cigar smoke drift to the ceiling.

'Harry, you've been in the news.' Jack winched his tone up a notch, preserving a bluff familiarity while hinting at professional interest.

'Like you told me before,' I said, 'not always a good thing.'

'We'd be interested in a feature.'

'On who? Me?'

'You're at the center of a story. A good one.'

I thought about how, just a week ago, such news would have made my heart jump. Not today. 'I don't think so, Jack. I've had as much publicity as I can handle.'

'Could be the start of another book.'

'Maybe so, but I know what my lawyer would say.'

Jack paused. I could picture him sitting there, eyes bright, planning his next move, his thumb marking his place in a tale of politics and murder and ambition.

'Harry, you have to be cautious, I appreciate that. But do one thing for me. Before you decide, think about this: who benefits from Rizzoli's death?'

'How would I know? I don't *want* to know.'

'Listen to me, who benefits? I've been doing my own research. Think about it and a few things will fall into place.'

He was winding down just as I caught up with his tone. I scrambled to snare the subtleties in his voice, but I was too far behind. I'd dropped my guard. I was on holiday; he was working.

'Look after yourself, Harry. I'll call you in the new year.'

'Jack. Hang on a second.'

But he was gone.

I pondered Jack's remarks for the next few days, but my own situation demanded full attention. Besides, Moe wouldn't let me forget it. He told harsh truths gently, but he did not shirk his responsibility as attorney and friend. He called every day, reminding me of the trouble I was in, preparing me for what was coming. On the Thursday after Christmas, he told me to pick out my best suit and get ready for a visit the following day. I had an appointment, he said tersely, with the US Attorney.

'Erpelding?'

'That's right.'

'The head coach.'

'However you want to characterize him. But he is tough and smart. And your pal Gurlick will be attending, you can count on that. I'm getting signals, Harry. The Feds have been putting together a corruption case for some time, and Bobby's death has them all hopped up. McCann's commission shut them out, and the murder lets them right back in. They think Bobby was involved in bigger things and they'll be fishing for whatever they can get.'

'They can fish all they want, they're not getting anything from me.'

'Because you don't have anything or because you won't give anything?'

I had always been candid with Moe. He was the kind of attorney who functioned best when he knew the whole story, even the details he didn't need to know. He didn't make personal judgments and he didn't stray beyond his brief. But it was unlike him to ask for the story so forthrightly, and I had to make a quick decision. 'What kind of question is that for counsel to ask?'

There was a pause at the end of the line. I could see him handling the baseball, fingering the seams and reading the autographs. Like he was handling me.

'You're not under indictment, Harry. There are no charges here. And you know whose side I'm on.'

The slight tone of injury was calculated. But there really was no decision to make. What did I know of except the list? And that didn't exist any more. 'You know all there is to know, Moe.'

'OK. Let's do it then.'

'Can we meet at your office?'

I didn't have to be with him to see his exasperation.

'Harry, do you realize what's going on here? When these guys call, you come running. Especially in your situation.'

We met at the JFK Building. Unlike Gurlick's bleak paneled space in the Statler, Erpelding's top-floor corner office was full of light and an old-world view of Beacon Hill. But the décor was flat and gray as government. Though trying not to show it, Moe looked around with distaste. We sat at Erpelding's desk, empty except for his computer and the compulsory snaps of wife and kids. On the wall behind him were the standard-issue diplomas and citations and the official portrait of President Reagan, looking more goofy and redundant than ever now that he was in the final days of service. I got the feeling Erpelding could hardly wait to get the Bush photo up there. I could tell from our State House confrontation that his political aspirations were defined by Bush the pseudo-maverick, Yale boy in a CIA suit, leader of the '88 Republican charge, vanquisher of the pathetic Dukakis. A mediocre man for a mediocre time, and Erpelding fit right into the scenario. His sweat smelt of ambition. Gurlick's chair was beside ours as we sat, but he slid it across to the other side, creating a geometry of confrontation. Moe tried some small-talk, but Erpelding was having none of it.

'Moe, we're not pulling any punches here. Your client should know that. Out of respect for you we're going to be very straight, but there's a murder case going on, time is crucial, and Mr Donohue does not have an outstanding record of co-operation.'

Before I could respond, Moe stayed me with a raised hand. 'Harry has had no official contact with you or the FBI over the last year,' he said. 'In October he had an *informal* request from Mr Gurlick here for information about a book project he was working on with Bobby Rizzoli. He did right to ignore the request. It was an inappropriate approach and arguably not without potential infringement of my client's civil rights.'

Erpelding's shoulders twitched with impatience, and he folded his hands on the desktop. His sleeves were rolled, exposing a coach's forearms (hair so thick you could have parted it) and a chunky, silver-banded watch. His tie was loose. He couldn't have reached his position without some subtlety of character, but right now all I could see was a pug-nosed bull with a jutting chin and a thick neck tight with straining tendons. He looked from my face to my cast and back. If we were going to lawyer him to death he was going to have to get more political. And, for that, he was going to have to control his disdain. Not easy for Erpelding.

'We would like your co-operation. *Appreciate* your co-operation. We have the ability to inconvenience you if that's the way you want to play it, but we'd rather work with you.' He nodded at Gurlick. 'Steven approached you out of a sincere belief that you may have had something to offer on a case we've been working on for over a year.'

'Seems like Steven forgot about the First Amendment,' I said.

'As a citizen,' Gurlick said, struggling for words, 'you as a citizen involved with someone under federal investigation. Perhaps unwittingly involved in areas outside your relationship as such.'

What was it about this guy that set my teeth on edge? The chemicals in his aftershave? The sheen of his bulbous brow? The wing-tipped circumlocutions?

'Was he being investigated for writing a book?'

'Of course not.'

'Then I have nothing that could have been of interest.'

'Have or had? What's our time frame here?' Erpelding said, hands gripped tight.

'Dick, please,' Moe said. 'Let's not turn this into an inquisition. Otherwise we have to walk out and it gets complicated for everybody. Harry does want to co-operate. But it has to happen under guidelines we all understand.'

Moe's strategy was simple: provide reasonable, carefully proscribed co-operation. Keep them from getting testy, but play it cautious. They were fishing, all right, but Erpelding now gave me a look that, strangely, seemed like the offering of a last chance. As if he had something *I* wanted. 'Any willingness you show to solve this crime and others associated with it will reflect well on how matters proceed in the future.'

His tone had shifted. Like an arguing lover, he was signaling beneath the surface. Taking soundings. He knew something. Something he wasn't supposed to know, maybe, but something he could use as leverage all the same. Gurlick sat with steepled fingers looking back and forth between us, the usually pale scar at his temple pulsing red in the bright light.

'What do you mean, "others associated with it"?' I said.

Moe swiveled and looked at me. A man of his intelligence and experience was quick to pick up the slightest changes in tone. He heard echoes of secrecy in my voice. Erpelding sat back in his chair. His eyes flared. I saw with storybook clarity that I had underestimated him. The bull look and short attention span disguised a carefully calculated interviewing technique. I could see the minute calibrations in his narrow eyes. He had sucker-punched me. He did know something. About me. About Bobby.

'Like I said, we're not here to play games or to hold back. We believe Bobby Rizzoli was involved in the exam scam. *Know* he was involved. Deeply. Four months ago we actually extended him an offer to co-operate, one in which he would have made out very well, and he was giving us every sign of taking it. Then he backed down. Just around the time that you came on the scene, Donohue. Am I to take it that was a coincidence?'

'Was what a coincidence?' Moe asked.

'Your client's appearance and Rizzoli getting cold feet.'

'You're implying something, Dick, and—'

'It's OK, Moe,' I said, my own hand now doing the silencing. Not fair on Moe, this whole thing. 'Yes, it was a coincidence.'

Erpelding rested his chin on his knuckles and lined me up. 'We've had surveillance going on Bobby for some time.'

Ah. Here was the revelation. Lucy and me. He was Mr Tan without the threat of violence. Or was Mr Tan his minion?

'Bobby and others we have been tapping for over a year,' he continued. 'RICO warrants going way back that Joe McCann's commission tried to subvert. Rizzoli was involved, we know that. You were in his sphere.'

'In his sphere? I didn't meet Bobby until he was in prison. Never had a conversation with him at his house or on his home phone. But let me tell you this. If you were bugging the prison phone too, then you know I only ever talked to him about the book. If I *had* known about the exams, if he *was* involved, I would've suggested a book on it. *There*'s a story that would've made me some dough.'

'Unless you couldn't be seen to know about it.'

Moe was writhing with irritation – at me for holding out on him and at Erpelding for the tenor of the interview. 'Dick, give us a break. This kind of speculation is ridiculous.'

Erpelding's lip curled as he stared at me. 'Is it?' he asked.

'What difference does it make now?' I said. 'Bobby is dead.'

I was giving him rope, and he knew it. I could see him relax in the chair. But I was getting fed up. I had nothing I was prepared to give these guys, nothing they could hold against me, and a life to reassemble. Yet my comment was ill advised. It betrayed a cynicism that an experienced prosecutor might see as an opening. He stood and crossed with his halfback's lope to a filing cabinet on the opposite side of the room. He took out a manila envelope and returned to his seat. Moe was watching us both very closely.

'You spend a lot of time with Lucinda Rizzoli?'

Gurlick peered slit-eyed at me, like a voyeur. He had been listening! It was him! Soft-palmed Steven Gurlick, with his spaceman cranium and cornfed gaze.

'*Spent*,' I said. 'And if you've been bugging her house, you don't have to ask, do you?'

Moe rubbed his forehead. Now I had let *him* down.

'I guess not,' Erpelding said. 'Did her husband know about your arrangement?'

'What arrangement?'

'Sleeping arrangement.'

'Fuck you, Erpelding.' I struggled out of the chair and bumped my cast-bound elbow against the arm. Pain shot up my shoulder like an electric shock.

'Careful there,' Erpelding said.

'C'mon, Moe,' I said, breathing hard. 'Let's get out of here.'

But as I moved to the door, Erpelding stopped me dead. 'It's your conversation with Paul Pallotta I'm more interested in.'

I turned slowly. 'What conversation?'

'The one you had on the second of December in the Lisbon restaurant in Somerville.'

'I don't remember any such conversation.'

He reached into a drawer and took out a tape recorder. He

slid a tape from the manila folder. 'I thought you might need reminding.' He put the tape in the machine and pressed the play button.

I could lay the whole thing out for you. Names, ranks, and serial numbers. And it is big.

'Big' is a word I hear every day, Paulie. You're going to have to be more specific.

Paulie's voice, a telephone voice for the ages, sounded natural. My own rang tinny and comic. Like a character in a bad movie.

Police chiefs all over Massachusetts owe their jobs to one guy. One guy they all got exams from and they all owe big-time.

'Dick . . .' Moe said.

He paused the tape. 'Perfectly legal, Moe. I can show you the court order if you want.'

'So what does this prove? That I had the bad taste to have dinner with Paul Pallotta?'

'That you were consorting with a known member of an established crime family and discussing matters germane to our investigation. You guys gonna sit down?'

We sat. Moe's head was tilted in a way that said he feared what else might emerge. There was no more strategy. He had given up on trying to look after my interests. I had left him so much in the dark there was nothing he could do. I was frantically trying to remember where the conversation with Pallotta had gone from the point where Erpelding had paused the tape.

'I'm not going to make you suffer,' Erpelding said to me. 'We all understand that what you knew was hearsay, that you were talking about a book project, that you and Pallotta have not spoken since. You can save your breath on those issues, Moe. But you also understand we could use this to make things tough for you, Donohue. Bobby sold exams. You knew that. Don't tell me you didn't talk to him about it.'

'Don't worry, I'm not going to tell you anything.'

'We could easily make a case for you being an accessory.'

Moe snorted in derision. This comment, at least, we both knew didn't deserve a response. Erpelding eyed us like a card dealer. He had one more to play.

'But Bobby is not the fish we're after. He's a dead shark anyway. And this worst-kept-secret-in-the-world is all a smokescreen. He was not the mastermind, much as everyone would like us to think he was.'

Moe looked at me. But this time I had no idea what was coming.

'So who was?' I said.

Erpelding looked at his partner. 'You know Bucky Quinn,' Gurlick said.

'Bucky Quinn couldn't mastermind a beer bust in a brewery,' I said.

'Quinn is working with us. He's in protective custody. And when this is all over he'll move into the witness-protection program.'

'Couldn't happen to a nicer guy.'

'He has reason to fear for his life,' Gurlick said.

'Well, he is working with *you*.'

Erpelding glared. It was a glare of victory. Gurlick continued. 'The story Quinn's telling us is that there are certain higher-ups in state, individuals you're intimate with, who have orchestrated this whole thing.'

· Moe stuck out his hand like he was holding up a building. '*Whoa* there. Dick, are you saying what I think you are?'

'We're only going to have this conversation once, Moe,' he said. His shoulders were tight and hunched, his jaw set. He was waiting for the hand-off so he could slam his way into the end zone behind Gurlick's block. 'We're giving your client one shot at a white hat. He works with us, he gets immunity. But no negotiating, no considering. Minds made up, here and now, before you guys walk out that door.'

Something shifted deep inside me. It was a movement such as only happens once or twice in a lifetime, at once physical and emotional, immediate and distant, tying past and present, a feeling that transforms the moment and its surroundings into a vista wide and unfamiliar, but also intimate, as in a dream. I waited, but time was suspended, as in the long moment of a car wreck. Moe stood and put his hands on the edge of the desk.

'Those are conditions no lawyer can accept, Dick. You know that.'

'Hear me out.'

Now I stood. 'Who are we talking about?' I said.

'Quiet, Harry,' Moe said.

'We'll get to names in a minute.'

'*Who are we talking about?*'

My elbow felt as if it had been rebroken. Gurlick tapped the desktop with a fingernail. I wanted to smash his glasses. Moe still leaned on the desk. Erpelding stood to his full six-four, the better to confront us.

'Bucky's ready to testify that Jimmy O'Leary fed exams to Bobby. Used him to build an empire of corrupt police chiefs with ties to organized crime and a network of drug dealers.'

'Bullshit!' I shouted.

'You corroborate this, then your own involvement will fade away. Total immunity.'

I laughed. I could feel my eyes popping wide in outrage. Moe had a hand on my arm, and, in spite of my anger, I knew what he was thinking: if they were looking for corroboration, they didn't have a case. Bucky's evidence was hearsay. I set my own jaw and pointed a finger at Erpelding in a way I knew would anger him.

'Listen to me, Erpel*dink*. And I will only say *this* once. My dad hired Bucky Quinn when nobody else in Boston would give him the time of day. Paid him well and bought eyeglasses for his mother. The guy repays us by stealing from the shop, and when my dad confronts him he goes apeshit and smashes our new Buick. None of us have seen him since, hadn't even *heard* about him until his name pops up in the *Globe* like a bad coin. You think I'm gonna work with a scumbag like that and back some crock-of-shit story he's telling about my oldest pal? You think I'm going to stoop as low as you? Forget he's the DA. Forget he could have you for lunch in any courtroom in the state. Jimmy was my *best man*! I know Jimmy never did anything that I would call wrong. And even if he did, I would turn on my brother before I'd turn on him.'

'What if he turned on you?'

I was already on my way to the door, clutching the cast. 'He wouldn't,' I said, over my shoulder.

'So why don't you ask him?'

'I don't need to.'

'*Why don't you ask him?*'

I turned and faced him, my face flushed, my heart thumping. Moe had his hand on my shoulder.

'Why don't you go to hell?' I said. 'We've considered. Fuck you and your white hat.'

Gurlick was still tapping the desk with his nail. As we left, Erpelding was shouting another offer.

19

I'd thought the worst was over. I'd thought I'd reached my lowest point. Then, suddenly, a precipice dropped out of nowhere, and I was peering into an even deeper pit.

We left Erpelding's office in silence. It was hard to tell who was angrier. Moe headed for his office without saying goodbye. I walked down to North Station and straight into the Shamrock. Apart from two bus drivers in a back booth, I was the only patron. I gulped three quick Scotches and paid the bill. Outside, the clouds were pillaring ominously above the skyline. The streetlights were on. I could smell snow. My topcoat wrapped tight, I walked through the heart of the city to the Park Street T station. The liquor in my veins was warm and dizzying. At the same bank of phones I'd used three weeks ago, I again called Jimmy O'Leary.

'Yeah?'

'I'm having trouble with Gary,' I said. There was a long pause. 'Did you hear me?'

'I heard you. I'll be there in ten minutes.'

He picked me up at the same spot as last time. It was snowing. As I climbed in I banged my head against the doorframe; I had not allowed for the effect of the booze after my abstinence. Negotiating the cast was difficult, and I struggled into the seat.

'What the hell happened to you?' His voice was shrill and edgy. He had the hard, intimidating focus he used to cultivate before wrestling matches.

'A story for another time,' I said, trying to close the door. He squealed away with my door still open. He was in shirt-sleeves, and the heater fan was roaring. The interior was all fogged up, and he kept swiping at the windshield with a dirty rag. There was a strange smell in the car, soap or antiseptic layered over old food odors. This time he stayed clear of the parkways. He sped through Kenmore Square and up Brookline Avenue without a word.

'I've got some questions, Jim.' I tried to speak forcefully, but my anger had scattered. He was at his most intimidating. Ignoring my comment, he gripped the wheel at its crest and raced the engine. His shoulders were raised higher than usual, and the acne scars beneath his jawline caught the pale light in bas relief. Whatever words I had been rehearsing in the Shamrock were lost now. Jimmy, as always, was in control and not, at least for the moment, inclined to talk.

He knew where he was going. When we reached Brighton he turned up Harvard Avenue and stopped abruptly across the street from our old house. After forty-five years of friendship, I should have been used to the silence and skewed behavior. But I was nervous. 'We gonna talk now?' I asked him.

Still he didn't answer. His forehead was pressed against the car window, and his eyes were on the third floor, where he and his family used to live.

'You know what my brother Larry's doing now?' he said finally, his voice muffled by the glass. He was looking two flights up, lost in his own set of memories. There was a coldness to his voice that was rare, even for him.

'Running a supermarket in Nashua, right?'

He laughed darkly. 'No. Stop'n'Shop's doing without good ol' Lar for the time being.' He turned and stared at me. A red oval marked where his forehead had touched the glass. The close-set eyes flashed with what might have been taken for desperation or despair or an abandonment to the most violent impulses. 'Larry's in jail,' he said. 'In jail for kicking the shit out of Carol and their boy one too many times.'

The stare demanded a response. 'That's too bad,' I said.

'What the fuck do you know about it? You, with your dream family and your pervert of a brother who makes women's underwear.'

'I think I know something about it,' I said.

I knew what I'd heard, year in, year out, during my childhood, until finally Larry, the eldest, stood up to his drunken dad, beating his old man senseless just as Patrick O'Leary had beaten Larry and John and Henry for years. Margaret O'Leary wailing. The thump of falling furniture. Jimmy, the youngest, protected from the violence by his older brothers but most affected by it, appearing at our door and pleading with his eyes for refuge. Much as they pleaded now.

'We have to talk, Jimmy.'

'Talk,' he said. 'What the hell is *talk* going to do?'

'Like I said, I have some questions.'

He stared at my chest. 'I'll bet you do.'

I had come to seek explanations, not provide them. Yet the

atmosphere promised some shift in our relationship, some coming-to-the-surface of old hatreds or recent secrets. It was a day for revelation. He gunned the car onto the slippery street, nearly side-swiping a pick-up, and within seconds we were beside a vacant lot where we used to play as kids. Still derelict after all these years, it was an ugly patch of rusted auto parts and slabs of broken concrete. Jimmy cut the ignition, leaned across me, and popped open the glove compartment. Still leaning, he let me see the gun, a standard issue .457. Cold and ugly and unexpected. The sight had no meaning for me: I couldn't connect it with Jimmy, our friendship, or our past.

'What are you showing me that for?'

He smiled the flattest, coldest smile you could imagine. 'So you know it's there,' he said. He took it out, hefted it, returned it and shut the compartment. 'Let's go,' he said, and stepped out of the car.

I didn't move.

He came around to my side and yanked open the door. 'You coming or what?'

'Why should I?' I said.

'I thought you said you had some questions.'

I swiveled my legs out of the door and peered up at him. 'Jimmy, what's wrong? Get back in the car. Let's talk.'

'What? You spooked? Never seen a piece before? Lucy Rizzoli never show you hers?'

He turned and walked onto the lot in his shirtsleeves, negotiating the rubble with difficulty in leather-soled loafers. I climbed out after him. It was snowing heavily now. I was relieved he had left the gun but still frightened by his mood. A layer of fresh snow covered the lot, and I walked very carefully, thrown off balance by the cast, the terrain, and the liquor. Old toilet seats and light fixtures lay stunned on the ground. Car tires, whitened by the snow, gaped at the sky. Jimmy slowed. The thick snowflakes were hitting my lashes and melting. Behind us a city truck with flashing yellow lights spread salt on the road. Jimmy turned as I got near him. The light colored his face as he fell on me savagely, reaching beneath my topcoat and ripping open my shirt.

'What the hell are you doing?' I shouted. I was trying desperately to stay on my feet. My elbow was already alive with pain, and I knew that if I fell it would probably be rebroken. I was trying to break free but the only thing keeping me up was his frenzied grasp of my torn shirt.

'*Who sent you?*' he screamed. He was crazed. 'Who sent you, you lying son-of-a-bitch!'

His lips were blue and sputtering. I couldn't reply: all my energy went on staying upright. When he finally realized I wasn't wearing a wire, his grasp slowly loosened. I clutched him round the neck with my good arm, and he slipped and fell backwards. I fell on top of him. I was inches from his face, screaming in pain.

'What's wrong? *What's wrong?*' he shouted.

I was always much heavier than Jimmy, and I pressed hard against him now to keep his pain-jarring movement to a minimum. Gradually I caught my breath as he struggled. 'Get off of me! *Get off of me!*'

'My elbow,' I said. 'Wait.'

We lay like lovers, the snow falling around us, the sweeping yellow light climbing our coupled form. I slid off him, onto my good side. From the ground I watched the snow swirling from the blackness above, thick and wet and dyed amber by the city truck's swiveling beacon. He stood, wiping off his pants, then helped me up. I was nauseous from the pain. My chest was bleeding where he'd scratched me. He buttoned up my shirt as best he could. 'I'm sorry, pal,' he mumbled.

'You thought I was *wired*? You think for one second I'm going to turn on you?'

His lips were swollen. His eyes were wet, with tears or melted snow, I didn't know. His own shirt had lost several buttons in the scuffle. He spat in the snow and looked away, his shoulders slumped, his hair matted and wet.

'Jimmy. What's going on?'

'What do you think?' he said, still looking away.

'Something's happening. What could make you think I'd wear a wire?'

He grimaced and looked at the ground. 'You think you know the whole story, don't you?'

'I only know what I know,' I said. 'I know Bucky Quinn is playing games. I know the Feds tried to get me to rat on you. Like there's anything *to* rat.'

He got agitated again, hitching his shoulders and rubbing his jaw. I was glad he'd left the gun in the car. He was reminding me of Lucy on the day when all this terrible stuff started.

'And now you think *I'm* a rat,' I said.

He bobbed his head slowly, another wrestling gesture, and hooked his thumbs into his belt. 'Remember we used to come down here with the Santini brothers?'

'Yeah.'

'When I was nine,' he said, 'nine years old . . . a couple times Ray Santini took me into the bushes on my own.' He pointed at the spot with his chin. 'Told me to pull down my pants to see what kind of a man I was. So I did, right? You would've too. Maybe you did. Felt me up, he did, no other way to put it. Felt me up good and did a few other things besides.' He hung his head. I thought he was weeping, but he was waiting out a sneeze, which came with sudden violence. He wiped his nose on his sleeve. 'You believe me?'

'Nothing about Ray Santini would surprise me,' I said.

'Guinea bastard with his stories about Gina Rappolo. Lying guinea bastard. By the time I realized what he'd done, he was gone. In the fucking marines.'

'He was never in the marines.'

'The hell he wasn't. Getting good dough for servicing some tight-assed colonel, I'd put money on it. If only I'd've had the guts to tell Larry, he would've killed him.'

'You wouldn't've been doing Larry any favors.' I was wet and shivering. I couldn't get the coat around my cast. The city truck was gone, and the only light came from a streetlamp in the far corner of the lot. Beyond, his car sat like an abandoned tank, the passenger door still open, the gun in the glove compartment. I imagined a gang of kids stumbling across it as we stood there, discovering the piece, coming after us. Not an unlikely scenario, these days, in this neighborhood.

'What's this all about, buddy?' I asked him. I was bone-weary and sick. I needed to get to a hospital to check my arm. But a greater despair beckoned.

'It's about not knowing people you think you know.'

'Like who?'

'Like anyone. Like Bobby Rizzoli. Jimmy O'Leary. Harry Donohue.'

I managed a weak smile he couldn't see anyway. 'You don't know me?' I said.

'I guess not. I took it you were bugged, right?'

'I *was* with the Feds today.'

'You think you know me, Harry?'

The only thing more intense than the pain in my arm was the hope that Erpelding was wrong. Last October I'd thought I'd lost plenty, but I'd had no idea. It had been a bad winter. But I could forget it all and start again if Jimmy was not what they said he was. Out there in the rubble and waste and cold, it seemed the only thing left to hold out for. 'Yeah. I think I do.'

He shifted from one foot to another – not the tactical shift of the wrestler, looking for an opening, but the resigned, meaningless movement of a man with nowhere to go.

'What are those pricks at JFK saying about me?' he said, his voice sliding out of the gloom.

'That you fed exams to Rizzoli. That you were using him to set up a syndicate.' I spoke in a low voice and gazed at the car. Just repeating the accusation made me feel disloyal.

'Bastards.'

'This is what Quinn's going to testify. So they say.'

'How the hell would Quinn know?'

Hope sprinkled from above. 'This was *my* point,' I said. 'If it was anything more than hearsay, they'd wouldn't look for corroboration. Right?'

But he was too far gone to allow me to try to convince myself. 'They won't need to look far for other rats,' he said.

'What do you mean?'

He shook – more than a shiver, it was the shake of anguish

and the worst of losses. 'Don't ask me why I did it, Harry. I don't know. I trusted people. I stepped in to have a look around, made a little dough, then suddenly I'm in up to my neck. I never meant to. You know me – I had ambitions. I was—'

'Jimmy, don't.' The familiar stain of failure was spreading through my guts like ink on blotting paper. I stepped back and slumped onto a concrete slab. The snow had let up. I was cold.

'Rizzoli and me, we were the same,' he said. 'Cells. Above, he talked to me and nobody else. Downward, he dealt with the chiefs. As far as they were concerned, he had stolen the exams. And that was the way it would've run if anybody talked: Bobby had broken into the McCormack Building, just like he broke into Hillbrook Savings Trust, taken the exams and sold them. For a few bucks, sure, but also for the kind of leverage no money can buy. Statewide.'

'Unless he talked.'

Jimmy shrugged. 'Why would he? Especially after he was in the clink. And if he did . . .'

'He'd be killed.'

He shrugged.

'Who killed him?'

'He was a casualty.'

I was trying to see through the darkness to his face. At this point every question had to be asked. 'Did you do it, Jimmy?'

He sighed deeply. 'No, Harry, I didn't. Didn't order it either. But you think the Feds are going to believe that?'

'Who did?'

He started to shake violently. I thought he was going to

attack me again. 'Why *wouldn't* you turn on me?' he shouted. 'Why wouldn't you rat on me like everyone else?'

'Tell me, Jim.'

'Tell you what? That I covered up tracks for everybody else? That I left myself exposed? That I made a patsy out of *myself*? Of course I didn't kill Rizzoli. He was the one guy in the world *I* could point a finger at.'

'So who did?'

He spoke softly, but with a hatred that was as tight as his jaw. 'Quinn and Rizzoli I could understand. *Accept*, even. Lowlifes from day one. But my own friends betraying me. Tell me the truth, Harry. Did they get to you?'

'*Who?*'

He was soaked with wet snow. His thin head was slick and shiny and silhouetted vaguely against the weak light across the lot. And then I understood his hesitation: he was still not convinced I wasn't working for someone else. He still didn't trust me. Because he trusted no one. That was where he'd arrived. I would have left him there, alone and unfriended for ever, but curiosity and an ancient sympathy kept me seated on the cold slab. 'Who?' I repeated. 'If you can't tell me, who can you tell?' It was a plea from the past.

'Remember, Harry, I was a cell too.'

He was a cell. So he had only one contact. I waited.

'I'll bet the Feds had nothing to say about Alex,' he finally said.

I couldn't believe what I was hearing. '*Alex*? Alex Lathrop?'

'If I turned him in, if I *could* have turned him in, who'd believe me? Who? Or he might kill me.'

'Alex would kill *you*?'

He snorted at my naïveté. 'He killed Rizzoli, didn't he? And he's ratting on me. He's working with the Feds, that son-of-a-bitch.'

I stood up. It was all too much to absorb, here on this lonely decrepit lot of all places. Alex, our old law-school pal. Friend of Gerald Ford, associate of governors and Washington policy-makers. Superior Court judge. Head of the Lathrop Commission. Too much, way too much. I had to leave. I felt hollow and alone. If my oldest, smartest pal Jimmy O'Leary could make such a mess of his life, what chance did I have? If Alex Lathrop was evil, then what was good? The world was upside-down. But something still didn't add up.

'I don't understand,' I said. 'How could Alex and you be working with Bobby? You guys sent him down.'

'For what? Ten years. On those counts? It was a slap on the wrist. Part of the deal. Rizzoli would get his cut, be out on parole in three years max, and have the book deal to keep him going until release.'

'The book deal?'

'Yeah. You think you getting the book contract was an accident?'

And so the last piece fell into place. It was all manipulated. All set up. That was why he had suggested the contract structure to Judy and told her not to tell me. That was why he had played hard to get on the initial phone call. That was why I was bugged and followed and made miserable when I thought I was grasping the best opportunity of my life. I was part of the deal and didn't even know it.

'You used me,' I said.

'C'mon, Harry. You were going to do all right.'

'Did you sic those two goons on me?'

'Nothing was ever going to happen there. I needed the list.'

I swayed in the dark, dazed. Everything else had been a shock; this had the unplumbed depth of betrayal. 'They were going to harm Gary.'

'C'mon, Harry. They weren't gonna hurt anybody. They were just scaring you. It was all a setup.'

'You turned on me, Jimmy. *You* turned on *me*.'

I stepped into the night, reeling and feverish. Every other part of his confession I could accept. But not this.

'Harry, what was I supposed to do?'

I stopped and turned around. 'I would have done anything for you, Jimmy. Anything.' I continued my trudge across the snow-humped lot. I was frightened of falling and not being able to get up.

'I'm all alone out here,' he shouted. 'Don't leave me by myself. *Don't leave me, Harry!*'

But I kept on walking as he yelled. I walked up to the car and took the gun from the glove compartment. I looked back. He was still shouting, though I couldn't make out the words. He had his arms extended to the sky. His small wet head looked like a seal's. I shut the car door and tucked the gun into my pants. I walked away from Jimmy and down to the end of the block. Every time I looked back, he was in the same position of empty prayer.

I kept walking until I reached Soldier's Field Road, passed through the riverside park, and edged my way down to the banks of the Charles. I steadied myself against the low wall. I heaved the gun as far as I could and watched it splash in the cold river. Then I caught a cab to the hospital.

20

The state police arrested Jimmy on New Year's Day. They nailed him like they nailed Bobby – at the worst hour and in the worst way. Five in the morning on the coldest day of the year, they hauled him from his Weston house in T-shirt, jeans, and light jacket. The troopers, bundled up warm in their parkas and ear-flaps, held him handcuffed for a good long minute in the glare of the blue police-car beacons and flat television lights. Later they'd watch the twelve o'clock news at the station house and hoot with locker-room bravado at their ten seconds of fame. That's when I saw it, anyway, from Gary's couch. Jimmy bore the humiliation with brooding disdain. Chin to his chest, cheeks sucked in, he stared at the scalloped snowbanks lining the sidewalk and rocked back and forth on his heels. His frozen breath came quick and shallow. I felt a little wrench in my stomach as he lifted a pointed shoulder and dry-spat at the snow with the same tongue-stopped style he used before a wrestling match, glancing at the camera as if at his opponent. I had to look away.

They bound him over to the grand jury, so the case against him had to have been as solid as it gets. The Feds had more than Bucky Quinn in the bag, even the wags in the street knew that, and the whole state wondered who their star witness might be. The papers, oh, the papers were braying with partisan righteousness, especially the *Herald*, and, on the news each night, Republican faces winced with the strain of concealing their glee. Gary's phone started ringing again. The radio talk shows were buzzing. It was public theater of a kind only the city of Boston can produce, a kind I usually relished. But it was no fun this time. The Lathrop Commission was disbanded, the Duke took more heat than he had losing the presidential election, and Joe McCann's gavel rapped and rapped as he tried to dam the tide of shouted questions flowing from the senate floor. The Bush inauguration flipped by unnoticed. All politics, Tip O'Neill would have reminded us, are local politics, and all eyes were on the O'Leary case and what it could have, *would* have, done to the state. As if it hadn't been done before.

In spite of my connection, I felt strangely removed from the affair. Gary's couch was the right vantage point. The police chiefs on my list – including Jake Cleary – were suspended pending Jimmy's indictment and trial. Class action suits were filed. The bank's insurance company got in on the act, sniffing blood, and several anti-corruption groups held frosty vigils outside the State House. I waited for the subpoena, but it never arrived. It slowly dawned on me that I would not be involved. Erpelding had pushed me so I'd push Jimmy. He'd never really considered me a suspect. Never expected I would work with him. And I had marched out and done exactly what he wanted me to do. So when Jimmy asked Moe if he would join the defense team, I told Moe to go ahead. I wouldn't be needing him after all. The defense was led by Mickey Taylor, of all people. Moe was doing little beyond conducting the discovery, but I pointed out that he was breaking his rule of civil suits only. He said he owed Jimmy a favor. Like we all did. Moe and I talked each evening, and though he was constrained in what he could say, reading between the lines I sensed that conviction was as inevitable as indictment. Erpelding had his ace in the hole.

The grand jury convened with much fanfare, and Bucky Quinn did what we all knew Bucky Quinn would do, which wasn't much. Pulling at his necktie, sucking at his teeth, he leaned over the witness stand for two long days and lisped his testimony with the palest conviction. Small-time when he trashed our Buick, and small-time at what might have been his hour of notoriety. The political cartoonists and columnists ignored him. Erpelding treated him, his own witness, with the jock's sneering disrespect for the weak. He was headed for the slammer unheralded and knew it, and how he must have hated not having the real goods on Jimmy. He was nothing more than a support act, a stage-setter, for the prosecution's star. Moe risked professional indiscretion and gave me the lowdown on the phone each night. He couldn't resist, and I couldn't bring myself to attend. It was bad enough watching the news.

Show-time arrived on day five, and the courtroom was packed. The first hour of that Thursday morning was spent in tedious protocol, as if the judge (Paul Shattuck, ex-Yale, ex-Marines, Reagan appointee and big-time Democrat ball-buster) was deliberately thickening the tension. At ten o'clock the state finally called its chief witness – Steven Gurlick. The high ceiling swarmed with whispers as Shattuck banged the gavel.

How was *he* involved? What was going on? The clerk swore in Gurlick, who sat straight-backed in the box and pushed his glasses up the bridge of his slippery nose. In response to Erpelding's first question, he announced in his nasal accent that he was there to convey the testimony of a confidential informant. The room exhaled in disappointment.

So Alex got the white hat. With full immunity and anonymity in the bargain. How bad Erpelding must have wanted O'Leary to let a deeply corrupt Dukakis-appointed Superior Court judge so cleanly off the hook. How galled Jimmy must have been to know he'd been shafted by his college pal, his partner in crime, a man who, in the end, knew how to fake loyalty as well as he could fake everything else. The only man in Massachusetts who knew what it took to send Jimmy O'Leary down. Who out-streetsmarted the smartest guy on the street. Who knew that Jimmy's weak spot was *his* loyalty. Ah, Jimmy. True to no woman but utterly faithful to those few men with whom he'd cast his lot. I had to admit, I felt sorry for the guy. But how else could the story end? Corruption was a chain, always had been, and Jimmy's sincerity made him the weak link. So he went tumbling to the threshing floor with those beneath him, while Alex and those others above reeled out of sight into the safe ceiling of the unknown and untouched. In the end, Jimmy wasn't a thorough enough scoundrel. Not ruthless enough, not willing to follow the hard logic of tyranny to its most violent conclusions. His tragic flaw his one redeeming trait.

News of Alex Lathrop's retirement didn't make TV. There were a couple of stories, buried in the metro section of the papers, that followed his PR company's release to the letter: he was calling it quits at the age of fifty-three to spend time with his family, pursue personal interests, and consider his future. It would have been too much, I supposed, to expect that, along with everything else, they'd let him keep his *job*. There were even limits to what the Feds could promise. To what they would risk. After all, Erpelding did have to live with himself. The *Globe* piece included a tribute from Joe McCann and concluded with the speculation that Lathrop was planning a run for governor in 1990. I read it aloud to Gary.

And when the television went silent and I lay with wheezing inertia on Gary's couch, the refrigerator whinnying in the kitchen and South End traffic coughing beneath the window, my thoughts usually turned to Bobby. Bobby lying frozen in his Hillbrook grave while Alex sipped seltzer and smoked Dominican robustoes at the Harvard Club. Bobby, whose greatest sin was knowing more than was safe. Bobby, whose last moments were spent listening to Hispanic curses while cold steel slid into his guts. Whose eyes, when they met mine on that last visit out at Concord, burned dully with that self-consuming combination of yearning and despair that I knew so well myself. The punishment of an overreacher. What of him? And his widow? He'd been offered a white hat, I knew that, and turned it down. He'd fallen for the greatest temptation of the inmate – to talk at the very moment he should most have kept his mouth shut. He had no one to blame, he'd be the first to say it, but himself. And Lucy, poor Lucy, was paying for it. Abandoned by everyone but her son and her strong-arm friend. Did she and Bobby get what they deserved? When I thought of Alex, his fortune and reputation intact, I didn't think so.

And me, hey, I'd have to say I was spared. Spared the grave and spared prison, though either fate might have befallen me as easily it had Bobby or Jimmy. Hell, *I* deserved worse. Maybe Jimmy kept me shielded. Maybe he rose above suspicion and personal dishonor long enough to keep my name off the chain. Or maybe I just got lucky. There I was, chasing all the wrong things – chasing them in spite of myself – and meanwhile failing completely to see the real story. I'd thought I was at the heart of the action? I didn't know what action was. I was the unwitting flunky who gets bumped off in the first reel. I was like Paulie Pallotta or Bucky Quinn, a self-proclaiming blowhard who sucks up the unwelcome attention while the real operators practice their voodoo off-camera. Yet the operators went down and I came out OK. Go figure.

I stayed at Gary's place for another month, and not once did he complain. My cast came off in February, and he helped me move back to Charlestown. Around the same time I also returned to the shop, where Johnny fixed me with his good eye and asked if I was looking for a job. He could afford to be playful. The Press was in receivership, Milt Solomon had cleaned up the books, and Judy had hired a new general manager. Frankie was cold-calling prospects for the print salespeople and, according to Maureen McCarthy, doing a half-decent job. Jeff sat in a carrel beside George Lapich proofreading legal briefs. Shirley had worked behind the scenes to make sure Johnny didn't fire him, but Jeff still wasn't happy. He claimed to have a senior-editor offer from Northeastern Press and was waiting only to see if I needed him. I told him to take what he could get from Northeastern. My old office had been left as it was. I moved back in, stared at the harbor, and wondered what I was going to do with my time. Maybe *I'd* do some proofreading.

On St Patrick's Day, Gary took me to see my mother, an annual visit I never missed. The day was dry and sunny, with thin cloud, a March nip, and a breeze that snapped the Irish tricolors hanging from city buildings and hotel flagpoles. Knots of young men with green face paint and dyed hair clustered on the street corners, yelling at us with meaty faces and upraised paper cups of beer. I sat back and watched the city pass, cradling my healing arm and thinking about the days when I, too, had the energy and poor sense to get hammered on a bright spring morning for reasons other than despair.

I enjoyed Gary's company. It was as if my own vulnerability brought out a calmness in him that he knew I needed, and he was a quiet, easy-going companion. He didn't ask me questions about the last few months, and he didn't try to tell me what to do. We spoke a little about Ann, who, to be fair, had kept a respectful distance. We talked sports. But mostly we just glided silently down the turnpike, past a skyline stitched tight against a clear sky, the buildings clean and solid in the March sun.

Judy was right – my mom was a lot better: sharper, at times even sarcastic, though still wheelchair-bound because of her ailing legs. We took her for a long walk in the nursing-home grounds. Ignoring my weak arm, I manned the chair handles. She was well bundled in spite of the sun, wrapped in a knit sweater and winter coat and a tasseled woolen blanket Judy had brought back from Ireland the previous summer. Her walking stick lay across her lap.

'How's your arm?' she said to Gary.

'Dad's the one with the bad arm, Grandma. I'm fine.'

'Why's he pushing the wheelchair, then?'

Snagged, Gary had to smile.

'It's therapy, Mom. It helps to push.'

'Keep pushing so.'

I laid my hand on her thin shoulder, light as a bird's. It trembled. Gary walked with his hands clasped at his back, glancing from me to my mother. She tugged at her green blanket. 'Are you married yet?' she asked, without looking back.

'Are you asking me or my dad?'

'It's you I'm asking. This fella here had his chance.'

'No, Grandma, I'm afraid not.'

'He's not without his prospects,' I said.

'Prospects? Sure, prospects are like money owed you. Damn all use when you go to the grocery store.'

Across the lawn, a delivery man carried a huge plastic shamrock into the social center. Ahead of us loomed the tall pines of the property's edge, buffeted by the wind. Peering over my mother's shoulder, I saw her grip the walking stick with hands veiny, thin, and determined. She spoke again in a cracked voice. 'He would've been eighty-five today.'

'Dad?'

'Well, I'm not talking about Johnny Keegan.'

'Eddie was hoping Megan would hold out till today.'

'The baby's healthy, that's the main thing.'

'How come Grandpa wasn't named Patrick?' Gary asked.

'You'd have to ask *his* mother that,' she said. She had a coughing fit. I stopped the chair but she waved me on. After she was settled she said, 'He wouldn't celebrate his birthday, you know.'

This was news to me. Even on the wagon, Dad drank all day on March 17th. 'What do you mean, Mom?'

'Wouldn't acknowledge it.'

'Didn't stop him drinking,' I said.

'Oh, he celebrated Paddy's Day, all right. But not his birthday. When we were first married, I'd give him his presents after breakfast. He wouldn't open them until the next day. Wouldn't let me bake a cake.'

'Why not?'

'Said it was a day for all the Irish. Didn't want to take away from that.'

'A day for the Irish, all right,' I said. 'Our day.'

On the way back Gary dropped me off at Court Street. I had arranged to meet Moe in his office. No day off for him.

He brought me up to date on Jimmy. 'Between you and me, Harry, we're resigned to the indictment. With Shattuck on the stand it was always going to be that way. We'll draw it out, but only to give us more time to prepare for the trial.'

'Which will be?'

He shrugged. 'May, June, if we can get away with it.'

'And this confidential informant?'

He gave me a cutting look. 'Confidential.'

Since our climactic meeting in Erpelding's office, our relationship had lost a beat. Moe knew what I was going through and stood by me as a friend, but he cut eye contact short and kept clear of certain topics. He would continue to represent me, but with care. There was less judgment than self-protection in this turn in our relationship, but its air of permanence disturbed me. I had not told him about my last meeting with

Jimmy, but he seemed to know about it. Maybe Jimmy told him; more likely he had made an educated guess. The past weeks had affected him as well. His gentleness and humor were lopped. He looked tired.

'Jimmy's also a suspect in the murder investigation,' Moe said, shaking his head sadly. 'I think we can keep that postponed until the first ordeal is over.' A man who had seen much of life yet was still shaken by injustice. And, in spite of the shift in our relations, he couldn't stay mad at me. Not when he knew the whole story.

'I hear Eddie's a grandfather,' he said.

'A girl, delivered on the fourteenth. He wanted a boy on the seventeenth, but he's putting on a brave face.'

'Name?'

'Jean.'

'Thank the world for girls.'

'Oh, I do, Moe. I do.'

'So you're enjoying a day off, huh?'

I laughed. 'Well, it's Paddy's Day. Besides, what else do I have to do?'

He smiled and shrugged. The skin on his neck showed an aging slackness I hadn't noticed before.

'Hey,' I said. 'How about some lunch? On me.'

'I don't think so, Harry. I got a lot going on.'

Through the window, the gulls hung in the air and the neighboring skyscrapers seemed to be slightly swaying. Thinking of my day ahead, I was aware of an emptiness that matched the breezy spaces thirty storeys high and a holiday vacancy on the streets far below.

'Tell me something,' I said. 'What does Jimmy have to say?'

'About what?'

'About me?'

Moe picked up the autographed baseball and twirled it in his hand. He was a man who knew something about change, about family tragedy and friendship gone awry. But he was in no mood to play the wise observer today. 'In truth, Harry, not much. I think he has other things on his mind.'

'Well, he would, wouldn't he?'

'Yes, he would.'

After a few moments' silence he got up from his orthopedic chair and stretched his back. I stood and put on my coat. The bright day filled his office and the sunlight lay in stripes across the carpeted floor.

'Not a bad day out there,' I said.

'No, not bad.' He blinked. Outside, the sweep of Boston Harbor lapped at the city's edge. 'Not bad for the end of winter.'